KYN KRONICLES BOOK 5

SHADOW'S DREAM

JAMI GRAY

Cover Art: Deranged Doctor Design, www.derangeddoctordesign.com
Publisher: Celtic Moon Press Revised edition, 2019
ISBN: 978-1-948884-24-2 (ebook) ISBN: 978-1-948884-25-9 (print)

First edition, June 2018, Black Opal Books ISBN: 978-1-626948-96-6 (ebook)
ISBN: 978-1-626948-97-6 (print)

SIGN UP FOR FREE READS FROM JAMI!

Join Jami's newsletter to be the first to hear about new releases, free books, special prices and other nifty events.

Sign up at: https://www.subscribepage.com/jami-gray-books

What Readers Say...

About Arcane Transporter:

"Taking a refreshing approach to fantasy magic, this fast-paced, economical thriller is told from a highly likable perspective." —Red Adept Editing

About PSY-IV Teams:

"This story is an emotional roller coaster, from betrayal, anger, fear, love..." —InD'tale Magazine

About the Kyn Kronicles:

"...a fantastic paranormal action novel is quite possibly the best book I've read this year. I could not put it down, and had to exercise serious self-control to keep from staying up all night to finish it." —The Romance Reviews

About Fate's Vultures:

"...if you like your characters with a bit more bite, with secrets, with hidden agendas, and all those sorts of things, and your worlds are a far more deadlier place, then this is for you." —Archaeolibrarian

ALSO BY JAMI GRAY

ARCANE WONDERLAND

Last Call

Bitter Spirits

Rune & Tonic

ARCANE TRANSPORTER

Ignition Point (*Prequel Novella*)

Grave Cargo

Risky Goods

Lethal Contents

Collision Course

Blind Spot

Terminal Drift

THE KYN KRONICLES

Shadow's Edge

Shadow's Soul

Shadow's Moon

Shadow's Curse

Shadow's Dream

Shadow's Fall

Tangled in Shadows (*Short Story Collection*)

FATE'S VULTURES

Lying in Ruins

Beg for Mercy

Caught in the Aftermath

Fear the Reaper

PSY-IV TEAMS

Hunted by the Past

Touched by Fate

Marked by Obsession

Fractured by Deceit

Linked by Deception

BOX SETS

PSY-IV Teams Box Set I (Books 1-3)

The Collapse: Fate's Vultures (Books 1-4)

The Kyn Kronicles Box Set (Books 1-6)

Arcane Transporter Box Set I (Books 1-3)

Arcane Transporter Box Set II (Books 4-6)

This is for all of you who've stuck around since the beginning—
Thank you!

ACKNOWLEDGMENTS

As always, none of my stories would see the light of day without the support and love of family and friends.

Any mistakes on translations are solely mine.

CHAPTER 1

Many nightmares haunted the most powerful witch in the Northwest, but none as disturbing as Cheveyo's recent visitations. As the head of the Kyn's Northwest Magi house, he was quite familiar with the varied forms monsters could take. From the kindly faced next-door neighbor whose horrific secrets were buried in the basement, to the terrifyingly grotesque beings who hid deep in the Kyn shadows, never to step into the light. Dressed only in his sleep pants, he stood on his deck overlooking the Oregon coast, concentrating on the bite of wood against his palms. A particularly strong gust cooled his sweat-soaked skin and triggered a hard shudder. For the briefest moment he considered going back in and getting a T-shirt, but he was locked in place by his lingering night terrors.

A flash of a female's face, the beloved features lined with pain and fear drove the dread perched in his aching chest to climb into a choking lump that settled in his throat. He shook his head, once, hard, and the features changed into softer, younger curves, this time etched with the more familiar signs of half-hidden disillusionment and hints of betrayal. His fault.

He slammed a fist against the railing, using the sharp spike of pain to help push the images aside. He focused on the roiling waves below, crashing into the rocky shore, willing his mind blank. The wind tangled his hair over his face, but he ignored it as he tried to regain his emotional footing.

Deep in his head, where a solid barred door stood guard on the psychic plane, someone knocked. Growling under his breath, he ignored it. He was in no shape to handle such an interaction right now. Not on top of everything else. A harsh, bitter bark of noise escaped, only to disappear into the night. If his people could only see him now—his mantel of authority nothing but a thin cloak hiding the Frankenstein patchwork of magical ability and sheer stubbornness—they'd panic. Hell, he couldn't blame them, not when he was busy doing a little panicking of his own.

Not only did he have his own dreams to contend with, but a bigger threat loomed on the horizon. A threat that three of his people, each one blessed, or cursed, depending on your point of view, confirmed. Since each held the ability to catch glimpses of the future and each had made the almost two hour trek from Portland to Canon Beach to share the details of it with him, it was enough to make anyone a mite leery.

Time was running out for the supernatural world of the Kyn. The meager curtain of secrecy keeping their presence from the humans was being devoured by the moths of technology and change. His visitors each bore the same message, either the Kyn came together and revealed themselves to the mortal world, or they would, once again, become the hunted. Only this time, thanks to the combination of rising discontent within the Kyn and humanity's sheer numbers, they would be eradicated.

Yet it wasn't those grim tidings that dragged him from his bed. Instead, it was the endless questions of "what if". Decisions made all those years ago were coming back to bite him in the ass, leaving him questioning his choices. Unfortunately, his doubt wasn't limited to just tonight, but every damn night for close to a year since he returned from Arizona. Since he left the woman who held his heart behind for the second time. Tala Whiteriver.

It made sleeping a fruitless, frustrating pursuit.

Another knock on the psychic door, this one a bit more impatient, left him raking his mist-laced hair back from his face as he turned his attention inward. Manipulating the magic he lived and breathed, he thinned the barrier enough to allow communication, but not enough to allow his visitor a peek inside the mess crawling behind the door. *"What, Raine?"*

There was a minuscule pause before she responded. *"What the hell is your problem, Cheveyo?"*

Even without her being physically there, he could practically see her—hands on her hips, a dark frown on her face. *"Other than you pounding at the damn door, not a damn thing."*

Her disbelief was palpable. *"Yeah, try again, because I'm not buying it."*

The nice thing about communicating on the magical plane was that his ability to project whatever he wanted was nearly infallible. Even to this warrior woman, who thought she knew who she was dealing with. Unfortunately, the time was coming closer to shatter her assumption. Just not yet. He wasn't ready to deal with the fallout, nor was there a real need for the reality check.

Mentally taking a defensive pose—feet braced, arms crossed—he reigned in his impatience. *"Then buy this: it's personal."*

"Fine," her mental voice all but growled. *"But if you're in trouble, you better—"*

"I'd better what?" Her response sparked his precarious temper and, for the first time in a long while, he decided to remind this admittedly lethal adult-child of her place. His magic rose in a thunderous wave held in check only by his control. *"Remember who you're addressing, Raine McCord."* He allowed the edge of his power to whip between them, anticipating her explosive reaction, which wasn't long in coming.

She struck back, not to harm but because, in the Kyn world, it wasn't about hurting, but dominance, and right now she was having trouble reconciling her perceptions with truth. A truth he managed to keep from her and her lover, Gavin Durand, for months now. He let her magic dance with his, making her work for it, but knowing in the end he would win.

When the pressure of her magic finally retreated, he drawled, *"Are you done?"*

"For now."

At her reluctant, yet cautious submission, he buried his smile deep. If she caught the barest whiff of his amusement, she'd go ballistic, and tonight he didn't have the time or patience to deal with her temper tantrum. Spectacular though it would be.

"What's happening?" This time her question carried more respect and wariness.

He sighed and gave her the only answer he could, *"Change."*

He could feel her turning his response over and over,

trying to fit it with the pieces she held. She was doomed for disappointment, because she was currently missing a few key segments. *"When?"*

"If I'm not mistaken—" And he wasn't. *"—soon."*

"I really wish you and the rest of the leaders would stop with your cryptic shit."

Her waspish complaint garnered an honest laugh. *"Wish we could, but it's part of our job descriptions."*

"Why am I not surprised?"

There was a wryness to her mental tone, one indicating they had skated beyond the flashpoint. It allowed some of his tension to slip away. *"Because you're nothing if not intelligent."*

"You might want to remember that," she warned. *"While you're hiding your secrets, Cheveyo."*

"If I need you, I'll let you know." It was the least he could give her, considering this bond existed because both of them had once made a choice to save the other.

"Promise?" Her question was soft, but serious.

"I promise." With that, he gently closed the psychic door between them.

Alone in his head once more, he drew in the cool night air and slowly let it out. The chaos in his head calmed. He let the night wash through him, taking what Mother Nature offered and letting it sink deep, soothing his ragged emotional edges.

Deep in the house behind him, a phone rang. He took a moment to take another breath and let it out before turning to head inside to answer. His bare feet whispered over the wooden floor as he reached for the cell phone on the kitchen counter.

Spying the familiar number, his momentary peace evaporated. "Hello, Natasha."

CHAPTER 2

As the cabin came into view a wave of hair-raising, déjà vu left Cheveyo white knuckling the steering wheel. Strange that such a benign image could make his heart race and leave his mouth drier than the desert. Especially considering he spent more years than he cared to remember facing down both human and inhuman nightmares that would break most minds. Yet this rustic three-room cabin housed his greatest joy and his deepest fear. Neither of which could be allowed to play a part in his current visit because he wasn't here for personal reasons, he was here for business. Specifically Kyn business. His shoulders braced under the settling weight of his role as the head of the Northwest Magi House as he brought the rental SUV to a stop next to a battered truck.

"Want me to wait here?" The question came from the man sitting in the passenger seat and held no judgment. An admirable feat considering the situation.

With a studied deliberateness, Cheveyo relaxed his grip on the steering wheel, forcing his tension back. "No need."

The other man undid his seatbelt, letting it retract as he shifted in the passenger seat. "You sure?"

Staring through the windshield, Cheveyo pondered Chay's question. The younger man was here as Cheveyo's bodyguard. Not because Cheveyo couldn't take care of himself, but because it was a political necessity created by the fallout from his last visit. Of course, fallout out might be over simplifying things a bit considering the bodies left in his wake, one of which belonged to the mate of the Southwest Alpha. Despite the fact she tried to kill Cheveyo, he couldn't quite squash his twinge of guilt over his part in her death.

A sigh came from Chay. "Not sure how many times this can be said before you listen, but this mess here, it's not on you."

If Chay could so easily follow his thoughts, then Cheveyo was slipping. He grimaced and blew out a hard breath. "I'm listening, Chay."

"But you're not hearing." Chay settled with his back against the door, his arms crossed over his chest. "Tomás's mate was a nut job, Cheveyo. Something which seems to be an epidemic down here." He added the last under his breath.

There, then, was the judgment and, for some odd reason, it scraped against Cheveyo's temper. "She was a grieving mother," he snapped, glaring at the other man.

Completely unruffled, Chay's dark gaze and voice remained rock steady. "She raised a Soul Stealer and came damn close to killing you, just to protect her dirty little secrets." A hard edge snuck into the last couple of words and added a baleful light to his eyes. "I may not have been there, but Gavin and Raine didn't pull any punches when they brought me up to speed. You came here last year with

Raine to help a fellow Magi leader uncover who was killing her people. You did your job, and now Tomás is out for blood."

"She was his mate," Cheveyo muttered, knowing there was no real way to refute Chay's statement.

"And now he's as crazy as she was," Chay shot back, his frustration finally breaking through. "Look, what happened then and what's happening now is not on you, it's on them. It's not safe for you here. Hell, even Natasha didn't want you to come."

"It's not her call." Something he made crystal clear during his last exchange with the Northwest's Demon Queen and the other two heads of Kyn houses.

Chay gave him a hard look. "Because of the shared visions?"

"Partly." There was no arguing with the fact that when a shaman, a high-ranking witch, and an oracle all shared the same damn dream, you needed to pay attention. A point he explained at length to the other Northwest leaders.

"And the other part?" Chay pressed.

He held Chay's dark gaze. "There was no other choice. Warrick couldn't come because Tomás would see his arrival as a threat to his pack—"

"Not to mention he holds our alpha directly responsible for his mate's death," Chay cut in unhelpfully.

Ignoring his comment, Cheveyo went on, "There are so few Fey here that sending Carys would do nothing to resolve the situation, and Rio specifically warned Natasha to stay the hell back." And it would be beyond foolish to ignore the Southwest Amanusa leader when he warned his Northwest counterpart to stay away. Besides, not only would the wrong people note Natasha's absence from the Northwest, but they'd very likely exploit it.

Chay's lips tightened. "I could take care of this myself."

"That isn't the issue." Since Chay was one of the highly skilled, covert Kyn warriors known as Wraiths, Cheveyo didn't doubt Chay's ability to hold his own. But justified or not, Cheveyo couldn't shake his sense of responsibility for the current unrest among the Southwest Kyn.

"Then explain to me what is," Chay demanded.

"I can't."

Chay canted his head as a shrewd light flared in his eyes. "Can't or won't?"

Holding his gaze, Cheveyo bit out, "Won't."

"Why?"

"It's personal." Cheveyo wouldn't give him more than that. Couldn't, actually, because his other, deeper, reasons were locked down tight. If everyone would stop picking at him and his decisions, he wouldn't have to waste time repeating himself.

Chay continued to study him, his face carefully blank, his thoughts hidden deep. "Can you do this?"

It was a question few would dare to ask Cheveyo, because questioning a Kyn leader could be detrimental to your health. As Chay was one of the privileged few, Cheveyo answered, "Yes."

A few more seconds ticked by before the tension in the SUV faded and Chay's arms dropped as he shifted in his seat. "Fine, then I'll wait right here while you explain your impromptu visit."

Grateful for the reprieve, Cheveyo followed his lead. "Scared, Chay?"

"Of accusing the Southwest Magi Head of not being able to keep her house in order?" Chay's lips twitched. "Merely exercising caution."

A small humorous huff escaped as Cheveyo shook his head. "Wise man."

He reached for his door and shoved it open before stepping out into the late afternoon sun. He stood next to the SUV, his gaze scanning their surroundings. The light drifted through the ponderosa pine painting the ground with dappled patterns. A breeze carrying the promise of rain tried to push back the blanketing heat as Arizona's monsoon season sought refuge in Flagstaff's higher elevations.

He shut his door and rounded the rental SUV, noting the sense of stillness hovering over the cabin. He stopped by the hood, and as previous tradition dictated, waited for the typical greeting—the rush of canine welcome followed by the occupant's appearance. When neither happened, unease crept in. Something was off. He took a moment to determine what was wrong. Turning back, he caught Chay's attention through the windshield.

The thump of the passenger door rippled through the yard, then Chay stopped at his side. "Want me to knock?"

"Might as well, her truck's here." But Cheveyo wasn't sure it would do any good. No one was here. Not Tala Whiteriver or her furry shadow, Ash. The quiet was too deep, too still. Chay jogged up the steps to the door and knocked.

As the seconds ticked by with no response, Cheveyo's waning patience and growing disquiet turned brittle. This wasn't right.

Heeding instincts honed by decades of experience, he tapped into the magic that made him Kyn, thinning the protective barrier until the world shifted and took on a sharper, clearer edge.

The cabin was no longer still, but surrounded by a

luminescent glow, the telltale sign of a complex ward. Not unexpected considering Tala's strength. Thankfully, there were no signs of intrusion or violence. Some of the tightness in his chest loosened.

Since he had no desire to clash with her protections, he called Chay back. "She can't be far, let's take a walk around." Because standing here and waiting wasn't working for him.

Chay came back down the front steps, a frown marring his lean face. "You feeling it too?"

"Yeah, problem is, I can't pinpoint what's behind it." Cheveyo waited until Chay stood at his side and kept his voice low, "You getting anything?"

When Chay shook his head, Cheveyo couldn't hide his grimace and silently cursed. If whatever triggered his internal alarms could elude two highly powerful witches, this already complicated situation was quickly graduating to completely screwed. *Or maybe it's just an excuse not to face her.* He ignored the snide voice, acknowledging that not even a year had passed since his last trauma-inducing visit. Not nearly enough time to forget what once hunted here. Or the havoc it left behind.

Together, he and Chay walked around Tala's cabin, all senses on alert. As they came to the wrap-around deck at the back, faint canine barks drifted to them. Not the friendly variety, but the deeper, warning sounds of trouble.

Exchanging a look, they took off, weaving through the trees and running through the surrounding forest. Despite the rush of air through his lungs and the heavy beat of his pulse, Cheveyo couldn't miss the sharp yips interspersed with deep growls growing in frequency and volume as they drew closer.

When a sharp feminine cry rent the air, Cheveyo's heart

stopped for a breathless moment in recognition. *Tala!* Having no idea what waited ahead, he locked her name behind his teeth and dug for more speed. A whisper of the earth's natural magic swept over him, lending speed to his passage as if Mother Nature shared his sense of urgency. At his side, Chay kept pace.

There was another deep, evil sounding growl quickly answered by a different, aggressive snarl. The warning yips changed to threatening rumbles, and Cheveyo gathered his magic close. There was a pained yelp followed by a short scream full of frustrated rage, the echoes of both leaving Cheveyo swearing under his breath. Every hair on his skin stood on end as the unmistakable energy of magic rode like lightening through the air as a powerful spell was cast.

"Shit." The muttered oath came from Chay even as the sunlight flashed off the blade in his hand as he leapt over a fallen log.

Cheveyo didn't bother agreeing, too worried about what they were running toward. Abruptly, they broke through the tree line and rushed into a small clearing. Cheveyo rocked to a stop, horror rushing through him. In front of him, a damning scene unfolded, shifting the situation from challenging to perilous.

Tala Whiteriver, the leader of the Southwest Magi, was crouched over a wolf, her fist wrapped around the hilt of a knife sunk deep into the furred chest of Tomás Chavez, the alpha and leader of the Southwest Shifters.

CHAPTER 3

"TALA!"

The sound of her name pierced Tala's adrenaline-laced haze and brought her head up, the demand in the familiar voice hard to ignore. Still reeling from the stunning blow delivered by the wolf currently pinned at her feet, it took precious seconds for the world to resettle. When it did, she wondered if the hit had done more damage than she suspected. Why on earth was Cheveyo here? Especially now?

A fiery lash of pain along her side wiped the questions from her mind, and she turned her attention back to the mortally wounded, but still struggling wolf. Gritting her teeth against the scream demanding freedom, she shifted her weight and wrapped her free hand around the wolf's paw buried in her side, holding his savage amber gaze and exerting pressure until his claws flexed and tore free of her skin. The resulting agony left black spots dancing on the edge of her vision, but she didn't dare give in. Not yet.

Breathing through the pain, she forced her chaotic thoughts into focus. She needed to get through to the rage-filled shifter. To ensure compliance, she sank as much power as she could into her command, praying it would work against the alpha. "Tomás, still."

If he didn't stop moving, her blade would nick his heart. Nearly immortal didn't equal immortal. When his struggles stilled, her hand trembled on the hilt.

Fingers shackled her wrist, squeezing hard, but not hurting, not yet. "Tala, what the hell is going on?"

She didn't dare look away from Tomás as she answered, "Something's wrong." That earned her a hiss of displeasure, which she chose to ignore. "He went after Ash, and when I went to intervene, he turned on me."

The fingers on her wrists flexed and gentled. "Why?"

"I don't know." And she didn't. Yes, she and Tomás had their differences, but this...She held the wild, maddened gaze while stunned panic clawed her mind. "This isn't right."

"Understatement of the century," Cheveyo growled.

Still struggling to comprehend what the hell happened to Tomás, Tala muttered, "Maybe he's bespelled? Or cursed?" Or his mind finally snapped. An option she wasn't quite ready to voice because the ramifications made her blood ice.

Cheveyo didn't answer, but his grip shifted, covering hers on the knife's hilt, keeping it steady. "You need to let go."

She shook her head. "If I move, he's dead."

"Is it silver?"

Swallowing against her dry throat, she nodded.

"If you want to find answers, you need to let go and get them while you can." It was an order, pure and simple. One not easily dismissed.

She finally looked at Cheveyo. New lines marred his

lean face, adding an edge to an already intimidating countenance. Between his piercing obsidian gaze, equally dark hair, sharp cheekbones, and bronze skin his Shoshone heritage was blatantly obvious. Strangely enough, his normally clean-shaven jaw was shadowed, but when her gaze went back to his, she couldn't escape the grim truth staring back. Tomás was dying, because of her.

Guilt rose in a choking wave and collided with the rancid nausea of panic. The caustic mixture settled in the pit of her stomach like a leaden, poisonous weight. Forcing her hand to release the hilt, she managed to dip her chin in a nod. Once sure Cheveyo held the knife steady, she turned back to the man she once considered maybe not a friend, but an ally.

Ignoring his constant growls, she cradled his furred head in her palms, ignoring the blood smearing her hands, and sank her magic into her touch. The familiar ache of working with natural, living magic burrowed into the marrow of her bones and burned. She held his feral gaze with hers and let the magic take her.

Unlike some of the other Kyn bloodlines, shifter magic was close enough to the Magis' power to be malleable. She settled her magic over Tomás like a protective cloak, all the while searching for anything that didn't belong. The combination of wolf and man was seamless, like the finest silk, and her magic slipped along, looking for purchase. It snagged over Tomás's chest, and she stopped, narrowing her power as she began a slow, methodical search. Nothing, except the ragged edges of his severed matc bond. It rasped against her magic, like sandpaper on an open wound, and she couldn't stop her reflexive flinch.

Nothing could be done for that injury, so she carefully moved on. She curled her magic's protective energy around the unforgiving presence of her blade, trying to provide a magical barrier between Tomás and the silver. It slid into place, even as cold knowledge swept through her. Silver and Lycos blood did not mix well as evidenced by the weakening magic seeping beyond the blade's touch. The barrier wouldn't hold long.

Another's magic slipped along hers, trying to reinforce the barrier. The familiar touch slipped into numb spaces and reawakened old aches. Desperate to stop the inevitable, she took Cheveyo's silent offer of help, weaving their energy together, slowing, but not stopping, the silver's deadly advance.

"Hurry, Tala." Worry laced Cheveyo's low voice.

Taking a deep breath, she placed her hand on the alpha's chest and once again sent her magic spinning through every inch of Tomás's body, desperately searching for the reason behind his incomprehensible behavior. Again, she came up empty. "There's nothing there." Refusing to look at Cheveyo, she ignored the tremor in her voice and held Tomás's glare. "Why?"

His lips curled back as a growl rumbled from his flared muzzle.

"We won't get anything from him unless we force him back into human form."

She snapped her head around to glare at Cheveyo. "We force him to change, and he'll bleed out in minutes."

There was no give in his obsidian gaze, and his face a merciless mask. "We don't force the change, you'll be facing a Tribunal with nothing but speculation. I'm not comfortable with that, are you?"

She remained stubbornly mute while fear tried to gain a foothold. The Tribunal would require witnesses and the only witness was currently glaring at her over the dying alpha. She was so screwed.

Reading her silence as an answer, Cheveyo continued with relentless practicality, "We don't have time to get a healer here, nor do we have time to get him to one."

He was right. Shoving her fear aside, she forced cold practicality to the fore. With Tomás dead, if she didn't have some answers for his pack and the other Kyn leaders, it wouldn't be long before she joined him in the hereafter. She was angry at having her hand forced, and there was no hiding her resentful consent from Cheveyo's glittering gaze.

His mouth tightened, but he quickly pulled the blade free.

Working against the clock, she gave him no warning, waiting only until the knife was free before drawing hard and fast on his magic, using it to bolster her own. She slammed it into the maddened wolf. Cheveyo's painful hiss was drowned out by Tomás's howl. Relentless and unforgiving, she drove her magic through the alpha, the combined wills of two strong witches struggling to override the will of the grievously injured shifter.

Tomás's wolf disappeared in a flash of heat and light, and when the burst faded, a man lay in the animal's place. Blood smeared his barrel chest, and Tala pressed her hands tight against the wound. Cheveyo yanked his T-shirt over his head and wadded it up. "Ready?"

She nodded.

Together they switched places until Cheveyo could press the cloth against the wound. The additional pressure made Tomás groan, his eyes fluttering closed while his hands feebly clawed at Cheveyo's wrists.

Tala caught them in her bloodied grip, holding them still. "Tomás."

At his name, the alpha's lashes lifted.

Tala was grateful to note some semblance of comprehending intelligence breaking through the lingering madness.

"Tala," he growled her name despite his labored breathing.

She leaned in, searching his face. "Why?"

Fury twisted his lips into a snarl as he jerked against her hold "You and yours—are playing—games with my wolves."

Despite his lethal wound, he managed a particular brutal shove rocking Tala back on her heels even as she tried to keep her grip on his wrists. Gritting her teeth, she held on. "I've never played any games with you or your wolves."

Her denial acted like an accelerant to the alpha's temper. "Liar!"

Despite Cheveyo's weight against his chest, Tomás lunged forward, catching Tala off guard. Her balance compromised, she lost her grip on his wrists, and barely dodged a wicked swipe of a half-shifted claw.

"Dammit, Tomás!" Cheveyo's voice whipped across the impending confrontation as he forced the wolf back to the ground. "Settle your ass down. I'm trying to keep you from bleeding out."

With a snarl, Tomás subsided, his face paling even as he shared his baleful stare between them. "Witches—ain't nothing but manipulative crones."

Unruffled, Cheveyo snapped, "And wolves are nothing but damn drama queens. What in the world possessed you to attack Tala?"

The alpha's chuckle was wet and choked. "Take her out first—before she—destroys us."

Shocked rocked through Tala. "You're mad."

Tomás turned his head toward her, his smile cruel and malicious. "Not mad—determined."

She shook her head. "I have never held any intention of destroying you or your pack."

"Bullshit," he hissed, only to fall into a painful coughing fit. When he finally stopped, his breathing was ragged and choppy, his complexion ashy and a thin line of blue surrounded his lips. "You took from me—just returning the favor."

"She had nothing to do with your mate's death." Cheveyo reclaimed Tomás's attention.

"Her—you—and that arrogant fleabag, Warrick—you killed my Lizzie." An ominous rattle sounded as he sucked in more air. "He promised me vengeance—"

Startled by that, Tala bit out, "He?"

Instead of answering, Tomás's lips curled in a fierce grin, revealing bloodstained teeth. "Not the only one you stole from..."

Ignoring the ominous shiver wrapping around her spine, she tried to appeal to the man who led the second largest pack in America. Grabbing his face, Tala forced him to meet her gaze. "You're dying, you fool. I can't save you."

For a moment sanity flickered. "Don't try..." Amber washed through his irises, and she lost him. "He'll make you all pay—"

Another coughing fit cut off his babbling, this one so fierce it dislodged Cheveyo's hold and curled Tomás's body. When it finished, Tomás's gaze was sightless, and one last harsh breath escaped before he fell eternally silent.

Stunned, Tala knelt next to him, her bloodstained hands in her lap, her thoughts chaotic. The warm press of fingers along her chin brought her back as Cheveyo forced her gaze to his, his fingers gentle but insistent. "Tala, you with me?"

Mutely, she nodded.

He searched her face, gave a short nod, and let her go. "We need to get to your cabin and get ahold of Andrew and the other alphas."

Andrew was Tomás's Second, but there were four other alphas who held the Southwest packs together. With Tomás's death, the power structure would shift, and it wouldn't necessarily be Andrew who took his place. Change had just bitch slapped the Southwest Kyn with a brutal backhand.

The enormity of the situation barreled into her and, for a moment, she floundered. Closing her eyes, she bowed her head and took a bracing breath. She couldn't afford to fall apart now. "We call Tobias in Tucson first."

"Why?"

Grateful for Cheveyo's focus, she answered, "Because he's the closest alpha, and the one most likely not to tear my throat out when this news hits."

"Tobias it is," he muttered.

CHAPTER 4

THE URGE TO TURN AROUND AND HEAD BACK TO PORTLAND WAS overwhelming, but Cheveyo knew he wasn't going anywhere, anytime soon. He studied the woman on the other side of the thrice-cursed dead body of Tomás Chavez, Southwest Lycos leader and Alpha of the Red Thunder Pack. A bruise rose along one sharp cheekbone, the skin darkening, her dark eyes were wide and a tad wild, even her blood-streaked hands held a slight tremor.

Whatever problems existed within the Southwest Kyn just took a mammoth leap sideways and threatened to drag Tala along for the ride. Considering her stunned, blank expression as she stared at the body, he knew the reality of the situation had yet to sink in. When it did, no doubt she would do whatever she could to push him aside. Too damn bad he didn't plan on budging.

When a canine whimper cut through the heavy silence, it jerked Tala out of her dazed state. She turned quickly and winced. "Ash?" She scrambled to her feet, her hand going to cover a crimson stained tear in her shirt.

Cheveyo reached out but missed her hand by

millimeters as she turned away. His fingers curled into a fist as his arm dropped, and he kept his concern silent.

Chay hefted Tala's pet wolf into his arms. "I need to get him somewhere where I can patch him up."

She hurried to Chay's side, her attention taken by Ash. "We can take him to the cabin." She rested a palm on Ash's head as the wolf tried to lick her hand.

Chay looked to Cheveyo in silent question. Understanding that Chay was reluctant to leave him alone and unguarded, Cheveyo said, "Go, I'll be right behind you."

Chay waited until Cheveyo, with Tomás in his arms, stood, and then he led the way back to Tala's cabin at a brisk pace. Tala stayed at his side, not touching Ash, but ensuring he could see her. Cheveyo followed behind, his mind picking through the various possibilities of what they would soon face. Considering how strong pack bonds were, he posed the most pressing question. "How long do we have before Andrew hits your door?"

She didn't even bother looking back. "If we're lucky twenty, maybe thirty, minutes, depending on where he was when Tomás died."

That wasn't very long to prepare for a seriously pissed off wolf, especially if Chay was busy playing vet. "How bad is Ash?"

"He's got a good sized slash along a foreleg and a couple of deep gouges in his neck that need stitching." Chay shifted his hold as he maneuvered around a log, causing Ash to whimper.

Tala made a soft shushing noise.

Obviously following Cheveyo's train of thought, Chay continued, "I'll need about twenty minutes to set the stitches."

"Make it fifteen."

Without bothering to answer, Chay picked up the pace. When they hit the edge of Tala's backyard, Cheveyo's arms were beginning to ache from the deadweight of Tomás's body.

Tala scrambled up the short steps to the deck, her magic sweeping ahead of her and the back door slid open. She led the way, throwing over her shoulder, "This way."

The men followed her inside. Tala stopped next to the entryway leading to the front of the house and motioned Chay in.

Cheveyo paused in the dining area. "Where do you want him?"

Small lines bracketed her eyes and her voice was rough. "Down the hall, last room on the left."

He nodded and turned. A sound from behind had him craning his neck to see her standing awkwardly between the entryway and the hall, her indecision clear. She wanted to go to Ash but felt obligated to take care of Tomás. That glimpse into her well-hidden heart brushed against long suppressed protective tendencies, and he made the decision for her. "Go with Ash, *bił hinishná-anii*," he urged. "I've got this."

She gave him a tiny, weak smile and headed to the front room.

Cheveyo went down the hall to the bedroom she indicated. He laid Tomás on top of the bed then looked around, unwilling to leave the alpha's body exposed. A quilt, its colors faded with age, lay folded on top of a wooden hope chest at the foot of the bed. Recognizing it, he brushed his fingers over the soft material. Just once. Memories tiptoed closer, but he lifted his hand and deliberately turned away. He wouldn't use that one.

He went to the end of the hall where the linen closet

stood and pulled out a different blanket. Shaking it out, he brought it back and gently draped it over Tomás. He left the room, closing the door quietly behind him.

He made a quick stop at the bathroom to wash his hands. As the rust color water swirled down the drain, he kept his gaze away from the mirror, reluctant to witness the upheaval created by this visit. He wiped away the crimson streaks on his chest and then waited until the water in the sink ran clear before turning off the faucet and drying his hands with the hand towel. When he stepped back into the kitchen, the teasing sense of rain wafted through the open sliding door. He went over to close it. Catching his reflection in the window, he decided perhaps he should find a T-shirt. There should be one left from his last visit. That was, if Tala hadn't decided to burn it.

He turned back down the hall and, once outside her closed bedroom door, a strange reluctance to invade her privacy made him pause. He turned the knob, and slowly pushed the door open. The familiar scent of sage touched lilac wrapped around him, slipping through unknown emotional cracks like haunting ghosts. Keeping his breathing shallow, he headed determinedly to the dresser taking up the far wall. He hit pay dirt with the first, low drawer. He snagged the familiar material, shut the drawer, and got out while he could.

Back in the hall, with the door safely closed behind him, he tugged on the shirt and headed to the front room. As he drew closer, he could hear Tala crooning comfort to her wolf. He leaned against the entryway, arms folded across his now covered chest and watched Tala cradle the wolf's head so Chay could carefully stitch the wounds.

Ash gave a sharp yip. Tala's hands tightened, keeping

him still. "Just a few more, *yázhí.*" She shot Chay a sharp look. "Hurry up."

He didn't bother looking away from his work. "I'm going as fast as I can. Don't want to leave your mutt looking like a junkyard dog." At Ash's low growl, Chay's hands stilled, and he met the wolf's gaze with a glare. "Knock it off, flea bag."

Cheveyo couldn't stifle his grin when Ash unsurprisingly subsided with a haughty canine sniff. "Best watch yourself, Chay, or that flea bag might bite you in the ass."

Tala lifted her head, her gaze flickering to his shirt, a tinge of color rising along her cheeks before she went back to Ash.

Chay, on the other hand, kept his attention on his task. "He does, and I'll bite back." His fingers were nimble as he made quick work of the last few stitches. "There, you're all done, you big baby." He set down the bloody needle on the towel at his side before picking up the bandages and setting them in place. "You're going to sport a few bald spots, old man." Which explained the small pile of shaved fur at his knee.

Ash shifted until he was half sitting, half lying in Tala's lap, then gave Chay an evil eye before turning to lick Tala's chin. She returned his affection with a gentle hug, then helped him get settled on a well-used doggy bed. "Stay put, big guy."

Chay gathered the emergency vet supplies and headed back into the kitchen. As he drew even with Cheveyo, he stopped and kept his voice low, "What now?"

Cheveyo watched Tala baby Ash, her affection for the wolf undeniable. "Until we figure out what the hell is going on, we kept the others off of her."

"Cheveyo." Chay waited until he had Cheveyo's attention, implacable resolve adding a depth of age to Chay's youthful face. "You're my primary, she's secondary."

Unfazed by Chay's pitiless expression, Cheveyo simply said, "She's my primary."

A pained wince broke through Chay's mask. "Dammit, man, you're bound and determined to make this as difficult as possible, aren't you?"

Cheveyo arched an eyebrow. "You expected differently?"

Blowing out a breath, Chay turned and went to the kitchen sink. "You're the least difficult of the big kahunas, so yeah, a man can hope, can't he?"

His woeful tone left Cheveyo shaking his head. "Perhaps you should heed the age old words of wisdom—"

"'Hope for the best, prepare for the worst'?" Chay offered over his shoulder as he cleaned the needle and rinsed out the stained cloths.

"More like, 'hope springs eternal,'" offered Tala as she slid past Cheveyo and took a seat at the table.

"Ha, ha, ha." Cheveyo moved into the dining room and joined her. "I was thinking more along the lines of 'False hopes are more dangerous than fears.'" Catching her arched brow, he shrugged and answered, "Tolkien."

At the sink, Chay turned around and leaned back against the counter's edge, drying his hands on a towel. "Hobbits, one ring, flaming-all-seeing eyeball of doom Tolkien?"

"That's the one."

"Huh, guess that explains it."

"Explains what?" Tala pulled one leg up and rested her chin on her knee.

Chay's smile was bright and playful. "Where he got his story ideas. Old man must have dealt with the Kyn."

The teasing that bordered on flirting irritated Cheveyo to no end. "We're going to be dealing with something a bit more serious than some agoraphobic salamander with kleptomania tendencies, any suggestions?" It came out more sharply than he intended and earned him a glare from Tala and a mocking grin from Chay.

Ignoring the sudden tension permeating the room, Chay drawled, "Got any silver shavings? We could spread them like salt along the doorways and windows." He tossed the hand towel aside and braced his hands on the counter's edge.

"Why are you here?" Tala's steel-laced question cut through the younger man's attempt at levity while her attention locked on to Cheveyo.

Cheveyo deliberately leaned back in his chair, shifted his legs out in front of him, and crossed them at the ankle. "You're aware of what transpired at the Council's latest meeting?"

She straightened slowly, but he still caught her wince before a small frown marred her brow as she tried to figure out what was coming. "I am."

Understanding that she wouldn't let him tend to her wound until this was out of the way, he stayed on point. Since caution was necessary when swimming in dangerous waters, he began wading in slowly. "So you know the decision to make the Kyn's existence known to the humans will be put to a Council vote at the next meeting in six months' time?" The eleven individuals composing the Kyn's Council were the ultimate decision makers, and, generally, their decisions became Kyn law.

She nodded.

He waded in a little more. "While it is too early to predict the outcome at this point, there are indications some of the Council may be blind to the larger picture. There are those who are concerned that this willful blindness may lead to the eventual extinction of the Kyn."

His careful wording earned him a sardonic snort. "Cut the bullshit political talk, Cheveyo. You and I both know that the Council likes hiding in the shadows. If they can keep the big, bad monsters off the humans' radar, all the better. Unfortunately, that's becoming harder and harder to do." She deliberately paused before adding, "Something the Northwest Kyn know all too well, don't you?"

He took her well-aimed jab with an acknowledging incline of his head and dove in. "We do, which is why, when a possible situation is brought to our attention and our help requested, we respond."

It didn't take her long to put two and two together. She grimaced. "Rio called you."

"Not me," he corrected. "Natasha."

Tala pushed to her feet.

Catching her pained wince, he followed suit, slipping around the table and capturing her arm in his determined grip. "We need to treat those."

She looked down and tried pulling his hand away. "Later."

He didn't move. "Now."

"Fine," she muttered ungraciously, allowing him to steer her to the sink.

Chay, who watched the exchange silently, moved off to the side and began rummaging through drawers.

"The top left by the stove," Tala directed him.

Chay found the drawer containing clean hand towels

and handed one over to Cheveyo. He took it and began running it under warm water.

"Well, Rio didn't call out of the goodness of his black heart, so why does he want you here?" Her tone was acerbic, but Cheveyo still caught the thread of worry she tried to hide.

He wrung out the now wet hand towel and motioned for her to pull up her shirt. She did so, exposing the raw claw marks along her ribs. He crouched down and began to gently clean the wound even as he crafted a healing spell. It wasn't particularly strong, but it would help ease the worst of it. "Because part of your problems started with us." He held on to her hip as he dabbed a particularly deep tear. Her quiet gasp was followed by the warm weight of her hand bracing against his shoulder. His stomach tightened, and he resisted the urge to stroke her hip in comfort, as she visibly held her breath. "Almost done," he said softly.

Her fingers dug in briefly, then released. Strain vibrated along her voice, "Tomás was the only one who blamed the Northwest. You don't owe us anything."

He wanted to growl at her use of "us," but concentrated on his task instead. "It's not a question of owing anyone anything." He rose, rinsed the towel, and dropped back down to resume his task. Time to come at this from a different angle. "You weren't at Mulcahy's funeral." His change of topic wasn't arbitrary.

"I wanted to come, but I wasn't comfortable leaving." Her fingers were absently brushing his hair from his shoulder.

He paused and looked up, meeting her gaze. "Why?"

Her fingers stilled. This close to her, he couldn't miss the slight flex of her jaw. "Someone started up that land deal business again."

He frowned. "I thought that deal died with Tomás's mate?"

"So did—"

"Tala!" An enraged bellow followed by a dull thump of something heavy hitting the front door cut her response short. "Open up, damn you!"

Chay didn't wait for Cheveyo, but rushed past to deal with the incoming threat.

Cheveyo rose, tossed the towel into the sink, and grabbed a gauze pad. Tala batted at his hands until he snapped, "Stop it. Let Chay take care of him. No sense in rushing in there yet." He taped the pad in place then tugged her shirt down. Keeping his hands on her waist, he waited until her gaze came to his. "Let us do our job."

Her spine snapped straight, and dull color rose under her skin. "I'm the Southwest Magi," she hissed. "I'm not hiding behind you."

He resisted the urge to shake her. "I'm not asking you to hide. I'm advising you to let us keep the enraged wolf from tearing your throat out." She opened her mouth to argue further, but he leaned in close. "Don't, or I'll lock your ass in your room."

Fury flared, and she went nose to nose with him. "You wouldn't dare!"

"Try me, *awéé*." Only when she finally pulled back, and he was certain she wouldn't test him, did he slowly release her.

"Fine."

Taking her less than gracious acquiescence, he gravely said, "Thank you."

"Don't thank me yet," she warned as she stepped around him and headed for the front room. "If I'm going down for killing one Kyn leader, I can just as easily go down for killing two."

CHAPTER 5

Knowing the importance of perception, Cheveyo stayed behind and to Tala's right. If he made the stupid move of standing between her and the pack's Second, she'd have to explain the deaths of two Kyn leaders, and that wasn't a situation he intended to create.

Chay stood near the stone fireplace, feet braced and arms crossed over his chest, his attention centered on the man barely holding it together by the couch. Lean and corded with strength, Chay barely topped the six-foot mark. With his impassive face and aura of coiled danger, like a snake preparing to strike, his ability to pull off dour and daunting wasn't difficult. The other man, however, was a ticking time bomb.

The two men were engaged in a staring contest, but as soon as Tala stepped into the room, the newcomer's attention whipped to her. "Where is he?"

"Andrew—"

"No!" Andrew cut Tala off with a sharp gesture, his voice verging on the edge of a growl. "Where is he?" He took a predatory step forward. Which in turn, triggered Chay to do the same.

Tala's spine stiffened, and her shoulders straightened. "Dead."

An amber sheen rolled over Andrew's dark eyes, the shifter's hold on his emotions tenuous at best. His upper lip curled, and a low, hair-raising rumble echoed through the room, only to be returned in stereo as both Ash and Chay responded to the primitive vocal threat.

Needing to take the current situation from lethal to survivable, Cheveyo softly commanded, "Enough." He didn't raise his voice. Instead, he looped his magic around the angry shifter like an invisible cage, leaving it poised to snap closed at a moment's notice.

When Tala stepped forward, deliberately adding a few inches between them, his patience cracked. If she wanted a reason to be pissed at him, he'd be happy to give her one. He tightened his magical grip and Andrew's growls cut off like a thrown switch. Ash and Chay fell silent. The quiet vibrated with the combined weight of Tala's resentment, Chay's wry amusement, and Andrew's fury, leaving Cheveyo stifling his beleaguered sigh.

"Cheveyo!" Tala gritted out.

He met her furious gaze, keeping his impatience in check. "What?"

"Let him go."

"I'm not hurting him, merely keeping him from making a mistake."

Her hands curled into fists at her side, and he swore he could her hear her teeth's enamel crumbling under the pressure of her locked jaw. "Now."

Without looking away, he slowly released his hold, conceding to her demand. Andrew gave a full body shake as

Cheveyo's magic receded. Although the room's tension slipped back, Andrew glared at Cheveyo. By the fireplace, Chay repositioned until he could rest an arm on the mantel, while Ash took his time laying his head back on his paws, his gaze never wavering from Andrew.

Tala pivoted back to Andrew. "Andrew," she called, regaining his attention. "What would drive Tomás to attack Ash and me?"

Lines creased his forehead as he frowned. "He attacked you?"

"And Ash," she reiterated.

He shook his head. "He wouldn't do that."

"But he most certainly did," Chay said.

Cheveyo shot him a quick look. As much as he appreciated Chay's willingness to back his protection of Tala, neither of them were there at the beginning of the attack. If asked to swear to who attacked who, they would be forced to tread a very thin line. Yet he did nothing to counter the impression Chay seemed determined to give.

Andrew's fury was slowly pushed aside by a grim acceptance. "Lizbeth's death has left our alpha..."

"Unsettled?" Tala offered gently.

"Unbalanced?" Chay's muttered opinion earned him a dark look from Andrew.

"Misguided," Andrew snapped, his fisted hands flexing.

The movement was probably meant to hide the fact Andrew's claws were out, but when a small bead of blood landed at Andrew's feet, Cheveyo knew the shifter's emotional state was volatile. He kept his question as empty of accusation as possible. "Misguided enough to attempt to kill another Kyn leader?"

An uncomfortable flush rose under Andrew's copper tone skin. "I don't know," he bit out.

"You don't know, or you don't want to answer?" Chay's brown eyes were cold.

"I don't know." Andrew visibly wrestled his emotions back. "If you had asked me a few weeks ago, I would have told you there was no way he would attempt such an idiotic move."

"What changed a few weeks ago?" Regardless of how calm her question sounded, Tala's question was layered in steel.

Andrew ran a hand through his shaggy hair, wincing when strands pulled against his torn palms. "He had a meeting down in Phoenix." His lip curled. "With one of the dickless mouthpieces of the BLM."

Tala cocked her head, puzzlement marring her brow. "The Bureau of Land Management? Why?"

Andrew's lips thinned, and he shook his head. "He didn't share, and I didn't ask."

The slight shift of Andrew's gaze revealed shadows of deception. He was lying. Before Cheveyo could call the other man on it, Andrew continued, "I want to see him."

Chay straightened, his silent disapproval unmistakable.

Before Tala could answer, Andrew closed in on her and snarled, "I'm not answering another damn question until I see him."

"Let the boy see him, child."

The new voice spun all three occupants of the room around.

A man stood in the entryway between the kitchen and the front room, his weathered hands holding a worn baseball hat. He tucked it into the rear pocket of a well-worn pair of jeans as he came closer, his hand-tooled moccasins silent against the wood. His thick silver hair lay in a shaggy cut around the sun burnished, clean shaven face. Faded flannel covered a white T-shirt and his bright, dark eyes framed the straight blade of his nose. Age didn't mark his features, but lay in the palpable aura he carried with him.

"Danny?" Her gaze went beyond him as if she expected someone else to pop into existence.

Reading her correctly, he gently chided, "I came alone." He turned and extended his hand. "Cheveyo, it's been a while."

Cheveyo clasped Danny's hand briefly before letting it go. "It has, sir." But the passage of years barely left a mark on the notable elder's face. "Time seems to be treating you well."

His politeness brought a flash of white as Danny smiled. "It has." Greetings done, the older man turned back to the silent Tala and scowling Andrew. "Please, Tala, allow the young wolf to see his alpha. There is time for mourning before change comes."

Normally such phrasing wouldn't set off Cheveyo's alarm bells, but as Danny was one of the most revered medicine men of the Southwest Kyn, his words carried more warning than comfort.

With a soft sigh, Tala stepped to the side, acceding to Danny's request.

Cheveyo caught Chay's eye and dipped his chin in silent command.

Chay pushed off the mantle. "Come on, I'll show you the way."

Tala, Danny, and Cheveyo waited quietly until the two younger men left, taking most of the tension with them.

Motioning to the couch, Tala said, "Danny, have a seat." Only after he did so, did she take a spot on the couch's other end, leaving Cheveyo the chair. She gingerly adjusted until she could draw one leg onto the cushion and brace her back against the couch's arm. "I'm always happy to see you, but your timing is…" She trailed off, obviously looking for a polite turn of phrase.

"Awful?" Danny offered.

When Tala's shoulders slumped, Cheveyo stepped in, "More like worrisome."

She shot him a dark look, but Danny reached out and touched her knee, gaining her attention.

"Why didn't you heed my warning, *sitsi*?" His gentle reprimand gained more of a reaction from the stubborn woman than anything Cheveyo had done to date.

She blinked rapidly as her shoulders rose and fell in a shrug. "I wasn't ignoring you. I had every intention of following through. It's just…" She drummed her fingers on her knee and slid a glance at Cheveyo. "Rio beat me to it," she muttered.

Her admission caught Cheveyo off guard, but he worried if he voiced his questions, she'd clam up tight. So he reined in his curiosity and listened.

"Ah." Danny shook his head, then looked at Cheveyo. "It's good you're here, then."

Holding the shrewd gaze, Cheveyo leaned forward, braced his elbows on his knees, and laced his fingers together. "I think I'll withhold judgment on that, if you don't mind. I'm still trying to figure out why Tomás went after Tala." He studied the woman in question then turned back to Danny. "There is something more at play in this than his grief." When Danny's mouth thinned, Cheveyo shook his head. "It was not why I am here, although I'm glad I came."

Tilting his head, Danny smiled, but knowledge swam in his gaze. Still, he asked, "Why have you returned?"

Recognizing the question for what it was, Cheveyo didn't bother to play word games. "I've come to ask you—what have you dreamed?"

Danny grimaced and exchanged a look with Tala. When he turned back to Cheveyo, a darkness dimmed his bright gaze. "Your people are sharing the same seeing?"

"Just the three most skilled at receiving such warnings," Cheveyo admitted.

Danny nodded. "The inevitable is coming on wings weighted by strife and violence. If we do not step into its path, we will become nothing but ghosts." He reached out and patted Tala's hand. "I did not see it starting like this."

Needing something more to work with, Cheveyo asked, "What did you see?"

Very little emotion leaked from the older man's expression, but the skin around his eyes tightened. "Dissension among our kind, while the humans band together in the shadows. Despite our unique abilities, humanity dominates us by numbers alone."

The stark words were unsurprising and eerily familiar. "Could you see any paths not ending in our extinction?" It was a question Cheveyo asked of his people, and they were unable to answer.

That earned him a raised eyebrow and a slow nod. "Paths exist, but they are shrouded in volatile darkness, hiding unseen dangers."

His unexpected answer stirred Cheveyo's waning hope. It was better than certain death. "Any guidance you could offer is welcome."

That earned him a highly amused look. "I don't mind offering guidance, but I'm not sure you'll find it any more welcome than Tala did."

Cheveyo spared a glance at the strangely silent Tala,

noting the mutinous set of her jaw. Recognizing her expression, he knew whatever Danny told her had set her hackles on end. "Perhaps, but I would still appreciate the help."

The medicine man nodded. "Then I'll share what I told Tala." His took a deep, his shoulders straightening even as his voice deepened. "The Kyn have long stayed hidden, but the time is coming where hiding will no longer ensure survival." He fell into the familiar cadence of story-telling woven in the memories of Cheveyo's childhood. "Unlike us, humans flit like lightning bugs on the world's landscape, able to change course on the tip of a wing. We, who are mired in our history and blinded by age, are slower to react. As much as Mother Nature loves her various children, she is still a Mother at heart, and her patience, while enduring, can be harsh and exacting. For the Kyn to continue, they too must change, faster than the world around them, faster than some are comfortable with."

Cheveyo settled in to wait, listening closely, while Danny captured the current Kyn situation in a nutshell.

"Long ago, there was one who saw much of this and began preparing for this day. He came to this new land to build a home far from eyes hazed by tradition. Despite the hunger of those left behind for his failure, he began to carve a new role for the Kyn. Each move he made, each deal he created with the humans, was done to build a safe harbor for his people when the winds of change became a storm."

Cheveyo blinked when he realized Danny was talking about Ryan Mulcahy, Natasha's predecessor and the previous head of the Northwest Kyn. The same man had not only been his friend, but had been murdered by a traitor's curse.

"His success angered those positioned on the other side

of the ocean. Jealousy began to fester among wounded pride, eroding the bindings of service to their people and replacing those ties with self-serving power and greed. Whispers and cunning have gained dominance, taking their place beside arrogance, and they now work in tandem to destroy him and all he built.

Danny's story stirred Cheveyo's simmering grief and anger because those forces were led by the current head of the Kyn Council, Leo DiMarcco, one of its most powerful members.

Not privy to Cheveyo's reaction, Danny continued. "When death took the man, those who privately celebrated his loss were taken unaware by his legacy's unexpected strength of spirit and determination not to lose what he built."

When Mulcahy fell, the Northwest struck back with lethal focus, refusing to falter under their grief. Their leader had been well loved, even by Kyn outside of the Northwest. A fact made obvious when Danny met Cheveyo's gaze, not bothering to hide his dark satisfaction laced with grief.

Cheveyo permitted a grim smile. Natasha's gruesome message to Leo left no doubt on where the Northwest Kyn stood, and it wasn't at the Council's side. Cheveyo fully supported Natasha's decision to send the head of the traitor, complete with a gift box and bow to Leo. While the Northwest may not be able to prove Leo's involvement with Mulcahy's death, after the latest betrayal, they had no doubts he was playing games in their territory. Now, Cheveyo wondered if Leo's games were limited to the Northwest, or if they had stretched farther than expected.

"The lines have been drawn—do the Kyn step forward and take their place at humanity's side or remain forever lost to the shadows of secrecy? It is time to choose."

Danny's voice took on a timbre, which raised the hair along Cheveyo's neck. "The only way to survive the pending storm of humanity's fear is to set aside the wounds of old hurts and well-worn prejudices, turn our backs on the fears haunting us, and trust the unknown to lead us forward."

The ripple of prophecy hung in the air, leaving a ringing silence in its wake.

"Trust is not going to happen if we're killing each other." The harsh comment came from the archway behind them.

"Andrew." Tala scrambled to her feet, her hand bracing on the couch's arm, her face paling at the quick move. "If I'd had any other choice—"

He raised a hand to stop her and shook his head sharply. "I know, Tala." There was resigned grief in his angry tone. He came into the room and tapped his knuckles to the side of his skull. "I know, logically, but—" he fisted his hand and dropped it to his chest, "—this, needs more time." He dropped his fist and gripped the back of an empty chair. He studied her before shaking his head slowly. "And I can't explain why he choose to attack you."

Cheveyo rose and faced Andrew. "But you recognize he did attack her." He wanted to hear the wolf admit it out loud, making Danny another witness. Behind Andrew, Chay moved in to the archway and leaned a shoulder against the wall.

The look Andrew gave Cheveyo wasn't friendly. "I wasn't there."

Not willing to back down, Cheveyo waited.

A low snarl escaped Andrew, his eyes taking on the glow of the predator under his skin. Cheveyo didn't move and Andrew looked away first, turning his head to focus on Tala. His gaze flicked down to the bloodstained side of her shirt before coming back. "I can't testify to what I didn't see."

Tala arched a brow. "Will you confirm that Tomás's behavior has been erratic?"

He dropped his chin in a stiff nod.

His reluctant admission lessened her tension. Tala's stiff shoulders relaxed a bit, but her voice was rock steady, "You'll state as much to Tobias?"

Andrew gave another short nod before adding, "I would suggest you reach out to him first."

Danny cleared his throat, garnering everyone's attention. "Actually, let the Triune approach Tobias. It's best he hears it from them." He turned his attention to Tala, his face grave. "However, they will want to see you."

The Triune was the three person advising body for the Magi house and Tala was answerable to them, a fact that left Cheveyo worried. Normally the strongest member of a Kyn house ruled without question, but Magi leaders were power checked by an advisory body. A holdover from the Burning Times when the Magi leaders' unpredictable wrath and thirst for vengeance fueled humanity's widespread determination to wipe them out. If they decided against her, the situation in the Southwest could easily become unsalvageable.

"I know." She lifted her chin, no signs of concern evident. "I'll attend the Triune's meeting with Tobias, as I have questions of my own to ask. Do I need to worry about any others?" She directed her question to Andrew.

He flexed his fingers on the back of the chair. "For now, the pack will wait for Tobias's direction."

"You're not gearing up to claim the Southwest then?" That question came from Chay.

Andrew shook his head. "With Tomás's recent behavior,

there were rumbles Tobias would be challenging him for the position soon. The Red Thunder pack is mine, but the Southwest belongs to him."

The "for now" remained implied, and Cheveyo was happy to leave it at that. There was more than enough trouble to clean up without taking on tangled lines of Shifter succession. Besides, that was the Northwest Alpha, Warrick's, bailiwick. Cheveyo had enough on his plate, trying to get Tala out of the crosshairs of whoever was determined to throw the Southwest into chaos.

"I would suggest your friends—" Andrew gave Chay and Cheveyo a pointed look, "—stay close."

Offended pride washed over Tala's face, but before she could say anything, Cheveyo cut in softly, "We plan to."

Before the undercurrents could rise into a clash of tempers, Danny offered, "Then let me help you take Tomás home."

Andrew gave a reluctant nod, uncurled his grip on the chair, and left the room.

Cheveyo stepped up to Chay, and they both watched the stiff back of the wolf disappear down the hall. Without turning his head, Chay kept his voice low, "He knows more than he's saying."

"He doesn't trust her." Cheveyo looked over his shoulder to see Danny talking quietly to Tala.

"Or us," Chay added, following the direction of his attention. "Which doesn't bode well."

"No, it doesn't," Cheveyo admitted. "But then, I think that's exactly what someone wants."

CHAPTER 6

Tala closed the door behind Danny and Andrew then leaned her head against the wood. In the kitchen behind her, Cheveyo and Chay moved around, but she wasn't quite ready to join them. In fact, it was tempting to open the door and run far, far away. As if that would help. Her mind wheeled uselessly, trying to figure out why Tomás snapped. The sound of Cheveyo's deep voice triggered another silent worry—the timing of his damn, inconvenient visit.

As if she needed the added burden of dealing with the man who played a pivotal part in creating the woman she was today. Unlike his last visit, where he was the one being hunted, this time, it seemed, was her turn. The role reversal made her uncomfortable.

"Keep that up, and someone may answer."

The droll observation had her head halting in mid-thump. When she realized she was repeatedly hitting her forehead against the door in frustration, heat flooded her face. Closing her eyes, she mouthed a silent curse before turning to face Cheveyo.

She studied him, her lips pressed together in an attempt

to restrain the barrage of useless words threatening to spill free. He looked good. Too good. She ignored the tingle of relief when she couldn't find any physical signs of his last disastrous visit. Well, unless you looked close, and she was definitely looking. His inky hair, now brushing his shoulders, was longer than normal, and there were more shadows in his dark eyes. The rest of him, though, still tempted her to reach out and touch.

The silence stretched between them, taut with unspoken things. Strangely, he broke first, and held out his hand. "Let's go to the kitchen, and I promise to answer your questions."

The temptation proved too great. She forced her fingers to uncurl before taking his hand, an action she'd never permit in public, but here in her home, where no one could see, she could indulge. "Don't make promises you can't keep."

"I don't intend to." His fingers tightened then relaxed as he headed for the kitchen.

They met Chay coming out. He took in their joined hands, but other than a quirk of lips, ignored it. "I'm going to grab our bags and make sure the fur menace out front takes it easy." He didn't wait around for an answer, and soon the sound of the door opening and closing echoed in the quiet kitchen.

Tala tugged her hand free as she continued to the dining room table, muttering irritably under her breath, "Go ahead, make yourselves at home." She gingerly settled into a chair, her movements careful so as not to pull on the claw rakes decorating her side. By tomorrow, the worse of it would be healed.

Cheveyo sat across from her with an audible sigh. "Leaving you alone is not an option."

She refrained from taking his response in a personal direction and kept the conversation to business. A much safer approach. "Doesn't mean I have to like it."

"No, it doesn't," he agreed, unruffled by her temper.

Once, his ability to appear unaffected drove her to frustration. Now, thanks to her experience of leading the Southwest Magi, she understood it for the necessary mask it was. Leadership roles were a bitch to manage and an even bigger pain in the ass to maintain. Although being on the receiving end of his blank expression was still frustrating as hell. Which reminded her, "Did Rio really tattle to Natasha?"

He cocked his head. "Tattle?"

Bracing her elbow on the table, she rested her chin in her hand. "What else would you call it?"

Dry humor snuck through, and his lips twitched. "Not tattling. Rio is as far from a child as you can possibly get."

She refrained from rolling her eyes. The Demon Lord riding herd on the resident Amanusas could out whine and out manipulate any child she'd ever known. Normally, he kept his devious machinations within his own house, and she wasn't sure how she felt about being dragged into his games. Correction, she knew how she felt—irritated—but not enough to make it an issue. "But he's not above game playing."

"Obviously he's not the only one."

"No, obviously not." And that fact made her wonder. "Which leads me to my first question—what game are you playing?"

Cheveyo's gaze was serious, almost too serious as he shook his head. "Not me, Tala. Not with you."

That fast, he snuck under her guard, chafing against an age-old hurt. She bit her lip, the small pain allowing her a moment to construct her response. Before she could speak, the front door opened, and Chay crossed the floor, his hands filled with two duffel bags. He came through the kitchen, his step hitching as neither Tala nor Cheveyo broke their silent staring contest. He kept on walking.

It wasn't until he disappeared down the hall that she was able to push old hurts down and choke out, "Then who?"

"The Council."

The possible ramifications of his answer struck like lightning, burning away the echoes of the past and leaving her wondering if she truly knew the man sitting across from her. "Are you serious?"

"They've had no qualms about screwing with us," he pointed out calmly, as if he wasn't opening Pandora's box of chaos.

Us being the Northwest Kyn, she surmised. If what Danny shared was accurate, there was no way to deny that one. Which meant the Southwest was running out of time to avoid the upcoming conflict. "Yeah, but it isn't as if you didn't make it easy on them."

"What do you mean?"

She winced at his sharp question and dropped her gaze. "No disrespect to Ryan Mulcahy, but you can't argue that from the get go he put himself in the Council's crosshairs."

"Is that what you believe?" Something bitter and dark drifted through his face before it smoothed back to his previous demeanor. "He left Europe to escape the Council's manipulative eye."

Catching the hint of a story in his words, she nudged, "Guess America wasn't far enough away then." She waited, hoping he'd share details. When he remained silent, she sighed, a little hurt at his reticence. "Regardless of what sent him overseas, when the Kyn settled here, they put more than an ocean between them and the old guard. The Council isn't one to forgive perceived insults, and Ryan setting up shop, making alliances with the human government, allowing the original Nations' tribes to join the Magi house as an equal power, and pretty much thumbing his nose at the old laws, didn't win him any favors. It was only a matter of time before they decided to strike back."

Finally, frustration broke through Cheveyo's calm, a furious light burning in his dark eyes as he leaned in. "And you and the rest of the Southwest Kyn, you're all just happy to sit on the sidelines and watch the fallout?" His lips twisted into a cynical curl. "Or maybe you just want to see who wins."

Instead of pissing her off, his comeback stung. She sat back. Did he really think so little of her? "Is that what you believe?"

He shoved back from the table, the chair legs scraping overly loud across the floor. Pacing over to the sliding glass doors, he braced a hand against the frame, his grip leaving his knuckles white. "The woman I knew would never stoop to such a level, but the Magi leader might be ruthless enough to do so."

This bitterness was new, not part of the man she knew, and it left her worried that the damage from his last visit might go deeper than anyone could guess. As much as she wanted to get to her feet and close the physical and emotional distance between them, she drew on skills honed from dealing with powerful Kyn in tricky situations and stayed seated. "I was merely sharing an outsider's perception of the current situation between the Northwest and the Council." She stared at his back. "If the roles were reversed, wouldn't you do the same?"

A heartbeat passed, then another before his muscles uncoiled and his arm dropped to his side. He turned to face her, crossing his arms over his chest. "I would do what was needed to keep my people safe. Which is exactly what Mulcahy did."

She got it, she really did. It was a leader's responsibility to put the needs of those they called theirs before all else. For Mulcahy, she didn't doubt he carried the weight of responsibility for every Kyn on American soil. It was who he was and why he managed to succeed, despite the Council's repeated interference through the years. But, as with all situations, there were two sides, and it was the flip side worrying not just her, but the other Southwest leaders. "How's that working out so far? Mulcahy is dead. Both Natasha and Warrick escaped attempts on their lives by the skin of their teeth. The Northwest barely gets their feet under them before another blow hits."

"Not without cost," he snapped. He dragged a hand through his hair. "Warrick lost two wolves and almost lost his mate."

"Because his Third betrayed him and his mate," she added softly.

His dark eyes flashed, and his jaw tightened, signs she was finally making inroads with him. "He still counts Sebastian his, regardless of what his Third did." He moved away from the door, his arm slashing down. "No one expected Jamie to turn on Natasha."

Since he opened the door, she decided to plow through with a question she harbored since hearing the rumors during the last few weeks. "Is it true?"

Her question threw him, and he blinked. "What?"

"That Jamie was working with Leo?" She couldn't figure out what could entice someone who managed to make a place for himself at the right hand of the Northwest Demon Queen, to be stupid enough to throw his life away by getting tangled up with the Council. Had Jamie harbored a death wish? Because that was the only reason Tala could find for him to even consider betraying Natasha, much less actually being dumb enough to go through with it.

"Beyond a shadow of a doubt," the answer came from Chay as he reentered the kitchen. "Stupid dumbass lost his head over it. Literally." He flashed a fierce grin that was just disturbing as he headed for the refrigerator and pulled it open. "Anyone want anything to drink?"

She suppressed a shudder at that visual. Nice to know the rumors were true. "Water, please."

Cheveyo shook his head but came back to the table and reclaimed his chair.

Chay brought her water and his tea, then took the chair between them. "Jamie, who shall forever be known as Idiot, kidnapped Natasha, and, when he went to show off his brilliance to Leo, was shocked when our illustrious leader decided to wash his hands of the whole mess. But forgiveness isn't in Natasha's vocabulary, and she made sure Leo got the memo."

"Hard to miss it." Tala had nothing but admiration for Natasha's gruesome response.

Chay nodded. "I heard it made the last Council meeting very interesting."

"Interesting isn't the word I'd use," Cheveyo said.

"Me either," Tala added, trying not to dwell on that moment when Natasha faced down Leo, and the world held its breath. Whoever had been watching over the meeting had worked triple time to ensure everyone left alive.

Shaking off the unsettling memories, she rotated her glass on the table. "Which, if you're here to propose what I think you are, is why the Southwest will be cautious before making a decision."

Chay leaned back in his chair and laced his hands behind his head. "Too dangerous for you, uh?" A devilish grin accompanied his question.

Ignoring the younger man, she aimed her response to Cheveyo. "If it was up to solely me, the decision would be easy."

Unmoved, he drawled, "With Tomás's death, it leaves it up to you and Rio."

"Does it?" Her hands stilled, and she lifted her gaze to Cheveyo. "The Southwest's Shifters may disagree. Tobias will take Tomás's place, which gives him a voice in the final decision. We have no Fey house, so unless all three remaining houses can agree to ally with the Northwest and come out to the humans, you'll walk away empty handed. Besides, the Council's retaliatory threat is very real. To be honest, until Tobias is satisfied with why his alpha is dead and has proof that your sudden appearance isn't tied in with it, I don't think you're going to get him to make that choice."

"And if I pointed out that the timing of Tomás's attack is suspicious?"

"Is it?" When Cheveyo exchanged a long look with Chay, she couldn't suppress the feeling more passed between them than she knew. "Spill, you two."

Finally, it was Cheveyo who spoke. "The Council has proven it's not above using our own people against us. It wouldn't be much of a reach to think they may have used Tomás's grief for their own ends. Setting him on you would not only throw the Southwest into chaos but, doing so just as the Northwest would consider coming to you with an offer of alliance, would ensure furthering the division between us."

She tried to wrap her mind around the depth of manipulation such political games would require, and it almost physically hurt. Problem was, she was starting to believe the two men. "You think this is the Council's way of stopping any possible alliance between the Northwest and the Southwest."

"It's exactly what they would do, especially if it gets them the end results they want." Chay dropped his arms to fold them on the table. "The Northwest carries enough weight to worry the Council, but if you add in the Southwest, now you have the majority of the American Kyn in a position to block the Council's decisions." All his earlier teasing was gone and in its place was a stomach-clenching seriousness.

The picture he painted wasn't hard to bring into focus. "And the Eastern Kyn?"

"The major Eastern house is the Amanusa, and they like to play in the human's political arena," Cheveyo said. "If the Council has their way, their playground becomes severely limited."

Following that logic, it meant that a division among the Kyn wasn't just possible, it was fast becoming a reality. Studying both men's expressions left her with no doubt where they stood. "You really want to take on the Council?"

Cheveyo reached out and caught her hand with his. "It's not a question of taking on the Council."

Her laugh carried an incredulous edge. "Isn't it?"

He squeezed her hand. "No, it's about ensuring the Kyn's survival."

CHAPTER 7

The sun sank, leaving trails of pink, purple and blue in its wake as Cheveyo sat alone in one of the two chairs on Tala's porch. He scrubbed his hands over his face wishing he could forget the fear he caught leaking around Tala's earlier shock, but he couldn't. Even more, he understood where it came from. What they proposed involved a pivotal shift for the Kyn, one he knew needed to be made, or it would only be a matter of time before his people became the ghosts Danny mentioned.

It didn't help that his raging need to exact payment for Mulcahy's death and the chaos wrought on the Northwest simmered underneath, wearing against his control. More than anyone, he knew the dangers of going off half-cocked, but the driving anger, it didn't give a damn. He wasn't sure how much longer he could keep it in check. Hell, if he even wanted to keep it in check.

He dropped his hands and stared unseeing at the stunning sunset, mocking bitterness filling him. When the man known for his logical approach chewed at the bit to scorch the earth and leave nothing but ashes in his wake, it might be time to worry.

It didn't help that someone had Tala squarely in their crosshairs. When it came to her, his protective streak turned frighteningly lethal. A fact he tried very hard not to let show, considering if she knew, she'd string him up by the balls in no time flat. This resulted in his self-imposed exile to the porch, giving her the privacy she requested to call Tobias. Cheveyo wasn't sure he could refrain from stepping in should the discussion take a wrong turn.

The door behind him opened. Her scent hit first, triggering a familiar ache, one etched deep. He tried to keep his inhale soft as she closed the door and crossed in front of him to lean against the porch rail. He dragged the alluring mix of sage and lilac into his lungs, letting it soothe the ragged edges of aged dreams. All the reasons why he chose to keep her at arm's length ran through his head, but for the first time in years, they were weak, broken reasons, and darker, stronger ones rose in their place.

She broke the quiet first. "The Triune beat me to it. Still, Tobias wants to meet around eight down at Black Pines."

There was no missing the tension in her taut shoulders. "I hear a 'but' in there."

She half turned to him, a small frown marring her forehead. "I need to make a stop first."

"Why?"

Her frown deepened. "I need to meet with someone."

Color him curious. "Who?"

"One of mine."

Holding her gaze, he waited.

Eventually, she huffed out a breath. "He works with the National Parks Service, and he called yesterday requesting a face-to-face meeting."

Leaning forward, he rubbed his temple, a futile attempt to ease the beginnings of a headache. "About what, Tala?"

When she didn't answer, he dropped his hand and looked up. Her tilted chin and mutinous expression tore one of the few threads left on his patience free. "What about?" The steel-edged question came out sharp.

Her eyes flashed, and her answering tone was equally hard, "He didn't say."

Pushing to his feet, he forced his legs to take him to the end of the porch. Frustration mixed with worry while he fought down his instinctive need to keep this stubborn woman under lock and key before anything more could happen to her. If he didn't get his ass under control, she'd go around him, and right now things here were too unsettled and unknown for her to be on her own.

He gripped the porch railing as he stared out over the yard and forced his voice to remain level. "Perhaps you should consider rescheduling. This may not be the best time for this."

That earned him a short, humorless laugh. "You know better than that, Cheveyo." He turned, and she moved closer until they were standing toe to toe. "Right now there is no good time, we both know it."

Unfazed, he folded his arms over his chest so he wouldn't reach out and shake her. "And yet you still plan on going."

She simply held his glare, her silent response resonating between them.

He clenched his jaw, his molars grinding together, but he spat out, "Fine. Where are we going?" When she opened her mouth, he cut her off, "Don't even think about arguing. Need I remind you? You go nowhere alone."

Her mouth snapped shut, but her lips curled in a silent

snarl of defiance. "Mesa Creek Road, it's about a half-hour drive."

Without breaking their staring contest, he raised his voice, "Chay."

The door opened, and Chay stuck his head out. "You rang?"

"Get Ash settled, we're going for a drive."

"Got it." He disappeared back inside.

Tala cocked her head to the side, her eyes narrowed as she studied him. "Be very careful," her warning was soft, but very clear.

He closed the distance between them, forcing her back until he could cage her against the railing, his hands gripping the wooden edge on either side of her hips. He leaned in until she was forced to put her hands on his chest to counter her balance. The heat of her touch left him stifling a groan, even as the feel of her appeased a darker part of him. "You should take your own advice."

"Don't." Arrogance turned her voice icy, but couldn't disguise the flash of hurt that was there and gone.

"Don't what?"

"Don't you dare pretend." Her words carried a sibilant edge of fury, and her nails bit into his chest in an unconscious reflex. "Your role as my mentor is long past, and I am worlds away from that girl. Your protection isn't needed anymore. This is my house, my rules. If you don't like it, leave."

There was no escaping her underlying bitterness, but he wasn't ready to confront it or the reasons behind it. Not yet. He forced a smile and knew it was cold. "Wanted or not, me and my protection aren't going anywhere."

Fury washed under her skin, adding a rosy glow, but before she could say anything, the sound of a throat clearing cut off her response. The both turned their attention to Chay, who stood on the steps below the door. Had to give the man credit, he barely flinched under their combined regard. "I'll be in the SUV, whenever you two are finished."

The bite of Tala's nails disappeared from Cheveyo's chest, only to reappear on his arm as she forced his hand off the railing and escaped from his hold. "We're finished."

Watching her storm away, he muttered, "Keep dreaming, sweetheart, because we're nowhere near finished."

With Ash settled safely behind Tala's daunting wards, Cheveyo reclaimed the driver's seat and followed Tala's directions to the home of one Rory Ellis. Chay lounged in the back after courteously giving Tala the passenger seat.

"Who is Rory Ellis?" Chay poised the question.

Tala shifted so she could see both men. "He's a druid, works for the U.S. Forestry service. His current assignment is in Picture Canyon Preserve. His wife is an empath and teaches at one of the local elementary schools. They have a son about six."

"How many druids do you have here?" Chay's curiosity was evident.

"Just a handful. You may have met a few. They're the Juniper Clan, and fall under the Cascade Order."

"Actually, a couple of them were at the last conclave." Cheveyo moved into the center lane of the freeway. The Northwest was home to a group of twenty druids, who called themselves the Cascade Order. While they gathered throughout the year for various celebrations, they hosted an annual conclave, inviting all those who lived east of the Mississippi. They worked closely with the smaller groups, known as clans or groves, scattered along the west coast. And, it seemed, into the Southwest area.

"Huh," Chay said.

Cheveyo risked a glance in the rearview mirror. "You sound surprised."

Chay shrugged. "Guess I am. Doesn't seem like this terrain would garner much druidic attention."

Tala laughed. "They may be nature based in their beliefs, but they don't need a forest to claim land." She motioned to the passing scenery, indicating the white aspen and pines stretching along the highway. "Although we do have our own forests, a little younger than yours, but still..."

"Point taken." Something bumped the back of Cheveyo's seat, and then Chay was leaning between the front seats, his shoulders braced. "So Rory's a druid and his wife is psychic?"

Tala nodded. "She's fairly sensitive, and genealogical research uncovered a Fay or two further back in her family lines."

"She didn't know?" Cheveyo asked.

Tala shook her head. "Nope, didn't have a clue."

"Must have made for an interesting conversation," Chay commented.

"Yeah," Tala said. "It took a bit before Anne got past her shock, but with her ability, believing us wasn't difficult. It was altering her current view of the world that took a bit longer."

Having experienced similar situations when a human married into the Kyn, Cheveyo winced in sympathy. "At least it ended well."

"That it did," she agreed.

"Any idea why Rory wants to meet?"

Since it was the same question Cheveyo put to her earlier, he silently thanked whoever was listening for Chay's ability to casually slip it in to the conversation.

Sure enough, instead of raising Tala's hackles, she took Chay's question in stride. "I'm not sure, but he wouldn't ask if it wasn't important." She went quiet for a moment, then added, "The only thing I can think now, after Andrew's little revelation, is that it may have something to do with the land deal."

That damn land deal seemed to garner quite a lot of unwanted attention. During Cheveyo's last visit, a Phoenix-based development corporation wanted the land that belonged to the Southwest pack, land they weren't inclined to give up. Especially the alpha pair, Tomás and Lizbeth. When the developer raised a host of evil spirits that resulted in the death of the alpha pair's son, any chance of a deal disappeared. That it was back in question now was worrisome, but not as worrisome as the fallout from Tomás's death. Which reminded him, "Are you going to have enough time to meet with Rory and make your appointment with Tobias?"

"Hopefully." She shifted in her seat until she faced front again. "Tobias set a reservation for the Pines's back room."

Keeping his attention on the surrounding traffic, he negotiated around the slower cars. "Better to meet him now than hash it out in front of the Triune." He was checking the passenger side mirror and caught her wince. "What?"

She cleared her throat. "They want to meet tomorrow morning."

A subtle tension in her voice caught his attention. He

risked another glance to find her focus wasn't on him, but on something only she could see, as she absently played with the tail end of her blonde braid. Keeping his voice even, he said, "Not surprising."

"No, it's not."

"But you're still worried?"

His question stilled her restless movements, and the weight of her gaze landed on him. "I'd be a fool not to be."

Since she was far from a fool, if she was worried, there was reason to be, but asking her outright wouldn't work. He sighed and drummed his fingers on the steering wheel. Time to take a roundabout approach. He asked the most important question, considering the situation. "Who's serving as Triune?"

"Teagan Greenstone, Hadley Begay, and Wyatt Reid."

He recognized two of the three names. Teagan was Tala's cousin, and, while they grew up together, they hadn't hung in the same circles for years, but the lack of closeness shouldn't impact the upcoming meet. He knew Hadley's name because while he was mentoring Tala all those years ago, the two women had been best friends. But the third? "Wyatt?"

"Wizard from the Karrow Cabal," she answered easily. "He joined the Triune about three years ago after Danny stepped down."

The quickness of her answer didn't indicate concern, but the Karrow Cabal was one of the largest American wizarding groups. Since they could trace their bloodlines back to one of the founding European families, they held a great deal of weight in the Kyn community. "Is he the one that worries you?" Catching her shrug, he shot her a narrowed eyed look. "Tala?" he prompted, while Chay watched on.

Her jaw firmed, and her lips pressed tight, but she turned her head and looked away. "No."

His fingers tightened on the steering wheel, and he waited until he passed the van in front of them before asking, "Who?"

"Teagan."

Her cousin? "Spill."

She made her reluctance obvious, her voice tight. "Jenny's loss hit her hard. They were close and the way it went down…"

Yeah, the shit between the Shifters and the Magi houses just kept getting deeper and deeper. The young witch, Jenny, had been involved with the alpha pair's son. Something that hadn't sat well with his parents. In fact, when grief-stricken Lizbeth decided to trap her son's soul as a Soul Stealer, she fueled the black spell with Jenny's death, and the death of her unborn child, the alpha pair's grandchild. "Teagan holds you to blame." Not really a question.

It was Tala's turn to sigh. "She's struggling with it. She helped raised Jenny."

He picked his way through the emotional minefield, trying not to set off any triggers. "How were you supposed to stop it?"

"It's my job as the Magi head to keep them all safe, Cheveyo."

Even now, the guilt she carried over the whole, twisted situation rang through loud and clear. As much as he wanted to comfort her, that wasn't what she was looking for. "Lecturing to the choir here, but you and I both know it's not that easy."

"But she doesn't."

Her quiet answer snuck under his skin and scraped

across his nerves, but it was Chay's voice that came out sharp. "Then she shouldn't be serving on the Triune."

That startled Tala, who twisted around to face him. "That's harsh."

No, it wasn't, but maybe if she heard the truth from someone other than Cheveyo, she'd listen. He wasn't surprised when Chay didn't back down. "She shouldn't hold you responsible for Lizbeth's actions."

Her chin jutted out. "My position means I'm responsible for my people and their actions."

"Lizbeth wasn't yours," Cheveyo tried to point out.

Tala went to respond, but Chay cut her off. "There's such thing as free will, and you can't control everyone's decisions. If you follow that logic, then it's Tomás, not you, who's responsible for Lizbeth's actions."

"If I was paying closer attention—"

"What?" Impatient with her self-flagellation, Cheveyo's question came out short. "You could have stopped Jenny from getting involved with Eric?" Their exit was coming up, so he maneuvered over to the ramp. "You're going to tell me that telling a teenager they can't see someone guarantees they'll stay away? Ever heard of Romeo and Juliet?"

"That's not the point."

Damn, she was stubborn. "Isn't it? You did the best you could. Lizbeth's decisions are not yours to bear."

"Stop." She held up a hand, her eyes flashing. "I get it."

"Do you?"

"Yes, can we change the subject now?"

"Fine." Based on her crossed arms and mulish expression, he could only hope they got through to her. For now, he'd drop it as she had enough on her plate. He moved on. "What about Hadley? You two still close?"

She shook her head, her expression wistful. "Not so much."

"What happened? You two used to be thick as thieves."

Her smile was fond, but sad. "We grew up."

His heart ached for her, but he wasn't surprised. Not only did time test the bonds of friendship, but Tala's position set her apart, making it doubly difficult to hold on to such things. He made the left, and the conversation switched to driving directions.

Tala took them into a fairly new home development filled with modest cookie-cutter homes lying on the very edges of Flagstaff. They made their way through the neighborhood's maze and turned on to Mesa Creek Road.

Chay's quiet curse filled the car as Cheveyo began to slow.

At the end of the cul-de-sac, a state trooper's car was parked outside Rory's house. Dread pooled in Cheveyo's stomach as he turned into the slightly curved driveway and stopped in front of the double car garage. Tala already had her door open and was stepping out before he could shut off the engine. He and Chay followed her to the front door blocked by the recognizable uniform of a state trooper.

"Anne, what's going on?" Tala barely nodded to the state trooper as she slipped around him to stand near the tear stained and pale young woman gripping the doorframe.

The younger woman clutched her arm, her voice shaky, "It's Rory. He's been in an accident."

CHAPTER 8

Shock rocketed through Tala as she held Rory's petite wife close, scared that, if she didn't, Anne would collapse to the ground. "An accident?" She aimed her question at the grim faced trooper standing silently by.

"Ma'am, perhaps we should go inside?" In contrast to his appearance, his voice was kind.

Tala led Anne inside, leaving the men to follow. She guided the young woman through the open floor plan common to so many of the newer homes and led her to the spacious kitchen overseeing the brightly lit living room.

"Talala!" A childish voice piped up, and a young boy rose from the Lego covered rug and zipped around the couch to catch her around the knees.

She dropped her free hand to ruffle his brown curls, while keeping Anne tucked close. "Hey Pax, how's things?"

He tilted his head back and beamed. "Mom bought me new Legos. It's the Jungle Tree House cuz we're reading the Magic Tree House." His attention switched with breakneck speed to his mother and the men slowly following. Pax frowned. "What's wrong, Mom?"

Anne slipped out of Tala's hold, visibly pulling herself together before kneeling in front of her son and wrapping him in her arms. "I promise to share in just a little bit, but for now, why don't you work on that tree and let me talk to Tala, okay?"

"Okay." His response was muffled as he buried his face against her neck and returned her hug. The mother and child clung to each other for the space of a few heartbeats before Pax uncurled his arms, kissed his mom's cheek, and went back to his Legos, his mood much more subdued.

"Come on, Anne," Tala urged softly, helping her to stand with a hand at her elbow. "Let's sit at the counter." They did just that while the three men took up positions in the kitchen.

Once everyone was situated, Tala addressed her questions to the trooper. "I'm sorry, I didn't catch your name."

"Sergeant Willows."

The sergeant looked to be in his late thirties, maybe early forties, but his gaze was decades older. Probably a result of other visits such as this. Not a job she envied. "Sergeant Willows, what happened?"

Willows looked to Anne, then back to Tala. "Before I answer, are you family?"

"No, a close friend of the family's. Rory asked me to stop by so he could give me some references for my research."

"Research?"

"I'm an herbalist, and with Rory's background in botany, he's one of my main go-to's for research questions." When the trooper's gaze switched to Cheveyo and Chay, she added, "My two graduate students, Cheveyo and Chay." Hands were shaken, and greetings murmured, before the sergeant turned back to Anne and Tala.

Behind his back, Cheveyo mouthed, "Grad student?"

Fighting the urge to roll her eyes, she raised an eyebrow before turning her attention to the trooper's conversation with Anne.

Willows stood on the other side of the counter facing Anne, compassion easing the hard lines of his face, his voice pitched low so not to disturb Pax. "Your husband was in an accident and was taken to Phoenix General." A soft sob escaped Anne, and she covered her mouth with a shaking hand. Sympathy washed over his face. "Is there anyone you can call to stay with your son?"

Tala rubbed gentle circles between her trembling shoulders. "Anne, why don't I call Sara and have her pick up Pax? He can spend the night with Tyler."

Anne nodded, and Tala excused herself to make the call. After Sara assured her she'd be over in fifteen minutes, Tala left the trooper with Cheveyo and Chay, trusting them to get the details of Rory's accident.

Once she explained the impromptu sleepover to Pax, he started picking up his toys. She used his momentary distraction to usher a stunned Anne into her room where she started packing an overnight bag as they waited for Sara to arrive. When Tala checked on Pax, he was finishing up in the living room. She helped him tuck the box away, and followed him to his room.

Covered in images of far-flung galaxies populated with space knights and warrior raccoons, Pax piled a stuffed floppy eared dog, and a crumpled pile she soon discovered were his pajamas, on his pillow. She kept a light conversation going as they picked out clothes and went in to the bathroom to gather the necessities. Once everything was safely tucked into a camouflaged backpack, she took his small hand to lead him to the living room.

They were almost to the living room, when he tugged her hand, bringing her to a stop. "Tala, why was mom crying?"

Looking down into his scared face, her heart broke. She dropped into a crouch so she was eye-level with him. "Well, sweetpea, she's worried about your dad."

"Is he in trouble?"

"No, honey, but something happened, and he had to go to the doctors." When the boy's gaze dropped, and his bottom lip began to tremble, she gathered both of his hands in hers and squeezed carefully. "Pax, look at me." She waited until he did so. "The doctors are taking really good care of him, so you just keep him in your prayers, okay?"

"Okay." His voice was small.

She pulled him in for a hug, letting him hold on as long as needed. When he finally wiggled to be free, she rose and keeping his hand in hers, headed back into the living room.

Sometime while helping Pax pack, Sara arrived. She now followed Anne out of the master bedroom. When she caught sight of Tala and Pax, she flashed a sad smile at Tala and a brighter one at Pax. "Hey, kiddo, ready to go see Tyler?"

The next handful of minutes became a subdued rush of getting Pax out the door, then listening to Anne's scattered directions and reassurance that her mother, who lived in the valley, would meet her at Phoenix General. With the house shut tight and Anne ensconced in the trooper's passenger seat, Tala waited until the trooper's car drove away before turning to Chay and Cheveyo. "Were you able to get any information from him?"

Both nodded, but it was Cheveyo who came up to her and with a warm hand at her back, nudged her toward the SUV. "We'll fill you in on our way to Black Pines."

She let the quiet settle, anxiety for Anne and Rory setting up shop among her growing pile of worries, while she ignored the faintly panicked voice muttering what the hell else could go wrong because that would just jinx it. It didn't stop her stomach from roiling with dread. Once Cheveyo was back on the main road heading for the restaurant, she broke the heavy silence. "What happened?"

Chay answered, "According to the sergeant, they found Rory's car just past Stonelake Road. Do you know where that is?"

Shifting in her seat so she could see him in the dim interior, or at least, catch glimpses of him from the streetlights illuminating him in disjointed splashes. "If it's where I think it is, it's near where the road goes into a series of curves as it comes up the mountain." Which didn't bode well for Rory's health.

"Okay, that would make sense then. They think the front tire blew, causing him to lose control, and then the car went off the side and down an embankment."

Chay's answer left her reeling and her imagination working overtime to supply the horrific images. "Oh, dear gods."

"Rory was med-evaced to Phoenix and the last time the trooper checked," Cheveyo joined in, "Rory was listed in critical condition." He spared her a quick look before turning back to his driving. "Willows said when he got to the scene, he was surprised to find Rory still alive."

Even as the two men filled in what details they could, her mind spun through various scenarios. "I'll check in with Anne later tonight, once she has a chance to see him. If she's okay with it, I'll ask Danny to go down and visit." Danny's healing ability might keep Anne from becoming a widow.

"You may want to contact his clan as well," Cheveyo offered.

"Actually, I can do that now." She pulled out her phone, thumbed through her contacts, and located Ken Black, Rory's best friend and fellow druid. She made the call, grateful when Ken picked up. After passing along all the information they had, Ken assured her he'd reach out the other druids and Danny. Knowing those closest to Rory would be there to help Anne and Pax, allowed some of her turmoil to recede.

Unfortunately, trepidation about her upcoming meeting with Tobias took its place. She pocketed her cell, and stared unseeingly out the window, her thoughts as chaotic as the day's events. While she'd been able to push everything but the immediate happenings aside, now she was right back on the hamster wheel of questions.

No matter how much her worried thoughts twisted and turned, they kept snagging on the one question she desperately needed an answer for. What had instigated Tomás's attack?

She and Ash had been hiking the well-worn trails behind her house, collecting herbs and plants that needed restocking. One moment things were fine, the next Tomás burst from the underbrush hitting Ash mid-body. Stunned by the unexpected attack, it took her precious seconds to recognize Tomás's wolf form.

She tried yelling at him, then hurtled defensive spells, hoping to snag the human half of the shifter's mind, but gave up when he turned on her. Maybe she could have fought him off with just magic, but under the whirlwind of claws and teeth, her survival instinct kicked in with a vengeance.

Remembering the feral light in his amber eyes, the

doubts haunting her retreated to whispers. There had been nothing sane for her to connect with, not then, and certainly not when her knife was buried hilt deep in his chest.

Still she wondered as she searched for an answer only to come up empty. Desperation set in. She needed something to give Tobias and the Triune, something more than Tomás had lost his fricking mind.

Warmth pressed against her hand, startling her back to the present and gently stilling her mindless picking on her jeans.

"You okay?" Cheveyo's question was low, but the sincerity behind it brought a lump to her throat.

Unable to speak around it, she shook her head.

"One thing at a time, *awéé*. We'll be okay."

Unable to resist the devastating combination of comfort and tenderness, she turned her hand palm up and held tight, wishing he was right.

They made it to Black Pines with time to spare. Not that it mattered, because, as they stepped into the backroom, they found it already occupied. Two men and a woman were seated on one side of the table, and a waitress was setting drinks in front of them. Tala noted the three empty seats situated on the closest side and moved to the one in the middle. Cheveyo and Chay followed—one to her left, and one to her right.

They stopped behind the chairs and waited while the man in the middle pushed back from the other side of the table and stood. "Tala."

"Tobias."

"Toby, please." He motioned to the empty chairs. "Have a seat."

Everyone settled in while the waitress took their drink orders.

Tala studied the man who would be the new Southwest Alpha. Toby was the opposite of Tomás in more than just looks. Blond, light eyed, with a muscular frame that harkened back to his northern European heritage, he gave the impression he would be comfortable, regardless of his surroundings, be it a boardroom or camped out in the Alps somewhere.

Her previous interactions with him had been limited to various meetings, most of which involved regional Kyn politics. He struck her as fair and strangely levelheaded, an anomaly for most Shifters who tended to let their more primitive natures take the lead. His companions—a clean-shaven male sporting shaggy brown hair and glasses, and a sliver-streaked dark-haired female dressed in corporate professional—were complete unknowns.

When the waitress left, a stilted silence settled around the table. Toby braved it first, giving a round of introductions. "My Second, Will, and my Third, Leticia."

Tala returned their polite nods. "I appreciate you making the time to meet with me on such short notice, Toby."

The wolf wore an inscrutable mask. "Andrew managed to catch me before your Triune, so, given the situation, I felt it would be the most judicious decision in my attempt at gaining answers." His gaze turned to Cheveyo. "However, I wasn't expecting to see you here, Cheveyo." There was no missing the underlying territorial growl in his last statement.

Given his recent change in powers, Tala figured the wolf was entitled.

Obviously so did Cheveyo since his relaxed position remained undisturbed. "My visit was very last minute, and I did not have the time to notify the necessary parties. Natasha requested I deliver a—" Here, he paused, making it obvious he was carefully choosing his words, "—delicate, but urgent message to the powers that be. Unfortunately, my plans were unavoidably changed."

Toby's smile was more a bearing of teeth. "Funny, today seems to be the day for such things." He turned his attention to Chay. "And you are?"

"Chayton." The fact that Chay remained unruffled under the alpha's regard, when most would show some sign of intimidation, solidified a few of Tala's assumptions. Not only was Chay here to protect Cheveyo, but chances were damn high he was one of those sneaky Wraiths, a group of elite warriors at home in the shadows. Wasn't it funny how when a Wraith hit town, things suddenly detoured to hell? Or maybe that was just having Cheveyo in the picture. Whatever it was, she was really beginning to hate it.

"He's mine," Cheveyo added, reclaiming Toby's attention. The two men engaged in a staring contest, neither willing to back down. At least not until the waitress returned, her perkiness cutting through the tension.

Tala stifled her sigh as orders were given. Cheveyo's claim was like some sick version of deja-fucking-vu. The last time he claimed someone as his, it was that freaking hellcat, Raine McCord. Before that...well, Tala had no intentions of going there. Not now. Not ever, because the past needed to stay in the past.

The waitress finished taking Chay's order and turned to Tala. "And you, ma'am?"

"The Southwest salad, dressing on the side, please."

"Of course." With another professional smile and a quick scan of drink levels, the waitress left.

The polite smile Toby donned for the young girl faded, and he studied Tala. She couldn't miss the banked fury in his brilliant gaze and knew his patience was at an end. "What happened?"

She relayed everything as matter-of-factly as possible—starting with how she and Ash were on her land, harvesting herbs, when Tomás attacked, all the way through to her and Cheveyo's futile attempt to save Tomás. When she finished, the roiling anger from all three wolves made it hard to breathe. Still, she kept her heart rate level and her breathing even, knowing the slightest change might trigger a messier situation than what they currently faced.

It was Leticia who spoke first, forcing out the question, "Magical traces?"

Cheveyo shook his head. "Neither Tala nor I could find traces of anyone or anything else at work."

Will leaned forward, bracing his balled up hands on either side of his bread plate. "So what? Our alpha just decided to attack Tala for the hell of it?"

"No." Chay shifted in his chair, his face hard. "He intended to kill her, then Cheveyo, and then Warrick Vidis."

Will snarled, his fingers flexing, the nails scraping against the table. Toby set a restraining hand on his wrist, leashing his Second. He gazed intently at Chay. "He told you that?"

Chay nodded.

"Damn it," Toby muttered, letting go of Will and rubbing his forehead as he sat back.

"You don't seem surprised," Cheveyo noted.

"We're not," Leticia said quietly, ignoring Will's glower. She then turned to Toby. "I hate I-told-you-so's as much as the next person, but I did warn you he was too far gone over Lizbeth."

Toby's jaw tightened. "And I told you, challenging him while he was obviously grieving would give those looking for it an excuse to cause problems." It had the tenor of an old argument.

Leticia folded her hands in her lap and gave her alpha a telling look.

It was Will who said, "Well, thanks to Tomás's insane attack, we now have even bigger problems."

Not quite catching the unspoken conversation, Tala frowned. "Bigger problems?"

The three wolves exchange a look, and Leticia urged, "Since we can rule them out, you may as well share."

Toby grimaced. "Fine." He sat back in his chair, his arms crossed, and met Tala's gaze. "In the last three weeks, it's become apparent someone's decided I'm better off dead."

CHAPTER 9

Further conversation ground to a halt as their food arrived. Cheveyo waited until everyone was served and the wait staff retreated before getting back to the conversation. "Do you have any idea as to who's decided to come after you?" In an attempt not to ruffle Toby's fur any more than necessary, he focused on his meal to avoid tempting a direct challenge. Such things never went over well with alphas.

"Initially, I thought it was Tomás."

That wasn't the answer Cheveyo expected. He paused with a bite of steak half way to his mouth and met Toby's gaze. "Seriously?"

"Completely." Toby took a huge bite of hamburger and chewed, closing his eyes with a soft hum of appreciation.

Shaking his head, Cheveyo turned back to his meal. If everyone down here knew Tomás was bat-shit crazy, then Tala's meeting with the Triunc tomorrow should be a cakewalk. Unfortunately, he knew better, so, instead, he'd stay quiet and see what else was at play.

When the steak hit his taste buds, he understood Toby's

gastronomical bliss. The steak damn near melted in his mouth. He dug in for another bite.

Next to him, Tala picked up the conversation, "What happened?"

"A missed shot," Will answered since Toby's mouth was full. "During a monsoon storm, when the pack was out on a run. They nailed him in shoulder." He waved a fork at his alpha, his expression exasperated, but resigned, as if Toby lived to drive him crazy. "If it hadn't been for the weather and that pup, West, stumbling over his damn paws and bowling into Toby, the bullet would've been a headshot."

Chay narrowed his eyes. "Silver?"

"Yes," Leticia answered, patting her mouth with her napkin, then setting it in her lap. "Initially, we thought it was a trespassing poacher, but either the rain managed to wipe away the scent, or they used something to cover it, because our Tracker came up empty."

Tala turned to Toby. "If you thought it was Tomás, did you confront him?"

Cheveyo enjoyed another bite, silently thanking the gods she asked that question instead of him.

Toby gave a slow nod. "He called me some choice names and made some, what I figured at the time, were paranoid accusations and basically threw me off his ranch. Andrew stepped in and try to calm us both down, but not before Tomás challenged me."

"Should've accepted, would've served him right," Will mumbled.

Toby narrowed his eyes at Will and continued, "It was obvious to me Tomás was in a sorry state, and as much I wanted to take the challenge issued, I couldn't." But going by the flare of amber in his eyes, it was clear walking away was the last thing he wanted to do.

"Why?" Tala asked, genuine curiosity in her voice.

"It would have started a series of back-to-back challenges from the other packs," Leticia said. When she caught Tala's puzzled frown, she explained, "If Toby accepted and won, there are those wolves who wouldn't shy away from claiming Toby took advantage of a grief-stricken wolf to gain power." Her tone made it clear she wasn't one of those wolves.

Remembering Tomás's clear hate and churning desire for vengeance, Cheveyo decided it was safe to insert an observation. "I wouldn't consider Tomás grief stricken. He was bound and determined to take out everyone he could and to hell with the consequences."

Toby used a French fry to scoop up some ketchup. "Be that as it may, unless we could provide proof that Tomás was working against the good of the Pack, such an argument would simply be a matter of opinion."

Cheveyo thought about mentioning the fact that Tomás indicated he was working with a partner then decided not to. Not with someone still targeting Tala, and he wasn't comfortable in completely eliminating the three possibilities sitting across from them.

"After that, things stayed quiet for about a week, then there was an accident on the construction site I'm overseeing." Toby's ketchup-covered fry disappeared and was quickly followed by another. "My crew was working on a new corporate plaza development down in the foothills area when one of the steel I-beams fell." His face darkened, and his eyes glittered. "I managed to dodge the worse of it, but it put two of my crew in the hospital."

"Construction accidents happen all the time," Chay observed.

"They do," Toby agreed. "But after, when I went to recheck the crane, I found a snapped cable."

"Which happens when they get overstressed, right?" Chay prompted when Toby paused.

Toby's jaw flexed. "Sure, but this particular cable was just replaced two weeks ago. Despite the frayed edges there was no way in hell it snapped from being overstressed."

Chay frowned. "So you're thinking what? The break was caused by a chemical reaction?"

Toby shook his head. "There was no chemical scent so I reached out to a local witch and she found traces of a spell."

"Definitely rules out accidental then," Cheveyo murmured before stabbing another piece of steak. He paused with his fork raised, his mind slipping through the possibilities. "I'm assuming you checked to see where Tomás was during both occasions?" He wouldn't put it past Tomás to have hired out a hit. Witches might love their Three Fold law, but there were some who didn't quibble on ethical lines if the price was right.

"We did." Leticia traced the condensation on her glass with one glossy nail. "During our run, he was supposedly with Andrew shoeing a horse. Then he was out of town on business in the days leading up to the construction mishap." She lifted her gaze, her lips curved with a hint of cynicism. "Again, no proof of his involvement beyond a gut feeling."

"Gut feelings work for me," muttered Chay.

"You and me both," Will agreed, clearly not happy with the whole situation. "But then came the latest incident which came the closest to killing Toby."

Chay turned to Toby. "What happened?"

"A surprised gift left at my office from a supposed client," Toby growled, shoving his now empty plate away.

"A bottle of poisoned wine." He paused, his gaze going to Cheveyo. "Not just any poison, mind you, but that nasty-ass shit Warrick sent the warning out about."

Stunned, Cheveyo carefully set his fork down and rocked back in his chair. "The one that turns Shifters feral?"

Grim faced, Toby nodded. "That's the one."

"You don't seem feral." Despite the rather flippant tone of his comment, Cheveyo was quite serious.

When Toby looked up, his eyes were pure wolf, and a savage predator stared back. "I almost lost one of my electricians. The only thing that saved her was she didn't drink much."

"Because she's a wine snob," muttered Will.

"She's not a snob, you plebeian," Leticia shot back. "She just has good taste."

Cheveyo ignored the byplay. "Regardless, that's worrisome." How the hell had that evil potion gotten down here so fast? The last he heard, both the human geneticist behind the drug and the remnants of the drug itself had been destroyed.

"It's downright frightening, actually," Toby corrected, and Cheveyo silently agreed. "According to the information Warrick sent, that shit shouldn't exist anymore."

Reading the alpha's statement for the challenge it was, Cheveyo calmly answered, "That was our belief as well."

"Well, someone's playing us all for fools then, aren't they?" Will snapped, his fork bending slightly in his tight grip. When he noticed, he forcibly relaxed his hand and set the crooked fork on the table.

"Three different attempts in three different forms," Tala mused. "Either you have a group hunting you, or..." She trailed off and looked at Cheveyo.

It was easy to follow the speculation in her gaze. "Or

someone is bound and determine to set you all at each other's throats," he finished softly.

"Which means they aren't just playing with your house," she agreed.

"Perhaps you two would care to share?" There was a note of warning in Leticia question.

Cheveyo inclined his head in acknowledgement and did just that. "The first attempt was direct—a silver bullet. It says 'we know what you are and how to hurt you.' The second wasn't as focused on harm, more of making a point. Using a spell to weaken the cable would throw suspicion on the witches. If it managed to hurt Toby, all the better."

"And the drugged wine?" Toby asked when Cheveyo stopped speaking. "What does that tell you?"

That his visit here was anticipated. "It tells me that whoever is targeting you, isn't done yet." He looked at Tala and back at Toby. "They're playing with both of you."

Toby cocked a brow. "And who do you think is running the board?"

Even though Cheveyo had no doubt Toby had suspicions about the answer, he still gave it. It was why he was here, after all. "The Council."

Toby's lips curled into a mirthless grin. "So the rumors are true then? The Northwest is setting itself against the Council."

Cheveyo buried his frustration at the light speed of the damn rumor mill. "Not the Council as a whole, just those who would destroy what the Kyn have built here in America." He held Toby's gaze and waited.

The wolf leaned forward. "You're looking for allies."

A statement, not a question, so Cheveyo treated it as such. "Change is coming, we can't outrun it, but we sure as hell can get in front of it before it tears us to pieces. Staying in the shadows is a death sentence, for all of us."

Leticia cleared her throat with a delicate cough, causing both men to turn their attention to her. "I'm not sure how neighborly relations fare with the Northwest pack, but I can tell you that if you tell the ranchers in this region that their neighbors sprout claws and teeth, you're asking for them to come hunting us."

Cheveyo inclined his head in acknowledgement. "Humans are already hunting us, but if we can control how our presence is made known and leverage the partnerships currently in place, we may stand a chance of surviving as a race."

"Maybe," Will said, his skepticism loud and clear. "Maybe not. Right now, knowledge about us is only shared among a select group. You tell the entire world we're real, and we're done before we even get our heads above the tide. They not only outnumber us, they fear us. What they fear, they kill. Period. Our history proves there's no mediation, no compromises. Hell, so does theirs."

Toby raised a hand, cutting off the age-old argument before it could start. When Will fell silent, he lowered his hand to the table and addressed Cheveyo and Tala. "Until we find out what the hell is going on here that discussion will have to wait." His gaze centered on Tala. "I appreciate you meeting me tonight and sharing what happened, Tala. While I apologize for the situation Tomás's behavior has put you in, I must relay your version to the other alphas tonight and address their concerns as best I can." He switched his attention to Cheveyo. "Be assured, I'll pass along your theories as well." He pushed back and stood, dropping his napkin on the table. Will and Leticia followed suite.

Unwilling to remain seated, Cheveyo rose, offering Tala a hand before he could think better of it. Thankfully, she took it and rose, Chay slowly doing the same next to her.

She faced Toby, regal and composed, no signs of the chaotic mess Cheveyo knew was tumbling through her. "I will gladly answer their concerns tomorrow in front the Triune, Alpha Greene."

He inclined his head, and Cheveyo caught the gleam of calculation in his gaze. "A bit of advice, if I may?"

Tala waited with a polite smile.

"When hunting, it's best to follow your prey with care. You'd be surprised how alert they are to who is on their back trail."

CHAPTER 10

Hours later, Cheveyo gave up on the idea of getting any sleep. Since he was wide-awake, he decided to take Chay's place on watch. He padded down the dark hallway, pausing at the living room.

A table lamp's soft light provided enough illumination to confirm Ash was still curled up on his plush bed near the fireplace. He raised his head, met Cheveyo's gaze, sneezed once, then reburied his nose in his paws and closed his eyes. An obvious canine dismissal.

"Love you too, mutt," Cheveyo muttered, then continued out onto the porch.

"Couldn't sleep?" Chay's low question came from heavy shadows to his right.

Not quite ready to settle, Cheveyo shook his head and went to lean a shoulder on the left porch post. "Figured I'd keep you company, or if you'd rather, you're welcome to go on in."

The shadows shifted and stretched, then slipped back as Chay stood up to mirror him on the other side. "Nah, I'm good."

An easy quiet settled between the two men. The tension riding Cheveyo crept away as the night's peace seeped in.

When Chay finally spoke, it startled Cheveyo. "Can I ask you something?"

Letting some of his humor free, Cheveyo shot back, "Can you?"

"Smartass," the younger witch muttered without any heat.

Grinning, Cheveyo simply shrugged as he waited for Chay's question.

It wasn't long in coming. "What happened to you?"

Cheveyo's earlier tension came back with a vengeance. Slowly, he turned to Chay. "Excuse me?"

The predatory move barely fazed Chay, who understood the reasons behind Cheveyo's reaction better than others. "Before you decide to burn my ass, know that I'm asking as a friend. Not as a member of your house, not as a Wraith, but as a friend." He studied Cheveyo before muttering, "Something I'm thinking you have too few of."

Chay's observation hit too close to home for Cheveyo to deny. After standing witness on how deep betrayal could scar, Cheveyo wasn't one to encourage close ties. Besides, as he told Tala earlier, a leader needed to maintain a necessary distance to ensure order within their house. It made for a lonely position. Yet tonight, when the doubts of his past collided with his worry of the future, he found himself answering his friend, "I'm still figuring it out."

"I'm happy to lend an ear." A depth of understanding stared back as Chay made the offer.

"Why?" As much as Cheveyo hated it, suspicion at such an offer was hard to shake.

Chay's answering smile carried a hard-won knowledge. "Because if I've learned nothing in the last year or so, it's that if we're going to survive this...whatever it is...we need to start thinking of ourselves as a whole, instead of separate pieces. Otherwise, we've done the majority of the Council's work for them." A militant gleam flashed before quickly being doused. "Much like you, I'm not at all comfortable with being led by the blind and arrogant."

Although startled by Chay's depth of perception, another part of Cheveyo was secretly pleased. "When did you get so damn smart?"

Chay grimaced and turned his face back to the night. "After spending endless hours holding Axel from death's nasty-ass embrace." Dark memories carved deep grooves into his face. "That spell was a bitch, but the mind that set it was twisted as fuck." Fury lay under his words, making them a harsh whip. "I didn't think Axel would make it. Hell, at one point, I wasn't sure if I'd make it."

Cheveyo didn't doubt that for a second. While both Chay and Axel were part of the Wraiths, the spell laid on Axel had tied his spirit to the Side, the realm belonging to the Amanusa. Didn't much matter how strong you were, being trapped in a realm you were never meant to see was a hellish nightmare even Cheveyo didn't want to imagine.

Much like the shifters, the demons were dual in nature. However, only demons could survive in the Side, and when the castor anchored the spell laid on Axel in the Side, it had trapped his wolf in the demonic realm, while his human body lay in a coma. The only reason Axel was alive today was because Chay was a powerful witch in his own right, and just happened to be a stubborn-ass bastard. How he managed to hold Axel through the long flight from Alexandria to Portland stood as testament to the depth of his strength—both mental and magical. Yet doubt could weaken even the strongest warriors.

"But you did."

Chay dipped his chin. "Yeah, I did, but something like that, it changes you." He turned, his gaze serious. "Which is why I'm asking you this question now."

It was Cheveyo's turn to look away as memories circled.

Undaunted, Chay kept pushing, "The last time you were here, you spent days at the mercy of the Soul Stealer, and when you got back to Portland, you were quieter, darker." He fell quiet, not needing to say more.

Cheveyo knew the whispers circulating through his house. Yet with the betrayal of Warrick's pack, Mulcahy's death, and Natasha's accession, he had chosen to ignore them. Especially since his patience hit an all-time low, along with his tolerance for petty tyrants. At least, he ignored them until someone forced him to defend his position.

In the last year, he managed to put down a handful of challengers, rather brutally, actually. It hadn't stopped the rumors, only made them softer, more careful. But it sure as hell made potential challengers think long and hard before stepping up. As much as he didn't like this harsher aspect of himself, he didn't deny it had its place in this new reality. "What's coming can't be fought with diplomacy."

"No, it can't," Chay agreed. "But you better know what weapons you're wielding, or you may find more than your enemies lying at your feet." Chay's dire warning held a grim ring of truth.

Cheveyo wasn't comfortable with revealing everything, but giving Chay some of it? Yeah, that was doable, especially as Chay had more than earned it. If it wasn't for the fact that Chay's position with the Wraiths exempted him from being a head of house, this was the warrior Cheveyo would name as his successor.

Studying Chay, Cheveyo started in, "When Raine and Gavin,"—the Witch-Fey warrior who now served as the captain of the Wraiths and his lover—"cut the Stealer's ties to me, they weren't worried about the long-term ramifications. And to be honest, neither was I." Funny how long held beliefs fell by the way side when your survival was on the line. "The problem was the Stealer managed to do some serious damage to certain aspects of my magic."

Memories rose in a choking cloud, cruel claws digging deep, tearing through bonds once considered unbreakable. The Soul Stealer's most grievous damage wasn't to Cheveyo's magic, but to his sense of self. He breathed through remembered horror until it receded, chasing it back with the reminder he was still here, different, but stronger than before.

When he found his voice, it came out rough. "Between Tala and Raine, they did the best they could to repair the damage."

Unfortunately, Tala's insistence that Raine fix him, forced Raine, with Gavin's help, to do what was considered by some as unnatural. As much as they tried to deny it, the Kyn weren't that far from their human cousins, and they too feared things they couldn't understand or control. Including the fact that the magic the Kyn called their own was evolving with each new generation.

In Raine's case, she could not only see magic but manipulate it in others. Something she discovered when Tala forced her to repair the Stealer's damage to Cheveyo. And what the couple did to him was far enough outside the realm of what should be possible magically that keeping their abilities quiet wasn't just a matter of protecting them, but the Northwest as well. Theirs wasn't the only new ability to show itself, but it was one of the most powerful.

"But the scars go deep." There was no judgment in Chay's voice, but it brought Cheveyo out of his thoughts and back to the present.

"Very," he agreed. He tilted his head back and stared at the star-studded sky. "In the course of rehabbing my magic, I discovered while I'd lost some things, I gained others." He dropped his head and rubbed the back of his neck.

It was as much as he could give Chay without betraying Raine and Gavin, something he was loath to do. Even Tala was unaware of what the two had done to keep him alive, and he wasn't sure if he'd ever be able to tell her. Hell, he hadn't admitted it to Raine or Gavin, not even to ease the guilt Raine tried so hard to hide. Admitting knowledge gained him nothing, but staying quiet kept the couple on their toes, something that could be critical to their survival.

Chay watched him closely, something working behind his eyes. "So is that why you came back here?"

Frowning Cheveyo looked to the younger witch. "What do you mean?"

"Did you come back here to find what you lost?"

At first, he thought Chay's question carried an unintended dual meaning, but when he caught a depth of intensity that wasn't there earlier, he wondered if it was intentional after all. "I'm not sure," he answered slowly, picking his words carefully, "that what I lost can be found."

"But?"

The single word erased any lingering doubt Cheveyo carried, because Chay wasn't asking about Cheveyo's magic, but the woman sleeping in the house behind them. "Maybe I'll get lucky."

A soft creak of wood underfoot spun Cheveyo around to see Tala pushing open the screen door. The shadows made it difficult to read her expression. "Is that what you think?

That you lost me?" Her voice was soft, but there was no mistaking she'd been listening.

"And that's my cue." Chay straightened. "Good luck."

Cheveyo couldn't determine if it was pity or amusement, or a combination of both in Chay's voice, but whatever it was left him silently cursing the younger witch for putting him in this situation.

As Chay moved past him and up the steps, Cheveyo caught his rueful expression. Clearly, Tala had been standing there when he answered Chay's question. Chay drew even with Tala, who was holding the screen door open, and murmured something to her that Cheveyo didn't catch before he disappeared inside. With a soft whine of the hinges and the dull thump of the aluminum frame hitting wood, she let the screen door close behind him.

Cheveyo didn't move as Tala went to the rocking chair and took a seat, drawing her feet up until her chin could rest on her knees. Her hair, the curious mix of gold and sable, freed from her normal braid, fell around her like a living cloak and shielded her profile.

The quiet stretched as he fought through his tangled knot of emotions. Frustration at finding himself in this uncomfortable position of facing things best left in the past, anger at Chay's unexpected interference, resentment at how unaffected she appeared, and under it all, the reawakening of an old ache that never truly healed.

She turned her head, resting her cheek on her knees. "Are you going to answer me?" Instead of the expected demand, her question came with an unusual mix of gentle teasing and wry poignancy, the combination leaving him powerless to resist.

"Will it make a difference if I do?" He sank down to the

top step, not sure he could say what needed to be said if he sat next to her.

"What do you mean?" Her wary puzzlement made her words cautious.

"Don't," he warned her softly, not looking at her. "If you really want to get into this now, don't play this game."

"I'm not the one who likes games, Cheveyo."

That small bite of temper gave him hope. "Despite what you think, neither do I."

Her disbelieving snort preceded her, "Don't you?"

"No." Her accusation stung, and his denial came out sharper than intended. "At the time I did what I thought was necessary." And leaving her then, it hadn't been easy. Far from it, but it was the only path he saw to ensure she became the woman who sat across from him now. A woman who knew exactly who she was, with the strength to wield the enormous weight of authority she carried. Had he stayed then, or asked her to come with him, it would mean this Tala, the one who embodied all he saw those many years ago, wouldn't exist.

When she didn't say anything, he turned to find her watching him from the shadows. Her arms were wrapped around her legs, and she was absently rubbing her chin over her knees. Her gaze drifted over him like a phantom touch, but he didn't look away. Finally, she asked the million-dollar question, the one that haunted his nights. "And now? Looking back, would you make the same choice again?"

He wished he could offer her a comforting lie, but he promised the truth. "Yes." Despite the scars it left on his soul. His answer dropped like a stone into the night, falling between them.

She stilled then dropped her feet and rose.

He held his breath, his body strung tight, waiting for her to walk away and take whatever slim chance he thought he had with her. Instead, she walked toward him, and, as she came close, he turned to keep her in sight.

When she sank down beside him and laid her head on his shoulder, his breath left his body in a rough sigh. He didn't dare move, even though it took a hellish amount of strength not to wrap his arm around her and pull her in tight.

His tension slowly eased as the moments ticked by, and she held her position.

Finally, she murmured, "Hindsight is a merciless bitch."

"On that, we can agree."

She gave a soft laugh. "That's something at least." She fell quiet, and he waited, knowing more was coming. "You were right, though, to leave. It took me a while before I could admit it, but I did need time to be on my own, to be seen as me, not part of you."

"You were meant to be a leader, Tala." Finally daring to move, he curled his arm around her, taking comfort in just holding her. "It was why you were chosen to lead your house. You just needed the space and time to prove that to yourself and your people." He rubbed his chin against her hair. "My presence diminished your authority, and even worse, made your people doubt your strength. When I realized how bad it was getting, I couldn't stay. I never meant to hurt you."

She tilted her head back, and her hand cupped his jaw, her thumb gently brushing over his lower lip as her dark gaze roved over his face.

He bent his head at the slight pressure of her hold, and she met him halfway, brushing her lips over his in a butterfly touch. That barely there kiss sent heat streaking through him, bringing his body to life.

She dropped her hand and drew back, her smile sad and wistful. "But you did."

He caught her hand and pressed a kiss into the center of her palm before holding it against his chest, the warmth of her palm a brand against his skin. "I'm sorry for that, Tala."

Apologizing for how his decision hurt her wasn't much in the overall scheme of things, but it was all he could offer. There was nothing more he could say or do for the past, but the future...well, that was different. Because, forgiveness, if she chose to give it, was her choice.

Just as it was his to decide if pursuing a future with her would be worth the fight he knew would follow.

She searched his face, but whatever thoughts were racing through her head remained well hidden. "So am I."

CHAPTER 11

The next morning, Tala sat in the backseat of the SUV, Chay claimed the passenger seat, and Cheveyo once again played chauffeur as they headed to the Triune meeting. This time, Ash shared the backseat with her, his blocky head in her lap as she absently stroked behind his ear.

Years of practice, allowed her to maintain her mask of serenity even as her emotions raged under the surface. Last night's talk with Cheveyo left her torn between the familiar mix of resentment and anger and the new, unsettling fragile rise of hope. She was far from naive and knew damn good and well that love did not conquer all. And she did love Cheveyo, always had. Otherwise, even after all these years, she wouldn't still hurt so much.

The physical distance he put between them allowed her to step back emotionally as well. Which turned out to be a great survival tactic and a necessary skill for any Kyn leader. Yet, last year, when she had been at her wits' end trying to uncover who was killing her people, reaching out to him for help was a foregone conclusion. Because when it came down to it, he was one of the few she could trust.

Unfortunately, she hadn't been prepared for the overwhelming impact seeing him had left. Thankfully, his time here had been blessedly short and packed with enough drama to drown out her emotional upheaval. When he went back to Portland, part of her had been hugely relieved, but a more important part ached.

In the wake of his visit, she was left to reexamine her past choices. Choices driven by insecurity, guilt, and shame, but as she told him last night, hindsight was a bitch. Regret took anchor in her battered heart and sank its sharp teeth deep. The secret she carried would kill their chances of a future more surely than any known curse. Once he found out, it would be her turn to beg for forgiveness, and she wasn't certain she deserved it.

Her phone vibrated in her pocket, startling her out of her dismal thoughts. Shifting carefully, she managed to dig it out and answer before it stopped. "Hello?"

"Tala, it's Danny." The medicine man's voice was both tired and drained.

Concern rose. "Hey, Danny. Are you at the hospital with Rory and Anne?"

"I am, I just stepped outside to give you an update on his status." He paused, and she braced. "Rory's in a coma. The doctors can't say if he'll wake or not, but if he does, they're worried there'll be lasting damage."

Her stomach sank under the combination of worry and grief. "Is there anything you can do to help?"

"I've tried, and I'll keep doing so. So will his druid brothers. I wanted to let you know that I couldn't find any magical traces during my healings with him."

She wasn't sure if that was a positive or a negative at this point. "So it was just an accident?"

"Maybe," Danny's one word answer was heavy with doubt.

"What aren't you telling me?"

His sigh echoed through the line. "Nothing, I just can't shake the feeling I'm missing something."

Considering his depth of knowledge, such an admission was concerning. "What can I do to help?"

"Come to Phoenix," he answered. "I have an idea, so bring Cheveyo with you. And Tala?"

When he paused, she prompted, "Yes?"

"Get here as soon as you can, I don't know how long Rory will hang on." The grimness in Danny's voice scared her, even as her mind spun through the reasons for his request.

She raised her gaze and met Cheveyo's in the rearview mirror as an idea began to form. "We're on our way to the Triune, so it will be a few hours."

"As soon as you can, *sitsi*."

His gruff endearment left tears welling, but she held them back. "We will, Danny." With that, she hung up.

Even though Cheveyo's attention was back on the road, he asked, "What's going on?"

"Rory's in a coma and Danny wants us in Phoenix as soon as possible."

Chay half turned in his seat, a frown on his face. "Did he find something?"

She shook her head. "No traces of any magic, but he thinks he's missing something."

That earned her a skeptical glance from Cheveyo. "If Danny's missing something, why does he want us down there? I'm not sure we'll do any better."

She worried her bottom lip and offered cautiously, "I think he wants you to dream walk."

The SUV jerked a bit, then resumed its normal pace. "Rory's in a coma, he's not sleeping."

"I know that, so does Danny," she couldn't hide her frustration. "But if Danny's asking, there has to be a damn good reason."

"There better be," he growled back. "Because I'm not even sure it will work."

"How dangerous is this?" Chay cut in.

For a moment, silence filled the SUV, then Cheveyo answered, "Very."

Based upon the dark look that came over Chay's face that answer didn't sit well. "Then why the hell would you even consider it?"

In her lap, Tala's fingers tightened on the phone as she waited for Cheveyo's response. He didn't owe her a thing and, if she was right, what Danny asked for wasn't something for Cheveyo to undertake lightly.

"Because Danny wouldn't ask it of me unless it was important," Cheveyo ground out even as he turned off the freeway.

"For fuck's sake," Chay snapped. "Are you trying to get us both killed here? I let anything happen to you, and I might as well slit my own throat rather than try to explain to Gavin and Raine, hell even Natasha, how I got you killed down here."

"It won't kill me," Cheveyo shot back. Tala opened her mouth to disagree only to snap it shut when he glared at her through the mirror. "It won't."

"Well, it sure as shit doesn't sound like a walk through the damn daisies either, Cheveyo." Chay wasn't backing down.

She caught the edge of a grim smile as Cheveyo made another turn. "It's not, but it's not a walk through hell either, Chay. Regardless, something is going on down here. We're here to help, and that's what we're going to do."

Chay's mouth thinned while a militant light sparked deep in his eyes, his disapproval louder than ever. A tense minute ticked by before he finally spoke, "Fine, you can help to your heart's content, but the second I determine you are at risk, I'll drag your ass back however necessary."

Cheveyo arched a brow and murmured, "You're welcome to try."

As soon as Cheveyo parked next to a white sedan in the blacktopped rest stop, Tala had her door open, grateful to escape the suffocating tension in the SUV. Based on the crushed fast food bags littering the back seat, she was fairly certain that the sedan belonged to Toby and his entourage considering shifters had notorious appetites. She recognized a couple of other cars in the lot—Teagan's bright yellow Bug and Hadley's conservative Prius.

The state park might not sound like the ideal place for such a get together, but when meeting with volatile personalities, an enclosed conference room could be problematic. This early on a weekday morning, they were less likely to be stumbled upon by unknowing hikers or families out for a picnic.

Coming around the hood of the SUV, she waited while Chay helped Ash down, the injured wolf's movements still stiff despite the basic healing spell Cheveyo had casted early this morning. She kept a slow pace with Ash as Cheveyo and Chay fell in beside her, staying close.

Despite their casual demeanors, both men remained alert. With her nerves stretched tight, she sent her magic out in a gentle wave testing their surroundings, unsurprised by the solid strength echoing back from the two men at her side. Loosening her hold a bit more, she let it slip farther out until the hum she normally associated with shifters drifted back, followed by the pulse of witching energy. Her shoulders loosened and only when the low-lying headache eased up, did she grasp how tight her nerves were strung.

"Anything?" Cheveyo's question was low, not going farther than the two of them.

She shook her head, sinking her fingers deep into Ash's ruff, a comfort-seeking habit she couldn't seem to break. In response, he bumped her thigh, causing a slight twinge on her still healing side. "Just the expected responses."

She led them beyond the anchored picnic tables and followed one of the side trails as it wound its way through the trees. Any other time, this would be a perfect morning for a hike.

Nature's music drifted along the light breeze, and the sun played peek-a-boo with the leaves. They rounded a bend, and the sound of water tumbling over stone joined the chorus. They followed the creek up a little further until they reached a scenic spot screened by trees. Stepping through the tree line, Tala felt the combined weight of the gazes of those gathered as conversation petered out.

"Tala." The greeting was reserved but pleasant as Hadley rose from the fallen tree doubling as primitive bench seating and made her way around a cold fire pit to meet them. Moving with a quiet confidence, she held her hand out in welcome. Blessed with generous curves and subtle beauty, a beauty that Tala once envied, Hadley was dressed in casual jeans and blousy T-shirt.

Taking her offering, Tala offered a smile. "Hadley." She

let go and continued with the introductions. "This is Chayton, and you remember—"

"Cheveyo," the woman's voice softened, and her smile grew. "Yes. Surprised to see you here again."

"Hadley." Cheveyo inclined his head, his smile polite. "Nice to see you as well, despite the circumstances."

Hadley's smile dimmed, and her gaze flickered to Tala, but she stepped back and waved them forward. "We're just waiting on Wyatt, but everyone else is already here." Everyone being Teagan, Hadley, Tobias, Will, and Leticia. "Feel free to sit wherever. There's a couple of thermoses with coffee, if you're interested."

"Thanks, but I'll pass for now," Tala declined, not certain dumping a bunch of caffeine on her stressed-out nerves was wise.

Hadley nodded, concern replacing her earlier smile. "Danny filled me in on Rory. Have you heard anything more?"

"I just spoke to him on the way over. He said Rory's in a coma, and the doctors are still concerned."

"Gods, poor Anne." Hadley half turned, giving them her profile as she looked back to those gathered. "When it rains, it pours."

Considering the mess she was stranded in currently, Tala couldn't argue.

Hadley turned back to them, her pleasant expression strained. "Well, maybe it's a good thing Cheveyo's here, then."

Before Tala could process the unexpected sting of her comment, Hadley went back to sit next to Teagan, who was currently giving the three of them a gimlet eye.

"Wow, that was..." Chay trailed off.

"Bitchy," Tala bit off under her breath, trying not to let Hadley's barb settle and failing miserably.

"In a completely passive-aggressive way, yeah," he drawled.

"Welcome to my life," she muttered and led them over to where Toby, Will, and Leticia were gathered. Off-balance and on edge, she wasn't quite ready to tackle Teagan's attitude and merely nodded at her cousin.

Toby and Will both rose to their feet as they approached. Leticia simply dipped her head in acknowledgement.

Tala returned their murmured greetings.

Toby's gaze dropped to Ash who was holding a protective stance at Tala's side. "Got yourself quite the protector there."

"This is Ash."

Toby dropped into a crouch until he was eye level with the natural wolf. A silent staring contest ensued before Ash turned his head to the side. Toby chuckled and scratched under his chin. His gaze rose back to Tala. "You do realize he considers you his."

More than the alpha knew, but it was okay because it was mutual. "As much as I consider him mine."

Toby rose and stood beside them his attention drifting over to where Teagan and Hadley sat quietly talking. "I get the impression you don't have much of a fan club here, Tala." His gaze came back to her, and she was surprised to see the genuine worry in his eyes. "Are you sure this meeting is wise."

Nope, but her actions meant it was unavoidable. "The Triune's responsibility is to ensure its leader is serving their people first and foremost." She kept her voice pitched so their conversation stayed as private as possible. "The last year has seen quite a bit of unexpected and unwelcome change. This meeting will reassure my people that my actions have not damaged them in the Pack's eyes."

Before Toby could answer, Hadley sprang up from her spot and skirted the fire pit. "Wyatt."

Dressed in dark jeans and a button-down collared shirt open at the neck, the newcomer, and last member of the Triune, stilled at the edge of the clearing. "Hadley." He nodded to the other woman. "Teagan." He surveyed the others before moving forward. "Are we all here?"

Taking his question as her go-ahead, Hadley began a round of introductions.

Tala studied Wyatt as he exchanged greetings with everyone. Dark brown hair, light gray eyes, and of average height and build, he could easily blend in with any gathering. Nothing about him screamed scary-ass wizard with an equally intimidating heritage, unless you could sense his level of power emanating on the magical plane, then you might reconsider tangling with him.

Yet in the three years since he joined her house, he had become the unofficial voice for the Southwest Wizards and the one they turned to for guidance. Maybe it should have worried her, but it didn't, because he'd proven over and over again that he had no problems acceding authority to her, so long as she remained fair and objective. It made for a refreshing change of pace from the games others incessantly played.

"Tala." His pleasant baritone interrupted her thoughts as he offered his hand. "Craptastic circumstances, but nice to see you."

She took his hand with a genuine smile and small laugh. "Well put, Wyatt."

"And this is Cheveyo," Hadley chirped in an annoyingly

bright voice, and Tala braced for another one of her irritating verbal swipes. "He came to h—"

"Speak to the Triune," Cheveyo finished smoothly. "Natasha sent me. It's nice to meet you." The two men shook hands. "Despite the circumstances."

That got a grimace from Wyatt. "Yeah, death tends to stir shit up," he murmured which earned him a sharp look from Hadley while Tala fought to hide her amusement at Wyatt's unconventional response.

"Danny speaks very highly of you, Cheveyo," Wyatt offered. "It's nice to have a face for the name." He turned back to the group at large, clapped his hands and rubbed them briskly together. "All right, if we're all here, let's get this show on the road." Catching the shifters' surprise, he explained, "Formalities are archaic. I prefer a much more direct approach."

He walked over to Teagan, Hadley on his heels. When he got to the other side, he turned, put his hands on his hips, and said, "So what the fuck is going on around here?"

CHAPTER 12

Cheveyo wanted to laugh at the matching stunned expressions on Teagan and Hadley's faces as they stood next to Wyatt. With his blunt question, Cheveyo understood why Tala hadn't been worried about Wyatt's position. The two women behind him, though, were another story.

Hadley's behavior, stupid and childish though it was, wasn't unexpected. Even when Tala claimed her as a friend, Hadley's personality was soured by jealousy. He tried to warn Tala about it early on, but she remained willfully blind. Obviously, that changed somewhere along the line and probably added to why they were no longer close.

But he could see why Teagan's attitude hurt Tala. Teagan's icy reception cut like a well-hone blade against Tala's self-inflicted guilt. Although Teagan hadn't said much since their arrival, she had watched them. And while she did so, he watched her.

It didn't take him long to recognize the anger she portrayed was a brittle shield hiding her tormenting mix of grief and guilt. It seeped out in the sharp lines adding years to her face and in the fractured pain haunting her eyes. Even more telling, her magical signature alternated between swiping and clinging to Tala's, a reflection of Teagan's emotional state.

Cheveyo only noticed because he witnessed such a thing once before, between Raine McCord and her now dead uncle, Mulcahy. Just proof that family could be more damaging than any enemy's weapon. He tucked his concern away, knowing there was nothing he could do to fix things between the two cousins. Not yet.

Following Wyatt's lead, Tala stated bluntly, "I killed Tomás."

"Figured that much," Wyatt said. "Why?"

"Self-defense."

Finally, Teagan spoke, "Why a blade? Why not something less lethal?"

Tala's chin lifted, but her voice remained level, "He's the alpha," she said, her emphasis on the, "and, he attacked Ash, then turned on me while in wolf form. While he was busy digging through my ribs for my heart, I tried to get his attention. Unfortunately, he wasn't inclined to listen, and I less inclined to let him kill me. I made my point known."

Although Teagan paled, she didn't back down. "You used a silver blade."

Tala nodded. "I was harvesting ritual herbs, not planning on killing a shifter."

"But," Hadley interrupted, "what reason would he have to attack you?"

Toby stepped up to Tala's side, gaining the Triune's attention. "Revenge."

Hadley blinked and put a restraining hand on Teagan's arm when she took a step forward, her hands fisted at her side. "Revenge?" Color flagged Teagan's cheeks, and her eyes glittered. "For what? Doing what he couldn't and taking out his certifiable mate?"

Wyatt held up his hand and gave her a sharp look. She reluctantly subsided. He turned back. "Everyone sit, it looks like we need to get a few things clear before we go any further."

Everyone picked a nearby seat and settled in while Wyatt stretched out his legs and waited. "So, who wants to start?"

From Tala's left, Toby spoke first. "As far as the packs are concerned, what Tala did was self-defense. Since the death of his mate, Tomás's behavior has—" He grimaced and corrected himself, "—had been rather..."

"Questionable," Leticia offered diplomatically from his other side.

Toby nodded and continued, "He was very clear on who he held responsible for Lizbeth's death, and his behavior has been a source of concern for some time. As such, if this hadn't happened, I'm not sure Tomás would have been held his position for much longer." He paused. "After speaking with the other alphas, we find no reason to question Tala's version of events. As the alpha of the Southwest Kyn, I offer to the Triune our reassurance that no ill will follow Magi Whiteriver's actions. We accept it was self-defense."

Sitting shoulder to shoulder, Cheveyo didn't miss Tala's soft exhale at Toby's words and subtly shifted his hand until he could cover hers on the rough bark between them.

Her fingers laced with his and tightened once before she broke their contact. She turned to Toby and cleared her throat, her voice soft but her remorse more than evident. "As much as I appreciate the Pack's understanding, please know I am truly sorry for his death." She drew her authority close and offered, with the same formality, "The Magi House of the Southwest extends their deepest sympathies on your loss and would like to assure the Southwest Lycos our friendship remains yours."

"Great, so at least we won't have to worry about a blood war," Wyatt said, breaking the solemn tension. "I, for one, greatly appreciate that." He looked at Teagan and Hadley. "So, are you two satisfied?"

"Hold up," Toby cut in before either could respond. "I'm all for keeping this as simple as possible, but while the situation between Tomás and Tala may be satisfactorily resolved, the alphas and I have a few more concerns to address with the Triune."

Caught off guard by Toby's declaration, Cheveyo's muscles coiled as the previous tension resumed its position.

Wyatt leaned forward, his eyes narrowed. "Like?" Gone was the wise-ass tone and, in its place, was an unsettling intensity.

Unruffled, Toby held his gaze. "Like the possibility someone from your house convinced Tomás to not only go after Tala, but reinitiate the BLM land deal."

Toby's bombshell produced a visible reaction from the Triune—Wyatt's gaze narrowed with laser-like focus, Teagan's anger disappeared under a wave of shock, and Hadley simply appeared stunned. Next to him, Tala stiffened while Cheveyo's gut tightened in dread.

Hadley was the first to speak. "No one from our house would go after Tala, much less support the sale of land we've shared with the packs for centuries."

"If anything," Teagan added. "Our people would be more likely to target Tomás for what his mate did." She shot an accusing glare at Tala before turning back at Toby, her chin lifted defiantly. "Except our Magi made it brutally clear what would happen if any of us even considered such a thing."

"Which is why she's our Magi," Wyatt snapped at her.

"Enough!" Tala's sharp reprimand cut through their bickering with authoritative precision. She stood and moved between the Triune and the now standing Toby, her gaze landing on each Magi until all three subsided. "This is not the time nor place to air personal grievances."

Teagan flushed under her pointed reprimand, but she didn't drop her gaze.

Tala's smile was far from friendly, but her voice lowered ominously. "If you have something to say to me, cousin, I'll be happy to listen—later and in private." She waited until Teagan grudgingly nodded, before turning back to Toby. "Apologies, Alpha. If you wouldn't mind sharing why you and your alphas feel this is a possibility, I'd appreciate it."

Watching Tala reclaim her authority sparked Cheveyo's amusement. It was like watching a mother putting her toddlers in time-out.

And he wasn't the only one, going by the humorous glint in Toby's gaze as he tilted his head at Tala's polite request. "As much as I'd like to offer you specifics, unfortunately, all we have are whispers."

Tala studied him, her face still. "Do those whispers include why a Magi would set your alpha against me? Or what my house could possibly gain from selling the land in question?"

"Just the normal—power and revenge." He sighed. "Look, I'm not willing to give you the names of the ones sharing. Not without some concrete evidence."

Reading between his unspoken lines, Cheveyo wondered who their main focus was on. For Toby to phrase things in such a vague way could mean a number of things, including the fact that they didn't want to tip their hand because whoever they were looking at could be close to Tala. If that was the case, how close became Cheveyo's biggest worry.

Will, who hadn't risen from his position, added, "Which we are in the processing of collecting."

Toby spoke over him as he slid a telling glance at Cheveyo, "Especially, considering recently shared theories."

Proving he wasn't slow on the uptake, Wyatt's gaze went from Toby to Cheveyo as he cut in, "What theories?"

Taking his cue, Cheveyo rose. "That the Southwest is being manipulated."

A snort of disbelief brought all eyes to Hadley, who stood there rubbing her brow. Seeing she was the center of attention, she dropped her hand and waved it. "Let me guess. You're going to tell us we're being played by the big, bad Council."

In answer, Cheveyo crossed his arms over his chest and waited, curious to where she was going with this.

Her gaze skated over the group, her amused disbelief morphing into exasperation as she registered everyone's expressions. "Don't get me wrong, the Council is not a bunch of fluffy kittens, but there is no reason for them to mess with us." She made her way over to stand next to Wyatt and face Cheveyo. "Now you and yours, that's another story. Especially considering all that's happened lately in your neck of the woods. Then there are the rumors that whenever Natasha and Leo are in the same room, the chances of the next ice age appearing rise drastically. But the Southwest has nothing to do with whatever is going on between those two, and I, for one, would like to keep it that way."

Surprised by a flash of unexpected anger at Hadley's flippant attitude, Cheveyo didn't try to hide it, and his voice came out cold, "Which is why Natasha's message wasn't for you alone."

Embarrassment and offended pride fought for dominance on her face, leaving her flushed. Tala interrupted before Hadley could respond. "Whether it's the Council or someone acting under their own misguided opinions, we still need to figure out who is trying to sow dissension among our people. Then, and only, then will we consider Natasha's request."

"Which is what?" Wyatt pushed.

"To choose," Toby answered. "Stay hidden from the humans or take our place in the world."

Wyatt studied the shifter, then slowly turned to Tala. "Have you given Cheveyo your decision yet?"

Undaunted, she shook her head. "I can't. Not until we can clear up what's happening here."

Wyatt turned away and shared a long look with Hadley and Teagan. Whatever passed between them, it was Hadley who finally spoke, her words directed at Tala. "Prove who's betraying us and the shifters. Once we have that answer, we'll go from there."

Tala dipped her head in acknowledgement and turned to Toby. "What can we do to help?"

A little over an hour later, Cheveyo was back behind the wheel of the SUV, Tala riding shotgun and Chay in the backseat. Surprisingly it was Teagan who offered to take Ash back to Tala's so the three could head down to Phoenix to see Rory. Wyatt and Leticia followed behind in Wyatt's silver truck. Toby and Will were off hunting down their end of the rumors, while Hadley returned to her position as a paralegal, promising to use her expertise to look into the BLM contract from the Magi's end.

As if it wasn't challenging enough to try to unearth who could be working against the houses, they were also up against a deadline. Toby explained that when he found out about the contract, he sicced one of the pack's lawyers on it. The lawyer noted the looming deadline set by the BLM, which bought them a week to figure out how to break it.

"Dammit," Tala muttered, laying her head on the headrest, her eyes closed. "A week isn't nearly long enough."

"It's better than nothing," Chay said. "And considering both the Shifters and Magi are sniffing around, I don't think your mole is going to stay secret for much longer."

"I'm more concerned with who Toby targeted." Cheveyo switched over to the carpool land and set the cruise control.

Tala's lips curved, but she didn't open her eyes. "Caught that, uh?"

"Hard to miss," he agreed. "Too bad he won't share."

Chay shifted in his seat, resting his arm on the door. "You think it was one of the Triune?"

Cheveyo shrugged. "Maybe, maybe not."

"Not helpful, oh wise one," Chay muttered.

"It's a waste of our time worrying about it since we have nothing to work with. Yet." He tapped a finger on Tala's knee. "Unless you have some ideas?"

She opened her eyes and stared out the windshield with a small frown. "Like?"

"Like any gossip about possible entanglements between the Magi and Shifters?"

That earned him a snort. "It's not as frequent as you think, but I'm sure we can rule out Wyatt."

"Why?" Genuine curiosity lay in Chay's question.

Tala shifted her position, twisting around to see him. "Because the magical majority in my house lies with the shaman, and they are not the biggest fans of wizards, for obvious reasons."

"Ahh." It didn't take long for Chay to understand. "Got it."

Unfortunately, the shaman were naturally wary of the wizards. Shifters were considered part of the natural world, and even the witches, who sometimes got a bad rap in many of the Nations' oral traditions, were accepted, since they drew their magic from the earth. But the wizards, who relied heavily on spell work and potions were viewed with a jaundiced eye, as were the Amanusa house. This ingrained wariness carried over into hard to shake biases for some of the older traditionalists. While such prejudices were stronger in the older generation, there was hope in the more tolerant attitudes of the younger generations. It was the same issue he faced in his house, except his magical majority was more evenly composed of witches, wizards, and druids.

Chay drummed his fingers absently against the armrest. "Is that why Danny's not on the Triune?"

That seemed to startle Tala. "No, in fact, Wyatt studied under him for a bit." She explained further, "Danny's personal beliefs don't follow the norm. Maybe because he's been around for so long, but he doesn't share that particular viewpoint."

Cheveyo caught Chay's gaze in the rearview mirror. "Danny's like our Cassandra." Cassandra Miwa, an older witch, held the respect, not only of the Northwest Magi but every Northwest house. When she spoke, you listened.

Chay's face softened with genuine affection. "Yeah, I can see that."

"If it's not Wyatt," Cheveyo got the conversation back on track, "what about Hadley and Teagan?"

Tala shook her head. "I just can't see it."

Unfortunately, he could, but that might just be him. "Every time Hadley's around you, her little green-eyed monster claws her bloody. And Teagan's so angry, I'm surprised she hasn't come after you yet."

"She won't," Tala said, sorrow and surety making her voice soft.

"Why?"

"Because that anger you see, it's self-directed. She's more inclined to hurt herself than me."

Maybe, maybe not, but until he could find that same certainty, he'd make sure not to leave Tala alone with her cousin. He moved to the next threat. "And Hadley?"

"Seriously?" Arrogance mixed with skeptic humor. "Hadley's all talk and no backbone. Always has been."

"Doesn't mean she can't be a threat."

She sighed. "Look, neither of them gains anything if I'm dead. Not power, not money, not a damn thing."

His hands tightened on the wheel as frustration roiled through him, and, despite Tala's dismissal, he added Hadley's name to the list of who to watch. Determined to dig a little deeper, he pushed, "If you're out of the picture, who takes over?"

"For the Southwest Magi, it would be a toss-up

between Amelia out of the Colorado coven or Joseph from New Mexico."

Chay leaned forward. "And for here?"

Her jaw flexed. "Wyatt."

At her grudging answer, Cheveyo silently cursed and added a third name to his mental watch list.

CHAPTER 13

Cheveyo watched Tala lead Anne out of Rory's hospital room in an attempt to give the worn out young woman a break, before turning to Danny. "Any changes?"

"No." Exhaustion and silver scruff lined Danny's face as he sprawled in the chair set to the far side of Rory's bed and rubbed a hand over his face. He slumped farther down in the chair, until his head could rest against the top edge, and closed his eyes. "The doctors believe the longer he remains in a coma, the less likely he is to awake from it." His *if he awakes* remained unspoken.

Moving aside a crumpled scratchy blanket and thin pillow, Cheveyo settled on Anne's abandoned chair. He studied the man lying so still in the bed, his left leg and arm held in place by rigging and casts. Soft chimes and beeps kept a rhythmic pattern as machines fought to help him breathe. The left side of his face was battered and heavily bruised. Various cuts and swelling marred the dark discoloration making it hard to identify distinguishing features.

Where they shaved his head to get in to reduce the

swelling on his brain was starkly pale against the bandages. It was a miracle Rory was still alive.

Disinclined to break the hushed quiet, Cheveyo kept his voice low. "Are you sure you want me to do this, Danny?"

"Yes," the older man answered, without opening his eyes or moving. "As much as I respect the doctors here, this isn't entirely natural."

Cheveyo cut him a sharp look. "You said there were no traces of magic."

"There aren't." Danny opened one eye. "But—"

"But it's bugging you." Leaning forward, Cheveyo braced his arms on his knees and studied the floor. There were many ways to hide magic, some dating back centuries, well before Danny took his first breath. However, Danny wasn't a lightweight when it came to identifying the unusual powers the Kyn could wield. "You're sure he's awake?" He didn't want to deny Danny, especially if there was a chance to help, but dream walking held its own inherent dangers, especially if one of the parties wasn't able to be an active participant. Dangers that would piss Chay way the hell off, Cheveyo acknowledged with a small flash of amusement.

Danny sighed and sat up, drawing Cheveyo's gaze. "Rory's in there. He just can't find his way out. He's like an exhausted fish, too tired to continue forward, instead slowly sinking to riverbed." There was no doubt in his eyes. "You need to show him the way, give him a line to follow."

"If you're wrong—"

"I'm not." Danny's gaze went to Rory, and he patted his hand. "Something's just not right about this, but I can't quite see it."

The underlying worry in his voice did more to convince Cheveyo than anything else, and he nodded. "Okay." He gave silent thanks the number of visitors allowed was limited. It kept Chay out in the waiting room with Wyatt, because there was no way he'd let Cheveyo go through with this. Not on Danny's word alone.

Not about to waste time, he sat back in the chair, resting his arms on the thinly padded arms, and let his body sprawl until his head could rest against the back. If anyone should come in, he'd appear to be napping, albeit uncomfortably, but enough to be left alone. Plus Danny could run interference if needed. With his eyes closed, Cheveyo moved into a meditative breathing, slowly letting the distraction of the hospital room fade as he transitioned from the mortal to magical plane with relative ease.

Unlike his connection with Raine, there was nothing familiar to build on, so he used the two most important images of Rory's life he could think of—Anne and Pax—to create a bridge. As it began to take shape, he sent his magic out ahead like a wave, testing for a shore. Finding purchase, he slowly started out across the mental construct, careful of his footing. Initially the planks were awkwardly spaced, the bridge resembling the frayed rope-rotten board types found in bad action flicks.

The first hint that he was on the right track came with his receding tide of power that now carried the touch of earth magic, the primitive kind unique to druidic workings. Then the space between boards shrank, the questionable rope railing became tough vines, then thickened into carved wood to match the solid pieces underfoot. The bridge lengthened and began to curve to a mist shrouded shore, anchored by the two magics—his and Rory's. The trip could've taken a minute or an hour, hard to tell in this space between worlds, but, finally, Cheveyo stepped off the bridge and onto shore.

Trees, the kind Cheveyo recalled from decades ago in a land far from here, gathered together while mist danced above the grass covered ground. The air carried the bite of sea and wind, instead of sand and heat, and the sun shone through the leaves. He continued forward, following the instinctive tug of magic. When he looked down, he discovered he was on a hunting trail. As the path took him farther away from the bridge, the sound of rushing water gained strength. The trees gave way, revealing a crystalline river tumbling over eon-aged stones. The power drawing him forward slowed, then stopped. Heeding the magical indicator, he stopped at the river's edge and looked around.

The surrounding trees shimmered, as if viewed through a watery lens, distorting his ability to gauge how deep they ran. The leaves danced, their movement adding to the confusion, and he could feel the breeze, but there was no rush of air, no sound at all. Instead, a heavy silence lay over the surreal scene, as if waiting for something or someone.

Turning in a slow circle, he searched his surroundings and seeing no one, called out, "Rory? Rory Ellis?"

Unexpectedly, his voice echoed, the eerie returns gaining strength and depth until the actual words became low, reverberating rumbles. The sun dimmed the sky—what could be seen overhead—and began to darken into a threatening gray, light dancing high above the branches.

The heavy silence broke with a thunderous crack that left Cheveyo's ears ringing and his teeth clenched. Energy, laced with the sting of defensive power, scraped over Cheveyo's skin, leaving a sharp pain in its wake. Looked like his presence was triggering a protective ward. Great.

Knowing time was short before the ward gained strength and became a hell of a lot more detrimental, he adjusted his magic, and sent it out to meet the rising storm head on. His power hit the air, igniting a stunning multi-colored light show as the two energies collided. Not wanting to rip apart the ward and have the magic rebound on Rory, Cheveyo maintained a defensive stance only. Then he sank more power into his voice, "Rory Ellis, answer me."

His command cut through the deafening storm like a warning bell and left a ringing silence in its wake. The scene around him shimmered, broke, and reformed, as if it was a reflection caught in a rippling pond.

When it settled somewhat, Cheveyo frowned.

The trees reached for the sky with endless branches, elongated and curved. The river now flowed above him, providing a watery barrier between him and the forest, as if he stood in the river's bed looking up. Sunlight hit like diamonds in blinding bursts of lights. Even the stones hung perilously above his head, as if, with the slightest flick of a feather, they would bury him in an abstract collapse.

"Who are you?" The question came from behind him.

Cheveyo went to turn only to discover sand held his feet in a sure grip. Forgoing comfort for visual confirmation, he torqued his head until he could see the speaker. At first, they were hard to make out. Light and shadows created a camouflaging mosaic. Instead of fighting the seizure-inducing light show, Cheveyo adjusted his perception. As the one who instigated this dream, the control of it remained his, so long as he could hold it. He exerted his will, and the light show stopped, then winked out, leaving behind a barefoot man dressed simply in jeans and a T-shirt.

Some of his apprehension about this quest slipped away. Looked like he found his missing druid. With another flex of will, Cheveyo forced the sand to release him and stepped free from the riverbed's hold before turning to face Rory "My name's Cheveyo, Danny Ayze sent me."

"Cheveyo?" Rory frowned as he scratched the side of his nose. "I know that name, I've heard it before."

Nice to know his reputation preceded him. "I'm the Northwest Magi."

That widened Rory's eyes. "Why did Danny send you?" Then comprehension dawned, and he answered his own question. "You're a Dream Walker."

Cheveyo nodded.

"Well, damn," Rory muttered, his gaze going to his feet. "Danny called in the big guns?"

Not sure how he felt about being considered a "big gun," Cheveyo answered anyway, "Yes."

"How bad is it?"

With that one question, Cheveyo knew Rory understood what was happening, so he didn't mince words. "Bad."

Pain—emotional, not physical—swept over Rory's face, the intensity of it causing Cheveyo's heart to wince. The druid ran a hand through his hair, no sign of the damage his physical body bore evident, and half turned away, his attention on the river running overhead. "Anne and Pax?"

"Anne's here, Pax is staying with Sara."

"I want to go back." He looked back to Cheveyo, anger and frustration a mask for his underlying fear, his hand fisting at his side. "I've tried, but I can't get through. Why?"

"We're not sure, but we can't detect any magic involved, which means it's natural." While not completely sure what he just said was true, it was a small comfort he could offer Rory. At least until they could discover what was keeping him here. "Hopefully, between the two of us, we can figure this out."

Rory's hands went to his hips, and he blew out a harsh breath, his face pale but resolute. "Right, okay then." He looked at Cheveyo and motioned to a matching pair of smooth flat stones that suddenly took shape between them. "Let's do this."

Walking over, Cheveyo took a seat, while Rory did the same. "First, tell me what you remember."

Rory sat tailor-style on the stone, one elbow braced on his thigh, chin in his hand. He closed his eyes. "I was coming back from a meeting in Phoenix, heading up the highway. Traffic wasn't bad, the sun had gone down. Even though night hadn't completely moved in, it was dark. I was worried, anxious..." his voice trailed off and frown lines inched over his forehead, slowly deepening.

When he stayed quiet, Cheveyo prompted, "About what, Rory?"

Rory's eyes blinked open, his gaze unfocused, his confusion clear. "There was something I wanted to tell Tala." His frown grew, and he tilted his head as if listening to invisible voices. "I saw someone—they shouldn't have been there—" His pale face grayed, his eyes widened, then his breath hissed out as he winced. He pressed the heel of his hand into his eye. "I can't—see them."

Hearing the agitated panic creeping into Rory's voice, Cheveyo kept his voice low, soothing, "It's okay, let's focus on the accident, okay?" Because whatever it was Rory wanted to share with Tala, his inability to capture it would do nothing to help get him back to Anne and Pax, only agitate him. Better to leave that for the moment. When the druid's breathing evened out, Cheveyo nudged him again. "So you're driving home, it's dark, what next?"

Rory began speaking, and, as if dropped by an invisible

hand, a movie screen filled with images appeared behind him, a visual accompaniment to his retelling.

A dark highway, curves cut by headlights, Rory's hands on the steering wheel, his wedding band winking in the dash's light. A quick check of mirrors as he switched lanes when, from the other side of the road, a bright explosion coincided with a muffled report of a...gunshot?

Cheveyo wasn't sure on the sound, but he kept his attention on the images, letting Rory's voice provide the narrative.

The bright light faded, leaving behind burning afterimages. Rory instinctively jerked the steering wheel away from the light, the receding afterimages making it near impossible to see. The point, obviously, since the scene's perspective tilted wildly, the car careening out of control as it bounced off the asphalt on to the rough easement.

Rory's voice rose as he fought the steering wheel, desperate to stop the inevitable. Sharp cracks sounded in time to the spreading spider web of cracks creeping across the windshield. Metal groaned and wailed. Rory's curses went from shocked to angry to panicked. The airbag burst forth in choking cloud of suffocating white, while a searing punch of burning air carried chemical overtones. The scene turned and continued its sickening spin, horrific noises supplying nightmarish accompaniment. Pain bloomed in an unrelenting wave, then blessed darkness descended, the images fading to black.

Cheveyo shook free of the phantom pain while across from him, Rory breathed heavily, his head hanging, his fists curled against his knees. Cheveyo gave Rory space to regather his composure and decided to play back the images. This time with no sound, no emotional resonance, just visuals. He kept his attention focused on the scene playing out, slowing it down so it crept by in a strange freeze frame. The flash of light that triggered the accident. Could be an oncoming car with its brights engaged. But there was something—there! He stopped the memories.

Cheveyo inched back the memory, as if hitting rewind on a movie, going over each individual moment carefully. In that moment, as the afterimages faded and the car initially tipped, while the tires lost traction, he found what bothered him. There was no car attached to the sudden appearance of light. This wasn't a careless use of brights because there was no car coming down the other side of the road. If there was no car, what was behind the light?

CHAPTER 14

"A SPELL," RORY ANSWERED CHEVEYO'S SILENT QUESTION, HIS voice tight, angry. "It's subtle, but there. I wasn't looking for anything, was too caught up in getting home." He stood up and pointed out an area to the left, by the side mirror. "Anchored, I think, in the mirror."

"Mirror magic?" Cheveyo wondered aloud. It would be a dangerous spell to master, thanks to the distorting properties of the mirror, but it could be done. If the witch or wizard was talented enough, subtle enough. He could think of a couple of names in Tala's house that fit that particular bill. The suspicions he harbored gained teeth.

"Maybe," Rory muttered, his head canting as he peered closer. "Probably," he corrected. When Cheveyo moved to stand beside him, he asked, "But why me?"

"That would be the question, wouldn't it?" Cheveyo murmured. "Perhaps it has something to do with what you saw."

Rory shot him a puzzled look.

"Whatever it was you wanted to tell Tala?" He let the

images inch forward, checking to see if they had missed anything else.

Next to him, Rory turned and began to pace, his hand gripping the back of his neck.

Cheveyo let him go, giving him time to pull his fragmented memories together. Not that he held out much hope on getting much more, not now. The accident and the spell would wreak havoc on Rory's recall ability for a while.

Finally, Rory stilled, frustration radiating from him like a heat wave. "The more I try to remember, the more it slips through my fingers."

The pained obsessive note in Rory's voice triggered an instinctive warning. "Then stop," Cheveyo advised sharply, letting the memories drift away. There was nothing more to learn, not here. Better to concentrate on getting Rory out of this dream and back to the real world. "It's enough, Rory, you've given us enough."

"But—" he protested.

"No," Cheveyo cut the younger man off, pieces coming together on one possibility of why Rory was in a coma.

He stepped into Rory's personal space and grabbed his upper arms, forcing the druid to focus on him and what he was saying. "You have a wife and son who need you. Anne and Pax." He waited until recognition inched out the driving confusion. Picking up on his intensity, Rory's gaze clung to Cheveyo's even as he wrapped his hands around Cheveyo's arms, his fingers digging in deep. Taking that sign as a positive, Cheveyo kept pushing, "You can't afford to remain here, trying to capture the pieces. Let them go, and let's work on finding your way home."

Standing so close, gave Cheveyo a ringside seat to Rory's internal struggle and the barely there shadows clinging to the energy surrounding him. Strain was visible in the taut lines of Rory's neck, and a shudder wracked his frame.

That damn mirror spell must have contained a weakened compulsion spell, one keeping Rory focused on what he couldn't remember, instead of the loved ones waiting for him.

Using his hold on Rory's arm, Cheveyo wrapped his magic around the druid like a protective cloak. He didn't break eye contact as he offered, "I promise you, Tala and I will figure out the rest. That's not on you."

Rory swallowed, hard, and gave a jerky nod. With Cheveyo's magic standing guard, the druid managed to gather his frayed energy together, the thin shadowy tendrils pulling like taffy strands before breaking. Each time he sucked in a deep breath, another strand broke. Then another, until only a fragile few remained. His body gave another shudder before he finally spoke. "You swear you'll figure out what's going on? I don't like being used, especially against Tala."

Recognizing that Rory would use Cheveyo's vow to break the remaining holds of the compulsion, he lifted his hand from Rory's arm and place it over his heart. "I swear to you, I intend to figure out what is happening here, and I will do everything in my power to keep Tala safe."

He didn't make the vow lightly, and even here in this non-corporal realm, his promise rang with power, tying him more tightly than any crafted spell. He didn't mind, because he meant every word. He couldn't leave Rory here to die, and he had absolutely no intention of leaving Tala until her safety was assured and the threat eliminated.

"Thank you," Rory choked out, his body slumping as the last of the compulsion snapped under Cheveyo's promise. "Damn, I'm sorry I didn't sense it."

"No apologies needed." He kept a steading hand on Rory. "We need to get you back."

Rory straightened slowly as if pained. He stepped back, and Cheveyo let him. Despite its paleness, grim determination colored the druid's face. "Let's do this."

Taking him at his word, Cheveyo didn't waste time in forcing the world around him to shift. Ensuring his magic was tethered securely to Rory, Cheveyo brought the rest of his power to bear, forcing the river to slowly sink into place. Using the floating stones, he climbed out of the river, Rory on his heels. It should've been easy, but it was like climbing through cement. Each step was a fight, but eventually they made it to shore.

The sunshine from earlier was gone, replaced by the ominous threat of a raging storm. Frigid wind tore at them as they fought their way back to the hunting trail, and Cheveyo bit off a curse, recognizing the signs for what they were.

A few times he was forced to help Rory to his feet as the natural elements took savage pleasure in fighting them. By the time they made it to the bridge, Cheveyo was bent double under the gale-force winds and punishing rain.

Rory dropped to his knees, even as he kept his grip on Cheveyo's belt.

In front of them, the bridge swayed violently. Getting across would be a bitch. Cheveyo knew he could make it, but it was the exhausted and drained Rory that worried him. The spell was determined to keep the druid, but Cheveyo was equally determined to wrest him from the magical hold.

The faint scent of lilac and sage snuck under the ion-singed air and curled around him before slipping away. He raised his head, searching for the woman behind the magic.

No one was there, but he could tell she was doing what she could to help.

Sure enough, behind him, Rory found a new strength and pushed to his feet. Leaning in, he shouted in an effort to be heard over the screaming wind. "Keep going, I can make it!"

Registering Tala's unexpected support of the druid, Cheveyo took Rory at his word and began crossing the bridge. Each step a fight. Clawing one hand over the other, he used the bridge's railing and the combined effort of their magic to pull them both along. In between the brutal gusts of wind and rain, he could barely make out Rory's voice repeating the names of his wife and son, a talisman against the spell's hold and a focal point as he continued to give what energy he could to Cheveyo's fight.

Only as they stumbled over the bridge's midpoint did the insidious mirror spell shatter and break. Around them, the winds died, and the rain drifted away. No longer worried about being tossed off, Cheveyo let go of the railing and half turned to wrap an arm around Rory's waist. The poor druid was exhausted. "Hang in there, Rory," Cheveyo murmured even as Rory continued to whisper Anne and Pax's name. "We're almost there."

They crossed the last of the bridge and stopped. Fog hung in thick curtains, obscuring everything. To their right, the fog thinned and lightened.

Next to him, Rory stiffened then lifted his head. "I can see her." His voice was hoarse, but his wan face lit from within. "Anne!" He jerked away from Cheveyo and lurched forward, disappearing into the bright mist.

Knowing he couldn't follow, Cheveyo let him go, a sense of gratitude rising that Anne and her son would soon have their husband and father back. Like a taut line being snapped, he felt the moment Rory returned to the mortal realm.

The scent of lilac and sage grew stronger, wrapping around him like a physical touch, pulling him forward. "I'm coming," he told the woman demanding his return.

One moment he was walking through the fog, the next he was blinking his eyes open while alarms blared a hectic cacophony, blending in with a rush of bodies and voices. Blinking his way back, he found himself staring into Tala's beautiful eyes as she crouched before him. Without thinking, he reached out and cupped her check. "Demanding woman."

Her smile chased away the worry in her eyes as she turned and pressed a soft kiss to his palm. "Stubborn man."

"You back?" The question came from above and behind him.

Letting his head fall back, he found Chay glaring at him. "Yeah, I'm back."

As Tala shifted to get out of the way of hospital personnel rushing around Rory, she stood and tugged at his hand. "Let's get out of here and let them work."

He stifled a groan as he got to his feet and stumbled after her, Chay bringing up the rear.

Out in the hall, they were met by a smiling Danny. "Good job, son."

Feeling battered, Cheveyo shook his head carefully and turned to Chay. "I need you to check something out for me." Catching movement farther down the hall, he adjusted his request. "Actually, I want you and Wyatt, to check something out."

Tala's hold on his wrist tightened then relaxed, but he was grateful she didn't let go. Instead, she stayed quiet, listening.

Hearing his name, Wyatt sauntered up and joined them. It was a risk to send the wizard, but even if he was the one behind the mirror spell, Chay could more than handle him. Besides, best to know where your possible enemies were than worry about where they weren't. "Go find out where they took Rory's car and check the driver's side mirror for magical traces."

Chay frowned, putting the unspoken pieces together with lightning quick accuracy. "A mirror spell?"

"That's what I'm thinking, but I want you two to confirm it." Cheveyo split a look between them both. "Track it if you can, but let me know what you find."

"On it," Wyatt said before lifting a hand to Danny and starting down the hall.

"Hold up," Chay's voice brought Wyatt to a standstill, but Chay wasn't watching him, he was staring at Cheveyo with a frown. "And where will you be?"

"Tala and I are going to figure out who Rory was meeting, then head back to her home."

Chay was shaking his head before Cheveyo finished. "Nope, Wyatt can go check it out on his own."

"No, Wyatt can not," Cheveyo snapped. "You will go with him and ensure that whatever was left behind won't harm anyone else."

Chay's face darkened and he took a step forward. "My job is here."

Chay's clear challenge caused Cheveyo's temper to slip a bit more. He pulled free of Tala's hold and got into Chay's face before growling, "Right now, your job is whatever I tell you it is."

"Think again. My assignment is to keep you safe." Chay's voice dropped lower, keeping their conversation between the two of them. "Even from yourself."

His implication swept through Cheveyo, lighting worn fuses until a white-hot conflagration swept away his tenuous hold on his temper. Despite the drain of dream walking, he called a flow of power with a flex of will. Ensuring the magic touched only Chay, Cheveyo ruthlessly sank controlling barbs deep. It was time to remind this admittedly lethal warrior who really was the biggest threat in the room. "Best you remember that I am your Magi, Chayton."

With each word, his power forced Chay to step back, his physical body under Cheveyo's control. "And I protect myself." Despite the younger witch's impotent fury, Cheveyo forced Chay to turn until he was facing down the hall toward the exit door. Coming up behind him, Cheveyo whispered into Chay's ear. "Lest you forget a recently learned lesson, before there were Wraiths, there was the Order." He released his hold and added, "You were not the first to be feared."

Then he stepped back.

Chay's eyes widened in shock, and he turned his head carefully toward Cheveyo. The questions swirling in his eyes held mute behind his clenched jaw.

Holding his gaze, Cheveyo waited a heartbeat, then two as Chay readjusted his worldview, before asking calmly. "We good?"

Chay gave him a stiff nod, his reluctance obvious, then stretched his neck side to side with an audible crack. "Watch your ass."

Despite the fact the warning could be taken one of two ways, Cheveyo simply returned Chay's nod.

Chay studied him a moment longer, opened his mouth, rethought whatever he was considering, shut it, and shook his head. Instead, he turned to their silent witnesses.

"Tala. Danny." Then he headed toward where Wyatt waited.

As he walked away, Cheveyo warned softly, "Be careful."

Chay raised a hand in acknowledgement and kept walking.

Cheveyo watched the wizard and witch disappear down the hall, aware of Tala and Danny standing silently nearby.

Only after the swinging door at the end of the hall closed, did Tala speak, breaking the heavy quiet. "Know that I'm not making aspirations on your authority, but what the hell, Cheveyo?"

Catching the mix of worry and puzzlement in her voice, he sighed, trying not to wince from letting his temper get the better of him. "Chay takes his responsibilities too far sometimes."

"Be that as it may, he had a valid concern," Danny pointed out. "You've not fared very well during your visits here." When Cheveyo glared at him, Danny raised his hands in a conciliatory manner, a small smile playing over his lips. "Through no fault of your own, but still…"

Between Tala's exasperation and Danny's gentle reprimand, Cheveyo couldn't escape the niggle of remorse for his behavior. "Look, he means well, but sometimes he needs to remember who he's dealing with."

Tala's eyebrows rose until they nearly touched her hairline. "Oh, I'd say he won't be forgetting who you are any time soon."

Behind them, Rory's door opened and a nurse pushed out some sort of monitor on wheels. Amusement fading, Tala waited until she passed, before she asked, "You going to share what has you so on edge?"

Not wanting to continue this conversation in the hall, he motioned for the two to follow him in the other direction to the small waiting room. Thankfully, no one was in there.

They sat around a low table, and Cheveyo relayed what caused Rory's accident in succinct detail. When he was done, Danny was shaking his head, his worry evident, and Tala was frowning.

"A mirror spell takes a delicate touch," Tala stated.

"Very delicate," Cheveyo agreed, watching her turn the information over in her head.

"And strength to hold at that distance," Danny added. "Since it was anchored to the car, it also explains why I couldn't pick up on it."

Cheveyo nodded, but Tala cut in before he could say anything more. "But why target Rory?"

"Because he saw something he shouldn't have."

She gave him a gimlet eye. "Stop being cryptic and spill, Cheveyo."

"If you'd let me finish, I'd be happy to," he drawled. When she mimed zipping her lips, he continued. "The reason he was in the coma was two-fold—the accident caused physical trauma, but there was a compulsion spell woven within the mirror spell."

Tala's mouth fell open, but she held her tongue. Next to her, Danny gripped the arms of the chair until his knuckles turned white.

"Every time he tried to move forward, the spell held him back, telling him he there was something he needed to tell you, warn you about. Unfortunately, he really couldn't remember, so he ended up stuck in an endless loop. He couldn't break it because he has no memory of what he wanted to tell you, just that he needed to warn you."

"Which makes the mirror spell the initial attempt to ensure he never spoke to me." She leaned forward. "There are those who could do one spell successfully, but not both."

"You sent one of the few people we have who could've cast such magic with Chay." Danny turned to Cheveyo and his next question proved he hadn't missed a damn thing. "Why?"

"Don't ever mistake underestimating Chay." Cheveyo warned. "If Wyatt is involved, Chay will sniff it out."

Danny's eyes darkened, obviously not liking Cheveyo's implication. "And if he's innocent?"

"Better to know either way. At this point, we can't afford to overlook any possibility, no matter how unpleasant."

Tala and Danny exchanged a long look, before she sighed and agreed, "No we can't." She took a deep breath. "All right, what's next?"

"You and I need to find out who Rory was meeting and work our way backward. Maybe we'll get lucky and figure out who or what he saw."

"Or we come up with nothing," she muttered, her frustration evident.

"Got a better suggestion?" Because he was all for something easy, right about now.

Danny rose, drawing their attention. "How about you start with the bag of Rory's stuff the nurses gave Anne? I don't think she's had a chance to go through it. Maybe they'll be some clue there."

Amused by Danny's obvious attempt to stem an argument before it could gain traction, Cheveyo got to his feet. "Brilliant as always, Danny." He offered Tala his hand. "Shall we?"

She took it and let him help her to her feet. "Fine."

When they got to Rory's room, most of the hospital personnel had cleared out, but one nurse stayed behind, making adjustments and notes. Anne's tear-stained face was lit with joy as she sat by Rory's bed, his hand wrapped in hers, his eyes open.

Tala tugged her hand free and slipped into the room, while Cheveyo and Danny waited by the door. Anne turned, her smile huge. Tala murmured their request. Anne nodded her head and pointed to the small side table. Tala gave her a hug then went and pulled the bag out of the drawer. As she passed between them, she muttered, "Let's go do some snooping."

CHAPTER 15

Cheveyo's loss of temper with Chay worried Tala. It wasn't the carefully controlled reaction she was familiar with, but one indicating there was more happening beneath the surface than he was sharing. Was he closer to the edge than she initially thought? The fears she harbored since his last visit crept closer.

Last year, despite her worries that all was not right with him, she let him return to Portland, unwilling to risk undermining his position. Something she would never willingly do to him. Their personal history aside, Cheveyo was a leader she not only respected but understood. There was much more to him than he ever shared with anyone. She hadn't understood his carefully maintained emotional distance until she carried the mantle of the Southwest Magi, then his choice became crystal clear.

The Kyn leaders walked a thin line between fear and respect, a necessary path to control the powers in their respective houses. Unfortunately, sometimes fear became the more productive motivator. Much like today's exchange with Chay. Even if the young witch was a Wraith, questioning Cheveyo's authority could be detrimental to one's health.

But where Chay couldn't tread, as Cheveyo's peer, she could. And she would. Just not right now. Later, because she had a feeling their impending conversation would wander into much more private areas. She pressed the bag of Rory's things harder against her churning stomach as she headed back to the semi-private waiting room with Cheveyo and Danny at her back.

Once everyone was settled, it didn't take Tala long to find out why Rory was in Phoenix. After confirming his lock code with Anne, Tala accessed his emails first, but nothing raised any red flags. Up next was his calendar. On the day of his accident, he attended an all-day forum at the local university on proposed revisions for the Tonto National Forest's management plan. Since all Rory had was the event title, time and location she went to the internet and found the posted agenda. Pulling it up, she scanned the listed topics. Everything from hunting to wildfires to water rights to conservation issues seemed to be covered.

Sitting next to her while reading over her shoulder, Cheveyo asked, "Any idea of where to start?"

Holding back on her snarky comment regarding crystal balls, she shook her head and continued to slowly scroll through the agenda.

"You could try tracking down every person who attended the seminar." The unhelpful suggestion came from Danny, who lay on the couch, an arm over his eyes and his feet propped on the far armrest.

She didn't have to look up to know Cheveyo was shooting the older man a dirty look.

"Wait," she murmured, clicking on the topic 'Arizona Land Management and Collaborative Organizations.' She pointed to one of the listed panelists. "I know this name."

"Mason Atwood, ALMA?" He frowned in puzzlement. "What is ALMA?"

"Arizona Land Managers Association," Danny clarified and slowly sat up, rubbing a hand over his face. "Atwood." His gaze narrowed in thought, then he looked at her. "Isn't he the one who met with Tomás a couple of months back?"

Tala slowly nodded. "I think he's the one Andrew had to escort off the ranch, actually." To give Cheveyo perspective, she explained, "A couple months ago, Hadley swung by to drop off some papers for Tomás to sign. She said she barely got to the door before it was swung open and Tomás was all but screaming at Andrew to get 'that piece of government shit Atwood' off his ranch."

"Hadley have any idea of what was going on?" Cheveyo didn't look up from his phone as his fingers flew over the screen.

"Not a clue," she answered, wondering what he was looking for. "She only mentioned it because she found Tomás's behavior more erratic than normal."

"Or what had become his normal," Danny corrected.

"'Mason Atwood, Director of Arizona Land Managers Association for the last seven years,'" Cheveyo read aloud. "Looks like he straddles the bridge between the local land managers and various organizations and the federal government. Seems, along with his current job, he sits on a couple of sub-committees in Washington. Busy man." He turned to her, a shrewd light in his eyes. "Thinking what I'm thinking?"

"The land deal," she murmured, notching this latest

information in with what they currently had, which wasn't much. "Considering his position, if anyone has information on that land deal, it would be him."

Cheveyo nodded even as he hit his screen and then brought his phone to his ear.

It took less than three minutes to confirm Atwood was available and for Cheveyo to charm his way onto Atwood's schedule. When he hung up, his smile was all teeth. "Shall we?"

Mid afternoon was closing in as Cheveyo and Tala made their way to Atwood's office in the heart of downtown Phoenix. The location meant parking a couple of blocks away and hoofing it. The area served as a home to an eclectic mix of corporate businesses, entertainment venues and the local university campus.

Tala couldn't help but notice the covert looks she and Cheveyo garnered as they made their way through the mix of college students and young professionals. As they passed a glass-fronted building, she caught their reflections—a statuesque blonde and the strikingly handsome male—but it wasn't so much their looks catching attention as the auras they carried. Most of the time she wasn't sure if it was a blessing or curse, but regardless, the mantles of leadership left a lasting impression.

Finding the building housing Atwood's office, Cheveyo held the heavy glass door open for her to pass through. As they walked into an airy atrium bustling with activity, he took off his sunglasses and hooked them on his collar. The bright burst of laughter, the murmur of conversations, the clicking of heels over tile, and the background dings of elevators all combined into the typical business soundtrack.

They joined a handful of people on the elevator and took it to the ninth floor. When the doors opened, they stepped off, leaving behind the last three occupants heading to the higher floors. The short hall played gallery to a series of photos capturing pieces of desert scenes. There were the color-drenched canyon walls, the twisted beauty of Joshua trees, noble guards of saguaros, and haunting scenes of ancient dwellings, all mixed with breathtaking shots of the Colorado River as it carved its way through sheer walls.

They stopped at the long counter spanning the front and the young man who sat in front of the wall with the list of offices behind him.

He flashed a professional smile. "Hello, can I help you?"

She moved in front of Cheveyo. "Yes, we're here to see Mr. Atwood. I believe he's expecting us."

"Of course, if you would give me just a moment to let them know you're here?"

She nodded then joined Cheveyo where he stood next to the last picture. Done in black and white, it showed a half drained small canyon from Lake Powell and the Anasazi petroglyphs still visible on its wall. "Such history drowned," Cheveyo murmured, his gaze on the image.

"Change is inevitable," she offered sadly, her heart aching as she studied the image.

"I'm not sure it's worth the cost," he answered.

It was an argument initiated when Lake Powell first came into being and submerged the ancient Native American sacred burial sites, and it still raged on today. But there was a depth to his response, which left her wondering if they were talking about the same things.

"Mr. Cheveyo and Ms. Whiteriver?"

They turned to find a woman, dressed in a tasteful blue blouse paired with inky slacks, waiting to the left of the desk. Tala put her age somewhere in her mid-forties. As they drew closer, she held out her hand. "I'm Olivia, Mr. Atwood's executive assistant. If you'd follow me?"

They exchanged handshakes and greetings before heading down the hall. Olivia led them past a series of other offices until they reached a corner office. She knocked on a door set into a wall of tinted glass before opening it and motioning them in.

Tala stepped through first, her attention caught by the wall of windows overlooking the downtown cityscape. She wasn't aware she stopped moving until Cheveyo's hand at her back gently nudged her forward.

"Mr. Cheveyo. Ms. Whiteriver." Atwood came out from behind his paper-strewn desk, his smile relaxed, his dark hair streaked with silver. Sporting a collared button-down shirt, no tie, and tucked into gray slacks, he looked like any other businessman. Again, with the round of handshakes before he motioned them to sit at the chairs clustered in a casual manner around what appeared to be a highly polished tree trunk supporting a glass top. "Could I offer you some water?"

Tala and Cheveyo both demurred and took their seats. Atwood took a seat, hitching his foot to his knee as he leaned back. "I'm sorry, your names sound familiar, but Olivia was a little vague on why you wanted to meet. What can I help you with?"

On their way over, she and Cheveyo discussed how best to approach Atwood and decided to play it from the worried business partner angle. To justify his presence, he would be playing the role of her concerned fiancé.

She took the lead. "Mr. Atwood, we were wondering if you currently had any business dealings with a Tomás Chavez?"

His polite expression dimmed a bit, and his voice lost some of his affability. "I'm afraid I'm not comfortable answering that. May I ask why you would like to know?"

"Mr. Chavez is—was—" she made the slip deliberately, gauging his reaction, "—a business associate of mine—"

"Wait," he interrupted before she could finish, dropping his leg and sitting up. He leaned forward, his gaze intense. "What do you mean 'was'?"

She bit her lower lip, snuck a quick look to Cheveyo, before turning back to Atwood and offering with a touch of hesitancy, "I'm sorry, didn't you hear? He passed away yesterday."

Atwood's shock, real though it was, couldn't hide a flash of calculation as he templed his fingers under his chin and frowned. "What happened?"

"A heart attack," Cheveyo cut in smoothly. "He was out on his ranch when it hit. By the time his ranch hand found him, it was too late."

"My god. I just spoke to him a couple weeks ago." Atwood shook his head, before raising it, a sheen of remorse in his gaze. "I'm so sorry for your loss."

She nodded and dropped her gaze to hide her flare of cynicism. Unfortunately, due to the brief glimpse of the ruthless executive she caught earlier, Tala wondered at the sincerity behind it. She did manage to murmur a soft, "Thank you."

"You mentioned you're a business associate of Mr. Chavez," Atwood said.

"Yes." On their way in, she made a quick call to Toby to prepare for just this question. "I'm one of the majority partners in Rojos Lobos Limited." A legitimate business front for the myriad of Southwest Kyn businesses, one where each of the leaders held a seat, and if there was a land deal on the table, Tomás should have informed them before starting any negotiations—if he hadn't been bat-shit crazy and out for blood. "Are you familiar with us?"

His eyes widened as if he was finally putting the pieces together. "Of course, now I recall your name. Rojos Lobos's partners are listed as Whiteriver, Castle, and Chavez. I believe my office has mediated a few conversations between your company and the BLM over the years," his voice oozed political savvy, setting her teeth on edge. "I'm sorry I didn't put it together sooner."

Ignoring the fact that his apology rang insincere, she inclined her head. "It's come to our attention that Mr. Chavez may have been in the midst of negotiating a land deal we were not made aware of."

A practiced frown of concern creased Atwood's face. "As much as I appreciate your concern, I'm not sure how I can help."

This time it was Cheveyo who spoke, "We were hoping you could confirm if this is the case or not."

Atwood turned to him, "And your interest in this?"

Tala put a hand on Cheveyo's wrist. "I apologize, this is my fiancé, Cheveyo. We were visiting a friend in the hospital when Mr. Castle asked me to stop by and talk with you." She studied him carefully as she dropped that nugget of information and caught the minute tightening around Atwood's eyes, as if he tried to stifle a wince.

"I see," he murmured then pushed to his feet and paced to the window, hands in his pockets. With his back to them, he said, "Normally, I'd be reluctant to discuss my conversations with Mr. Chavez, but—" He paused and half turned to face them. "As you represent Rojos Lobos, I can confirm that, yes, Mr. Chavez had approached me to serve as a mediator between him and the BLM. We were in the midst of discussing the particulars of not only the land's ownership, but water and mineral rights."

"Which land parcels were included in this discussion?" she pressed, stifling her rising anxiety.

He removed his hands from his pockets and linked them behind his back, his shoulders stiff. "If I remember correctly, the land in question belonged to the ranch Mr. Chavez owned, plus fifty acres to the north of his property."

Stunned, her mind scrambled to put his answer into context. "Doesn't that border the reservation?"

Atwood's nod was stiff. What he described belonged not only to the Red Thunder Pack, but to the Magi house as well. Some part of her still held out hope Tomás hadn't completely lost it, but hearing how far he'd been willing to sell out both houses, left Tala reeling.

While she fought to regain her footing, Cheveyo stepped in, no sign of anything other than general interest in his voice, "How would that work if the land belonged to Rojos Lobos. Wouldn't it require agreement from all three partners?"

Atwood came back and perched on the edge of the chair, his hands clasped between his knees. "Mr. Chavez assured me he had all partners on board." He looked at Tala. "This is not the case, is it?"

Finally finding her voice, she shook her head. "No, Mr. Atwood, it is not."

He sighed. "This is not good."

"I'm sorry." She leaned forward. "We didn't intend to put you in a difficult situation. We were hoping it was an unsubstantiated rumor."

He gave her a wan smile, one at odds with the dark storm in his eyes. "I suppose there's no chance of changing your or your partner's mind?"

Forcing a semblance of sympathy, she said, "Right now, I can assure you that both myself and Mr. Castle would not be interested in moving forward with any sale."

"I don't think you understand, Ms. Whiteriver, when I say this is not good, I mean that the BLM may take issue with this. Especially as they entered the negotiations in good faith."

"A threat, Mr. Atwood?" Her question carried a dangerous bite.

He paled but remained resolute. "Not a threat, Ms. Whiteriver, simply stating a fact."

Obviously, this pending deal carried more weight than they realized. Wanting to ensure that this politically inclined opportunist didn't convince himself to keep pushing the issue, she allowed some of her anger at Tomás's betrayal to leak into her voice, adding a cutting edge. "You may want to remind your contact at BLM that the lands given to the Nations are federally protected. As part of this deal includes their land, and we value our relationship with the tribes, you can rest assured that Rojos Lobos is prepared to make it very, very painful for the BLM, or any other interested party, to pursue this matter any further."

Atwood swallowed, color seeping along his cheeks, but no matter how much he wanted to push, he chose the wiser course, even as frustration leaked through his voice. "I will be sure to pass your message along."

"Be sure you do." She stood, and, next to her, Cheveyo did the same.

Atwood rose as well and cleared his throat. "May I inquire as to who will be taking Mr. Chavez's position?"

"That would be Tobias Greene, out of Tucson." Catching a heightened interest in his gaze, Tala's smile grew razor sharp. "Rest assured, Mr. Atwood, he will not be following in Mr. Chavez's footsteps."

CHAPTER 16

"So what did we learn?" Cheveyo kept his eyes closed as he reclined in the passenger seat while Tala headed out of Phoenix. The effects of dream walking were finally catching up, and his body craved some serious down time.

"Tomás is a dick."

He didn't bother to hide his grin at her clipped response. "Besides that, *awéé*."

"Tomás is a really big dick."

He cracked an eye open and turned his head. "Careful, your temper's showing." And it looked damn good on her too. Color rode high in her sculpted cheekbones, and when she turned her glare on him, her dark eyes sparked with a not-so-hidden fire.

"If I had known what the bastard was planning, I would've skinned him, instead of making it quick." She hissed a curse and yanked the SUV into the next lane, zipping by the sedan doing the speed limit. She thumped her fist against the steering wheel—twice. "How was he planning on getting away with it?"

'It' meant selling the land out from under the combined

noses of the other two Kyn leaders. He closed his eye and returned to his previous position, his burst of amusement fading. "Unfortunately, I can think of a couple of different ways he could've done it."

"Without being caught?" Disbelief rode her question like a tick.

"Yep." He left it at that because the paths his thoughts traveled were dark and twisted.

When he didn't say anything more, she lasted a full minute before demanding, "Spill, Cheveyo."

His hands, clasped over his stomach, tightened, and when his knuckles began to ache, he forced them to relax. He didn't want to be the one to upend her life. Not again. Resentment clashed with practicality. Gods, he didn't want to put this out there, but Tala couldn't protect herself if she didn't know where the danger was coming from.

Still, he couldn't keep the hard edge from his voice, "Be very certain you want to open this particular box, Tala."

Eyes closed, he waited for her answer, feeling the tension skyrocket between them.

"Don't."

One word, all but vibrating with age-old anger and resentment predating the current situation, snapped his eyes open. When he turned, he found her looking at him, the emotions in her eyes a raging tempest that tore into his chest and left an icy ache in its wake.

She waited until she knew she had his attention before adding, "I haven't needed your protection in a very long time, Cheveyo."

The dismissal in her tone rankled, making his response sharper than intended. "You've made that crystal fucking clear, but right now, when you don't know who you can trust, you do."

Her hands tightened on the wheel, and a muscle jumped in her jaw. "And if I can't trust you?"

The verbal bullet slammed home with brutal force, the impact shattering bright pieces he hadn't known existed.

She paled, then flushed, "Dammit, Cheveyo, I'm—"

"Stop," he snapped. Fighting back his knee-jerk reaction to return fire, he locked his emotions down and chose to deal with the fallout later, when she wasn't driving a damn SUV up the mountain. "Tomás wasn't stupid. He knew he would need your and Rio's approval to go through with the land deal. Based upon what Atwood shared, and Tomás's unprovoked attack, it's safe to assume Tomás's plan to get that approval was to kill you."

"Even if I was dead, Rio wouldn't let him go through with it." She followed his example and stayed on topic.

"Rio doesn't matter," his voice remained detached and cold, mirroring the icy chill of his emotions. "If you step back and look at recent events—the attacks on Toby, the attack on you, Tomás's indication of a partner—the emerging pattern is simple, but effective."

"Say Tomás did manage to kill me, then what was his next move?"

"If the attacks on Toby were successful, Tomás could claim self-defense in attacking you."

She stiffened. "Because it would look like a Magi's spell killed one of his alphas." Her fingers drummed on the wheel. "Even if he got rid of me, Amelia or Joseph would step in, and neither one would be inclined to make a decision on the sale of the land without input from my people."

"There's nothing that guarantees your seat goes to either one."

She slid him a look. "You're talking about Tomás's

supposed partner." She turned her attention back to the road, shifting lanes as they overtook a semi on the uphill curve. "I thought you were convinced his partner was Leo."

"I never said he was my only suspect."

She snorted. "That's the impression you gave." Her lips curved into a bitter twist. "Playing games, Cheveyo?"

Anger simmered under his ice-enshrouded emotions. "I told you before, I don't play games."

"Then what would you call it?"

"Acknowledging the possibilities, since focusing on a singular assumption is liable to kill you." Okay, maybe he wasn't above striking back.

Her mouth thinned, and her voice turned brittle. "Who else do you think is his partner then?"

"Wyatt, Hadley, or Teagan." He ignored her sharp inhale and relentlessly continued, "Your choice if it's one or a combination of all of them."

Her laugh held disbelief. "Please. You may as well add Danny to that list."

"Who says I haven't?" His question fell between them like a stone.

Her hands jerked on the wheel, causing the SUV to jog in its lane before she recovered.

He ignored the surge of remorse at taking the last of her security away. There was no room for illusions when you ruled a house, and Tala was more stubborn than most. He knew her, knew that no matter how deep she hid it, her faith in those who she called friends ran deep. Unfortunately, experience was a cruel teacher. Better it come from him than a blade buried in her back.

In the console between them, his cell rang, slicing through the tension-laden air. He picked it up and saw Chay's number. "Hello."

"We're going to be stuck here for the night," Chay said without any preamble.

"What happened?"

"They sent us to the wrong salvage yard." Chay's frustration came through loud and clear. "By the time we tracked down the right one, they were closed." The familiar sound of car locks releasing came through the open line. "Won't open until seven tomorrow."

Chay's implication hit and Cheveyo caught a glimpse of grim satisfaction in his reflection from the passenger window. Looked like Tala was running out of escape options. Tonight it would just be the two of them. Well, them and Ash. "All right, then you'd better get checked in to a hotel for the night and hit it first thing in the morning."

"Will do." On Chay's end a car door slammed shut.

Before Chay could hang up, Cheveyo said, "One more thing, swing by the hospital and see if the name Mason Atwood rings any bells for Rory."

"Mason Atwood?"

"He's with Arizona Land Managers Association and was at the forum Rory attended yesterday. Seems he was brokering a land deal between Tomás and the BLM."

"Is that right?" The question was followed by an engine turning over.

"Yep, but it may be best to keep that piece to yourself for right now."

"Understood. And Cheveyo?" Chay paused, soft electronic dings going off in the background. "Watch your ass."

Chay's implacable warning raised the hairs along Cheveyo's arms. "I will." He hung up and stared out the windshield as streaks of purple and pink stained the sky.

"What happened?" Tala's question cut through his preoccupation.

He dropped his phone back into the console. "They got sent to the wrong salvage yard, and can't get into the right one until tomorrow morning."

She didn't say anything, and he resettled in his seat, letting his eyes close in a vain attempt to block her out while he tried to get a handle on the devastation she left in her wake.

Behind the mask of his feigned sleep, he began untwisting the knots of his volatile emotions. There was one thing he knew beyond a shadow of a doubt, unintentional though it was, the hurt he caused her by leaving had done more damage than he even imagined.

Tala wasn't a woman who easily forgave or forgot—a fact he witnessed many times, and it was a bone of contention they fought over when they were together all those years ago. If he had to guess, the passage of time had simply refined and strengthened that aspect. She might understand the logic of his decision, but forgiveness of it? The phrase "when hell freezes over" became an apt descriptor.

The thing he couldn't grasp was why that angry reaction remained so strong for her. The bond dragging him back here, the one refusing to let her go, it wasn't one sided. He caught glimpses of it when she wasn't trying to keep him at a distance. But the minute he started getting close, out came the verbal claws, and they were merciless.

The memory of her touch, of the yearning ache she tried to hide last night during their conversation, teased him with the promise of possibility. But it was her smile, full of wistful heartache haunting him. Instinct whispered she was hiding something, hiding it deep, leaving her afraid to share. And it had nothing to do what was currently happening, because whatever it was had existed long before this situation.

But what was it? What could she possibly fear when it came to him? He was the last person who would ever mean her harm. Hell, he was constantly battling his need to wrap her up and keep her safe. Not because she needed it, but because he did.

"I'm sorry." It was a hesitant peace offering.

He blinked open his eyes and turned his head to see her focused on the road. The last of the evening's light was disappearing, replaced by dusk and its entourage of shadows. In the dim light of the dashboard, light and dark played chase over her face.

He didn't pretend to not understand, and he kept his voice equally soft, unwilling to disturb this fragile truce, but determined to get some answers. "What did I do that you can't forgive?"

Her face blanched, stark fear and pain striping away the Magi leader and leaving only the woman behind. Her throat worked, her mouth opened then closed, without anything escaping.

"Tala?" Concern had him sitting up.

She turned to look at him, and he barely caught the sheen of wetness in her eyes before they went back to the road. "I can't." It came out choked.

His heart took on a heavy beat as her reaction sent dread coiling through him. Whatever secret she carried, it was daunting. When she brushed a shaky hand over her eyes, as if wiping away tears, he frowned, dread twisting to worried concern. "You can't what?"

She shook her head, blinking furiously. "We can't do this now."

Since he had no desire to reenact Rory's accident, he didn't push, but he also wanted it clear they weren't finished with this conversation. "No, not now, but Tala—" he waited for her to acknowledge him. "Tonight we're going to talk, agreed?"

Her hands flexed on the wheel, but her answer, when it came, was husky with tension and unshed tears, "Agreed."

CHAPTER 17

The remainder of the drive passed in uneasy quiet. Cheveyo feigned sleep to give them both a break from the tense undercurrents. By the time Tala pulled into her drive, Cheveyo was ready to crawl out of his skin. When the crunch of gravel sounded from under the tires as she parked, he sat up, noting the VW Bug.

The SUV's headlights fell over the porch, mixing with the soft light spilling around the curtains shielding the front windows. Tala turned off the headlights just as the front door opened, and Teagan stepped out onto the porch.

Tala pushed open her door and stepped out, meeting her cousin at the top step. Cheveyo remained in the car, giving the two women some privacy. They exchanged words then Teagan handed a key over. Tala took the last step up and wrapped her arms around Teagan.

At first, her cousin remained stiff, then she hesitantly wrapped her arms around Tala's waist. There was enough light from the house to see Teagan close her eyes, but not enough to reveal the expression on her face. They stepped back and let go. Tala turned to watch Teagan make her way down the stairs.

Cheveyo got out of the SUV, stretching his stiff back. He returned Teagan's nod as she got into her car and left. The red taillights disappeared down the curving drive and when he turned back to the house, Tala stood on the porch, her arms wrapped around her waist. He closed his door and headed her way. When he got to the top, he curled an arm around her shoulders and nudged her inside. "Let's go see Ash."

She didn't pull away, but she did nod. Together they went inside. Ash looked up from his cushiony dog bed with a soft woof of greeting. Tala pulled away and dropped next to her unlikely pet. She spent a good amount of time scratching his ears and cuddling the furry monster.

Cheveyo left her there and headed to the kitchen. As much as he wanted to figure out what the hell was going on, it didn't hurt to get something put together for dinner before they tackled the elephant in the room. Besides, a part of him was relieved to avoid the looming confrontation for a little while longer.

He rooted around the fridge, pulled out a pound of hamburger and dumped it in the microwave to defrost. A search of her spice cabinet produced the right combination for tacos. He set the head of lettuce, an onion, a couple of tomatoes, and an avocado on the counter, then proceeded to unearth a cutting board and knife. He didn't waste time, simply diced the onion first, then moved on to the rest. By the time the microwave dinged, the vegetables were prepped, and he was ready to brown the beef. He knew the minute Tala stopped into the archway, but continued to work on dinner. "Tacos work for you?"

She left the archway and walked closer, stopping on the other side of the counter. "Sure. Want any help?"

"Nope, I've got it covered." He dumped the meat into the pan, flicked on the gas stove, and shot her a quick look. "You've got time for a shower, if you want."

"Um, okay." An unusual hesitancy in her voice had him looking back.

Exhaustion lined her face, not the physical kind, but the type that sank into your bones when you just didn't want to deal with the world. If he was a better man, he wouldn't push and give her the rest she sorely needed, but he wasn't that good. "Go, Tala, get comfortable, we'll eat, then we'll talk."

She nodded, turned, and headed down the hall, presumably, to her bedroom.

He let the air out of his chest with a quiet sigh. A few minutes later the sound of the shower coming on drifted down the hall. Instead of letting his brain run around in circles about their impending conversation, he focused on the next steps needed to weed out who was trying to destroy the Southwest Kyn.

While his gut was more than certain the one behind all the current chaos was close, probably too damn close, he couldn't nix the merciless fist twisting his guts. Dragging that person or persons into the light wouldn't be enough to stop the threat. Not if it the Council was involved, and he was pretty damn sure it was. Too much rode on the upcoming Council vote. Eleven high-ranking Kyn from all four houses sat on the Council, and Leopold DiMarcco was their unofficial leader.

After centuries in power, he wasn't about to lose an ounce of it. Especially not to the remnants of Mulcahy's rebellion. Currently, the Northwest had one rock-solid ally in another council member, Zane Aimeric, and he was doing what he did best—working behind the scenes to gain more support.

The results were frustratingly slow, but as Natasha had made clear, if the Northwest was to face down the Council, they needed more than brute strength, they needed the addition of a political edge.

Yet Leo wasn't standing idly by while the Northwest tried to align their support. In fact, thanks to an unexpected and very recent partnership between Natasha and the shadowy Darius Abazi, the Northwest was now privy to the fact that Leo was mining fissures from within the American Kyn houses in a masterful manipulation designed to splinter the Kyn.

While the traps Leo laid in Portland failed to create the damage he yearned for, his games had left deep scars and an even deeper hunger for vengeance. Because of Darius's help, Natasha had taken up Mulcahy's torch and begun moving her pieces on the Council's board. One such move resulted in Cheveyo's current visit. The fact that he shared a personal tie to Tala was frosting on Natasha's devious cupcake, and she expected him to exploit it.

The spicy bite of pepper and cumin rose from the pan as Cheveyo let the taco meat mixture simmer. He grabbed two plates from the cupboard and began putting the tacos together, moving on autopilot. Arguing with Natasha was a pointless exercise in frustration, but since he wasn't a chaos-loving demon, he warned her to prepare for disappointment since he had no intention of using Tala. The Demon Queen's response had been a teeth-grinding, canary grin and a murmured, "Never say never, Cheveyo. It's not good for you."

Maybe not, but a man had to draw a line somewhere, and, for him, it was Tala.

The shower shut off and a sudden quiet descended. It was broken by the soft click of nails coming into the kitchen. Cheveyo looked over his shoulder to see Ash sitting by the counter, eyes glued to the stove. Catching his wistful look, Cheveyo wiped his hands on the towel. "Hungry?"

Ash gave a soft chuff and flicked a glance his way before going back to staring at the stove, as if will alone would bring the deliciousness to him.

The very telling response made Cheveyo grin. He folded his arms over his chest and stared down at the wolf hybrid. "I don't think you're allowed to eat at the table, Ash, no matter how good your manners are."

That earned him a disgruntled shift of ears.

"C'mon, show me where she keeps your stash, and I'll get you fed."

Casting one last mournful look at the simmering meat, Ash reluctantly got to his feet, head and tail down, heaved a heavy sigh, and led the way to the small pantry off to the side of the kitchen. A little snooping confirmed his food and bowl were inside. A few minutes later, Cheveyo set the bowl on the floor.

Tala came in from the hall, braiding her wet hair. She took in the scene as she flicked the end of her braid behind her. "I see someone couldn't wait."

Cheveyo straightened and moved back to the kitchen sink, where he washed his hands. "He tried to convince me he had reservations, but alas, I had to inform him we were booked for tonight."

Tala's laugh was soft. "It smells good."

"Thanks." He finished the tacos he started. "Take a seat, I'll bring your plate over."

The sound of chair legs scraping over the floor came a few moments later. He brought both plates over and set them on the table. "Drink?"

"I can get it." She half rose, but he gave her a stern look, and she settled back down with a frown. "You don't have to wait on me."

"I'm not waiting, I'm offering to get you something while I grab a drink." Recognizing she was pushing for an argument, he kept his voice patient and level. "So, drink?"

"Tea, please," came the ungracious response.

Turning, he hid his grin. Some things never changed. Drinks in hand, he set hers down and then took his place at the table. The tension from earlier still lingered, but wasn't as heavy. They ate dinner in a relatively companionable quiet. He finished before her and pushed his plate to the side. Sitting back, he propped his sock-covered feet on the empty chair to his side, content to sit there with her.

With Ash curled at her feet, she finished off the last of her taco and licked her fingers cleaned, before using her napkin. When she caught him watching, a tint of blush hit her cheeks. "You're staring."

"I am," he agreed.

She set her elbow on the table and put her chin in her hand. "Why?"

Recognizing the achingly familiar exchange from years before, his answer came out husky, "Because."

A small smile peeked out, and her eyebrows rose. "Because why?" Her question held a teasing undertone.

And there she was, the young woman he'd fallen so disturbingly fast and hard for, hidden under the years of responsibility, but there. Memory-tangled emotions flooded him, adding undeniable weight to his voice, "Because I want to."

Her soft smile faded, and she blinked, her internal barriers coming up as she retreated. But not before he caught the flash of fear she tried to hide. Regret wound through him. Looked like their reprieve was over.

She looked away. "Cheveyo, you can't—"

"I can," he stopped her, his tone implacable. "But you don't want to. Why?"

"Stop it," she snapped. "Why are you so intent on pushing this?"

"Because you refuse to address it," he shot back.

"So, what?" She shifted back in her seat and threw her hands in the air. "What's in the past, stays in the past."

"Like hell it does." He dropped his legs and leaned across the table, ensuring she couldn't avoid his gaze. "Every time you forget to be angry with me and let me in, I catch a glimpse of what we once shared. It's still there. But there's something you won't let go of, and you're using it to keep me away. Why?"

Her gaze slid from his as she worried her bottom lip and folded her arms over her chest, leaning as far back as the chair would allow. "This won't work between us."

"Because you won't let it," he said. She was so damn stubborn, but then so was he. "Why?" If she would just answer his damn question, maybe they could untangle this mess.

Her jaw tightened, and she met his gaze. He was thrown by the mix of anger, grief, and love staring back. "Because you won't stay." Her sharp accusation could cut glass.

Heeding his instinct to tread carefully, he circled her answer, knowing it hid her real reason. "It was different before, Tala. Not only did I need to solidify my hold on my house, you needed to grow into your position. We couldn't do that together, not then, not without creating cracks others could exploit." Her chin lifted, but he kept going, "But it's not the same now. Our houses are ours, our positions are set. Things are changing, and if we want to pursue a relationship—while challenging—it is possible."

The militant line of her jaw softened, the turbulence in her eyes receded, and, for a moment, he thought he'd gotten through. "No, it's not." Her answer was soft and carried a pain that hurt to hear. She dropped her gaze and her arms to the table, her hands curled into fists.

Unwilling to give up, he reached out and covered one of her fists, gently stroking her knuckles. "Tell me why." When she lifted her gaze, he added, "Please."

"If I tell you," she choked out and looked back down at the table. "I'll lose you for good." She lifted her gaze, and he was stunned by the agony staring back. "I don't know if I can live with that."

His stomach pitched, and the recently ingested tacos threatened to rebel. He swallowed hard, bracing for whatever she was hiding—because, regardless of what she thought, he couldn't imagine any secret that would leave him walking away forever. He searched for the right thing to say to ease the deeply entrenched fear staring back and came up empty. Instead, he took a chance and laid himself bare. "I love you, Tala. I've loved you for a very long time, whether it was right or not. Rest assured, there's not much you could do to destroy it."

"You can't promise that," she whispered, pulling her hands away and tucking them in her lap.

His hand curled into a fist, and he drew it back. "Actually, I can."

She lifted her head, her voice a curious mix of wistful and bitter. "Love doesn't conquer all, Cheveyo."

"Trust me, I know." A lesson he learned the first time he walked away, and not something he wanted to repeat. "If it did, you and I wouldn't be here now. I may have screwed up by leaving you, but at the time, I couldn't see any other way to give you a chance to be who I knew you were destined to be. Hurting you was the last thing I wanted, but if it meant you would grow into the power lodged deep in your bones, I'd do it a thousand times over, just to ensure you would always survive."

"But I didn't."

Soft though they were, he caught her words and frowned. "Didn't what?"

"Survive." She met his gaze and visibly braced. "When you left—" She stopped, cleared her throat and started again. "When you left, you broke more than my heart."

Gods, it hurt to hear, hurt even more not to be able to ease her pain. He wouldn't lie to her—he couldn't do it then, and there was no way in hell he was going to start now. A lump settled in his throat, making it ache and his heart beat with a heavy ache, his voice came out choked, "Please, *awéé*, find that trust you once gave me and just tell me how to fix this."

"This isn't something you can fix, Cheveyo." The finality of her answer sliced through his heart, but before he could recover, she kept going, desperation making her words ragged. "I lied to you that night when you came to me."

Uncertain of where this was going, he cautiously felt his way through, like a blind man in a minefield. "About what?"

"I wasn't fine that night. I didn't want you to leave, but I refused to keep you here, so I lied." The tears she tried to hold back escaped and one trailed down her cheek. What she said next tore through his soul. "I was pregnant, Cheveyo, but I couldn't keep her safe, and I lost our daughter four months later."

CHAPTER 18

TALA DIDN'T DARE MOVE, MUCH LESS BREATHE AS SHE SAT ACROSS from Cheveyo, waiting for his reaction.

"Pregnant?" The one word came out flat. His face was wiped clear of any emotion, the only indication of fallout from her confession was the stygian darkness gaining depth in his eyes.

Unable to speak around the suffocating weight on her chest, she managed to nod.

"You knew, that night, when we spoke?"

Another nod, her body so tense she was on the verge of shattering.

He shoved back from the table with such contained violence, she couldn't stop her instinctive flinch. He grabbed his empty plate, reached across the table for hers, and stalked into the kitchen.

As soon as his back was turned, she scrubbed shaking hands over her face, wiping away the traitorous tears. The sound of stoneware shattering jerked her head up and her eyes widened when she realized he had thrown the dishes into the sink with such force they were nothing but puzzle pieces. She swallowed, hard, while he stood with his arms braced on the counter, fingers curled into a whitened grip on the edge, his head down, and his shoulders rigid.

If she was braver, she wouldn't be trapped in her chair. Instead, she would go over and make him listen. The wave of his suppressed anger grew, making the air heavy. She wasn't that brave. She couldn't even find her voice to begin explaining, so she waited. Waited for him to demand the answers he deserved.

His head lifted, and, with night playing backdrop, the window above the sink acted like a warped mirror. Roiling power seeped around the edges of his control, like a fire seeking purchase, and brushed against her with stinging nips. She reached for her magic to shield from the approaching storm. She knew the minute he realized what she'd done because his energy disappeared between one breath and the next. She didn't drop her gaze, even as his burned. Nor did she release the hold on her magic.

"Tell me."

It was no less than a demand, but she heeded it. In this, his anger was justified. She reached for her voice, found it, and gave him what he asked for. "I found out a few days before you left, but I was trying to figure out how to tell you. Especially since things between had been so..." She paused and frowned, trying to put the right words to that long ago scene. "...strained between us. You were pulling away, which at that point, I didn't understand why."

He straightened and turned, his face dark, but thankfully he stayed quiet, letting her talk.

"I thought you were bored with me, and when you told me you were going back to Portland, you were so distant." And looking back through the lens of years and experience, she now recognized it for the protective shield it was at the time.

Her admission cut through his anger and ignited a look of disbelief. "Bored?"

The little bite of censure underlying his question eased some of the pressure on her chest. "Yes, bored. Think about it, Cheveyo." He was her first lover and her mentor—mixing the two hadn't been smart on either of their parts. "You were the first man I ever slept with, the first one I let into my heart. To have you tell me that I needed time to grow and stand on my own, felt like you were telling me I was too young for you, too weak to be with you."

Some of his stillness melted and he shifted his feet before running a hand through his hair. "That wasn't it, at all, Tala."

"Yeah, I know that. Now." And she did, but at the time, scared and hurt, it had been a completely different story. "You broke my heart, and, angry and hurt, I wanted to strike back the only way I knew how." A childish reaction, sure, but she had been relatively young at the time and trying to find not only her place with the Magi, but who she was as a woman. To have the man she loved tell her she wasn't enough tore through hopes she hadn't even realized she carried. "So I made the decision to say nothing, to let you leave. If you didn't want me, there was no way I was going to tie you to me with a child neither of us expected."

"It was my child, too." Though he kept his voice soft, the implied accusation made her wince.

She dropped her gaze, old shame coming back for a visit. "I know," she whispered. Taking a shuddering breath, she lifted her head, determined to get it all out as the time for secrets was well and truly past. "I would've called and told you." And she would have, once she worked through the fallout from his rejection. "I just never got the chance." Her stomach clenched, and she wrapped her arms around her waist.

Whatever he saw on her face dulled the edge of his anger, the harsh lines softening. "What happened?"

"At first the pregnancy was going along just fine, and I didn't share it with anyone. I wasn't ready." For their questions or their whispers, and there would have been both, in spades. The young, newly instated Magi being seduced by the charming and powerful older witch, was not a story she could afford to have bandied about when she was trying to establish her position. "When I finally did tell someone it was Hadley, and eventually Teagan and Danny. I made them swear not to say a word, not until I had a chance to tell you and make sure I could protect my baby."

"We could have protected our baby." His correction was strangely gentle.

And that possibility haunted her even now. The damn tears were back, but she refused to let them fall and dipped her chin in a jerky nod. "I knew the minute I told you, you'd be back, but—"

"But reaching out for help might make you look weak," he replied, saying what she couldn't, grasping the merciless truth of the situation.

"And I wasn't ready to make the announcement." Young though she was, she hadn't been blind to what having a newborn meant in regards to her position as the head of the Magi house. "I was four months along and making plans to call you and tell my house what was happening, when I got this twinge in my back. At first, I thought I pulled something, a muscle maybe. Then, that afternoon, I started bleeding. Hadley took me to the hospital, but by morning, the baby was gone." Even now, years later, the agony of that morning clenched her heart and she couldn't even begin to try and explain it to him. She drew her legs up, wrapped her arms around them, and buried her face in her knees, unable to fight back the memories or the sobs.

When his arms slipped around her, she uncurled enough to turn, wrap her arms around his neck, and press her face into his chest as hot tears seared her cheeks and dampened his shirt. "I tried to keep her safe, I swear," she choked out, her voice muffled.

"Shh, *bił hinishnáanii*." He kept moving, taking her to the living room. He settled on the couch, keeping her in his lap, one hand gently stroking her spine. "It's not your fault."

But it sure as hell felt like it, and it chased her into nightmares—that something she'd done, the choices she'd made, cost her their child. It didn't matter how much therapy she underwent, that guilt remained, and would probably always do so. Keeping it from Cheveyo hadn't helped, and after his visit last year, that guilt grew to choking proportions. It was the same caustic mix of shame and guilt that drove her to blackmail Raine into saving his life from the Soul Stealer, regardless of the cost. She couldn't face the possibility of losing him, too.

As the minutes passed, he continued to hold her. Exhaustion took over, replacing tension's hold and softening her locked muscles. Her tears finally stopped, and her ragged breathing evened out, but under her cheek she could feel him, coiled and tense. She finally looked up to find him staring out into the room. Cupping his jaw, she nudged his attention to her. "Cheveyo?" A hundred questions spun in his name.

His dark gaze drifted over her, harsh lines adding an

unforgiving cast to his face. He traced a line along from her temple to chin, his touch butterfly soft. "You said, 'she.'"

Needing to give him something after taking so much, she managed a shaky smile. "A little girl. The doctor tried to say it was too early to tell, but I could sense her, just a couple weeks earlier, like a fragile butterfly. I named her Aponi."

He traced her fading smile with a gentle finger, his eyes turbulent. "Aponi," he repeated softly, grief seeping through his harsh control, "is a beautiful name."

His gaze continued to search her face, while his thoughts remained locked behind an impenetrable mask.

She could no more stop her doubts and insecurities from rising than breach his mask. Tension crept back in, creating a distance touch couldn't bridge.

He dropped his hand and began to shift her off his lap. As he set her aside, she swore she could feel him shutting down on a level she couldn't reach, leaving her off-kilter and unsure. "Cheveyo?" She pressed a palm against his chest in feeble protest.

He covered it with his hand and gave a careful squeeze, before drawing it back to her lap. "I'm going to go for a walk." He pushed up from the couch and stood.

"You'll be back?" Feeling raw and exposed, she couldn't hide the tremor in her voice.

Keeping his back to her, he said, "I will." He looked at Ash who had followed from the kitchen and now watched them from the entryway. His, "Stay close," was answered with a soft woof. Then she watched the man she loved walk out of the house, taking her battered heart with him, and wondered if either would make it back.

CHAPTER 19

CHEVEYO'S LEGS COULDN'T CARRY HIM AWAY FAST ENOUGH, BUT HE refused to run. Instead, he kept his pace under ruthless control, striding out into the darkness and away from the cabin and the woman huddled on the couch inside. He needed space, from her tears, her guilt, and his anger. The emotional devastation held captive in his chest scraped against bone and beat against his skin, demanding escape. The whirlwind of shock, anger, grief, and disbelief mocked his earlier assumption of Tala's secret.

A child. They created a child, a small being of infinite possibilities, and he never knew. Was never given a chance to celebrate the existence, brief though it was, of his daughter. His reactions swept across the spectrum, from white-hot anger that Tala dared to keep this from him, to surging grief at their loss. In between, he bounced from understanding the why's behind her logic to self-directed disgust at not reaching beyond his pride to pick up a damn phone in those early years, to resenting her immature and admittedly selfish decisions.

As he moved deeper into the night-shrouded

wilderness and further away from the oasis of reality, his rioting emotions triggered a duplicate reaction from his magic. He held the storm back through sheer force of will until he found a spot he considered safe.

Jerking to a halt, he stood, stiff and brittle, among the fallen tree trunks who surrendered to the relentless combination of time and age. They lay as if tossed by a giant hand, leaving the younger wooden giants standing guard over their fallen comrades. With the ease of familiarity, he raised a warded circle, ensuring what he freed within the magical boundaries, would stay safely separated from the rest of the world and undetectable by even someone of Tala's strength. Warding in place, he dropped all pretense at control.

Magic and emotion clashed in a near silent wave, creating a devastating force, one he directed toward the fallen sentries. Emotion-driven energy washed over the clearing. Thick, hoary skins tore under invisible claws as the energy stripped the wood from the thick logs. As each curling piece came free, it floated in the air, the wood taking on deeper tones while eerie flames in gold and browns licked over the edges with a voracious appetite. Other logs burst apart as if ripped from the inside out by silent explosions of gold-lined light and were reduced to deadly slivers held back by the magic standing guard.

In the midst of all the destruction, he stood, his hands weaving power that he sent out into the hapless deadfall, to scorch, to tear, to give silent voice to the overwhelming storm tearing him apart.

Here, within the warded circle, he didn't hold back, didn't have to, because his magic wouldn't seep past his protections and hurt those he held dear.

Eventually, the storm in him began to subside, and the

magic he wielded began to retreat, letting the real world come back in pieces. As the last of his magical temper tantrum subsided, he stood, hands fisted at his side, sweat layered along his spine, his chest heaving. He stood still, strangely empty.

Around him, there were no more logs littering the forest's floor. Instead, in some places, there was a thin carpet of ash, and, in others, a mat of stripped bark. Catching sight of marred trunks of the standing trees, he gathered his power once again, but this time he sent it out in a healing wave, soothing the wounds he unintentionally created. Once the wounded trees were tended to, he dropped his circle and the night's air swept through, taking with it the lingering traces of ozone left from over-used magic.

He stood there, letting nature sooth the ragged edges of his soul. It might not be the familiarity of the ocean from home, but even here in the high desert, Mother Nature didn't shy from offering what comfort she could.

He let the quiet and calm find its way into his hollowed out parts, and his muscles slowly unknotted. He lifted his head back and took in the stars shining high above. It would be so much easier to be up there than down here.

A vibration in his back pocket interrupted his musings. He heaved a sigh and retrieved his phone without looking at the screen. "What?"

"Are you quite through now?" an unexpected voice asked drily.

He grimaced and wrapped his free hand around the back of his neck. "Are you checking up on me Raine?"

"Would you prefer I contact you via our personal line?"

"Oh hell no," he barked, not when he was basically standing emotionally naked in the woods.

"Yeah, I didn't think so." She paused. "You okay?"

"No, but I will be." Because he had no other choice. "Chay called you." It wasn't a question.

"He gave us a head's up. Said he was down in Phoenix with a wizard, checking on a car wreck?"

"Yeah," he confirmed, then he gave a quick run down on the current situation.

She let out a low whistle. "Sounds like Leo's already got his nasty-ass claws into someone. Any idea who?"

"Not that I'm willing to share yet." Mainly because he didn't want to give her or Gavin an excuse to come running down here when they realized just how many suspects he had in mind.

"How's Tala dealing with having you back?"

He found a relatively flat stump to sit on and took a seat. "Are you fishing, Raine?"

There was a muffled curse, then a sigh before her reluctant, "Maybe."

His lips twitched, but she wasn't done surprising him.

"Look, Cheveyo, normally I'd stay the hell out of whatever it is you two have going, but our shared door is a little worse for wear and things leaked through—"

"Like?" he prompted when she paused. He didn't bother explaining that it wasn't the door, but the fact that each of their magic had changed, evolved into something unexpected and much stronger than when he first forged their psychic connection.

"Like the kind of pain you get when someone betrays you." Her answer was weirdly hesitant and unsure.

It was so out of character for Raine that he actually pulled the phone from his ear and frowned at the screen, wondering if this was some stress-induced hallucination.

He put it back to his ear and caught the rest of what she was saying.

"...or not, I promise whatever she did, it wasn't to hurt you. That woman loves you something scary." The last part came out in a less than gracious tone.

Faintly amused by the entire situation, he murmured, "I wasn't aware you and Tala had become best friends."

That earned him a snort. "Please. That's definitely one thing you don't ever have to worry about. That woman is beyond ruthless, trust me."

He shook his head and rubbed at the lingering ache in his chest. "And you're not?"

"I am, which is why I hope you're hearing me." The gravity in her voice gave him pause. "I've watched her with you, and I got a front row seat to how far she was willing to go to keep you safe. Tala would use anyone, do anything, to protect someone she considered hers. It may not be pretty, and it may be hard to accept, but whatever she did, she did it because she was trying to keep you safe."

And that fast his temper spiked, his hand tightened on the phone, and his voice deepened with anger. "Perhaps others should worry less about my protection and more about their own." He didn't wait for her response. "I know you and Gavin think you have me pegged, and I know why." He ignored her sharp intake of breath and kept going, "But you two need to remember, in the scheme of things, you're rookies. Powerful rookies, no doubt, but there is a difference between power and experience. It might serve you both to remember who came before you."

There was a heavy silence broken by a burst of static, a telltale clue that Raine's hold on her temper was slipping "Don't let age blind you with arrogance, Cheveyo," her voice carried a brittle edge. "Because more than one leader has made that mistake."

He gave her credit for not backing down. It was admirable—foolish, but admirable. "I've never been one of them." He let his statement hang between them for a moment like an unsheathed blade, before going back to her original concern. "Look, Raine, I appreciate you reaching out, and even coming to Tala's defense. However, I'm dealing with it." His voice lost the contrary edge and gentled, knowing it hadn't been easy for this very private woman to reach out the way she had. "As I told you before, some things are personal."

"Whatever," she snapped. "Just do me a favor and don't get your ass killed. Dealing with an irate Natasha is not on my to-do list." With that, she hung up.

"I'm trying," he muttered to himself as he pocketed his phone. Then he shifted to the psychic plane and reinforced the door, ensuring there would be no more leakage, as Raine put it.

He had no intention of playing his relationship with Tala out in front of an audience, nor was he inclined to reveal the existence of his lost daughter. Either one would present too tempting a target for those willing to exploit it. Not that Raine would betray him, at least not intentionally, but as he warned, she and Gavin were about to step into the ring with some frighteningly heavy hitters, and those were enemies you couldn't afford to underestimate.

With the door reinforced, he shifted back to the mortal world and began to work his way through the emotional quagmire.

If Tala had told him about Aponi years ago, what would he have done? He knew himself well enough to answer with brutal honesty. He would have demanded Tala come to

Oregon with him, to leave her new position. How fair would that have been? To either of them? Hell, he wasn't sure Tala would've come anyway. And if she had, how long would it have taken before resentment replaced love? She wasn't wrong when she said he had started pulling back. Torn between what his heart wanted and what Tala needed, he put emotional distance between them, justifying it with ruthless practicality. A purely self-defense move, but one he regretted.

Instead of driving himself nuts with the what-ifs, he accepted that perhaps Tala's decision was justified. And once he admitted that, he could put the rest of her actions in perspective and start to come to terms with what she shared.

Now, for a relationship to work for them, he needed to be able to accept exactly what Raine pointed out, Tala was a power to be reckoned with, and she wouldn't hesitate to do whatever she deemed necessary to protect the one she loved. Considering he'd be hard pressed not to do the same, if not worse, he couldn't blame her. Which left him with one last question—could he forgive her?

Yes. The answer came from his heart, echoing deep in his soul and settled into his bones.

Unfortunately, a haunting whisper that held Tala's familiar voice chased the echo, a reminder there was one question still left—

Would she be able to forgive herself?

CHAPTER 20

When Cheveyo got back to the cabin a few hours later, he opened the door to find the light of a table lamp keeping watch in the living room. Ash lifted his head from his bed and watched him come in and lock the door behind him. When he turned back, Ash had resettled.

Cheveyo left his shoes by the door and the light on, exhaustion weighing him down. He moved down the hall, his steps quiet. There was a night light in the hall, its soft glow revealing the invitation of Tala's partially opened door.

For a moment, he debated if he should stay in the room she gave him, but the lingering ache in his chest propelled him forward. What he needed lay in that room. Besides, he wasn't the only one hurting here. Tonight he needed to hold her in his arms, and maybe it would ease the ache for them both. He stood in her doorway, nudging her door wide enough to see her. She lay on her side, back to the door, knees bent, her unbraided hair glowing under the minimal light.

Instead of slipping inside, he turned and went to his

room where he gathered his sleeping pants and headed for the hall bathroom. It was another twenty or thirty minutes before he emerged from the steam-shrouded bathroom, hair damp, and padded back to Tala's room. He slipped inside, careful to close the door most of the way, leaving it open just enough so if Ash decided to relocate, Cheveyo wouldn't be forced to get up and let him in.

He lifted the quilt and sheet then slid in behind her, fitting his body to hers, his arm curling around her hips. His body began to relax as her warmth met his. He expected her to murmur and shift, regardless of how deeply she slept. When she didn't move, he frowned. Her unnatural stillness sent off a series of internal alarms. Disquieted, he called her name softly as he braced on one hand to lean over her, "Tala?"

When she didn't respond, he nudged her onto her back even as his sent his magic toward the side lamps in silent demand. The lights came on, chasing back the shadows, and fell over the woman lying so unnervingly still.

Shaken, he sat up and placed his hand on the center of her chest—the reassuring rise and fall was shallow, but there. A visual check assured him there were no obvious signs of violence, no cuts, bruises, or any other wounds. She appeared to be simply sleeping.

He cupped her face in his hands and leaned in close. "Tala, wake up."

Nothing. His alarm spread. Protected as they were by Tala's wards, they should be safe from harmful magics, but logic failed to reassure him. Sinking power into his voice, he called her again, this time invoking her full name with an inescapable combination of command and power, "Wake, Tala Isolde Whiteriver."

His magic-laced demand clawed for purchase but found

none and slid away, proof that someone managed to breach her protections. Narrowing his eyes, he lifted his head and with a soft utterance, sent his magic out to scour the room for spelled traps—something he should have done in the first damn place.

His detection spell swept through the bedroom and turned up nothing. Muttering a soft curse, he got off the bed and widened the search to include the closet and bathroom. Like running an invisible hand over every inch of the room, he searched every corner.

And, still, he almost missed it.

He took a step toward the bathroom before caution tugged him back. "Ash!"

In moments, Tala's wolf was nosing his way into the bedroom. "Guard her."

Despite his recent injuries, Ash didn't hesitate to leap onto the bed. He stretched along Tala's side, alert and watchful.

Knowing not much would get by the wolf, Cheveyo headed into the bathroom. He stood in the doorway and flicked on the light. Nothing appeared out of place, an easy tell as Tala carried a touch of the neat freak gene. Concentrating on the detection spell, he narrowed its focus in order to better pinpoint the unusual bump in the existing energy's weave. For those who worked with magic, the world was an ever-changing landscape of energies. Controlling and manipulating those energies were the basis for most Kyn abilities. Not all, but most.

Like a psychic game of hot and cold, he started at the door and worked his way in. He found what he wanted at the bottom edge of the mirror behind the sink. Like an annoying, barely there thistle, the spell was buried under the mirror's edge.

Another damn mirror spell. This one much more disturbing, considering where it was located and who had recent access to Tala's home. At least he knew who would be the first person he would be hunting down after he woke Tala up.

Unfortunately, he couldn't undo the spell or use a counter spell because the insidious nature of mirror magic was based in trapping its victims with their own heart's desires and minds. Breaking it in this realm was more likely to leave Tala forever held wherever she was, with no way back. Something he was certain the castor hoped for when putting this nasty piece of work in place. However, he could ensure no one else tripped it. Encasing the mirror in a holding spell didn't take long. Keying that protection to recognize himself and Chay took a bit longer. Call him cynical, but he didn't trust anyone else not to either destroy the evidence or the mirror itself in an attempt to get to him and Tala.

With the protective spell in place, he went back to the bedroom. "Ash, I need you to stand guard at the door."

The wolf got off the bed and took a guard position inside the door, his gaze watchful.

Satisfied he had done all he could to ensure the protection of their physical bodies, Cheveyo took his spot on the bed and pulled the non-responsive Tala into his arms. He turned his head to meet Ash's lupine gaze. "Don't let anyone but Chay in, understand?"

Taking Ash's soft chuff as an affirmative answer, Cheveyo called his magic and wove his strongest protection ward. The lethal safeguard snapped into place ensuring that while he dream walked to get Tala, should anyone get past Ash that would be as far as they got. They were as safe as he could make it.

He tightened his hold on Tala, closed his eyes, and shifted worlds.

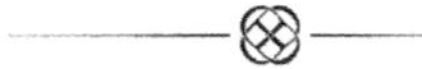

Feminine laughter, interspersed with childish giggles caught his ears first, and he opened his eyes to find he was standing next to a picnic table, the sun shining over a campsite. He laid his hand on the sun-warmed surface and looked around, recognizing by the surrounding forest that he was still in Flagstaff. There was a blue tent pitched off to the side, and two camping chairs were positioned around a fire pit while a cooler chest played side table. A fishing pole was propped against a nearby tree, and a netted bag hung from one sturdy branch.

"*Ape'*, you coming?" a young girl called.

He turned toward the young voice calling him father in the language of his birth, his heart beating hard in his chest. Sunlight danced in playful abandon over a nearby river, blinding him with a dizzying portrait of colors and shadows.

"We're waiting, Cheveyo." Tala's teasing addition left him bracing against the picnic table. The light show dispersed revealing a bittersweet vision patched together from a half-remembered dream.

Tala stood next to a girl about ten, her hand on the girl's shoulder, a fishing pole in the other. Standing next to each other there was no denying the family connection. Where Tala's hair was a lighter mix of browns and blondes with a few inky strands, the girl's hair was the opposite— midnight strands interwoven with gold and sables. The sight of them slammed into his heart, boring a deep, unfathomable hole in its wake.

"Aponi." Her name came out on a choked whisper before he could call it back.

Tala's smile dimmed, replaced by puzzled concern. "Cheveyo?" She stepped away from their daughter, breaking his frozen state.

He reached out for the lone pole by the tree, grateful his hand didn't tremble, and forced an answering smile. "I'm coming, *awéé*." Despite his shaky legs, he managed to walk over and join them. He turned to the little girl watching him. "So, *baide*, what are we planning on catching today?"

She giggled and grabbed his hand, the simple touch sending painful fissures through his heart, even as her joy cauterized the wounds. "Rainbows."

"Rainbows?" He fell into step as she tugged him toward the water.

Over her head, he caught Tala's soft smile as she looked on. The peace and joy in that single look seared right through him, leaving behind icy tendrils of dread. The spell had done its work well, maybe too well.

Aponi continued her chatter about the rainbow-hued trout and her certainty at catching one. He joined in Tala's teasing as he helped Aponi bait her hook and showed her the best way to cast a line, his mind churning over escape plans even as he relished this moment out of time. Hard as it was, he reminded himself that this wasn't real, that the bright, enthusiastic child at his side wasn't real. His soul clenched in denial, but no matter how tempting this was, he couldn't afford to forget that. Otherwise, he was signing his and Tala's death warrants.

Whoever cast the mirror spell knew enough about Tala to anchor the magic at a deeply personal level. It spoke not only to a devious mind, but one bent on causing as much hurt as possible. The one behind this was banking on trapping her spirit here with the false promises of what could've have been. On one hand, it confirmed who composed their suspect pool—Teagan, Hadley, or Danny—and he knew who was his top choice. On the other, the betrayal by any of those three would scar Tala.

To break through the spell's hold, he needed to get Tala to see beyond her guilt and the illusion's deceitful promise for what it was, a lost dream. Just blurting out the truth wouldn't work. In fact, it was more likely to trigger secondary spells, ones designed to ensure no one left this realm and returned to the waking world.

This reality was built around Tala's hidden desires, which meant, to be able to change things here, he needed to merge her dream world with his and make it a shared one. For that to happen, he would be forced to reveal dreams he kept buried. Fragile, half-composed desires for a family he could call his own, a life free from politics, intrigue, and lethal power games. Standing here surrounded by proof that Tala shared those same hopes and dreams, he prayed for strength. Strength to see the carefully constructed lies for the lethal lure it was, strength to find an escape before they were both lost in their shared dream.

Sitting on a riverbank with the warmth of his child sitting in front of him and the woman who held his heart laughing at his side, it was difficult to ignore the temptation to stay right here. He didn't want to lose this.

Aponi bounced in front of him, her pole dancing in the water. He reached around her to help her steady it and couldn't resist pressing a kiss to the back of her head, inhaling sunlight and joy, as he fought back his rising tide of anger and grief.

He captured the moment with crystalline clarity and tucked it away for later, knowing he would need its comfort, then resolutely turned his attention to the magic woven around them.

Being careful not to trip any traps, he began slipping pieces of his dreams into Tala's. It was slow, exacting work, but necessary to avoid detection. Weaving in his desires gave him a chance at controlling some aspects of the world around them. It might be a thin thread to anchor their escape on, but he'd take it.

He unlocked the newly imagined moments he could've shared with his daughter, layering more and more details, adding another dimension to the world Tala created. In the meantime, Aponi had caught two small trout to Tala's one and declared herself Queen of the Fish as she did a little dance along the riverbank.

"I concede victory, my queen." Tala solemnly took Aponi's pole and sketched a bow, complete with hand flourishes.

"It's okay, *Amá*, you can have some of my fish." Aponi's dark eyes danced, and, despite her attempt at a queenly air, her lips twitched. "They said it was okay."

Getting to his feet, Cheveyo brushed off his jeans. "Well, oh Queen of the Fish," he teased. "You can't leave your subjects without saying good-bye." With that, he swept the little girl up in his arms and strode to the river.

She squealed with laughter and threw her arms around his neck. "No, *ape'*! I don't want to go for a swim!"

He waded into the cold water, letting it lap around his ankles and soaking the cuffs of his jeans, pretending to let her go. The magic hidden within the quiet waters rippled around them, but sensing no true threat, simply kept a wary eye on them. It was enough to confirm where the secondary spells were anchored—in the surrounding elements.

"All right you two, enough," Tala called from behind them. "Let's go make some dinner before it gets dark."

Staying in the water, he turned, holding Aponi easily against his chest and noted the gathering clouds on the horizon. As the last of his magic slipped into place, the clouds darkened and a rumble of distant thunder crept forward, recognizing a change, but uncertain of what. He caught Tala's gaze and held it, his voice softening, "*Bił hinishnáanii*, I think it may be time to leave."

A flicker of unease crawled through her eyes. "Not yet, Cheveyo." It came out as a plea.

Reacting to her emotional upset, the water at his feet gained strength, the gentle nudges morphing into grasping tugs. He didn't waste time stepping out onto the bank.

He closed the distance between them, their daughter watching silently in his arms, her earlier laughter gone as she picked up on the undercurrents. "We're running out of time, *awéé*."

Tala shook her head, her gaze darting from him to the darkening sky behind them. "No, it'll pass." But doubt crept into her voice. Behind her, the sun inched back from the trees, and the shadows lengthened and darkened, reacting to her unconscious rejection.

He didn't dare continue arguing with her, instead he bumped her shoulder, indicating she should lead the way back to the camp. Unfortunately, since he could no longer see the campsite, he knew the dream world had shifted, and he wasn't the one behind the change. He stayed at her side, a silent Aponi held in his arms. The light was slipping away faster than Mother Nature ever intended and a chill rode the air, pebbling his skin and crawling down his spine. The first icy drop of rain struck his arm even as a low, mournful howl chased the rising wind.

"What's that?" Fear made Aponi's voice small.

Recognizing the song of the hunt, he picked up the pace, forcing Tala to do the same. "Wolves." A physical manifestation of the tripped secondary spells, designed to keep them here.

The hair-raising howls and answering yips competed with the approaching storm as they rushed down the path. He almost barreled into Tala when she stopped abruptly, blocking his way. He sidestepped, shifted Aponi in his arms, and regained his balance.

Next to him, Tala shot out her arm, barring his way with the fishing poles she still held, as she stared forward. "Don't." Her warning was a hiss of sound.

He followed the direction of her attention and found they were in a standoff with four bristling wolves, their heads down, haunches curled for a leap, forepaws dug deep into the dirt, canines glinting from snarling muzzles.

Yep, the dream didn't want them going anywhere.

"Dammit." He quickly set Aponi down, tucking her behind him. Her small hands clutched the back of his shirt as he grabbed the poles from Tala. "Get her out of here, Tala." She opened her mouth, her intent to argue clear, but he cut her off, "Take Aponi and leave. We aren't making it back this way."

"I'm not leaving you," she shot back as she began looking around even as she moved closer to him and their daughter. Apprehension warred with confusion. "Where's Ash?"

Her out-of-place question threw him and, intent on keeping his attention on the threat in front of them, he snapped, "Standing guard in the bedroom, making sure we get out of here alive."

"Bedroom?" Her question was soft, but he still caught it

before lightning ripped through the storm-ridden sky, leaving an eye-searing wave of white in its wake. As the light faded, the edges of the forest warped and twisted before recapturing their previous shape.

He wasn't the only one who caught the ripple. Tala's hand clutched his upper arm in a tight vise. Risking a glance down, his heart clenched at the mix of confusion and furious denial staring back as her acceptance of the dream began unraveling.

He was running out of time to reassure her. "Tala, take Aponi and get out of here. When I tell you, run."

Resolution stole over her face, and she nodded. She reached for their daughter, tugging her close as they inched backward, leaving her hand on his back as long as she could.

When her touch dropped away, Cheveyo shifted his stance, braced his legs and with a flex of magic the fishing poles flowed into a solid wooden staff. "Ready?"

"Cheveyo." His name came out choked in an emotional tangle. "Don't leave us."

He clenched his jaw, his hands tightening on the wood. "Don't worry, *awéé*, I have no plans to leave here without you. I promise." He kept his attention on the wolves slowing stalking forward. They might not be real in the true sense of the word, but any damage they inflicted could be, especially if the victim's belief in the world was strong enough. "Now, go!"

He didn't wait but lunged forward, catching the lead wolf in mid-leap, nailing its heavy shoulder with the staff. His hit sent the wolf tumbling off to the side, but the other three didn't wait around and charged.

With the ease of skill, he shifted his hold and swept his staff back, jamming the end into the throat of one wolf before quickly reversing and nailing the one coming in from the side. The fourth wolf darted in low and managed to rake his claws against Cheveyo's exposed calf. Pain burst in a bright bloom and, shifting his weight, Cheveyo half turned and punched down, his fist's impact with the wolf's skull reverberating up his arm in a numbing wave.

There was no way to take all four wolves, not to mention in this particular sphere, he might not be able to, but he needed to give Tala enough time to get Aponi out of reach. He continued his brutal dance with the now-more-cautious wolves. He scored a few more solid hits before knocking one of the wolves out, causing the others to back off for a moment.

Taking advantage of the unexpected breathing room, he called on his magic and threw up a curtain of flame. Snarling, the wolves retreated, amber eyes filled with lethal intent burning as bright as the flames keeping them from their intended prey.

Ignoring the complaints of his injured leg, Cheveyo ran back toward the river, praying Tala and Aponi would be there. Behind him, the wolves howled. When answering cries came back from in front of him, Cheveyo gritted his teeth and pushed harder.

The once relatively clear path was now a maze of ankle twisting stones and holes determined to slow him down. But he wasn't a stubborn bastard for nothing. He gathered his power and started manipulating the dreamscape, not an easy thing do to begin with, but especially difficult when you were running for your life and panic was a ruthless monkey on your back.

The howls drew closer, and the trail under his feet disappeared. Dark, ominous skies unleashed a torrential downpour, reducing visibility to inches and the wind scoured his skin. He pictured the river, Tala and Aponi, and forced the dreamscape to shift. Another eye-searing streak of light danced crossed the sky, but this time he caught the outlines of Tala and Aponi just ahead.

The afterimages played hell with his vision, and he almost missed the deep fissure bisecting his path. Using the staff, he jammed it into the earth and, with a harsh yell, leapt, arching his body.

He hit the ground hard, and his injured leg buckled, sending him tumbling forward, his shoulder taking most of the impact as he rolled. When he stopped, he was on his back, rain falling into his face, his shoulder and back bruised as he sucked in air.

Hands wrapped around his wrists and tugged. "Come on, get up!"

He blinked his eyes open to find Tala, trying to get him to his feet. Together they managed to get him upright, and she kept an arm around his waist as she led them to where Aponi huddled against a large boulder. Behind her, the river's proportions had exploded.

No longer dancing over stones, water tore over the riverbed with barely leashed violence, and the once sloping shores were now sharply defined drop offs. When they reached the stone, Aponi latched on to his waist.

He rubbed a comforting hand along her slender back as shudders wracked her body. Tala came up behind her, keeping the child between the two of them, the move more instinctive than practical since they couldn't offer much in way of protection from the elements as both adults resembled drowned rats.

"We can't get across, and we can't go back." She had to shout to be heard over the deafening combination of the rising storm and raging river.

As another shiver wracked her body, he wrapped his arm around her and pulled her close, keeping Aponi tucked between them. Her hands came between them, her fingers knotting in his shirt as she got as close as possible. Their position meant he didn't have to shout to be heard. "We can't stay here either." Because, despite the growing strength of the storm, he could still make out he wolves' song, and it was getting closer.

He twisted to look at the river behind them, and, when his gaze came back to her, she read his intent and shook her head. "Too dangerous."

Hardening his heart, he held her gaze. "Not if you help me create a bridge."

She pulled back in his hold. "Out of what?"

"This isn't real, Tala." His statement, soft though it was, struck with undeniable force. They were out of options. Before she could recover, he kept pushing. "It's your dream, so help me create an escape route."

She shook her head even as a soft whimper drifted from between them.

It tore at him not to acknowledge the scared child between them, but he couldn't afford to back down. Not now. His damaged leg twinged with breath-stealing pain, and he recognized the warning for what it was—Ash, trying to bring them back. "It's a mirror spell, like what was used on Rory. If we don't break it soon, we won't be able too."

His certainty clashed with hers, and he saw the rips of doubt deepen. She dropped her anguished gaze to Aponi then let go of him and gathered the little girl close. "We have to protect her."

He covered her hands on the slim shoulders of the dream he wished truly breathed. "You did, Tala."

Tala stepped back, taking Aponi with her, and shook her head violently. "No, I didn't, but I can now." Her gaze shifted then widened. She stumbled back, dragging Aponi along.

A snarl spun him around as a wolf leapt from the top of the boulder. He barely got his hands up before the wolf's weight knocked him back and to the ground. Using the momentum of the hit, he ignored the hot, fetid breath and glistening canines and managed to throw the wolf up and off. Twisting, he scrambled to his feet and sent a powerful wave of magic crashing into the wolf. The impact flung the wolf into a nearby tree, and he hit with an audible snap.

Tala's short scream spun him around.

He lunged, hands reaching to stop the inevitable, as she and Aponi slipped over the side and disappeared.

CHAPTER 21

WATER CLOSED OVER TALA'S HEAD, EVEN AS SHE KEPT HER ARMS locked around her daughter. Her heart raced, and her legs flailed as she fought the raging waters determined to drag them under. She kicked hard, propelling them upward, never losing her hold on Aponi.

Her head broke the surface, and she blinked the water from her eyes, searching for something to use as an anchor even as she shifted Aponi up, keeping her head above the tumbling water. She took comfort in the girl's harsh coughs. It was difficult to fight the drag of the river, but Tala refused to let it have her child.

Something slammed into her back. Fighting the current, she turned to find a thick log churning along. She looped her free arm over it. Muscles straining, she managed to drag Aponi over. "Grab on, baby."

The young girl struggled to follow directions, and it wasn't until the log jammed against an outcropping of rocks jutting from the rushing water, that she was able to get her upper body on the log and out of the unforgiving grip of the water. She continued to cough, clearing the water from her chest.

Tala tried to stay between her and the worse of the river's temper. Her feet scrambled for purchase but the water was too strong, the current too fast, and she didn't dare let go to test the depth. More debris pummeled her back with bruising force, and she gritted her teeth even as it forced her body against Aponi's smaller frame. As soon as Tala could breathe without hurting, she shifted carefully to the side so she wasn't crushing the girl.

"*Amá*, I'm scared." Face bleached white by their near drowning, Aponi gamely held on to the log, even as the river and rain kept up their relentless assault.

"It's okay, *yázhí*." The fear in her girl's voice hurt, but it also pissed her the hell off. Her baby shouldn't know such fear. "Your *ape'* is coming. We just have to get to the shore. You think we can do that?"

Without letting go, Aponi turned and eyed the steep shore just out of reach. "Sure." Her answer came out shaky.

Tala couldn't blame her, what should be a simple stretch of water easily waded through was now a churning divide between them and the relative safety of the shore. A particularly vicious wave washed over them, leaving them coughing out more water in its wake. Under her arms, the log shifted, and she lost her hold.

As Tala went under, the roar of water drowned out Aponi's shrill scream. Tala's lungs ached and burned, but she fought the current, her fingers reaching blindly. Rough bark met her touch, and she clawed her way back out of the river's reach. Her head broke the surface, and she sucked in air, the resulting coughs tearing through her already abused throat.

"*Amá!*" The little girl's cries anchored Tala.

"I'm okay, baby." Her voice came out in a hoarse croak. Muscles in her arms screamed as she dragged her battered body closer. "Shh, it's okay. I'm here." She blinked the water from her eyes and realized she was now between Aponi and the shore. An ominous creak from the log warned they were running out of time. Turning back to the hiccuping little girl, Tala forced a smile. "Aponi, baby, look at me." When her daughter's dark eyes met hers, Tala forced every ounce of belief she could into her voice. "I want you to get on my back, and I'm going to swim us across."

Aponi bit her lower lip, worry lining her face. "Like Scorpion and the Fox?"

Tala choked on an unexpected laugh. "Kind of, but let's not sting *Amá* when we're half way across, okay?"

Aponi managed a weak smile. "I wouldn't hurt you, *Amá*."

Seeing her daughter's faith lodged a heavy knot in her throat, but she managed to squeeze out, "I wouldn't hurt you either, *yázhí*. I'm going to keep you safe, promise."

'Don't make promises you can't keep.' The insidious whisper crawled through her, gathering doubts in its wake and scarring gouges on her heart. She tried to ignore it as she kept one arm on the log and used the other to help Aponi settle against her back. Once Aponi looped her thin arms around Tala's neck, Tala reached up and gave her daughter's hands a squeeze. "Hang tight, baby."

"Okay, *Amá*."

Tala turned toward the shore and dragged air deep into her lungs, steeling herself for the fight ahead. Fear for her daughter dug into her strained muscles with icy intent. In front of them, the water boiled, wood and leaves caught in the determined currents, the distance to shore daunting. Staying here was out of the question.

Gathering her courage, she blocked out the fear and focused on the shore. She let go of the log. The current rushed over her, threatening to tear the child from her back, but her daughter wrapped her legs around Tala's waist, clinging tight. Her choppy breaths were audible, even above the rush and noise of the river.

Kicking hard, Tala fought for every inch. They were about half way to the shore, when the sharp crack behind them made Aponi cry out. Tala didn't bother looking back, knowing their last bastion of safety was now gone, the log lost in the raging torrent. All they could do was move forward. Her arms and legs were leaden, but she refused to stop kicking, stop reaching for a shore that seemed even further out of reach.

'*We're running out of time.*' Cheveyo's warning slipped around her, and the doubts she managed to push back rushed forward. The odd behavior of the wolves, the shifting landscape, the treacherous river, and the painful truth circling the edges of it all, even the feel of her daughter's weight against her back.

A wave washed over her, shoving her down while the pressure of Aponi's legs at her waist disappeared and her arms loosened. Instinctively, Tala clutched at Aponi's arms, refusing to let her go, and scrambled back to the surface. Her head broke the surface. Next to her ear and against her spine, she could feel and hear her daughter coughing. "Hold on, baby," she choked out.

"Don't let me go, *Amá*."

The frightened girlish whisper sent cracks spiraling through Tala's heart and brushed up against old wounds. Her doubts settled into the tiny fissures and took root, but she couldn't stop her vow, "I won't, Aponi."

A shout from shore caught her attention. She looked

over to see Cheveyo jumping into the raging current. He fought his way to them, his face lined with grim determination.

Digging deep, Tala forced her legs to move, kicking toward him. She couldn't stop the harsh sob as she reached for him, her shoulders burning. Their hands met, and then he was dragging her closer, his muscles straining as his grip shifted to her wrist.

Pain slammed into her side, stealing her breath and wrenching her out of Cheveyo's grip. Aponi's startled scream was cut short, and her grip on Tala's neck disappeared.

Fear roared through her.

Ignoring the agony searing her side, Tala spun as best she could in the twisting current, her gaze frantic. "Aponi!" The little girl was desperately trying to stay above the water, and Tala didn't hesitate to lunge for her, catching her wrist. "Come on, baby, reach for me!"

The river was relentless, tearing at both of them. Tala barely registered when a strong arm wrapped around her waist, her focus on the girl struggling against the unforgiving water. With Cheveyo holding her, she used both hands to hold on to Aponi's arm, trying to reel her closer. Another wave crashed into them, this time driving Aponi under and ripping her from Tala's grip.

"No!" Tala clawed at Cheveyo's arm, deaf to his shouts. Freed from his hold, she dove into the river. She kept her eyes open, searching the murky waters. Her lungs burned, and blackness threatened, but she stayed under.

A darker shadow drifted ahead, and she grabbed it, bringing it closer until she could see Aponi's pale face, eyes closed. Despite the girl's dead weight, Tala aimed for the surface and swam. Light danced in front of her eyes. Just when she thought the darkness would claim them both, she was thrown up, and her head broke through. She sucked in air, choking even as she turned to her back and pulled Aponi's head out of the water.

Suddenly Cheveyo was there, pulling them both toward the shore. She did what she could to help, but it wasn't much as she was more concerned with keeping their daughter's face out of the water. She tried not to notice the blue tinge around Aponi's lips, but the cracks in her heart widened to terrifying depths.

Her feet touched ground for the first in time in what felt like hours, but her legs were slow to respond. Only Cheveyo's arm around her waist kept her upright.

They stumbled onto shore, and Tala dropped to her knees, her daughter cradled in her arms. She laid her down, then tilted Aponi's head back to confirm her airway was clear, terror crawling through her bones. Tala began chest compressions, keeping count to stave off the fear. She couldn't lose her daughter again. She'd never survive it.

Cheveyo knelt on Aponi's other side, and when Tala's arms began to visibly shake, he locked his hands on her wrists.

Her gaze shot to his. "What are you doing? Let me go, Cheveyo."

"No."

Stunned, she reacted, striking out with her magic, but he deflected it, his jaw tightening. "Let me go, you bastard. This is our daughter."

"Dammit, Tala, listen to me." His voice was harsh, cutting. "This is not real." His grip on her wrists tightened until it threatened to bruise bone. "Aponi is not real. This is a spell designed to trap us here."

His damning words joined the whispers in her head,

circling tighter and tighter, adding sharp edges to her doubt. "No. I can save her."

The pain in his eyes killed her, but he didn't back down. "This is not our daughter, *awéé*."

"It is." Her denial fractured under his ruthless certainty.

"In another life maybe," his voice gentled, softened. "But not this one."

The truth of his words reverberated like a bell as the last of her dream fell apart, shattered under the weight of reality and she knew. She looked down at the little girl under their joined hands, her hot tears hidden among the rain.

She tugged against Cheveyo's hold until he let go. Then she cupped Aponi's face and pressed her forehead to her child's, closing her eyes against the agony tearing through her. "I'm so sorry, *yázhí*." Grief, as fresh as the first time she lost their child, crawled through her. The warm weight of Cheveyo's hand brushed over her spine. She opened her eyes, pressed a kiss against Aponi's forehead, and whispered, "*Ayóo-anííníshní*, Aponi. I'll always love you."

"*Pinnanku tease em puinnuhi, baide'.*" Cheveyo said. "Until next time, my daughter."

Even as anger and grief rose, Tala couldn't fail to miss the deep pain in Cheveyo's husky voice. Still, she couldn't look at him. Not yet. While her mind could grasp their situation—a trap devised of a spell fueled by her deepest desire—her heart couldn't find the same cold comfort. Even after an icy wind swept between them, taking the image of Aponi with it, old resentments rose. In her lap, her hands curled into fists.

"Tala."

She ignored him, trying to get her ravaged emotions in check.

Of course, Cheveyo wasn't one to be ignored. He moved until he was in front of her and lifted her chin, forcing her to look at him. "Tala." His gaze searched her face, and the skin around his eyes tightened. She caught his flash of hurt before he tucked it away. He let her chin go and turned away with a small shake of his head. "We have to leave."

She knew that wasn't what he had planned to say and knew why he switched his words. She sat there, her voice flat. "Give me a minute, Cheveyo."

His shoulders straightened, but he gave her a stiff nod and walked a bit away.

She fought her way through her tempestuous emotions, her gaze focused not on the still raging river but inside her battered soul. She worked her way through the facts Cheveyo had given her.

A mirror spell, one anchored with the ghost of her unborn daughter and fueled by her inability to save her spoke to someone who knew her. Maybe even more than the man who haunted her heart. The list was extremely short.

She pushed to her feet, her body stiff. Absently, she wondered if she could walk without shattering. The first step was difficult, but with each one that followed she came back to herself and the woman she created. Coming up behind Cheveyo, she brushed her fingers along his back, a silent apology. "Where was it set?"

He turned his head, giving her his profile. "The spell?"

She nodded.

"In your bathroom mirror."

She absorbed the hit with blink, the betrayal another lash among many. A chorus of howls rent the air, even as lightning struck a nearby tree with a deafening crack. Her hand fisted in his wet T-shirt. "Teagan?"

His jaw flexed, and he turned away. "Maybe."

There was something in his voice that had her moving around until she stood in front of him. "Maybe?" Her question came out sharp. "She's the only one, besides you, who was in my house and behind my wards today." Wet strands of hair whipped over her face, leaving small stings behind.

"That we know of," he shot back, his face matching the ruthless bite of his words. "But unless we get the hell out of here, we'll never find out for sure."

"Fine, then let's go." Another howl, this time so close she spun around and backed into Cheveyo. "Well, damn," she muttered. "Now what?"

His hands clasped her shoulders and shifted her to the side as they faced down the amber-eyed menaces between them and their intended path out of this nightmare. The four snarling wolves began a slow stalk forward, forcing Tala and Cheveyo to mimic them in retreat.

"Go back to the river and build the damn bridge, Tala. I'll hold them as long as I can."

Lightning struck another nearby tree, causing them both to flinch. Her nose wrinkled at the overwhelming stench of ozone, but her feet remained frozen. "I'm not leaving you here."

An unexpected fierce grin answered her. "I wasn't planning on staying."

Swallowing hard, she gave him a nod and rushed to the river, leaving him to hold back the wolves. It wasn't easy crafting the bridge, especially with the snarls, yips, and pained grunts coming from behind her, but if she didn't get her shit together, they'd both die here. The bridge wavered into place as her magic forced the dream world to its will. The wooden arc reached across the river and disappeared into the fog-enshrouded bank on the other side.

"Cheveyo!" She didn't dare take her attention away from the bridge.

"Go!" His harsh command seemed close so she clambered over the boulder-strewn shore and onto the bridge.

The river raged higher, waves sweeping over the structure. Creating their escape route triggered the mirror spell's secondary defenses. She clutched the railing and used it to pull herself along. She risked a glance back to see Cheveyo fling one wolf into the raging waters before scrambling over the boulders and lunging for the bridge. As soon as his hand touched the railing, her magic flared, looping around him like a safety line.

Just in time, too. A wailing gust of wind slammed over the bridge and knocked Tala's feet out from under her. Only her grip on the rail kept her in place.

Cheveyo fought his way to her, his lips pulled back in a ferocious snarl. As soon as he got close, he caught her gaze and yelled, "Go, Tala!"

Behind him, the wolves regrouped and rushed the bridge. Tala reacted. Her magic began unraveling the wooden planks, leaving her and Cheveyo no choice but to run forward. Together they fought their way over, battling brutal winds, blinding waves, and rain.

She almost sobbed when she made out the faint golden light just within the fog bank. The storm around them grew to demonic proportions, lightning striking so close it raised the hair on her arms and left an ache in her teeth. When the end of the bridge appeared, she threw her body forward.

Lightning struck the bridge where she had been, and she covered her head with her arms as she rolled away.

When she came up to her knees, she saw Cheveyo struggling the last few feet. She scrambled forward only to be forced back by another vicious lightning strike.

"Open the damn door, Tala!" Cheveyo's shout barely rose above the storm's rage.

She looked behind her, and, sure enough, a door hung there. She pushed to her feet and stumbled forward, reaching for the ornate handle. She pushed, but it didn't budge. Desperate now, she slammed her shoulder against the unforgiving surface. The door inched open. She did it again and again, ignoring the numbing pain from each impact, until the door was wide enough for her to slip through.

She turned back to see Cheveyo a few feet from shore. She set her back against the door, dug her heels in, and reached out to him. "Cheveyo!"

He lifted his head—his hair plastered against his skull, his face thinned down to brutal determination—and reached out. Their fingers brushed. A harsh frustrated sob escaped, but she shifted her position, bracing a hand and a foot against the door so it wouldn't close and stretched as far as she could with her other.

Their hands touched just as a wolf leapt out of the gathering darkness behind him. Her heart clenched, and she screamed, "Cheveyo!"

CHAPTER 22

Cheveyo jerked upright with a gasp, only to choke as he inhaled smoke. Harsh coughs doubled him over even as pain streaked along his back and leg in phantom waves. Trying to get his brain on track, he looked up to see Ash standing on the mattress at the foot of Tala's bed.

Tala's pet lifted his paw from Cheveyo's shredded pant leg and woofed in question.

"Yeah, I'm awake."

"Good."

He barely registered Tala's hoarse voice before she grabbed him and yanked him over the side and down in to the narrow space between the bed and wall. He grunted at the impact and barely managed to escape smashing his face against the unforgiving floor. Pushing up into an awkward plank position, he turned his head and found Tala on her stomach beside him.

A rush of displaced air preceded Ash's appearance on his other side as the wolf leapt from the bed to the floor.

Cheveyo turned to his side, trying to make more room. "What the hell?"

Tala's face was pale but resolute, and she pointed to the window above them. "Fire."

Sure enough, now that he was paying attention he could see the dancing shadows on the wall and the hazy pall of smoke in the air. "The cabin?"

She shook her head. "The forest." Her voice was hoarse. She winced and rubbed her throat, then added, "Someone decided if they couldn't breach my wards, they'd burn through them."

"Son of a bitch," he hissed, rapidly assessing various plans. "Are they still here?"

Her eyes went opaque as she reached out to check her wards. "Not nearby."

"Good."

She gave him a sharp look. "Excuse me?"

"If they aren't watching, that gives us a chance to get outside undetected." And once outside, he might be able to hunt down whoever was determined to take out Tala. First things first, they needed to get out of the cabin rapidly filling with smoke. "Head to the sliding glass door."

Tala pushed up into a crouch, reached over the bed, and dragged down a pillow.

"We don't have—"

His mouth snapped shut when she lifted her head and pinned him with a hard stare. She yanked the pillow free from the pillowcase. A flare of magic preceded the sound of the cotton ripping in two. She handed him one piece and then tied the other over her face. "Now, we go." He didn't miss the bite in her voice even though it was muffled.

She reached out and tapped Ash's shoulder. In seconds the wolf was slinking toward the bedroom door, Tala crab walking behind him, her hand on his tail. Cheveyo stayed right behind them.

In the short time they were on the floor, the smoky haze grew thicker, and, even with the makeshift mask, he could still taste the ash on his tongue. They crept through the house, the flames outside shifting the homey interior into a nightmare of distorted shadows. Unwilling to chance a surprise attack, Cheveyo sent his magic out in search of hidden threats but came back with nothing.

They made it to the kitchen, and Tala reached up for the sliding glass door. He caught her hand before it could touch the metal and shook his head. He grabbed a hand towel hanging from the stove, wrapped it around his hand, then pulled the door open. Fresh air rushed in, displacing the choking haze.

Cheveyo tugged the back of Tala's shirt, and she looked back. "Concealment." He kept his voice low, but didn't wait for her nod before setting the spell that would weave a curtain of shadows to mask them from anyone watching. Once it was in place, he said, "Go."

Ash went first, then Tala. Cheveyo followed them out. They stuck close to the cabin as they went down the deck's steps. Hidden in the shadow spell, they made their way down the side of the cabin. At the corner, they stopped. When Tala turned and leaned toward him, Cheveyo met her half way.

"If we merge our magic, we can cast a wider circle." She inched back to study his face and offered her hand.

He didn't hesitate but wrapped her hand in his. After ensuring the concealment spell was solidly in place, he dropped the ironclad protections keeping others from touching his magic and let Tala in. Her magic slid along his, latching into place with a disconcerting ease, even as the power between them grew. He let her take the lead, adding his strength to hers as she cast the magical net in ever widening circles.

The flames brushed against their combined power. While it was started by magical means, it had taken on a more natural life, finding fuel in the surrounding woods. He picked up Tala's relief at the cabin's isolation and echoed it. No nearby neighbors meant they might be able to stop this with minimal damage. When the detection spell reached a mile beyond her wards, she reeled it back in. They were as alone as they could be. Whoever set this in motion was long gone.

Shoving his frustration aside, he shifted his magic to align with hers as she began crafting a spell to utilize the surrounding elements. Together they built the hint of an approaching storm into a reality, manipulating the moisture gathered above. Rain began to fall in a soft mist, slowly gaining strength as they continued to shape the storm's energy, building it higher and higher until a deluge poured from the skies.

Keeping the storm focused was draining work, but he kept funneling his power into Tala so she could direct the rain. Long minutes passed as they fought the fire, but bit-by-bit the rain snuffed out the flames. Eventually, they managed to drown the last ember leaving a heavy silence in its wake.

He did one last sweep, ensuring no threat lingered, then he helped Tala re-strengthen her wards. By the time they finished, only the cabin's wall at his back held him up. Tala slumped against his chest, her breathing ragged as if she just finished a marathon.

Their magic slowly untangled, and he found he was strangely reluctant to let her go. It took an effort of will not to fight her retreat, but he couldn't resist pulling her closer.

Her arms tightened around his waist, and she stopped pulling away. Grateful, he pressed his lips to the top of her head, stealing a moment to relish having her in his arms.

As the storm receded, soft breezes replaced the rain, and the acrid bite of smoke drifted away. Against his chest, Tala sucked in a shuddering breath and his skin pebbled. "We need to go inside."

"In a minute," he murmured. "Not sure I can stand just yet. It's been a long night."

That earned a weak laugh from Tala, but it shifted into sobs as the night's events finally hit her. His heart ached, and he didn't bother denying the tears seeping down his face as heart-wrenching sobs were torn from the woman in his arms. She needed this. Hell, they both did. Real or not, losing Aponi left him hollowed and hurting. He could only imagine what Tala was dealing with. Well, besides her obvious anger at him for forcing her to leave their daughter.

He rested his head against the cabin's side and continued to hold her. When her shudders and soft hiccupping sobs stopped, he let the night's hush settle over them. After long minutes he finally asked the question battering his soul, "Are you ever going to forgive me?"

She stilled, then shifted in his arms, pulling back so she could see his face. Even wrecked by soot and tears, she still made him catch his breath. Her dark eyes studied him and, although his heart stalled, he appreciated that she didn't rush to answer him. He had no idea what she was looking for, but would've willing given it had she asked.

A complex combination of remorse and discomfort flitted over her face. "Shouldn't that be my question?"

Unable to resist, he brushed a touch along her cheek. "I won't lie. It hurts you never said a word." She flinched, her eyes dropping away. He nudged her chin up until her gaze came back to his. "But, right or wrong, the decision was yours to make. Given our situation then, I can't blame you for making it either." He searched her face, hoping his words were getting through. "So, I'm going to ask again, do you forgive me?"

She caught his hand and drew it to her heart. "Here, yes." Then she tapped her head. "Here, I'm working on it."

He blew out a soft breath. "That's a start." That earned him a questioning look, and deciding now was as good as a time as any, he decided to push his luck. "Maybe you can add forgiving yourself to your to-do list."

She jerked, but anticipating her reaction he kept his arm locked around her waist so she couldn't jump up and leave. Finding her escape attempt thwarted, she narrowed her eyes and frowned, her jaw set with mulish intent. "You don't understand—"

"You're right," he cut her off. "I don't, but it won't stop me from getting you to admit that our daughter's death was not your fault, Tala."

She sat in his lap, facing him, body rigid, whether with fury or disapproval, he didn't know, and wasn't sure he gave a damn right now.

"I promised you I'd never lie, and I won't, not even to spare you further pain, so listen close." After what went down in the dreamscape, he was more determined than ever she let her unfounded guilt go before he lost her. "You didn't kill her. Your decisions didn't cause her death. You are not being punished for whatever imagined sins you think you carry. There is nothing I can give you to explain why she died, why it had to be our daughter, but she's gone. You named her Aponi in honor of the butterfly, so open your hands and let her fly. Cherish her memory and let her laugh among the stars, but don't trap her here."

He could feel Tala's tremors, and his chest loosened when she clutched at his wrist, holding his hand in her lap. He watched her fight through her emotions, her throat moving as she swallowed, and then she blinked to keep the pooling tears at bay.

He cupped her face, his voice softening as he added, "Let her go, *awéé*, and honor her with your strength."

Tala let out a shuddering breath and slowly leaned forward until her forehead pressed against the center of his bare chest. Warm puffs of air fell against his skin and a long minute passed before she choked out, "I'll try."

Relief left him tightening his hold, but it was short lived. Ash, who had been sitting in front of them, suddenly rose to all fours. His focus aimed at the lingering haze drifting along the dark edge of the woods. His low growl rumbled ominously as he lowered his head, the fur along his spine rising in warning.

The soft woman in his arms disappeared, replaced by the warrior as she rolled out of his arms and to his side, coming up in a crouch. They rose to stand side by side, their magic moving in tandem toward the unseen threat. Recognition flowed back as their power lit up the night and revealed the two wolves standing just outside Tala's wards. The larger of the two sat first, before the second followed his example.

"Toby." There was no trace of Tala's previous emotional upheaval, just a cool greeting from one leader to another. "Kind of late for a visit, isn't it?"

The larger wolf canted its head, tongue lolling to the side as his lips pulled back in a canine grin.

Tala considered the alpha, and only Cheveyo heard her sigh as she stepped forward, moving away from him and out into the yard. Ash fell in at her side while Cheveyo held his position and played silent sentinel. When Tala stopped and opened her wards to let Toby in, Cheveyo's magic slipped into position.

Proving shifters were every bit as sensitive to magic as the Magi, the alpha turned his stare to Cheveyo who simply raised his eyebrow in challenge. After everything that went down tonight, his trust of late night visitors was at an all time low.

Toby sneezed then rose and stepped over the ward. He and his companion stopped a few feet from Tala and Ash and waited.

Cheveyo wasn't surprised when Tala asked, "Cheveyo, could you grab a couple pairs of sweats for our guests?"

He shot the two wolves a pointed look and reconfigured his magic to narrow its focus to the shifters.

Toby's lips pulled back in a silent snarl.

"Consider it a precaution, Alpha," Cheveyo advised with lethal intent. "We've had a damn long night, and I'm not feeling all that social right now."

Toby gave a full body shake and resettled on his haunches.

Taking the move for consent, Cheveyo made quick work of unearthing a couple pairs of sweats for the two shifters. He stopped just behind Tala, who turned to face him in an attempt to give the two shifters a modicum of privacy for their shift. He waited until the two wolves were replaced with naked men, before tossing over the sweats. "We'll meet you inside." Then he turned and followed Tala back to the cabin.

He nabbed a couple of towels from the bathroom before rejoining her in the kitchen. They didn't say anything as they tried to mop up the results of the night's storm. He left his towel hooked over his neck, and Tala managed to blot most of the rain from her face. Thankfully her clothes were light enough they were already drying out. They left the sliding door open for the shifters and to air out the cabin.

By the time Toby and Will padded in barefoot, she was pulling down glasses from the cabinet. "I've got tea or water, or I can start a pot of coffee."

The two wolves took their seats at the dining room table. "Water's fine," Toby assured her. "Last thing I need is coffee."

"Same, please," muttered an exhausted looking Will.

Cheveyo leaned against the sink's edge, facing the dining room, content to play observer.

Tala set a water-filled glass in front of each wolf then shot him a chiding look. Heeding her silent reprimand, Cheveyo stifled his beleaguered sigh and joined them at the table.

"What happened?" Tala was the first to break the faintly tense silence.

"Shouldn't that be my question?" Toby leaned back in his chair.

Tala didn't pick up his volley, simply stared at him and waited.

Toby ran a hand through his hair, then dropped it to scratch at his bare chest. "We were out running, saw the smoke—"

"And where there's smoke, there's fire," Will finished in a laconic drawl.

Toby shot him a look, before continuing, "We figured we'd better swing by, just in case."

Tala shook her head and drew absent patterns on the table. "I appreciate your concern, but we're fine."

Toby eyed her. "Uh huh, which explains why you look

like someone dragged you through hell backward." He turned to include Cheveyo. "Both of you."

"It's been a long night," Cheveyo said.

"Very long," added Tala, earning a sharp look from Toby.

"Funny, that seems to be a reoccurring theme up here."

Will's sarcastic observation brought Tala's head up, and her eyes narrowed. "You two weren't just out for a run, were you?"

Unsurprised by Toby's headshake, Cheveyo prompted, "Care to explain?"

The two wolves exchanged a look, then Toby answered, "After this morning's Triune meeting, we decided it might be best to keep an eye on things."

Had the Triune only been this morning? Damn. Rubbing a hand over his face, Cheveyo braced for more troublesome news.

Tala's head snapped up, color riding high on her cheeks. "You've been spying on us?"

Cheveyo gave Toby credit, the alpha barely blinked at her lash of temper. Nor did he disappoint as he confirmed, "You can consider it spying, we consider it being prudent."

"And it wasn't just you," Will offered unhelpfully.

The knot in Cheveyo's gut tightened. At the Triune, the wolves indicated they had suspicions of who could be working against Tala, and Cheveyo had a sinking feeling that things were about to take a very nasty turn. "Who else?"

Toby didn't fail to deliver. "Teagan and Hadley."

CHAPTER 23

Torn between fury and hurt disbelief, Tala sat there for a moment, absorbing Toby's words. Since fury offered surer footing, she went with it, not bothering to hide the edge of power slipping into her voice. "What gives you the right to spy on me or my people, Alpha?"

Toby straightened in his chair and leaned forward, forearms braced on the table, and his face wiped clean of his earlier amicable demeanor, in its place was unyielding surety. "The safety of my wolves will always trump diplomacy, Magi Whiteriver."

An alpha in her own right, and undaunted by his banked anger, she held his furious gaze. "I am no threat to you or your wolves."

His smile was tight. "Perhaps, but the same can't be said of your people."

Calling on every ounce of control, she pulled together her battered patience and gritted out, "Why those two?"

Will cleared his throat, and when both Toby and Tala turned to him, his face tightened, but his voice was rock steady, "Both of their names came up when we went digging through the rumors we mentioned at the meeting."

Unable to stay seated, Tala pushed up from the table and stalked to the glass patio doors. The night wind drifted through, laced with smoke. Her reflection stared grimly back, and, in the dark surface, she could make out the three imposing, bare chested men at the table as they watched. Any other time she might actually appreciate the scenery, but right now, not so much.

If they were waiting for her to break, they could wait until hell froze over. Thanks to the thrice-cursed spell that tore open her soul, the possibility of betrayal by her cousin and friend barely made a ripple. "And since both are part of the Triune, you didn't mention their names at the meeting."

"Discretion and valor and all that," Toby said. "After this morning's meeting, I wanted to make sure we didn't have to deal with any more possible 'misunderstandings.'"

She couldn't fault his logic. Realistically, if their positions were reversed, she would've done the same. And it was something she should've realized earlier, except between the Triune, rushing to Rory's side, and that damn spell, her capacity for crisis management had long passed critical mass.

"How long have your wolves been on watch?" The intensity behind Cheveyo's question had her turning.

Toby looked at Will, who answered, "Since we left the meeting." He looked at Tala. "After spending a couple hours in her realtor office, Teagan came here. She didn't leave until you two returned."

Tala shared a look with Cheveyo before asking, "Did she have any visitors?"

Will nodded. "Danny stopped by, stayed for about an

hour. Hadley dropped in for about twenty minutes during the afternoon." He grimaced and grudgingly added, "Can't tell you more than that."

Because her wards were too strong to get through. She allowed a tight smile.

Unfortunately, Will's recitation didn't do a thing for thinning her and Cheveyo's suspect pool.

"And Hadley?" Cheveyo inquired.

Will sat back and folded his arms over his chest. "After visiting Teagan, she spent the rest of her day at her office then headed home."

Catching the drift of where Cheveyo was headed, Tala turned to Toby. "How long did your wolves watch my house?"

Toby shared a look with Will then answered, "Only until you returned."

"And yet, you just happened to be running by at..." She looked at the clock on the wall. "...two-thirty in the morning?"

Toby's lips curled with a wry twist. "Actually, yeah, since it seems to be the only time I get a little me time." He shot Will a sidelong glance and corrected, "Well, as much me time as a damn alpha can get nowadays."

His unexpected answer created a pinhole in Tala's temper, and she felt the night's tension drop a notch. Her shoulders relaxed, and she gave a soft snort. "Hate to break it to you, but you better get used to it. The whole mantle of authority is highly overrated."

"And does a number on your privacy," Cheveyo chimed in. "It's like your people forget why you ended up in the position in the first damn place."

"Considering Chay isn't hovering around, I bet you

drive your people nuts with the way you ditch your escorts," Will grumbled.

Cheveyo's answering smile was slow in coming and edged with sardonic humor. "My 'escorts,' as you put it, understand the best way to do their jobs is to give me space to do mine. It's an arrangement we've all agreed to live with." His smile faded under a return of seriousness as he turned back to Toby. "However much it rankles right now, it's probably best to continue keeping your First and Second close."

"No doubt," Toby agreed, despite the disgruntled look on his face.

Tala walked back to the table, retook her seat, and got the conversation back on track. "While you were on your run, did you happen to catch a glimpse of whoever may have set the fire?"

Will shook his head. "We weren't close enough. We didn't head over until we scented smoke. By the time we got here, you two seemed to have it under control."

She frowned. "No scents, no trail?"

"Nothing," Toby said, his voice grim. "Mixing rain and fire is a great way to wipe out scent trails, and we didn't see any signs of passage."

Fires weren't the only possible explanation. Under normal circumstances, she'd be reluctant to share, but this situation was so far from normal. Not to mention she wasn't comfortable leaving the wolves blind to a possible vulnerability. "A skilled castor could do the same with a complex concealment spell."

"Without leaving any signs?" Rampant disbelief saturated Will's question.

"Never forget that Magi work with natural elements," Cheveyo said softly. "Erasing scents or physical signs of a trail would be nothing to one who could craft the magic at a level to direct an element like fire. And believe me, it was directed. This was no random act."

Toby's jaw flexed, his voice emerged in a near growl, "And both witches have such capabilities?"

Tala gave a slow nod. "Don't underestimate either of them. Some of the most dangerous Magi are the ones you least expect. If we consider Cheveyo's theory that one, or both, may be working with a Council member, we need to be prepared for anything." Because Leo had centuries to perfect his magic, it was what made him such a formidable Magi.

A solemn quiet slipped around the table, and she broke it with, "You're certain they're both at home now?" Because, damn, she wanted a couple of hours to regroup before confronting either woman.

Toby canted his head, his gaze unfocused as he touched base with his wolves, one of the perks of taking the alpha position.

Tala fleetingly wished she could do the same, it would make figuring this out a hell of a lot easier.

After a few moments, Toby answered, "According to those on watch, there's been no movement since both settled in for the night." He looked between her and Cheveyo before adding, "Of course, based on what you just shared, I'm not sure how much stock we can put into that."

"At this point, I think we're good for the night." Cheveyo drummed his fingers against the table, a small frown creasing his forehead. "Between the mirror spell and the fire, whoever it is, has to be wiped. I sincerely doubt we'll need to fend off another attack tonight." He eyed the darkness lurking outside the patio door and grimaced. "Correction, this morning."

"Then—" Tala was caught unawares by a yawn then offered a polite, "Sorry. Then we'll plan on making some house calls first thing in the morning. Just be sure to let your wolves know not to let either one leave their homes and stay alert."

"Works for me." Toby shook himself and pushed back his chair. "Since there's not much more we can do now, Will and I will head out."

Will rose, and Cheveyo followed suit. Tala went to push her chair back, but Toby pressed a gentle hand against her shoulder, holding her in place. "Stay, Tala, and get some rest. Your protector here—" He jerked a thumb in Cheveyo's direction. "—can see us out. We'll leave the sweats with him."

She patted his hand. "Be safe, Toby, and let me know if anything changes."

He squeezed her shoulder briefly and nodded before heading out on to the deck.

Once all three men were outside, Tala slumped over the table and laid her head against her arms. Gods, she was tired and blessedly numb. Her eyes burned, gritty from exhaustion, and the longer she sat there the harder it became to keep them open. She must have fallen asleep, because the next thing she knew was the feel of Cheveyo's arms lifting her from the chair and the heat emanating from his bare chest.

It was too hard to open her eyes, but she did manage to mumble, "What about the mirror spell?"

"It's contained and can wait till morning."

With her head against his chest, the rumble of his deep voice triggered a cascade of chills that had nothing to do with temperature and everything to do with his proximity. As he carried her down the hall, he shifted his hold. She countered by looping her arm over his shoulder and burrowing closer. The tempting scent of sea and storms that defined him wrapped around her. Unable to resist, she pressed a soft, delicate kiss to base of his throat.

His arms tightened. "You're playing a dangerous game, *awéé*." There was an intriguing rasp to his low warning.

"Not playing games," she murmured just before another yawn stretched her jaw wide. Her lashes lifted as he paused, turned sideways, and nudged open her bedroom door.

He set her carefully on the rumpled bed. When he went to straighten, she latched onto his shoulders, holding him in place.

The hall light barely penetrated the shadows, but it was enough to see his face when he was only inches away. "Don't leave."

His gaze drifted over her face, and this close she didn't miss the hunger he kept ruthlessly in check. Still, his voice remained gentle, giving no sign of the battle she could see in his eyes. "You need sleep."

Maybe, but she also needed him to fill in the ragged holes the night's events had wrought. Something in her face must have given her away, because he shook his head. "Sleep, *bił hinishnáanii*. Otherwise, I'll go bunk in the other room."

She arched a brow. "Do you think I'm going to wake up and change my mind?"

His smile was rueful. "I wouldn't dare presume, but I do know it's been a hell of a long night, filled with a ton of shit neither one of us has had a chance to deal with. The last thing I want is you to come to me and then decide it was a mistake." His smile drifted away and what replaced it stunned her, a naked vulnerability she never saw before. "I meant what I said, Tala. I love you, and this time, I have every intention of following this relationship through. If you're just looking to dull the ache or scratch an itch, I'm not the man for you."

Stymied, she dropped her arms and lay back against the pillow. With no other place to put them, she laced her fingers over her stomach as she studied him. Even though he was in the dominant position, his arms on either side of her as he loomed above her, she got the disconcerting feeling all the power rested with her.

Since his honesty deserved no less from her, she said, "I love you, too, but if you're asking for a life-time commitment right this second, I'm not sure I can answer." When his expression began to close down, and he pulled back, she rushed on, "What I can tell you is that I need you with me tonight." Now it was her turn to smile ruefully. "Just to hold me, Cheveyo. I need help keeping the pain at bay. Just for tonight," she finished in a husky whisper.

She waited, braced for his decision.

It wasn't long in coming. "That I can do."

Her breath left in a shuddering wave as she shifted to her side, making room for him to lie next to her. Within minutes, he was curled around her back, and his arm draped over her waist.

She wove their fingers together and brought his hand to her chest. With each passing minute, her muscles uncoiled, and his steady breathing eventually deepened into sleep. Only then did she dare risk pressing a quick kiss to his knuckles and whisper, "Thank you."

She lay in his arms and relished the comfort she found. She hadn't lied, she loved him beyond reason, which scared her to death. With their positions, losing him was a constant cloud of worry. Considering how much Aponi's death wrecked her, she couldn't even begin to imagine what she would become if she lost Cheveyo.

He asked earlier if she would ever forgive him. What she couldn't find the courage to say was she already had. Years ago. Admitting that was difficult, mainly because it meant owning the fact he was, and always had been, her biggest weakness. Weak spots became death knells for Kyn leaders. A fact she blithely ignored when she took her position, but one hammered home time and time again as the years passed. Tomás was just the latest example.

Cheveyo's decision to leave and give her room to grow into her position left her hurt and angry. It hadn't helped that their situation had been riddled with insecurities and debilitating assumptions, on both sides. Unfortunately, she honed her initial anger into a thick shield, one that not only kept him away, but everyone else as well. All because she knew when she saw him again, she'd be tempted to reach for the possibility of them.

It worked too, at least until last year. It stunned her that one phone call was all it took to bring him back. His response made her reexamine her heart. He hadn't hesitated to stand at her side, despite their powerful positions. It was only when faced with losing him that the final barriers on her side had fallen. The threat of his death, stripped away all pretenses, leaving her heart raw and exposed. When he went back to Portland, she was left to struggle with the twins of guilt and shame over the secret of their child. It was a trap of her own making, but she'd been trying to determine how to tell him without losing him for good.

Now that the last of her secrets was out, there was nothing left to hold between the two of them but her own stubborn pride. She couldn't fight the glaring truth—she wanted Cheveyo however she could get him and regardless of the cost. Yes, their positions would make a relationship challenging, but then again their worlds were a study in the impossible.

Danger would always be a part of their world, more so with what was coming. His strength and integrity drew her as much as his heart. Even this momentary peace she felt lying in his arms was precious. He was a man who understood the strengths of a partner, and she didn't doubt that once she committed to him, he'd stand beside her.

Admitting that unfurled the tight knot of hope she nurtured. Maybe it wasn't just Aponi who needed to fly, maybe it was time for her to stretch her wings, to trust herself to be strong enough to stand beside him. Time to be the woman warrior he believed her to be. Decision made, she closed her eyes, the ragged edges of her soul eroding in the shelter of his arms.

CHAPTER 24

CHEVEYO WOKE TO THE FEEL OF WARM LIPS SLIDING OVER HIS chest. His hands were tangled in silky strands, and his eyes opened, only to go blind as those lips slipped lower. Lust roared through his body in a white-hot wave. If this was a dream, he didn't want to wake. Those wicked lips wreaked havoc, leaving behind streaks of fire, but they couldn't burn away the warnings slowly eating through his rising needs.

When a lash of tongue joined the soft press of kisses against his overheated skin, he groaned and tugged carefully until Tala lifted her head, determined to...do something. When her dark eyes, filled with heat and something more, met his, his brain short-circuited.

"Tala." Her name was all he could manage.

Shifting until she laying on top of him, every tantalizing curve and dip sinking against his harder planes, she folded her arms over his chest and rested her chin on them. "Morning."

His hands moved without prompting, cupping her face, his thumb brushing over angled cheeks then moving to her lower lip. When her tongue came out to meet his touch, he couldn't rein in his visceral reaction.

She didn't miss it either, considering how fast color rose under her skin adding a dusky hue, and the desire sparking in her eyes, melting into pools of fire-shot whiskey. The temptation proved to be too much, and his hips rolled against hers. Her lips curved with an enticing mix of wicked intent while her nails curled into his chest adding another layer to the desire rising between them.

His chest rose and fell as he tried to suck in air. He fought his way through the need screaming in his head to remember why pursuing this now was not a good idea. "What are you doing, *awéé?*"

Instead of the expected teasing response, her smile faded, and her solemn gaze drifted over his face. "You asked me a question last night."

There was an unusual hesitancy in her voice, one that managed to corral his body's demands quicker than the doubts circling his brain. Unfortunately, he asked her a couple of questions last night, and unsure of which one she now meant, he carefully nodded.

She must have caught his confusion. "You asked if I would ever forgive you." A wistfulness replaced the more somber shadows in her eyes. She licked her lips, and he forced his attention back to her and not the carnal images her innocent move ignited. "I forgave you a long time ago, Cheveyo." Color waxed and waned under her honey skin before her gaze dropped away. She turned her head and rested her check on the back of her hands, her shaky breath washing over his bare chest.

Unable to resist the temptation, he ran his fingers through her long strands in slow strokes, offering comfort even as he smoothed the warm tendrils into a decadent blanket.

She took a deep, shuddering breath. "I should've told you last night." Her voice stayed soft as if she feared rousing his ire. "Hell, I should've said something last year. It's just that I've been a coward for so long, I couldn't get out of my own way. I'm tired of being scared." The last came out in a shamed whisper lacerating his heart.

He rolled until she was on her back under him, his legs tangling with hers, eliminating any possible escape. His abrupt move forced her hands to latch onto his shoulders, her nervousness revealed in the tiny stinging bites of her nails against his sensitive skin. When she continued to hide her eyes, he used a finger to nudge her chin up until she couldn't evade his gaze. "You're not a coward." Certainty deepened his voice into a husky rasp.

She frowned and her mouth opened, her intent to argue clear.

He stopped it by laying his finger against her lush lips. "You're not. For lack of a better term, love, you're human." Thinking through of some of his past decisions, he didn't flinch from sharing hard won knowledge and pride-scraping wisdom. "It's easy to look back and judge. But, given the circumstances at the time, you did what you needed to do to survive." He held her troubled gaze, baring more than bruised ego. "We may be leaders, but we are not infallible. No one ever can be."

Comprehension fought against guilt, and she whispered, "Doesn't make it right."

"Depends on your perspective." His answer was ruthlessly hard. He dropped his forehead to hers until he couldn't take a breath without tasting her, and his voice softened. "If you want to rehash what we did or didn't do, then I should have paid more attention to what was happening around us before I left. And later? I could've reached out sooner, not waited until you called." Regret still shadowed her face so he dipped closer and stole a quick kiss. A delicate caress carrying the promise of more, a heated tease of tongue over damp curves rife with unvoiced apologies.

When he drew back, his weight held by the arms on either side of her, he couldn't help the burst of satisfaction as he took in her flushed face and dazed gaze. Even more telling, desire began inching out her remorse. Still, she asked, "Why didn't you?"

Recognizing she needed his unabashed honesty if they were to move beyond their shared history, he stuck to the unvarnished truth. "Hurt pride, bruised heart. Either one is just as culpable." Seeing her puzzled confusion, he opened the door to his heart and ushered her inside, risking her rejection. "You weren't the only one who was angry. I hate to break it to you, but the male ego is a fragile thing."

He looked away and shifted his upper half until he could brace on one arm. It gave her enough room to shift, which she did, so they were facing each other. He refused to let her go completely, keeping their legs tangled. He reached out and caught one long strand of her hair, the unusual mix of black, brown and gold stunning as he slowly drew it through his fingers before letting it curl over the edge of her breast.

He brought his gaze back to hers. "I announced my decision to head back to Portland, and you barely batted a damn eyelash. Then, as the months passed, and you never called, never reached out, I convinced myself that whatever we shared was one-sided."

Comprehension dawned. She reached up and brushed a soft touch over his face. "It wasn't."

He turned into her caress and pressed a kiss to her palm. "Yeah, I get that. Now."

The last of the shadows pulled away, and a tentative joy peeked out, her lips twitching. "We make quite the pair, don't we?"

He arched an eyebrow, his tone droll, "That we do." He searched her face, his humor drifting away. *Time to lay it all on the table.* His heart hammered in his chest, and he forced himself not to move. "The past is over and done. What's important now is where you decide we go from here. Do I stay and complicate your life, or do I leave you in peace?"

He didn't dare blink as she raised her arms and locked her hands behind his neck. "Stay, peaceful is damn boring."

A shudder of relief racked his body, and he wrapped his arm around her waist pulling her close, his heart and soul expanding, threatening to burst.

Her eyes shone brightly with an inner fire as she pulled him down. "*Ayóo-aníiníshní,* Cheveyo."

Her declaration of love washed away the last of his doubts, and his voice came out choked, filled with things no words would ever capture. "I love you, too, Tala."

Her lips brushed his once, twice, and that was all it took. The last of his restraint vanished under the heat of her kiss and what started out as a promise quickly became an inferno.

With one hand tangled in her hair and cradling her head, he rolled her under him. His mouth moved with devastating intent, as the fire of need roared through every nerve ending. This was what haunted his dreams for the last year. Their tongues dueled, the taste of her seeped into his bloodstream until he was addicted.

Her hand tangled in his hair, holding him tight as she met him stroke for stroke, nip for nip. The storm washed over both, taking them under, dragging them deeper into the depth of need and hunger until it was all that was left. Before he could drown in her heat, he tore his mouth from hers, searching for a modicum of control over his greed for her touch.

Tala was having none of it. Her hands ran over his back and clutched his ass, pulling him close as he ran an alternating line of nips and kisses along her neck. When she arced into him with a soft moan, he ground his aching dick into her softness. His groan echoed hers, relishing her heat, even through the annoying barrier of his sleep pants.

He lifted his body from hers until he could stroke his hands over the warm curves of her hips, dragging the thin barrier of her sleep shirt higher. What he uncovered tore another groan from him. A tiny scrap of material covered her, a deep, silky purple held together with ribbon. "You're a dangerous woman." He pressed a soft kiss above the edge of the material. Her breath audibly hitched and her hips rose. It was damn difficult, but he managed to lift his head. "Naked, now."

She huffed out a laugh but didn't argue. Instead, together they stripped each other with little finesse. When heated skin met heated skin, they both gasped then groaned. He held her against him as her lips traced destructive paths over his heaving chest. He retaliated by nibbling along her shoulders. She shuddered against him when his lips touched the soft skin where her neck curved. The unconscious move felt so good against his aching body, he did it again.

"Not fair, Cheveyo." However, she arched her neck

giving him further access, putting her husky complaint at odds with her silent commands.

He simply chuckled and this time drew the delicate skin between his lips, marking her. One last lick and he finally lifted his head.

Her hunger and voracious need stared back, a mirror to his firestorm clawing for freedom. "My turn."

Following her husky command, he rolled onto his back, giving her room to play. With one hand wrapped in her hair, he narrowed his eyes as he watched her taste him.

She held his gaze, looking at him through the screen of her heavy lashes. Her tongue darted out to circle one nipple, eliciting a hiss. A wicked smile curved her lips. "I missed your taste, and this." It was his only warning. Her clever, devious hand slipped down his body leaving a devastating hunger behind. Then she wrapped one searing palm around his straining dick.

His breath escaped on a low, rumbling moan as he widened his legs, encouraging her play. "Tease," he choked out.

But he wasn't about to let her have all the fun. Untangling his hand, he slipped his hands under the silky curtain of hair, and starting at her shoulders, slowly swept his palms down her back, following the delicate bumps of her spine.

The grip on his dick tightened, glided up, and unable to resist, his hips followed. Yet it wasn't enough to deter his own exploration. He continued his caress over her hips, brushing his fingers over the delicate crease between her hips and where he soon planned to spend an inordinate amount of time exploring.

Her breath stuttered, and, in retaliation, she began to

stroke him, her pace slow and steady, a sensual torment designed to keep him on edge.

Not to be outdone, he matched her pace. Mindful of her nearly healed wound, he carefully dragged his hands up her ribs, drawing soft tantalizing strokes along the underside of her beautiful breasts.

She arched into his touch with a whimpered, "Now who's the tease?"

His chuckle was filled with dark promises, but he didn't alter his tormenting sweep. "I'll get there, promise."

His gaze centered on her lush curves. He captured her breasts in both hands, holding them captive for his enjoyment. Then he proceeded to lick and lave until her gasps and moans filled the air. Her grip faltered, then disappeared as her hands rose to clutch his shoulders as she arched closer in silent demand. He reluctantly freed one hand, wrapped his arm around her waist and reversed their positions.

When he had her sprawled before him like a decadent offering, he ran his tongue over her curves, delicately circling her nipples until they were rigid points. Only then did he draw her deep into his mouth. The bite of her nails against his shoulders was lost in the pleasure as her legs shifted restlessly, then widened. Feeling her, warm and wet, left him beyond words, his dick throbbing in demand. Still, he continued to torment them both, driving their desire to impossible heights.

She fought to get closer, broken pleas falling from her. Her leg lifted and curled around his hip, attempting to capture him, but he had other ideas.

Memories rose, tangling with the now and left his mouth watering. Not about to deny himself the pleasure of her taste, he finally moved from her beautiful breasts and began a devastating path toward his ultimate goal. As he inched down, his hands swept over her thighs, and when he reached his intended destination, he nudged her legs further apart, making room for his shoulders and settling in.

She stared down at him, shudders wracking her body, need and love adding a luminous light to her dark gaze.

He blew a single breath over her damp mound.

A soft broken moan escaped. Her eyelids fluttered, her hips undulated under his phantom touch. Her hands kneaded his skull, the tugs leaving tiny stings in their wake. She managed to lift her lashes and plead, "Cheveyo, please."

"Please what, *awéé*?" His question was closer to a growl as the scent of her drifted to him, the temptation to gorge difficult to ignore, but he managed. Barely. He tortured them both by swiping his tongue through her dampness. Her shuddering moan fell, echoing his, as spiced sugar exploded against his tongue. Unable to resist, he did it again.

"Don't stop," she gasped. "Please, oh gods, Cheveyo, don't stop."

Obeying her passionate demand, he dipped his head and gave into his cravings. He licked and sucked, drawing her taste deep even as her moans turned to needy whimpers. He lost himself in her, her cries ringing in his ears. Only when she exploded around his tongue, did he press one last soft kiss to the inside of each thigh before lifting his head.

His heart clenched at the sight that met his eyes. The stunning beauty spread before him was his, and his alone. The enormity of her gift, the knowledge of how precious her heart truly was, humbled him and left his voice hoarse. "You are so beautiful, Tala."

Color rode under her skin, and her sensual satisfaction was mirrored in her glowing gaze. "So are you." Her fingers slid free from his hair and drifted over his face, tracing delicate lines along his jaw. "Come here."

Not needing any more urging he inched his way up. Desire kept a ruthless grip on his body, the ache for her touch barely soothed by the feel of her skin sliding over his. When she cupped his face and captured his mouth with hers, he sank into her.

She took her time, turning her kiss into a deliberate, sensual claiming. When she pulled back and pressed her hands against his chest in silent demand, he rolled to his back, his hands digging into her hips, dragging her close.

She rose above him, her hair tumbling over them both, the brush of silk strands an added caress. After nabbing a condom from the nightstand, she reclaimed his dick, her hand wrapping around him, stroking once, then twice, before she covered him. Only then did she slowly, inch by unbearable inch, sink over him. The feel of her, the heat, the tightness, the sense of completion, arched his spine, his head pressing into the pillow, every muscle strung tight. "Oh gods, yes, Tala." In a low groan, his voice squeezed out between clenched teeth as white starbursts exploded behind his closed eyes.

When she shifted to slide up, his hands caught her hips, dragging her down, hard. This time their moans sounded in unison. He forced his eyes open, needing to see her, to know this was no dream. His heart clenched, fractured, then reformed at the vision before him.

Tala straddled him, her head thrown back, her spine bowed, her hair flowing, the silken strands soft whips of sensation against his skin, her hands braced on his thighs, the bite of her nails a beautiful pain. Her chest rose and fell as she fought for breath, her breasts an irresistible temptation.

He bent his knees, providing a backrest for her as his hands slipped up over her ribs to cup her breasts. His thumbs brushed over her distended tips, and her hands covered his, holding him close. With a flex of his stomach, he curled up, slipping one hand free to cup the back of her head and bring her mouth to his. He ravaged her mouth as the shift in their position sent him deeper.

Her hands went to his shoulders, his went to her waist, then he dropped his knees and turned until his legs fell over the side of the bed. He held her steady as she found her balance astride him. With one last nip, he released her mouth. Their gazes met and held as she began to ride him in earnest.

White-hot fire seared through every nerve ending. The feel of her rising and falling, clutching him tight in the most intimate of embraces, it all collapsed into an inferno, leaving sensual devastation in its wake. The storm gathered strength, overtaking them both. His cries blended with hers as a brilliant soul-searing explosion swept through both of them.

CHAPTER 25

A COUPLE HOURS AND ONE VERY ENJOYABLE SHOWER LATER, Cheveyo stood at the stove, monitoring the bacon, phone pressed to his ear as Chay read him the riot act. "Are you even listening to me, Cheveyo?"

"Nope," he replied, as he dropped the bacon on to a paper towel covered plate. "Just waiting for you to finish."

"Fine," Chay snapped. "I'm finished."

"Good. So tell me what you found." He turned and brought the bacon filled plate over to the table where Tala sipped her coffee. She snagged a piece and nibbled, her brow arched. He rolled his eyes in response.

Chay didn't waste time. "Definitely a mirror spell, but there wasn't much left to trace. What was there, Wyatt and I both agreed, felt like witch, not wizard."

"Did you get enough to be able to identify the castor if you run into them again?" Heading back to the kitchen, he tucked the phone between his shoulder and ear so he could pour a cup of coffee. Mission accomplished, he repositioned the phone and brought everything back to the table.

Chay consulted with Wyatt and came back on the line, "We think so."

"Good. Then I need you and Wyatt to hurry the hell up and get back here." He checked the wall clock, it was closing in on eight. "Work fast, I want to match the two spells before ten."

"What the hell is going on at ten?" Chay grumbled.

"We're going to start making house calls." He shoveled some eggs on his fork and took a bite.

"We're heading out now." Chay paused, before warning in a low voice, "Cheveyo, swear to the gods above and below, if you try tracking that damn spell before we get back, I'm going—"

Cheveyo set his fork down, Chay's reprimand sending ripples of irritation through his good mood. "You're going to what, Chay?" There was no missing the icy bite in his question.

"Tattle to Raine," Chay finished.

The unexpected response startled a laugh and soothed his emerging temper. "You do that, and I'll bet I'm not the only one who ends up in her crosshairs."

"You're a mean bastard."

"Don't you forget it." Cheveyo hung up, shaking his head. He set the phone on the table and dug into his breakfast.

"Whose crosshairs?"

Despite her attempt to keep her question casual, Cheveyo didn't miss the sting of heat. "Raine's."

Tala frowned before taking another sip from her mug, keeping it cradled between her hands. "That damn bond you two share." She met his gaze, hers full of feminine possession. "What possessed you to connect the two of you?"

He stifled a sigh and chased his last bite of his breakfast with coffee. Funny, he expected this question sooner. Once he may have considered not answering, but now, with all the changes between them, he had no inclination to dodge it. Best to stick with their no-more-secrets agreement.

He sat back in his chair, legs sprawled, one hand idling playing with his coffee mug. "How much do you know about Raine?"

She shrugged. "Until she showed up with you last year, not much. Rumors abound, but I've never been certain how much stock they carry." She used her fork to move some eggs around her plate before looking back up. "Based on what I saw, I get she's dangerous."

He couldn't stop the wry twist of his lips if he tried. "Yeah, in that aspect, you two are like peas in a pod." When Tala's expression shifted to affronted dignity, he did laugh. "Raine's not much fonder of my comparisons either."

She shot him a narrow eyed glare. "Gee, I wonder why."

He shook his head. Tala and Raine were more alike than they believed, each an intriguing combination of formidable warrior and challenging female. Women who tolerated little and expected much. Such women were rare finds, and once a man was lucky enough to find one, he moved heaven and earth to keep her. Which is why Tala held his heart, and Raine held Gavin's.

"I won't share her entire story, just the basics." Because some details weren't his to share, nor was he totally certain of their veracity. "She was kidnapped as a teen and used for experimentation by a human scientist. The experiments killed her mother, but changed Raine at a fundamental level."

Pity moved in Tala's gaze. "Changed how?"

"No one was really sure. It took her a long time to get

through what happened. About a year and a half ago, Mulcahy asked if I could step in and mentor her." He didn't miss Tala's wince, which held equal parts sympathy and jealousy, as she was intimately aware of why he would be called in to serve such a position. "I agreed."

She searched his face, her question soft, "Why?"

There were more layers to her simple question, and despite their recently renewed commitment, he didn't mind soothing them. Some hurts took longer to heal than others. "Because Raine needed a chance to see what she could do before she hurt herself or those around her." Much like a powerful, younger Tala, Raine's attempts to master her abilities were similar to riding lightning—buck-naked.

"If he was so concerned, why didn't he mentor her?" Skepticism danced along her question as she broke off a piece of bacon and passed it off to Ash who was curled under the table for just such an opportunity.

"Two reasons," Cheveyo carefully kept his voice bland. "First, she was his niece and to describe their relationship as 'difficult' was putting it mildly." At that revelation, Tala blinked but held her tongue, so he continued and braced for the fallout. "Second, in order to save her life, I used a bastardized version of the *Naakishchíín* spell."

She stiffened, her face paling before she got out, "Why that spell?"

He couldn't fault her shock. The magic needed for that particular spell was ancient. In fact, the initial *Naakishchíín* spell allowed two people to share the same life force, draw on each other's strengths and weaknesses creating powerful twins. It also meant if one died, so did the other.

When he was trying to save Raine, he hadn't the luxury of picking and choosing a way to keep her from death's grasp. Normally he wouldn't explain his reasoning, but this was Tala.

He continued, "Raine went up against a half-demon with gypsy blood. She triggered a nasty spell, one that tied them together through death."

Tala frowned. "So the death of one, meant death for the other."

"Right, which meant there was no way to break it."

Comprehension crept in. "You had to counter it with a spell that worked in similar fashion."

He nodded. "I was running against the clock and didn't have much to work with. So I altered a known spell, made a few unique adjustments, and kept Raine breathing."

"Great, you kept her breathing. But now? How tight is this tie?"

Seeing the rising concern behind her question, he was quick to clarify, "Tight, but not at such an intimate level as required by the *Naakishchíín* spell. We can assist each other in times of need by drawing on each other's abilities, but, thanks to the thick psychic barrier anchored on both sides, we keep our individuality and privacy."

His explanation didn't appear to ease the worry darkening her gaze. "For anyone to have that kind of access to you or your magic, especially an unknown, that's worrisome, Cheveyo."

He couldn't deny her concern, but... "It's what ultimately saved my life with the Soul Stealer, Tala."

"No, I was there, Cheveyo," Tala argued. "I channeled the Ancestors to help with your healing. Granted Raine's ability to see your magic, like a piece of ripped cloth, allowed the two of us to weave it back together. She told me that your bond was messing with the healing."

He held his silence and watched her reconsider the events of a year ago.

Finally, she said, "What am I missing?"

"Are you sure you want to know?" If he gave Tala the truth, not only would it give her a dangerous insight into who and what the Northwest was protecting, but it was a crucial key in the upcoming battle with the Council.

She cocked her head to the side. "Why don't you want to tell me?"

"It's not a question of wanting to tell you. It's a question of how far are you willing to go to protect me."

Her answer was quick and rock solid. "As far as you're willing to go to protect me."

"This could pit you against the Council." He had to try and give her every opportunity to walk away. It was only fair.

She held his gaze. "And?" She studied his face, no doubt catching his worry. "I'm right here, *bił hinishná-anii*, and I told you before, I have no plans on going anywhere."

He believed her, but it didn't lessen the tension twisting his muscles. It wasn't just his life he was handing her, it was Raine and Gavin's. And ultimately every Kyn born in the last fifty years.

"Cheveyo." She waited until she had his attention. "I give you my word, I will not betray you with what you are considering sharing."

The weight of her promise hummed between them. He couldn't stop his retort. "You're making a vow about something you don't even understand."

She got out of her chair and made her way around the table. When she got to him, he shifted his chair so she could stand in front of him. She caught his face between her palms, bent down, and gave him the sweetest kiss. When she lifted her head, he couldn't avoid her gaze. Sincerity and love stared back. Her voice was soft, but rang with conviction, "I'm making a vow to you, the man who holds my heart and shelters my soul. I won't betray you."

The untarnished beauty of her gift humbled him. Unable to resist, he gently pulled her into his lap, sheltering her against his heart. "I love you, Tala Whiteriver, beyond all comprehension, I love you."

She curled into him and pressed a soft kiss to the base of his throat. "Same goes, warrior man." She lifted her head and faced him. "Now spill."

Ceding to her demand, he spilled. "When you asked Raine to help repair the damage from the Stealer, you didn't give her a chance to tell you that she couldn't repair what wasn't there."

"What do you mean, what wasn't there?"

"The Stealer fed off of magical life force. As much as I fought, I was losing the battle. The bastard managed to eat through my magic, and there wasn't much left." She shuddered against him, horror apparent on her face and he tightened his arms in comfort. "Raine kept trying to fix the wounds, but with nothing to anchor against, those repairs wouldn't hold."

"Right, because of your damn connection. It's why I let her in the circle. She had to act as the siphon for the healing magic. And it worked. I felt it."

"Because that's what Raine and Gavin wanted you to feel. Gavin is a master of illusions and he has no problems doing what needs to be done to protect the woman he considers his." Cheveyo rubbed his cheek over the top of her head. "You did something to Raine, something she still won't talk about."

The hand against his chest fisted and she stiffened.

Despite recognizing the signs of her discomfort, he waited. Finally, she admitted in a low voice, "I laid a geas on her, forcing her to keep a promise."

"What promise?" He was genuinely curious.

"To kill the Stealer and get your magic back," came the reluctant answer.

Something wasn't adding up. "Wasn't that what they were planning on doing in the first place?"

Tala nodded.

A geas was a compulsion, one that couldn't be broken without serious repercussions. Considering Raine's scalded cat routine any time Tala's name came up, he got a very bad feeling. "What did you tie the geas to?"

She blew out a hard breath, her shoulders straightened, and her voice was empty. "Her life for your magic and the Stealer's death."

The final pieces of the puzzle of the two women's cantankerous relationship fell into place. Taking hold of her upper arms, he leaned back and forced her away from his chest until they could face each other. "Oh, *awéé*, what in the world possessed you to make such a dangerous move?"

Tala lifted her chin but shrugged uncomfortably. "I could tell you I didn't think she would follow through."

Hearing the unspoken 'but' in her answer, he waited.

"But the truth was, I lost my temper. You were dying. Nothing I did helped and, from what I could see, she was taking her sweet-ass time fixing things."

Stubborn and protective made for a volatile mix, and Tala, like Raine, had the power to make their impatience a deadly thing.

Tala's brow furrowed and her eyes sparked with temper. "It was a simple geas, Cheveyo, and she acted like I set a death spell on her."

"Not her," he murmured. "Gavin." He watched comprehension slip in and replace Tala's irritation. "Those two are connected tighter than Tomás and Lizbeth ever were. And, honey, I hate to break it to you, but he is the one person you don't want to threaten if you want her help."

"Well, shit," she muttered, her remorse clear. "Dammit."

"What?"

She sighed. "Now, I'm going to have to apologize to her."

Her obvious chagrin surprised a laugh out of him, and he hugged her close. "Yeah, I think we can hold off on that momentous occasion."

For a minute they held each other. Finally, she spoke up. "If Raine and Gavin were able to fool me into thinking you were healing, then what was really going on?"

He stroked her spine. "She rewove my magic into something different then anchored it to her and Gavin until I could maintain it on my own."

"Different how?"

It was his turn to shrug. "My abilities are not the same as they were. They're stronger, less predictable, and some carry unique characteristics." Trying to describe the changes was difficult because each Kyn's magic was very personal.

Tala's eyes widened with understandable shock. "She changed your magic?"

He dipped his chin in acknowledgement.

The ramifications of his answer hit her with stunning force leaving her face white. "Oh, my gods," she breathed.

"Now you understand why the Northwest can't afford to kowtow to the Council." His voice was quiet.

She swallowed and nodded slowly. "If they find out

what she can do, the Council won't be happy until she's dead."

"And it's not just that. It's the fact that with every new generation of Kyn, new abilities appear. Abilities that the Council can't control."

"And what they can't control, they destroy," she added. "You're talking about the evolution of magic."

"Exactly." He studied her face. "It's not just a question of coming out to the humans, it's also about saving our future generations, from them and our own."

She worried her lower lip. "Mulcahy, he saw all of this, didn't he? It's why he came to America in the first place." She didn't wait for his answer. "Of course, he did, and it's also why the Council is so gung-ho about stringing up the Northwest. They're not the biggest fans of competition."

"Not competition—choice," he corrected. "So long as the Northwest exists, there is a refuge for those looking to escape the Council's persecution. Unfortunately, our numbers have visibly increased in the last century. Enough to worry the Council."

"Makes sense." She paused. "Why didn't you just tell Toby or Rio about this?"

He winced. "I think it's best to leave that job up to Warrick and Natasha." Even though he was fairly certain Rio was well aware of what was going on.

As if following his thoughts, her gaze narrowed. "You know if you told Rio, he would be all over it just for the chaos it would bring."

"Maybe," he agreed. "But unless Natasha feels it's worth the risk, I think I'll refrain and just stick to the whole, we-need-to-show-ourselves-before-we're-forced-to argument."

"That's no fun," she groused.

He snorted. "Since when are Kyn politics ever fun?"

That earned him a wry grin. "Okay, I'll give you that."

A knock sounded at the front door. Ash scrambled out from under the table and raced out of the kitchen with a low woof. In Cheveyo's lap, Tala leaned to the side to see over his shoulder. "Are we expecting someone?"

"Not that I'm aware of." He kept his hands on her waist as she scrambled off his lap.

Once on her feet, she squeezed his hand and he let her go. Another knock sounded. "Whoever they are, they're impatient." She headed toward the door.

Curious, he rose and followed. Tala pulled open the door and when a young voice started in on a spiel about a local food drive, he headed back to the kitchen and began cleaning up their dishes. After a few minutes of murmured conversation, the door closed. Bending over, he set the last plate in the dishwasher and then straightened.

"You know," Tala's husky voice had him turning to see her leaning against the arched entryway. "I think I like you like this."

Drying his hands, he re-tucked the hand towel on the stove. "Like what?"

She sashayed her way to him, her hands brushing down his chest, leaving fire in her wake, before lifting on tiptoe to nip his chin. Her smile was wicked. "All domesticated and barefoot in my kitchen."

He caught her hips, dragging her close. The desire in her eyes deepened as he pressed against her, making it clear he liked it too. "We still have time before Chay and Wyatt get back," he growled. "Want to see how domesticated I can get?" He wrapped an arm under her ass, bent, set his shoulder on her stomach, and straightened before she could blink.

Draped over his shoulder, hanging upside down with her hair trailing down, she laughed. The joyful sound seeped into his pores, filling the last of the hollow spaces with her light.

CHAPTER 26

"Whoever spun these, they're sneaky as shit." Sitting on the tile of Tala's bathroom, Wyatt leaned against the tub. He turned to Chay, perched on the closed lid of the commode. "Don't know about you, but I'm picking up the same signature as before."

Chay's mouth was a thin line. "Yeah, me too, but…" He trailed off, his brow furrowed.

Tala, who stood in the doorway, Ash at her side—because with three large men stuffed into the bathroom, space was a bit limited—could feel his magic reach out and encompass the trapped spell.

"Careful, Chay," murmured Cheveyo who sat on the edge of the tub next to Wyatt. "See this?" There was a change in the enclosed space's energy as he adjusted the magic the three men were working with. "I'm thinking we have two castors, not one."

Chay's gaze narrowed. "I think you're right."

Wyatt leaned forward, his gaze unfocused with concentration. "What is that?"

"That is a buried signature." Cheveyo's answer was

grim, a muscle jumping along his jaw. "And one I've seen before."

Unable to stay quiet, Tala piped up from her outside position, "Where?"

Cheveyo turned his attention to her, and her lungs seized at the depth of fury burning in his obsidian gaze. "On the spell that killed Mulcahy."

Her stomach pitched. Before she could process his answer or dig for more, Chay broke in, "Any way around it?"

Cheveyo refocused. "Yeah, just give me a minute."

"Be careful," Chay warned. "Remember what happened last time."

Cheveyo's only answer was a brief nod, but Tala needed more. Swallowing against her dry throat, she asked, "What happened?"

Chay looked at Cheveyo. Without breaking his focus, Cheveyo managed, "Don't look at me. You brought it up, you explain it."

Shaking his head, Chay did just that. "The spell that took out Mulcahy also managed to level an entire conference room at Taliesin, pinning our fearless leader here to the floor with rebar." He met Tala's stunned gaze. "Or so I was told."

Yeah, Chay's explanation wasn't helping the knot of worry in her stomach. Taut silence wrapped around the small space, leaving her white knuckling the doorjamb as Cheveyo continued to untangle the knotted magic. She breathed through her anxiety-fueled-by-ugly-overactive-imagination. Not an easy feat when she could do nothing but watch as he worked with a spell set by a castor with a proven lethal track record.

Finally, Cheveyo said, "Done." Relief swept through the room, tension slinking out on its coattails.

His expression decidedly not happy, Chay sat back and ran a hand through his hair as he looked at Cheveyo. "That signature mean what I think it does?"

"Probably, but it's not proof enough to bring before the rest of the Council." There was nothing comforting about Cheveyo's answer.

"What the hell do they need? A signed confession?" Chay grumbled.

She might not be privy to all the details, but could fill in the blanks with what she did know. If the Northwest thought Leo was behind Mulcahy's death, then Leo was behind the signature Cheveyo was concerned about. "Pretty much," Tala offered, not batting an eyelash at Chay's glare. "It is the Council, after all. If you want them to turn on one of their own, a signed confession, preferably in blood, would be a good start."

Wyatt watched the entire exchange closely. "I get the feeling I'm missing something important here."

Before anyone could answer, a knock echoed through the house. Ash, ever the dutiful furry butler, rose and headed out of the room, his nails tapping down the hall. Tala sighed and went to follow. Hopefully, it wasn't another high school student looking for donations for their holiday food drive.

"Tala, hold up."

Cheveyo's quiet command had her pausing just before she left the bedroom. She looked over her shoulder to find him right behind her. She arched an eyebrow. "It's the door, Cheveyo. I don't think someone bent on harm would bother to knock first."

Undaunted, he simply put his hand on the small of her back. "There's always a first time."

Okay, maybe someone was a bit more rattled than she

thought. Besides, it was a pointless argument and not worth fighting over, so she headed to the door, letting the six-foot-plus witch trail along. Ash sat by the entry, his tail sweeping slowly across the floor, his ears perked. He watched them come closer, and, when Tala reached for the doorknob, he gave a soft woof. She rubbed his head in silent thanks then opened the door.

Will stood on the other side, his attention unerringly on Ash. He lifted his gaze, his eyes carrying an amber glow. He didn't bother with a standard greeting. Instead, he said, "Got a call about fifteen minutes ago. Your girl Teagan's being squirrelly."

Opening the door wide, Tala motioned him in. "How so?"

Will stepped in the entryway, only coming in enough to close the door behind him. He scratched Ash's ear. "The wolf who's been watching her place says she talking to herself and pacing in front of the window. Has been for the last couple of hours. Says if he didn't know better, he'd think she was schizophrenic."

Alarm raced through Tala because such erratic behavior was so far from Teagan's normal state as to be scary. She turned to Cheveyo. "We need to get over there."

He didn't argue, nor did he waste any time in letting Chay and Wyatt know where they were headed and why. By the time Tala grabbed a heavy sweater, pulled on her shoes, and snatched up her car keys, Cheveyo and Chay were waiting by the door. She didn't bother arguing about who was or was not coming. "Where's Will?"

"He's on his way to update Toby. He only stopped by because he didn't have your number and was coming back after switching off with another wolf." Reading her expression correctly he added, "And no, I didn't ask who he'd been watching."

Not a concern right now. She looked at Wyatt who was standing next to Ash. "You do anything Ash doesn't like, and he'll be at your throat."

Undeterred, Wyatt grinned. "Don't worry, Tala, we won't leave bloodstains on your floors."

She huffed out a breath and headed out. When she went to go to her truck, Cheveyo caught her hand and pulled her to a stop. "We'll take the SUV, more room." She nodded and fell into step. They all piled in and headed to Teagan's to find out exactly why her normally solid and stable cousin was suddenly conversing with invisible friends.

Teagan lived a few miles from the local university in a cluster of two story condos that started a previous life as apartments. The boxy complex was set among the trees, providing a false sense of security when the main street was just on the other side. They parked in one of the uncovered spots for visitors.

Tala was out of the SUV and heading up the curving walkway, leaving Cheveyo and Chay to follow at their own pace. The unrelenting sense of urgency paced her as she strode up to Teagan's bottom corner unit and knocked. Behind her, Chay murmured something to Cheveyo. She turned her head in time to watch Chay head toward the green area where a lone occupant in a hoodie sat at a picnic table. If the books spread around them were any indication, whoever it was appeared to be in the midst of studying. She looked at Cheveyo. "Our wolf watcher?"

He shrugged. "Probably, but Chay didn't want to spook Teagan by tagging her en masse."

The sound of a lock releasing brought her attention back to the door. It inched open, and Teagan peered around the edge, her red-rimmed eyes widening. "Tala? Wha—wha—" She frowned and finally managed, "Why are you here?" Her attention went to Cheveyo, and she stepped out from behind the door, barring the opening. "What happened?"

"Hey, Teagan." Her cousin's skittish behavior made Tala appreciate Chay's assumption. Not wanting to get the door shut in their faces, Tala put a hand against the thick wood to keep it open. "Can we come in?"

Under the rumpled, short-sleeved T-shirt, the muscles in Teagan's arm gripping the knob, flexed, then relaxed. "Sure." With obvious reluctance, she dragged the door open, staying behind it as she did so.

Tala and Cheveyo stepped through and stopped just inside.

The condo was an open floor plan, so the living room and dining room shared a large space that flowed into the small galley kitchen. Off to their right, a patio door let in the morning light, dispersing the typical gloom of a garden level condo. The walls were a light sage, and the crème-colored furniture held pillows of deep forest green. Delicate Tiffany like lamps stood on side tables, while a combination display-slash-bookcase offered homes for a collection of framed photos and books nestled with various other knickknacks, including a stream-lined TV holding the middle position. Despite the modern touches, it was airy and light, like stepping into a comfortable cottage nestled in some long ago forest glade.

Teagan shut the door and flipped the security lock

before wrapping her arms around her stomach and stepping around them. She stopped by the patio doors leading to a covered porch, turned, and waved them to sit. "Make yourself at home."

Tala picked up the hand crochet blue afghan and draped it over one overstuff sofa arm, then sat. Based on Teagan's rumpled attire and the tea mug, mostly empty, on the white rattan coffee table, she decided to go with the most obvious question first. "You okay, Teagan?"

Teagan watched Cheveyo take up residence in an easy chair near the fireplace and answered absently, "I'm fine." Then she shook her head hard, frowned, and then with stilted movements, moved to the kitchen.

Clearly, she wasn't. "Teagan—"

"Would either of you like something to drink?"

The desperate casualness to Teagan's abrupt question, pulled Tala up short. She met Cheveyo's considering gaze and raised an eyebrow in silent command. Proving he was no slouch, he didn't waste time. Deciding it was best to keep Teagan distracted while Cheveyo scanned her condo for anything out of the ordinary, Tala rose to her feet and wandered over to the bar counter dividing the kitchen from the rest of the living spaces. "I'll take a cup of tea, please."

Standing in the kitchen, Teagan stared at her for a long moment before giving a jerky nod. "Chamomile work?"

"Sure." Tala pulled out one of the two barstools as Teagan began putting things together for tea. Based on her cousin's weird behavior, it might be better to take a roundabout approach to things. Folding her arms on the bar top, she waited as Teagan filled the teapot and set it to boil.

Teagan turned, leaned against the counter next to the stove, and beat her to the punch. "Why are you here, Tala?"

Following her cousin's example, Tala answer with the same bluntness. "Someone set a mirror spell at my place yesterday. Was it you?"

Teagan blinked, but didn't hesitate, "No." Her smile was a twisted grimace. "Guess I shouldn't be surprised you'd think it was me."

"You've made your opinions of me very, very clear, 'coz." Tala kept her voice soft, even as the words carried an obvious edge.

Teagan looked down, her dark hair mused, but long enough to provide a curtain. "Yeah, well, things change." She paused. "I've changed."

"Have you?" Gods above and below, part of her wished her cousin could get past Jenny's loss and the decisions Tala had been forced to make.

Teagan nodded without looking up. Her voice cracked. "Jenny's death—hurt. When you told me Lizbeth was responsible, I wanted to share that pain. You wouldn't let me."

"I couldn't let you strike back at the wolves, Teagan. I couldn't risk losing you as well, no matter how much we were all hurting over the twisted situation." It was an old argument, but she couldn't stop making it. Not if it finally got through to her stubborn cousin. "I was protecting you."

"I know." Teagan shoulders shuddered, and Tala didn't miss the fact that Teagan's grip on the counter's edge was so tight, her bones pressed white against her skin.

When she lifted her head, the warring emotions staring back took Tala aback, leaving her unprepared for Teagan's next move. Teagan lunged across the narrow kitchen and grabbed a knife from the butcher block.

Her gaze met Tala's, filled with a mix of guilt, rage, but over it all, a panicked plea silently screaming for help. "Now it's my turn to return the favor." With that, she spun away, and an ugly pain-filled grunt sounded.

Tala was off the barstool before she even realized she moved. She darted around the bar's edge, her gaze going to the spreading stain high on Teagan's thigh. She approached Teagan cautiously, her mind racing. "Teagan?"

When she reached out, Teagan's hand flew up in a warding motion, and she stumbled back, putting distance between them. Teagan didn't release her grip on the knife sticking obscenely from her thigh. "Don't, Tala."

"Tala," Cheveyo's low voice had her turning to find him right behind her. "Be careful."

"What the hell is going on?" Because something was really off here.

"I don't know yet," he murmured, his attention focused on Teagan. He stepped in front of Tala, blocking Teagan's access to her.

Wild-eyed and shaking, Teagan watched him approach even as she whispered to herself, but when her gaze skittered, it was obvious she wasn't tracking her surroundings.

Tala waited until Cheveyo was able to crouch in front of Teagan before regaining her attention. "Teagan." When her first attempt failed to get a reaction, she added a bit of power and raised her voice, "Teagan, look at me."

Teagan's head snapped up, her fingers going bloodless on the knife's handle. For a moment whatever tormented her stepped back, and sanity peaked through. "I didn't set the spell."

Her already pale skin went sheet white. Her spine arched, causing her grip on the knife to shift. Her jaw locked, tendons straining along her neck as a low groan broke free. It lasted a moment, maybe two, but when the strange seizure passed, Teagan slumped against the far wall of the kitchen, bracing a hand against the refrigerator. Harsh sobs echoed in the small space. "Don't touch me, please." It was a plea, not a command.

Shaken, Tala didn't wait for Cheveyo's next move. With a muttered incantation, she wrapped a protective spell around Teagan. Of course, without knowing exactly what she was offering protection from, it made casting troublesome. Still, she managed to get it in place.

He shot her a look over his shoulder. "You need to let me in so I can take care of that wound before she bleeds out."

"No, stay out," Teagan grated. "Didn't hit anything vital."

She slid slowly down the wall until she sat on the floor, one knee bent, her injured leg stretched out, one arm braced against the floor, the other curled into a useless fist at her side, her body shuddering.

Tala sank down in front of her, the protective spell a haze of pearlized gold between them. "Teagan, what's going on?"

Instead of answering, her cousin shook her head and remained mute. It wasn't defiance Tala saw in her face, it was fear. Under Tala's concern, anger began to simmer. Once again someone one was targeting those under her protection.

She turned to Cheveyo. "Did you find anything in the house?"

"No compulsion spells, no traces of any magic but hers." And based upon the dark look on his face, he wasn't happy with that discovery.

Of course, it couldn't be that easy. Determined to figure

out what the hell was going on, Tala didn't hesitate to sweep a magical eye over Teagan.

Tala couldn't see magic, but, like most Magi, she could feel it. Teagan's normal energy was like a cool breeze dancing through trees. It always brought to mind the first breath of fall.

As she examined her cousin, her attention was caught by tiny, icy pinpricks. Knowing how devious spells could be, Tala preceded with extreme caution, inching her way, until she could peel back the delicate skeins of magic. It took a moment to realize what she was looking at. When she withdrew her magical touch, she was beyond pissed and there was no hiding her fury as she snapped, "I think someone laid a geas on her."

"Any idea of the geas's intent?" Cheveyo's question was strictly neutral, his attention centered on the injured woman in front of them. "Because we need to get that knife out."

Teagan's earlier comment joined with the ugly suspicions swimming through Tala's mind, but she refused to voice them. Not yet. Not until they had Teagan somewhere safe, because depending on how the geas was laid, the simplest phrase could trigger Teagan. So she ignored his question and addressed his second concern. "I'll open the spell for you."

Teagan's gaze jerked to hers, eyes wide with a combination of panic and frustration.

Before her cousin could say a word, Tala added, "It's best I stay right here until you're done."

Even though she wanted to go to Teagan's side, Tala forced herself to turn away and pull out the nearby drawers until she found the hand towels. Grabbing them, she gave them to Cheveyo then suited action to words, adjusting the spell so Cheveyo could approach Teagan.

With a sharp look, he took the towels from her. When his expression went dark, she knew he was following her thoughts on the geas.

Tala stayed at the very edge of the counter, as far as she could get without losing sight of either one.

When Cheveyo pulled the knife from Teagan's thigh, her quickly stifled whimper made Tala wince. It didn't take him long to wrap the wound in towels, but Teagan's face was shiny with sweat, and Tala's nails were leaving half-moon marks in her palms.

He murmured something Tala didn't catch then rose to his feet and stepped to the sink to wash his hands. He looked at her. "Grab Chay, we need to get her to the hospital."

She gave him a nod, turned on her heel, and rushed outside. The next few minutes passed in a blur of activity as Cheveyo took Teagan to the SUV, Tala locked up Teagan's house, and Chay kept watch. When they piled into the SUV the guard wolf was long gone. Tala drove, Cheveyo sat with Teagan in the back, and a grim-faced Chay was in the passenger seat.

The ride to the hospital was filled with tension and a hundred unspoken things, but Tala was too busy concentrating on getting Teagan to medical help to fill the void. Ten minutes later, she pulled up to the ER entrance. Chay was out before the SUV came to a halt, opening the back door for Cheveyo.

A touch on her shoulder from the backseat brought her head around. Cheveyo dropped a quick kiss on her lips. "Wait for us."

"I was planning on it."

He nodded then, between him and Chay, they got Teagan out of the car. Tala watched the trio disappear through the door before parking the SUV. Finally alone, she took a minute to sit in the quiet interior, the ticking engine the only sound outside her own breathing.

Anger, guilt, and worry made for a caustic mix and her hands flexed against the wheel as she fought her way through it. She had to find her balance. Her earlier suspicions gained strength, making them hard to ignore. Yet she couldn't rush out and confront the one she was beginning to believe was behind everything. Not alone, because that's what they wanted. No way in hell would she make it easy. No, she'd wait for Cheveyo.

She got out of the SUV and headed toward the hospital, with each step her molten fury hardened into unbreakable determination. This whole twisted mess was going to end.

Since chances were damn good her appearance would trigger the thrice-damned geas on Teagan, Tala didn't rush crossing the parking lot. Geas were brutal, unforgiving compulsions and would force the bearer to complete the task given, no matter the cost to the bearer or those caught in the fallout. Teagan was a damn strong witch, as evidenced by the fact she drove a damn knife into her own thigh to protect Tala.

But Tala had no desire to test Teagan's strength any further because whoever set the geas had one goal—Tala's death.

CHAPTER 27

Cheveyo leaned against a tree in the hospital's courtyard as he watched Chay pace. "They want to keep Teagan overnight, and I'm not comfortable leaving her alone." He tried his damnedest not to growl, but the younger witch's attention to duty was starting to chafe.

"And I'm not comfortable leaving you two alone," Chay groused as he passed Tala sitting at a small table. "So find someone else to babysit."

This courtyard was supposed to offer visitors a peaceful retreat, but its intent seemed lost on Chay. Pushing off from the tree, Cheveyo intercepted Chay on his return route. "We are trying," he snapped, a whip of anger creeping out. "But if Danny's not available, you're up."

Chay wasn't mollified, "And who's going to watch your ass."

"That would be me."

Both men turned to see Tala standing behind them, a frown on her face. "Danny's not at home, so I left a message. I'm not sure when he'll get it."

Mindful they were not alone in the courtyard, Cheveyo motioned them back over to the table.

They all settled in, him next to Tala and Chay sitting across.

At least this way they could keep their voices low and not have to worry about being overheard.

Chay didn't waste time. "There are two ways to break a geas—complete the task or kill the castor. You better be damn certain you're going after the right witch."

Cheveyo held his tongue because Chay's comment wasn't directed at him.

Tala leaned forward. "That geas had to be laid by someone close to her, someone she would never suspect. Considering who her visitors were yesterday and what was left in my home, I'm about as certain as I can be with out a written confession."

Unsurprisingly, Chay didn't back down. "She had two visitors, Tala."

Her chin lifted, and her eyes flashed. "It's not Danny."

Chay's lip curled with mocking cynicism, revealing for a moment the hardened warrior. "Why? Because he's a medicine man, and he's been your trusted friend for years."

Even though Cheveyo couldn't fault Chay's suspicious nature, he didn't have to like his tone. "No," he cut in before Tala could. "Because if Danny wanted her dead, Teagan wouldn't have missed."

"Actually," Tala said before Chay could react. "If Danny wanted me dead, I'd be buried six feet under years ago." She eyed the younger witch. "Don't ever underestimate the holy men in our community. The Ancestors don't choose weak vessels. Just because their magic comes from a realm we don't understand, doesn't make it any less terrifying."

In a way, she was right. Those who chose to walk the

healing path of the Nations' tribes had to have a core of steel. Otherwise, the merciless forces known as the Ancestors would ride them like stalking horses. Instead, the medicine men and women made unbreakable vows to serve their people, much like the monks of the Far East. Danny, for all his unassuming looks, was a formidable powerhouse and even Cheveyo would hesitate before going against him.

Chay studied them both, his thoughts well hidden. "Be very careful your belief in him doesn't blind you."

Her smile was tight. "I'm far from blind, Chay."

He shook his head and blew out a harsh breath. "If you two are so determined to do this, may I remind you that if Hadley really is behind this mess, you showing up on her doorstep is not going to end well. Hell, what makes you think she'll even answer the door?"

"Because she's arrogant," Cheveyo said. "As far as she knows, the mirror spell at Tala's didn't work. The traces we did find on the spell harken back to Leo, not her."

Chay's fingers kept up a steady, slow rhythm on the table. "Leaving traces like that seems sloppy for Leo."

"More like sloppy on Hadley's part," Cheveyo corrected. "The magic used to create that spell is a tangled ball of witch-and-wizard-type spells, complex but easy enough to bury Leo or any identifying signatures in that mess. Including her's, which is why she expects to stay off our radar."

Chay looked at Tala. "Hadley have enough juice to do that?"

"Honestly? I don't know." She shot a look at Cheveyo, worry coloring her cheeks before she looked back at Chay. "We were friends once, but we drifted apart. Back then, I'd have said she didn't have the drive to hone her skills to that level. Hell, I'm still struggling to figure out why she'd do it in the first place." There was a hint of hurt in her voice.

Oh, Cheveyo had some damn good guesses as to Hadley's motivation, but it wouldn't help the current situation. Not really. He wrapped an arm around Tala's waist. When she sank against him, he realized how much the last couple of days had taken from her. "The why isn't important. We just need to stop her."

"And how, exactly, are you planning on accomplishing that?" Chay's question bordered on insolent.

"Carefully," Cheveyo drawled. "Very, very carefully."

Against his shoulder, Tala's head turned until she could see his face. "Cheveyo."

Hearing the warning under his name, he looked down at her, taking in the features he cherished. Despite the emotional battering she endured, her strength shone undeniably through. No way would he let Hadley or anyone else snuff that out, a vow he made sure she saw. "Enough is enough, Tala."

She studied him, her dark eyes shadowed with apprehension. "If she's working with Leo, you're in just as much danger as me. Maybe more."

"You're not helping to calm my nerves here," Chay muttered.

Cheveyo ignored him and focused on the woman in his arms, needing her to understand she would not be taking this on her own. "Whether their intended target was you or me, they started it, we end it. It's as simple as that."

He held his breath while her gaze ran over his face, not letting it out until her lips curved up. "Yes, simple, and dangerous."

Hadley lived on the edge of the city in a scattered collection of homes tucked into the forest. Each home had enough space to ensure privacy—a good thing, in Cheveyo's opinion, since he wasn't really up to keeping nosy neighbors blissfully ignorant.

"I'm going in with you." It was no less than a command from the woman sitting beside him.

He turned off onto a dirt road weaving its way through the trees and fought to hide his grin. "I figured as much."

"Hmmpff."

He found her disbelieving huff adorable. If she were anyone else, hell, if he were anyone else, maybe he would risk making her stay in the car, but he wasn't fool enough to risk his ass on her temper. Tala had every right to stand beside him as they confronted Hadley.

"Turn right up at that mailbox," she said.

Following directions, he bounced along the rutted road, grateful for the SUV's suspension. "Must make for a hell of trip during the winter," he observed drily.

"Yeah, I'm not quite sure how her little Prius does it," she muttered.

"Magic?"

His quip earned him a soft laugh. "Probably."

Spotting the aforementioned Prius tucked under a carport, he pulled into the drive of a modest ranch-style home. There was nothing here that screamed "evil witch bent on revenge." Through the ages, real witches pulled off the most-wicked shit under the sweetest guises. Take the old bat from the Brothers' Grimm stories. Mad as a damn hatter and corrupted beyond belief, she managed to fool local villagers for years before they caught on and burnt her ass to the ground.

Some of his thoughts must have leaked out onto his face, because Tala stilled in the process of releasing her seatbelt and asked, "What?"

He turned off the engine. "Just ruminating on how much can be hidden under a friendly smile."

Her gaze went to the house, and a vein of sadness crept in. "Wonder if the friendly part was ever real."

Since he refused to lie to her, he had nothing comforting to offer. Instead, he said, "Ready?"

She grimaced and opened her door. "As I'll ever be."

With that, they got out of the SUV. As soon as they started walking up to the door, the hairs on his neck rose. He clamped a hand on Tala's arm in warning. She turned to him in silent question. Uneasy, he sent his magic out to seek what was setting off his alarms. Nothing came back but the expected vibrations of Hadley's personal wards.

"Cheveyo?" Tala's voice was quiet.

"Something's off."

He felt when her magic joined his, their combined energy creating something richer, deeper. Together, their magic cautiously circled the home, neither willing to break through Hadley's wards, not unless given no other choice. Instead, they limited their scan to the surrounding area, keeping it as delicate as possible and trying not to ruffle Hadley's metaphoric feathers.

Tala picked up the first warning sign. "Where's Toby's wolf?"

It wasn't just the missing guard wolf that worried him. "Where's Hadley?"

No matter how soft they kept their scan, there was no way to keep it completely from a witch of Hadley's power.

He stepped in front of Tala and took the lead. He went to knock but paused when Tala touched his back. "Hold up."

As intertwined as their magic was, he had no choice but to follow as her power slid around Hadley's wards, in an effort to identify the protective triggers.

The intricate warding composing Hadley's protections was impressive, but not impenetrable. Tala spent a couple of tense minutes assessing what they faced. "This is going be tricky."

"But not unmanageable," he countered, already weaving his magic through Hadley's in an attempt to unlock the first level of wards.

"It's not these, I'm worried about." Even as she spoke, she worked with him to realign the wards so they could enter the house. "It's what we'll find inside."

He couldn't disagree because the same apprehension nipped at his heels. "Let's get inside and see what we're dealing with."

Together they disarmed the outer layer of protections, giving them safe passage into the house. Had Hadley been there to answer their knock, this wouldn't have been an issue. But since she wasn't at the door, demanding answers on why they were messing with her magic, he felt secure in assuming she was nowhere nearby.

With the primary wards down, he reached for the doorknob. He didn't realize he was holding his breath until it escaped in a relieved rush when his palm didn't burst into flame, and nothing tried to eat his face. He turned to Tala. "Ready?"

She nodded even as she curled her hand in his T-shirt, her knuckles brushing against the small of his back.

He tested the knob and was surprised to find the door unlocked. He shared a look with Tala, who shrugged.

Maybe Hadley felt her wards were enough of a deterrent. Using his other arm, he nudged Tala behind him as he moved to the side of the door. No sense in presenting an easy target. He gave the door a small push so it swung wide.

At the sight that greeted them, he muttered a curse. "Dammit all to hell."

Tala peered around his arm, sucked in a sharp breath, and whispered, "This is so not good."

CHAPTER 28

Cheveyo stepped across the threshold, being careful where he put his feet. Hard to do when the disaster that once served as Hadley's living room was nothing more than an obstacle course of broken furniture. Tala followed, choosing to step where he did. The chaotic wreckage made him uneasy.

It wasn't just the coffee table sporting a split down the center, as if a bar or body had landed on it, and now lay drunkenly in front of the slashed cushions of what once was a plaid couch. Or the glittering trail of glass shards from a shattered lamp marking its route from the side table to the front window. Or the smears of blood filling the scratched grooves marring the wooden floor. It was the dark spill of magic wafting from the hall and setting every warning bell he possessed clamoring.

Considering Tala was plastered to his back, she wasn't immune either. "I don't like this, Cheveyo."

Yeah, neither did he. Reaching back, he caught her hand and untangled it from his shirt. He gathered their magic, weaving a protective spell he settled over both of them, unwilling to step into a trap blindly. "We need to find out what that is."

She gave a reluctant nod.

He inched his way through the living room and down the dark hall, keeping her hand in his. With no idea of what they were about to face, he had no intention of letting her go. In an unnerving twist there were no further signs of violence as they crept down the hall's narrow confines and deeper into the still house.

They passed a bathroom and an untouched, but very feminine office, before coming to the last two rooms. The door on the right remained cracked open, while the door on the left was closed.

He turned to Tala and tilted his head to the left and then to the right in silent question. She pointed to the right. When she tugged against his hold, he reluctantly released her. She slipped to the right of the door, her back to the wall. Her energy spiked as she prepared for whatever they might encounter.

Angling his body so he wasn't approaching dead center, he pushed the door open.

For a moment, he could only stare, fury chasing horror as he took in the scene. They found Hadley's witching room and Toby's wolf. Her ceremonial circle was carved into the floor, melted puddles of wax evidence of where candles once burned. Strewn within the lines were the remains of what once served as her alter. But what turned his stomach and iced his blood was the figure held captive in the center.

"Oh my gods," Tala's comment was barely audible as she moved forward.

He raised his arm to stop her, "Wait!"

Rocking to a stop at the door's threshold, she turned to

him, her face pale, her eyes wide. "We can't leave him like that!"

"We won't," he bit out. "But we can't rush in there either."

Because if they did, it would trigger the dark, hungry magic prowling within, barely held in check by the waning barriers of hastily laid salt lines and poorly constructed confines of the circle. Sliding along their combined magic like a dark, icy wind, it held the twisted form of what once was Toby's wolf captive.

Cheveyo didn't take his gaze away from the maddened yellow gaze blazing from a grotesque mask created from a mishmash of wolf and human. An ugly suspicion crested. "I've seen this before," he muttered.

He didn't need to see Tala to feel her sharp attention. "What are we dealing with?"

Unable to fight back his anger, his lips curled into a disgusted sneer, "Magic and science."

"That doesn't sound good."

"It's not." In fact, the wolves who portrayed this kind of mutilated transformation were victims of a human-created serum. One that ended in horrific death. "Maybe since the poison didn't work on Toby, they decided to target a different wolf."

"This is the crap they used on Warrick's wolves?" Horror and pity filled her voice, but she didn't wait for his answer. "Tell me you can fix this."

He couldn't answer because somewhere in that twisted amalgam of wolf and human was a comprehending soul. The last thing Cheveyo wanted to do was crush whatever hope the poor wolf was holding on to. Unfortunately there might not be a way to save the wolf. "We need to get past the laid spell first."

When her lips thinned with displeasure and a steely glint appeared in her eyes, he reigned in his flinch. Yep, she picked up on his unspoken concession. "Fine," she snapped.

Together they stepped over the thin salt line, careful not to disturb it. Normally, salt lines would act as rock solid barriers but, considering the state of the room, it was obvious the wolf recognized the threat Hadley posed and fought back. Thankfully the lines were merely blurred, not broken because they were the only things confining the dark magic to the room. The minute he and Tala stepped across the threshold, the magic lunged forward with a disconcerting eagerness.

It hit their combined magic with enough force to send a shudder through his frame. Based upon her stifled grunt and locked jaw, Tala didn't fare much better. They worked in tandem with an ease of practice forged years ago. He let her lead because this was her territory and her witch, and she knew each intimately. Proof of that came when it took her mere moments to weave their energy together and create a solid cage, holding the hungry magic back.

Unfortunately, the dark spell clawed through Cheveyo, waking echoes of the Soul Stealer's attack. He white-knuckled his way through the nightmares, wrestling them back through strength of will. He would not leave Tala unprotected. Bolstered by determination he turned his back on the debilitating memories and focused on what Tala was doing.

Her magic carried the warm brush of sunlit forests, the cool air of rivers curling through canyons, and the whispered song of beauty sung by those who called the desert home. He added the wildness of ocean clashing against the shore in a never-ending battle cycle, the undaunted age of forests much older and wiser than their younger cousins, and under it all, the fire still burning beneath the shelter of mountains. Their powers came together into a wild beauty with savage teeth, tearing through the sticky tendrils trying to trap them.

Bit by bit they unraveled the spell, and only as the last layer emerged, did he step in. "Tala, hold up."

Pausing, she heeded his warning and turned to him, her normally dark eyes a pearlized white. Recognizing he was no longer dealing with just Tala, he barely choked back his snarled curse.

The Ancestors had arrived.

As a channeler, Tala became a reluctant host when the ancient power set up shop in Tala's body so they could take part in the world. Obviously, they decided to join in this little adventure.

He didn't flinch under her blind gaze, but he did adjust his tone to something much more respectful. "Ancestors."

"We see you, Stalking Wolf."

If he wasn't expecting it, the multi-tonal voice would have freaked him out. Instead, he dipped his head in acknowledgement. "Please, be cautious, Wise Ones."

Under the Ancestors' influence Tala tilted her head in a strangely insectacoid manner. "What do you see that we do not?"

"A blood ward." When dealing with disembodied beings who held enough power to snuff you out like a gnat, it was always best to err on the side of blunt politeness.

Turning her blind gaze back to the wolf, she began to slowly walk around him. When the wolf tried to lunge, she raised a hand, freezing him in mid-motion.

Cheveyo kept his wince hidden. Intervening wouldn't end well. Instead, he held his position and waited.

Tala made a full circle and stopped in front of him.

He bowed his head. The pressure of the Ancestors presence left him gritting his teeth. He locked his knees to keep from crumbling to the floor. Weakness tended to piss them off, and that was the last thing he wanted to do.

"This blood ward is not familiar to us."

Since it was modeled off of a blood ward normally used by the demons, he wasn't surprised. "I've seen it once before, or a version of it."

"Can you undo it?"

"Not alone."

"You wish for our daughter to help?"

"As much as I appreciate the offer, there is one with me who has held another through this. I would ask that you let me and your daughter call on him to help this wolf."

Chay, who managed to hold another wolf through the same type of attack, was this wolf's only hope.

Instead of answering, Tala made a humming sound and turned back to study the wolf. "What has caused such unnaturalness?"

How to explain genetic manipulation to a millennial old being? "The potion is human crafted and changes the basic nature of the two-souled."

The air in the room suddenly became heavy, making it hard to breath. "Humans." It came out on a hiss, but the Ancestors weren't done expressing their displeasure. "They are never satisfied with what they were given. They just have to keep picking at things."

He couldn't argue the truth, so he kept quiet.

Slowly the air lightened. "We'll leave the rest to you."

Relief left him lightheaded. Or maybe that was lack of oxygen. "Thank you."

"Stalking Wolf."

At the unspoken command, he lifted his head, holding Tala's eerie gaze. "Yes?"

"You and our daughter—" The Ancestors paused, and he waited, enduring their study. "This is a good thing." He blinked at the unexpected endorsement, but they weren't done. Her gaze shifted beyond him, a frown lining her brow. "The future holds many uncertain things, but one thing remains true." That disconcerting gaze came back to him. "Survival cannot be achieved alone. Something you need to remind the Weaver of before she loses everything she holds dear."

There was only one answer to give, so he dropped his head in acknowledgement. The obscene pressure disappeared, and he caught Tala as she stumbled against him.

"Dammit, I hate when they do that," she muttered confirming who was back in the driver's seat. Bracing a hand against his chest, she rested her forehead next to it. "Never a dull moment."

He wrapped his arms around her and held her tight. "At least you know they're on our side."

That got a small laugh. "Not sure that's as reassuring as you think it is."

"Probably not," he agreed, letting her go.

She stepped back, visibly recollecting herself. "Don't tell me, the Weaver is Raine?"

He nodded.

Tala rubbed a hand over her face before muttering, "Yeah, guess they knew all about her ability to mess around with magic."

"Part of the whole all-seeing thing, I guess," he agreed, shifting his attention back to the still frozen wolf. "We need Chay."

"I'll call Wyatt and have him go to the hospital to sit with Teagan, then we can call Chay." Her attention went back to the wolf, and she frowned. "Will you be able to hold him?"

"I'll do my best." He handed her his phone. "Chay's number," he explained when she took it with a raised eyebrow. "And you better call Toby, find out why he's not here looking for blood."

Because, as an alpha, Toby should know when his wolves were in trouble. Unfortunately, Cheveyo was betting the blood ward, while not an exact match to the one he dealt with before, was close enough, which meant Toby didn't know because the magic blocked the pack's connection.

"Got it." She took his phone and left because the cells wouldn't work so close to the spell. Magic and electronics didn't mix.

As soon as she left, Cheveyo took a moment to find an opening in which to anchor his magic with the wolf's. Not easy, but easier now that the other spell no longer blocked him. It would be draining to hold on to the wolf, but doable. Once Chay arrived, between the two of them, they should be able to work through the ward and hopefully allow Toby's natural connection to his wolf to do the rest.

Maybe.

Cheveyo made himself comfortable on the floor and began weaving his magic with the wolf's.

CHAPTER 29

After making arrangements for Wyatt to replace Chay at the hospital and then getting Chay's assurances he was on his way, Tala called Toby. After hanging up, she slipped both phones into her pockets and stood in the shambles of Hadley's living room, wondering when the hell the woman she once called friend had turned into a sick, twisted bitch.

Better yet, why?

Growing up, the two of them were close, almost like sisters. Granted, when Tala took over as the Magi leader, they began to drift apart. Tala with her responsibilities, Hadley with hers in her new role on the Triune. But when Tala found out she was pregnant, it was Hadley she talked to, sharing her fears and worries. Then when she lost Aponi, Hadley had been there, stubbornly sticking around even when Tala managed to run everyone else off.

Thinking back on that difficult time, Tala tried to remember when Hadley stopped being there, but couldn't pinpoint it. However, it took a couple of years for Tala to clue in that the emotional distance she put between herself and others finally managed to push even Hadley away.

At first, it was snide little comments on Tala's leadership, nothing you could take direct offense with, but they carried enough sting to make one wonder. Then Hadley began to use her position on the Triune to voice her "concerns" over Tala's decisions. Over the years they became, for the most part, friendly adversaries.

A pain-filled canine whine made her wince.

Correction, adversaries with nothing friendly about it.

Heading back to where Cheveyo worked to save Hadley's latest victim, Tala tried to ignore the sting of betrayal seeping beneath her guilt. Useless though it was, she couldn't help but wonder how she missed the signs. Could she have prevented this? Unfortunately, that was a question only Hadley could answer.

Tala hovered in the doorway, the wash of Cheveyo's magic drowning out the suffocating miasma of the lingering darker magic. At least her skin wasn't trying to crawl off her bones now.

"Come help me," Cheveyo said without turning.

Blowing out a breath she took a seat beside him, their knees touching. "What do you need?"

"Help with the healing spell." His eyes were closed, his face drawn in austere lines, but the power riding just below his skin was palpable, flickering with a comforting light like the beckoning flames of a campfire on a chill winter's night.

It called to hers, and, because it was his, she didn't hesitate to let her magic twine with it. It curled around her spirit, warming the icy holes of doubt. Between one breath and the next, her magic synced with his until they shared the energy load needed to keep the wolf alive. Closing her eyes, she sank into it.

"It won't do you any good."

Cheveyo's unexpected comment startled her, causing

her hold on the magic to wobble before she steadied it. She blinked her heavy lids open and looked at him. "What?"

He turned to her, his dark eyes solemn. "The second guessing you're doing won't get you the answers you seek."

Heat rose under her cheeks. "Reading minds now?"

His lips tipped down, the darkness in his eyes taking on new depth as he shook his head. "It's the same thing I'd be doing if our positions were reversed." He turned his attention back to the wild-eyed wolf panting on the floor, a hardness settling his face into a grim mask. "If it's any comfort, it's not your fault."

"Right." Disbelief dripped from the one word as she looked away.

"It's not," he restated firmly, reaching out and covering her hand balled up on her knee. "Leaders are not gods, Tala. We do all we can to keep our people safe, but even we can't keep them safe from themselves. That's the curse of choice. They choose to use their abilities to help or harm, and you have to stand by and watch the fallout."

She knew this, but hearing him say it, strangely, helped. "It sucks."

"Yeah, it does."

His soft agreement allowed her to set her internal debate gently aside and refocus on the immediate situation.

They continued to tether the wolf and minimize what pain they could. His occasional low-throated whines and yips became the only sounds to break the hushed quiet.

She slipped beneath the waves of magic, sinking like a small stone into the world of power and light, determined not to let Hadley's spite claim the shifter. Focus narrowed to directing the healing, time unfurled around her.

Chay's "Cheveyo, where are you?" filtered through, bringing the present back with a visceral yank.

"Back room."

Chay being Chay didn't make much sound as he appeared in the door, a wild storm of fury on his heels in the form of Toby.

As soon as the alpha caught sight of his wolf, he blanched. "What the holy fuck?"

"Explanations later." Cheveyo didn't waste time. "Chay sit on the other side of Tala, Toby to my right." He waited until the two men dropped into place before continuing, "We're dealing with a corrupted blood ward." He ignored Chay's vicious hiss and Toby's hair-raising growl. "Chay, I need you to work with Tala on the healing spell. Structured like you did for Warrick's wolf. Toby, you need to use your tie to your wolf to hold him still."

"What are you going to do?" The growl in Toby's question made it difficult to understand.

"I'm going to reconfigure the ward."

Reconfigure the ward? Tala barely stifled her shock at his answer. That meant he planned on manipulating the magic—and to do that he would need to reach out to Raine. Instead of voicing her worry, she simply said, "Cheveyo."

He looked at her. "I'll be fine, *awéé,* but if we don't do something fast, we're going to lose him."

Fine, but she refused to let him do this on his own. Not that she didn't trust the other woman, but...well, she didn't. Sue her. Tala uncurled her hand and laced her fingers with his in silent response. On the psychic plane, she tightened her hold on his magic, refusing to permit anything, or anyone, to separate them.

Her move didn't go undetected. Cheveyo's lips twitched, but he simply warned Toby, "According to Warrick, what happens next is going to get very uncomfortable for both of you. You need to keep your wolf—"

"Hollis," Toby bit out. "His name is Hollis."

Cheveyo nodded then corrected, "—keep Hollis in check for me. He and his wolf have to hold on until we can defuse the ward."

Toby's gaze didn't shift from Hollis. "That ward did this?"

"No, the ward is keeping his two natures from reconnecting. This botched transformation is the result of Hollis being poisoned. The only good part is, Hollis isn't feral." His 'yet' remained unsaid.

At that, Toby did look at Cheveyo. Tala gave Cheveyo points for not quailing under the yellow-eyed glare of the enraged predator next to him.

Their staring contest was cut short by Chay's, "You better hurry, Cheveyo."

No more conversation ensued as everyone got to work.

Tala worked with Chay and, together, they created a two-layer spell, one to contain the blood ward, and the second to try and bridge the gap between Hollis's two natures. While that took concerted effort, she could still feel the minute Cheveyo's magic shifted, becoming something more as he opened his psychic door and let Raine join their group.

Whatever conversation the two exchanged remained private, but when Cheveyo began directing them, they played their parts. Tala began to pray.

By the time they managed to undo the ward, every inch of Tala's body ached. Thanks to the depth of her magical well,

Hollis was still breathing, but she worried how much damage the wolf's psyche endured.

Tala wasn't the only one feeling the drain. Both Chay and Cheveyo wore a pale under-cast to their skin, and Toby's face seemed to have thinned down, bruises appearing under his eyes, but his gaze remained bright and focused.

Next to her, Cheveyo shifted his position until he could cradle Hollis's head, his voice calm as he warned. "Okay, Hollis, this is going to feel weird as shit, but you can't fight me."

Hollis panted, but it was Toby's low, warning growl that left Tala tense.

Cheveyo ignored it, closed his eyes and bent over Hollis, his focus intent.

Tala watched Toby watch Cheveyo. She knew Cheveyo was working with Raine to counter the effects of the drug, but they hadn't had a chance to explain exactly what that entailed to Hollis's alpha. Toby might not know what exactly was happening, but he could sense enough to know it wasn't normal healing magic at work.

The tension in the room crept up a notch, yet Cheveyo never wavered from his work.

In preparation for Toby to do something stupid, Tala braced. She carefully unwound her magic from Chay's, leaving enough to keep Hollis stable. Next to her Chay stiffened as the weight of holding the healing spell shifted to him. She was grateful when he remained silent but watchful, as she layered a protective spell over Cheveyo and Hollis.

"Cheveyo, what are you doing?" Toby's hands dug into the floor, his nails scraping over wood.

"What I can to get this poison out of his system," Cheveyo murmured without opening his eyes.

"That's not what it feels like," Toby snapped.

"Do you want your wolf back or not, alpha?" Tala cut in.

Toby turned his yellow-eyed glare to her and she recognized the combination of guilt and fury. "What I want is your witch's heart on a platter."

"And I'll deliver that, as soon as we save Hollis." Since she meant every damn word, there was no missing the weight of her vow.

Toby stared at her, his wolf disturbingly close. "Your word, Magi."

She didn't hesitate. "My word, Alpha."

"Now, Chay," Cheveyo commanded as Hollis's body began to convulse.

There was a rush of unseen energy. Suddenly Tala's magic jerked, then siphoned away to do Chay's bidding. She couldn't follow what was happening between the two witches and keep an eye on the rabid alpha, so she left them to it and stayed focused on protecting Cheveyo.

Toby's head whipped around, his jaw flexing. "Easy, Hollis." There was a wealth of power in his command, and Hollis's body slowly calmed.

Tala watched in stunned silence as the twisted mess of human and wolf slowly slid into sleek, dark fur. Finally, a panting wolf lay in Hollis's place.

Toby broke the silence first, reaching out carefully to run his hands along Hollis's heaving sides in soothing strokes.

Cheveyo gently set Hollis's head down and scooted back, making room for the alpha to attend to his wolf. He stopped when he was sitting between Chay and Tala.

She wrapped an arm around his waist, a bit alarmed at his pale coloring. "You okay?" She kept her question low.

"Yeah, it just takes a bit out of you," he murmured, watching the wolves.

Chay drew his legs up and rested his wrists on his knees. "That was a dangerous stunt to pull."

"More dangerous not to," Cheveyo answered with grim acknowledgement.

Guilt pricked at Tala. Cheveyo was cleaning up her messes yet again, but if he hadn't been here—she shuddered.

Proving how in tune he was to her moods, he bumped her shoulder. When she lifted her gaze, he said, "We were lucky that Hadley did a rush job with the ward. If we had gotten here any later, Hollis would be dead, and you'd be facing a bloody reprisal from the wolves."

"And I'd be the one leading the pack," Toby confirmed in a hard voice. "No matter how much I like you."

Cursing the sensitive hearing of shifters, Tala tried not to let his recrimination ruffle her feathers, but it was hard. "As much as I would like to lay all the blame on Hadley, I don't think she's the mastermind behind this. She's powerful and manipulative, but a blood ward?" She shook her head slowly.

Toby gathered Hollis in his arms and stood. "My understanding is that a blood ward is part of the demons' toolbox."

She rose, Chay and Cheveyo doing the same on either side of her. "That's a magic Hadley's never claimed."

"It's an old magic," Cheveyo corrected. "And the one set on Hollis didn't carry any taint of demon."

"Just very old, very corrupt magic," Chay confirmed as

he twisted his spine, setting off a series of soft pops as it adjusted with his stretch.

All of which pointed directly to someone old enough to remember such spells. Someone like Leo. She shared a look with Cheveyo. "I want her partner's name before I hand her heart to Toby."

"Tala."

Heeding the warning note in Toby's voice, she looked at the alpha, and her heart thudded painfully. Death stared back.

"Bring me a name and her heart," he ordered, "and I'll back whatever decision you make moving forward."

CHAPTER 30

Despite Chay's protests, Cheveyo sent him with Toby and Hollis. Once they were gone, he closed Hadley's front door with a barely disguised sigh of relief. He pressed his palms to the door and let his head hang down.

Arms wrapped around his waist as Tala stepped in behind him. "You okay?"

He dropped one hand and covered hers as they laced over his stomach. "You think anyone will be upset if Chay arrives back in Portland as a rooster?"

"A rooster?"

"Can't make him a hen, that's a bit too much transformation even for me."

His dry comment got a choked giggle before she said, "Maybe you could convince Natasha to make you a deal."

He turned in her arms, pulled her close, and rested his chin on the top of her head. "It's a good thing I like the kid, or your suggestion might prove to be too tempting for my sanity."

Her head lifted, and he raised his so he could look at her as her hands stroked over his spine. He drank in the softened lines of her expression as her chocolate gaze roamed slowly over his face.

Her lips twitched, probably due to the exasperation he wasn't bothering to hide. "He takes his job seriously," she said softly. "That's a good thing."

"Yeah, I know, but it doesn't make his hovering any less irritating." He dropped a chaste kiss on her forehead. "Ready to do some snooping?"

Like a fast moving storm, her softness shifted into ruthless anticipation. "More than."

His hold tightened, then dropped away. "Let's start with the most obvious then."

"Her office." Tala turned and headed toward the hall.

Unwilling to trigger any other unexpected surprises, they scanned the office before stepping inside. Hadley's protection ward took Cheveyo less than half a minute to disarm. Mainly because he recognized the base pattern from the perimeter wards he undid earlier. Still, the ease of disarming it left him frowning and wondering what he was missing.

Catching his look, Tala asked, "What?"

"Considering how complex her perimeter and alter room wards were, I was expecting a bit more difficulty with her personal warding."

Tala snorted as she pulled out the delicate looking chair and sat behind the desk. "There's one thing you can count on with Hadley."

He moved over to the shelves. "What's that?" He began pulling out books, thumbing through them, and setting them back. Even going as far as to nudge the knick-knacks out of position, just in case.

"She thinks she's all that and a bag of chips." Tala was bent over in the chair, rifling through the bottom drawer.

"And?"

Reaching up onto the top shelves, he moved a hand-carved piece out of position, and dislodged a monstrous dust bunny. He stepped back and shook his head, wiping his face free of dust.

"And, she's not."

Puzzled by her answer, he turned to look at Tala. She had a pile of folders in her lap that she was searching through. "What does that have to do with her warding abilities?"

His question pulled Tala from her task. She paused in what she was doing to answer. "You remember that Danny trained her and me, right?"

He nodded and wondered where this was headed.

"Initially, he trained us together, but it wasn't long before he decided to separate us. Hadley got upset and blamed me, claiming Danny was playing favorites." A blush rose under her cheeks, and her gaze slid away as she fiddled with the files in her lap. "At the time, I wondered if she was right. Eventually, I asked Danny."

Having trained enough young Magi to see where this was headed, understanding crept in. "He told you no."

Even though it wasn't a question, she shook her head. "He didn't answer straight out. Instead, he decided to show me."

Because Danny was a damn good teacher for a reason.

A fact born out when Tala continued, "He brought the two of us together for one more training session. This time, he wrote our assignments down, put them in sealed envelopes, and had us work in two separate areas. It was an elemental riddle, and the answer was a spell."

An elemental riddle had an obvious answer that could be used, but the correct answer was much more individualized, depending on an adept's instinctual understanding of their own magic. Cheveyo had used the same tool to gauge a young Magi's magical instinct.

"Instead of having us craft the spell, we had to write down each step of our cast and the reason why we decided to choose as we did. When we were done, he had Hadley go first."

"Which didn't go over well."

Tala's smile contained more grimace than mirth. "Her reasoning was sound..."

He leaned a shoulder against the bookcase. "But lacked depth."

"When I think back on it now, I get what Danny was doing, but at that time I was worried I had over thought the whole thing, so when it was my turn I stumbled through it. Hadley was pissed, but she hid it well. Just a couple of snide little comments on me showing off, but nothing out of the ordinary for her." She fell quiet, tracing a finger in an abstract pattern against the desk's surface, lines marring her forehead. "Hindsight's a bitch sometimes."

Because her story wasn't an unusual one, he picked up the story's threads. "How long before you realized how much she was mimicking you on spell work?"

She looked at him, no signs of her earlier compassion evident, just simple practicality. "The next session."

"I'm betting Danny didn't have to say a word."

She shook her head. "Once I put it all together, the more furious I became. How she always waited until I began, or how she used what I did, then tried to pass it off as if it was her thought first. When I approached Danny about it, he confirmed my assumptions weren't arrogant. Finally, even I had to admit that Hadley was great at following another's lead, not so great on thinking on her own. It made her a good tool, but a piss poor advisor and leader."

And that clarity of insight, Cheveyo thought, more than anything, testified to why Tala was the Magi leader. "Which means the ward work on the wolf and her alter room was Hadley following someone else's directions."

Tala tapped the tip of her nose then sighed. "Now we need to confirm whose directions."

"I'll give you three guesses, and your first two don't count." There was no hiding the bite of frustration in his voice.

She aimed a narrow eyed look at him. "We need inarguable proof."

He held her gaze as his anger turned pitiless. "We'll get it." Even if he had to tear if from Hadley, one bloody piece at a time.

After scouring Hadley's house and turning up nothing, Cheveyo believed that was their only viable option. There was nothing there. Not a damn journal or half scribbled note. And he wasn't the only one frustrated.

"Is it too damn much to ask for just one crumb?" Tala grumbled.

He shoved a box back in place in Hadley's bedroom closet. "Probably." He turned to see Tala press her fists into the small of her back and stretch. Wisps of hair escaped her braid, and a streak of dust marred her chin just under her mouth. He walked over and used his thumb to wipe it away. Unable to resist the silky slide of her skin, he did it again.

She turned and nipped his thumb.

Heat curled low and hungry, deepening his voice, "What was that for?"

"You're distracting me." Her husky answer raised more than an involuntary shiver.

Reluctantly, he let her go and refocused. "Fine. If there's nothing here, where else would she keep personal stuff?"

Hands on her hips, Tala slowly rotated, as if searching the bedroom for an answer. "Her office in town maybe?"

Maybe, but… "We're running short on people we can trust to check it out."

"Wyatt's still with Teagan, Chay's with Toby." She pulled her phone out and thumbed the screen. "And Danny hasn't called me back."

He leaned a hip against the dresser and folded his arms. "Try calling him again. See if he'll sit with Teagan and then we can send Wyatt to poke around Hadley's office."

Not only was Danny better equipped to help Teagan, Wyatt would be more in tune with the subtler signs of anything connected to darker spells. Contrary to recent events, wizards tended to play in the dark much more than witches.

Tala put the phone up to her ear. With each ring, the grooves bracketing her mouth deepened. When the voicemail kicked in, her message was abrupt, "Danny, call me." She disconnected with a soft frustrated growl.

Even though Cheveyo understood, he offered, "Maybe he's out visiting." A common thing for most who served as medicine men, since their roles were not restricted to simply healing the bodies, but also nurturing souls. When she nibbled on her lower lip, obviously unconvinced, he dug a little deeper, "What aren't you sharing?"

She gave a half-hearted shrug. "Nothing, it's just…I can't shake the feeling he might be in trouble." She winced.

"Problem is, I can't tell if it's just me being paranoid or not."

Her indecision made him pause and study her strained features. Small, but there were signs that the last couple of days had gnawed at her confidence.

He straightened, walked to her, and grabbed her hand. "Considering everything that's gone down, I vote for driving out to Danny's and checking for ourselves."

She took one last look at the room and her fingers tightened against his. "Works for me."

For the second time that day, Cheveyo pulled the SUV into a long driveway. This time, they were on the opposite side of town, nestled at the foot of rolling Kachina Peaks area. Afternoon sun played over the yellow flowers lining the paved roads and the areas between the scattered homes in the meadow. They pulled in behind a well-preserved truck parked next to a classic ranch style home. A simple white fence outlined the surrounding space and included a horse minding its own business. A small barn peeked from the back edge of the fence.

Tala peered out the window. "Truck's here, so if he's not, he has to be close by."

Cheveyo turned off the engine, then twisted in his seat to look back the way they came. "I'm not seeing anything strange which would indicate Hadley beat us here." He straightened and asked Tala, "Did you?"

She shook her head.

"Guess that's something." He opened his door and got out. When Tala met him at the walkway, clearly scanning their surroundings, he asked, "How's the gut?"

She met his gaze even as some of the lines around her mouth eased. "Still twitching."

They moved along the walkway and up the three short steps to the porch spanning the front of Danny's home. A pair of solid wooden rockers stood guard by the wide window blinded by heavy sun screening, a squat tree trunk serving as a small table. Cheveyo went to hit the doorbell when the warm weight of Tala's hand on his arm stopped him.

"The buzzer's broken," she warned.

Heeding her, he tugged open the screen door, using his shoulder to hold it open, and then rapped his knuckles against the wooden surface. His breath stopped when the heavy door swung quietly open under the negligent pressure.

Now it was his stomach's turn to knot. "Dammit."

Next to him, Tala caught his quiet oath and shared an uneasy look. Without speaking their magic rose, joined, and began searching for possible traps. Even as their magic came back empty, Cheveyo called out quietly, "Danny, you home?"

Silence answered, not the quiet of welcome, but the quiet of waiting. Unfortunately, he couldn't determine what it was waiting for. There were no signs of potential traps, but even more strange, no signs of personal warding.

He looked at Tala in silent question. Correctly reading him, she explained, "He doesn't use wards. Said he rather depend on his neighbors for warning."

Cheveyo leaned to the side to look behind her, pointedly taking in the fact that Danny's nearest neighbor was barely within shouting distance and only if they were listening for said shout.

Tala's hand pressed against his chest, bringing his

attention back to her. She was trying not to smile. "Not those neighbors, Cheveyo." She nodded her head to his right.

When he turned to follow, he found himself staring at a wide-eyed rabbit quivering in the bushes just beyond the edge of the porch.

"Those neighbors," she clarified.

Shaking his head, he said, "Unless it's sporting a serious pair of fangs, I'm thinking Danny might want to consider a security upgrade."

"You know Danny. He doesn't like locked doors." Slipping in front of him, she used the flat of her hand to push the door wider. "Danny, you around?"

When nothing came back, she stepped inside, leaving Cheveyo to follow.

Casting another look at the fluff-tailed guard, he told it, "Pipe up if the wicked witch appears, will you please?"

He got a nose twitch in reply.

Sighing, he crossed the threshold, letting the screen door close behind him. Unlike Hadley's place, there was no skin crawling miasma creeping around nor was there any obvious signs of violence. In fact, there was a half drunk cup of tea sitting on a folded napkin next to a book spread eagle on an end table next to an easy chair. The light on the table still burned.

With the open floor plan, Cheveyo could see the kitchen and dinning room just beyond the wide archway.

Tala disappeared down the hall.

If Cheveyo remembered correctly, the house wasn't very big. The living room, the kitchen-slash-dining room, a laundry room off the carport, two bedrooms down the hall and a bathroom. Which explained Tala's quick reappearance.

"No one's here," she confirmed. "And nothing seems out of place."

Cheveyo walked across the burnished hard wood floor and the scattered rugs in traditional Navajo patterns. He dipped a finger in the tea. "Cold," he confirmed.

She spun in a slow circle, and, when she was once again facing him, a puzzled frown marred her face. "His truck is here. There's no evidence of struggle. No fouled magic. So where the hell is he?"

Cheveyo headed into the kitchen, taking in the teapot on the cold stove, the plate and fork resting in the sink, and a neat pile of mail tucked on the counter. He dismissed those and focused on the phone hanging on the wall. A phone which was still attached to a hard line. Change came slow to most Kyn. Next to it was a note pad and a stubby pencil on a string.

An idea sparked, and he went over to the note pad. He ran his fingertips carefully over the blank paper. Sure enough, though nothing was written on it, he could feel the dips and curves of previous messages. He used the pencil to lightly cover the blank page and reveal the remnants of writing.

He tore the sheet off and brought it over to Tala. "Recognize this?"

She took the paper from him and went over to the patio door, angling it so the light would fall over it. "They're the ingredients for medicine bundles."

The medicine men, or *Hatałii*, spent a lifetime mastering a few chants, but they were skilled in the use of herbal remedies. Yet each remedy, or medicine bundle, was unique and Cheveyo couldn't place which one used the items listed. "Any idea of which one?"

She worried her lip as considered. "No, but a couple of

these help ease nightmares, and this one is for protection." She looked up. "You think he was called out to heal someone?"

"Maybe, I don't know." He was grasping at straws, but it was all they had. "Where would Danny go to perform a ceremony?"

"He has a spot he uses up the canyon."

"Say Hadley convinced him she needed his help with a healing, is it close enough to get to on foot?"

Tala shook her head, but movement out in the pasture caught her attention. "But he could go on horseback." She unlocked the patio door and rushed out to the deck. She came to a stop at the railing her hands curling over the edge as she scanned the backyard.

Cheveyo followed and stood next to her. "What are you looking for?"

"Danny has two horses. The paint is missing." Excitement lit her eyes. "If Hadley lured him out, he'd take his paint. There's a reason his truck is still running all these years later, and it has nothing to do with magic."

Even though a simmer of the same excitement bubbled in his veins, he cobbled it with caution. "Before we start chasing a possibility, do me a favor and call his phone."

She didn't bother with questions, but simply followed his directions.

Sure enough, an echo of the ring sounded from inside the house. He motioned for her to stay on the line as he went back inside, tracking the phone. He found it tucked in a drawer near the fridge. He held it up so Tala could see it.

She hung up, her earlier excitement bridled by worry. "He never takes his phone when he heads up the canyon."

Which only added weight to their nebulous theory. "Is it reachable by car?"

"No," she crushed the fragile hope. "It's three hours by horseback, maybe four by foot."

"Time's not on our side." Catching her expression, he asked, "What are you thinking?"

She held up her phone. "Do you know how to track someone's phone?"

Considering he was the Chief Information Officer for Taliesin Security, which provided a legitimate business front for the Northwest Kyn, it seemed like a redundant question. "You want to track Hadley's phone." Something he should have thought of first, if he hadn't been so wrapped up in the other threats they were constantly fielding. It was a long shot, but a good one to check out.

She answered, even though it wasn't a question. "If she's got on it on her, why not?"

"Give me a second, and I'll need her number." He used his phone and pulled up a customized app he used for work. "Okay, give it to me." Tala rattled off the number, and, within minutes, he cursed. "It's not pinging, which means she's got it turned off."

Disappointment tightened her lips, but she shrugged it off. "All right, then, moving on to option number two."

Curious he asked, "Option two?"

Despite the situation, she managed to give him a mischievous grin. "How long since you went horseback riding?"

CHAPTER 31

Cheveyo's answer to Tala's question was years, but much like riding a bike, it wasn't a skill you forgot, especially if it once served as your preferred transportation mode. After finding camping supplies in Danny's barn, he and Tala made sure to bring along the basics. Thankfully, when Cheveyo dutifully checked in with Chay, he got voicemail. After leaving a comprehensive message which included where they were heading and why, plus a request to have Chay or Wyatt check out Hadley's office and a warning not to leave Teagan unprotected, he climbed up behind Tala, and they got underway. It was mid-afternoon and chances were high they'd be spending the night up the canyon.

After the first hour, Cheveyo's ass was numb, but the ride up provided a cherished respite. There was something about riding with Tala in his arms that soothed the ragged edges of his soul. As the peace of the surroundings seeped in, his underlying anger and frustration at what life was currently dishing out, slipped away creating a moment out of time.

Tala leaned back, relaxing in his arms as she rode with natural grace. "I've missed this."

Catching the wistful note in her voice, he bent his head and nuzzled her ear, offering comfort. "Me, too."

She turned into him with a small smile. "As much as I hate what brought you back, I'm glad you're here now."

The sincerity in her voice warmed his heart. He lifted his head, hands relaxed on the reins, and used his knees to help guide their mount up the non-existent trail. "Maybe when this is finished, we can take a few days for us."

"Think we'll be able to ditch everyone that long?" she teased.

"I remain hopeful," he drawled.

The rest of the ride was uneventful, but it left Cheveyo with memories to tuck away.

They were getting close to where Tala thought Danny could be, when a rustling brought their horse to a standstill, his head coming up as he mouthed the bit with nervousness. Tala lost her comfortable seat and straightened. Cheveyo touched her shoulder in warning to stay silent. Another noise, then a soft neigh cut through the tense quiet.

Cheveyo dismounted, and, ignoring the protest of overused muscles, glided forward. He was careful to move quietly as he wound his way through the trees. Catching sight of something moving ahead, he stopped and waited.

Another soft chuff and then a riderless paint broke through the foliage. Not wanting to startle the horse, Cheveyo moved out of the trees slowly, murmuring reassurances. The horse sidestepped anxiously, but his ears flicked forward, and, eventually, he stretched his neck out to nuzzle Cheveyo's offered palm.

"That's it," he murmured as he gently laid his hand on

the quivering neck and stroked, despite the knot of dread twisting his stomach. No doubt this was Danny's horse, and it being here with no Danny in sight, did not bode well. "How'd you get out here on your lonesome?"

The paint stood under his comforting hands, his muscles jumping despite Cheveyo's care. There was no saddle and the simple leather reins were badly frayed, as if the animal had torn free from wherever it was tied.

Cheveyo worked his way around the horse, checking for any injuries. Just below knee height were some scratches, probably courtesy of the more hardy, low slung bushes crouched along the trail. As he continued his inspection on the other side, he pulled up short at the brown smudge just above the paint's shoulder. It was too dark to be dust. He scratched the edge of it with his nail, it flaked off.

Blood.

Since there was no injury to account for it, he was fairly certain it belonged to Danny. Gathering the reins, Cheveyo led the horse back to where Tala waited, still sitting on the other horse who let out a welcoming neigh when the paint stepped into view. Cheveyo stopped by the shoulder of Tala's horse. Her eyes were dark with worry as she looked down at him.

Before she could ask, he said, "No signs of Danny."

"But he's in trouble," she finished grimly.

He tugged the paint closer and pointed out the blood smear. "Not sure if he left it deliberately, but since it's the only unexplainable mark, I'm going to say yes, Danny's in trouble."

"Which makes him bait." Tala scrubbed both hands over her face and blew out a hard breath. "How the hell did she ambush him up here? Her car was at her house, we have the only two horses…" She trailed off, her frustration obvious.

"I think we can cross off broomsticks, but I'm betting Hollis had some form of transportation that didn't include paws."

Understanding sparked, and she muttered, "Motorcycle."

"Probably," he confirmed.

Tala's horse shifted, and she laid a calming hand against its neck. When it settled, she met Cheveyo's gaze. "It's illegal to bring motorcycles up here."

He arched a brow. "I don't think Hadley's sweating the legalities right now, *awéé*."

She gave him a gimlet eye. "I'm sure she's not, but considering all she's done, I think it's safe to assume she's waiting for me."

"Us," he corrected, no give in his tone. "She's waiting for us." Because anyone with half a brain cell wouldn't be able to miss the fact there was no way he'd let Tala ride to Danny's rescue without him.

"What the hell is her problem?"

Despite Tala's understandable anger, there was a ribbon of confused hurt underneath her muttered question. One he couldn't ignore. "Jealousy." He cupped the back of her calf, drawing her focus. "You have the position she wanted within the Kyn." Based on her puzzled expression, he figured the time for delicacy was long gone and tried to soften the brutal edge of truth, "She's always wanted what you have."

"Jealous or just selfish, it still doesn't explain her depth of betrayal." Tala's temper wasn't easily soothed.

He studied her pale face, and it hit him with bruising force that he couldn't afford to leave the woman he loved emotionally vulnerable, because Hadley was the type to capitalize on just such a blind spot. As much as it sucked, it was time for some cold, hard truths. He couldn't stop his hand from tightening on Tala's leg.

Tala wasn't anyone's fool and her gaze sharpened even as a shadow of reluctant knowledge swam beneath. "You promised," her voice was soft, but carried the bite of reprimand.

He had, and he wasn't about to break his vow to give her only the truth, but it didn't make this easier. "When you and I were together, Hadley made it clear that she would be a better fit for me than you." He held Tala's gaze, refusing to look away. "I turned her down, and, within a month, you let me walk away without an argument."

She sat atop the horse, statute-still, yet, in her eyes, he could see the ugly reality began to sink in. Finally, she tore her gaze from his and stared unblinkingly out toward the forest. Her hand tightened on the reins and the horse shifted, taking her from his reach.

He gave her space, understanding his simple statement was the trigger of an emotional avalanche.

After talking to Tala a couple nights ago, it wasn't difficult to stitch the pieces together. His rejection of Hadley coincided with the emergence of his and Tala's emotional drift. Unlike Tala, he wasn't blinded by years long friendship. He wondered if Hadley hadn't been whispering insidious doubts in Tala's ear during that time. Based upon Tala's current reaction, he had a feeling the answer was yes.

When her voice finally came, it carried an arctic chill. "Damn her."

There wasn't much more he could add to that, so, instead, he mounted the paint. Bareback wasn't fun, but it would help speed up their arrival.

Tala maneuvered her horse alongside until their legs brushed. "You never said a word." Her words carried a faint accusation.

Refusing to let the past interfere again, he held her gaze and gave her truth, "There was no reason to do so. Her offer never held any temptation for me."

She studied him carefully. "But it did influence your decision to stay."

That he couldn't deny. "It made me step back and reexamine our relationship, so yes, that's when I knew I had to give you room to grow. That decision I wouldn't take back."

"Fine." It was reluctant but accepting. She leaned over and pressed a quick kiss to his lips before straightening back up and giving him a sidelong look. "But the next time some female hits on you, I want to know."

Keeping his face expressionless, he murmured, "Only if I have bail saved."

His dry comment got a fierce grin, which soon faded. "How do you want to handle this?"

"'This' being the obvious trap Hadley laid out for them. Without knowing the details of what the trap entailed, it made things beyond tricky. It didn't help that Hadley was playing with a stronger, deadlier unknown partner.

"Let me go in first." She opened her mouth to argue, but he cut her off. "Hear me out. She's using Danny as bait. Up to this point, everything she's done is to get to you. Giving her exactly what she wants isn't how we take her out. We need her off balance. You said it yourself, she's a great tool, but not good at thinking on her feet, so let's make her improvise."

Tala's mouth shut, but he could see she was thinking it

through. "I don't like sending you in when we have no idea what traps she's laid."

Neither did he, but… "Since her main goal seems to be taking you out, I'm thinking the traps are tailored for you, not me. It gives us a slim opening to turn her magic back on her."

Her eyes narrowed. "That's a thin line of hope, Cheveyo."

"Maybe, but it's better than nothing," he argued.

Instead of answering, Tala nudged her horse's flanks and began moving back up the canyon.

Cheveyo smothered his sigh and sent the paint to follow. For a few minutes, the only sounds were the sharp clicks of the horses' hooves against the loose rock and the muffled thumps as they moved onto softer ground.

Tala twisted in her saddle. "If you go in, go in with Raine playing sidekick."

It wasn't the reaction he expected, but her logic made sense. "I can do that."

She shifted back around and her voice drifted back, "You may not need her, but better safe than sorry."

In less than hour, Tala slowed her horse. "We should go in from here on foot."

He tightened his legs on the paint, who obediently came to a halt. He slid off, and, together, he and Tala hobbled the horses. When they were finished, he followed Tala through the woods.

The tree line broke on a ridge overlooking a tiny meadow. Because of the lack of cover, they were forced to move to the overlook's edge on their stomachs. Lying side by side, they studied the clearing. He recognized the familiar rounded roofline of a hogan built on the far edge. A thin line of smoke curled from the roof, but there were no other signs of life.

When Tala began to gather her magic, Cheveyo stopped her with a simple press of fingers to her arm. She looked at him, eyebrows raised.

He lowered his head until his mouth was near her ear, wanting to ensure their voices didn't carry. "Let me, she may recognize your energy."

Tala nodded, and he didn't hesitate. Using the lightest touch he could, he sent his magic out to merge with the soft breeze already dancing along. Using nature's patterns to disguise his own, he began the delicate work of identifying where Hadley anchored her spells. He hit the first one on the closest edge. Its simplicity almost made him miss it. The magic was woven in a fine strand strung along the inside edge of the clearing, set to vibrate a warning if tripped. Easy enough to get by undetected if he wanted.

He kept going.

The next one lay just outside of the hogan's entrance. While he recognized the presence of the spell, the particulars of it were harder to determine. Layer upon layer of magic created a protective barrier. Not only that, but it made trying to detect what lay inside impossible. Sneaking in was definitely out.

He turned, met Tala's gaze, and shook his head. Her face hardened. In silent agreement, they made their way back to the protection of the forest, and a fast and furious discussion ensued.

Based upon the layered spell, it was a given Hadley was working with a complex magic normally outside her reach. Tala didn't want him waltzing in, but when he pointed out how limited their and Danny's options were, she finally relented.

"I don't like this," she snapped, her voice low. "Swear to the gods, Cheveyo, you get yourself killed, and I'll bring you back and kill you again."

Wrapping his arms around her waist, he pulled her in tight and hid his smile against her hair. "I love you too, *awéé.*"

She leaned back against his hold and cupped his face. "Stay safe."

He took her lips, pouring his commitment and love into a heated rush of a kiss. When he raised his head, her eyes were shiny. "I will come back." He brushed his thumb over her lush lower lip. "Your promise you will stick to the plan."

She swallowed, and her voice was choked, "Promise."

But there was more in her dark gaze, something he recognized because it lived in him as well.

A promise of retribution should anything go wrong.

CHAPTER 32

Cheveyo and Tala made their way down toward the clearing, being careful to stay just outside of the view of the hogan. No sense in making it easy for Hadley. Hidden behind a screen of trees, Cheveyo thinned the barrier he held between him and Raine, and sent out a summons. Hopefully, he didn't catch her in the midst of her own drama.

"You rang?"

There hadn't been time to explain much when he demanded her help with Hollis, and considering how their last, real conversation ended, he didn't fault her for the wariness in her mental voice. *"I'm about to walk into a trap."*

His comment was met by a moment of stunned silence, quickly broken by the hard bite of, *"Why?"*

He didn't waste time and shared the highlights with Raine, ending with his promise to Tala.

Raine's response was immediate. *"At least someone over there is thinking straight."*

Ignoring her comment was his only choice. *"Can you*

and Gavin hide the connection, so Hadley doesn't pick up you're there?"

Silence stretched through their link, an undercurrent of concern lapping at his mind. Not much, but enough to clue him in.

He was stepping out onto the minefield of what she and Gavin were trying so hard to keep quiet, but the time to spare feelings was long past. *"Raine, can you and Gavin repeat what you did to me or not?"*

"Yessss." Her caution was obvious in the drawn out word. *"But you do understand it won't just be me in there. I need Gavin's help to create the illusion."*

Yeah, he got it. He didn't like it, but there wasn't much about this entire situation he did like. *"Understood."*

"Do you?" There was a sharpness to her question.

"Yeah, I do, Raine." Time to put it all on the table. *"I know what you two did to save me."*

A tense silence stretched, filled with unspoken fears and worries.

"Peace, Raine," he soothed. *"Unorthodox as it may be, it kept me alive, so I'm thankful."*

"It's not normal." Her answer was barely there.

He didn't bother hiding his chuckle. *"Yeah, well, what of our world is normal?"* He didn't give her a chance for a comeback. *"Can you two repeat it?"*

Instead of answering, Raine sidestepped his question. *"Your assumption that Hadley is in league with Leo means there's no telling what kind of magic she's going to be flinging about."*

"Which is why I want you on standby."

"You want me to mess with her magic." Resentment flared along the edges of her statement.

No one liked being considered a tool, especially not this woman who already considered herself an outsider with the unusual world of the Kyn. Yet Leo's past machinations proved inherently lethal, and Cheveyo had no intentions of being taken out of the upcoming fight.

All of these thoughts made his response gentler than their weight. *"As a last resort."*

"You trust us?"

And there was the heart of it all. He didn't hesitate. *"Yes."*

Raine's mental sigh came through loud and clear. *"You do realize it would be simpler to bring this to an end before it gets to that point?"*

Maybe taking Hadley out first was the best option, but, even now, all his suspicions were just that—suspicions, with nothing concrete behind them. Nothing they could use to sway the Council or the other Southwest leaders. Which meant making a judgment call was just shy of playing god. And that was crossing a line even he wasn't ready to break. *"Worried about the danger?"*

"Not from some psycho-witch with a hard-on for you." It was an expected answer, but then with cold, merciless practicality, she added, *"But from Tala or Natasha if we don't get your ass out of there in one piece? Yeah. Neither Gavin nor I want to die for you, Cheveyo."*

He was torn between offended pride that she would think it would come to that and black humor. *"Not asking you to, girl. The only reason I'm inviting you in—"*

"Is because you promised The Wicked Witch of the South," Raine cut in. *"Yeah, yeah, I get it. Fine, we'll make sure the connection stays invisible. How soon are you going in?"*

"As soon as you stop bitching at me."

"Good, means I have enough time to make some popcorn to share with Gavin while we play audience to your showdown."

He choked on a laugh.

"Cheveyo." Her tone softened, losing the sarcastic edge. *"Be careful."*

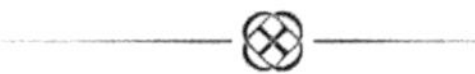

Breeching the first ward left the merest vibration in its wake, but when Cheveyo lifted the old blanket hanging in the doorway and stepped across the hogan's threshold, every internal warning system went on red alert.

He stood still in the only opening as his eyes adjusted to the dimly lit interior, his magic hovering around him in a protective cloak. He couldn't do much about what lay in wait, just ensure that whatever it was didn't slip past his protections.

The one room structure left no place to hide, and although no one jumped out of the shadows, he remained leery. Something was here.

The fire stove squatted in the center, its long pipe chimney disappearing through the hole at the roof's center. A camping lantern, sitting off to the right, provided most of the light. Enough to see someone lying on their side, back to the door, on a sleeping pallet against the far side.

"Danny?" Cheveyo called out softly as he stepped farther inside.

A soft groan from the bundle on the floor brought Cheveyo the rest of the way. Trap or no trap, he wouldn't leave his friend. Bracing a knee against the ground, he kept his touch gentle as he encouraged the person on the ground to roll over.

When the light spilled over the features revealed, Cheveyo sucked in a sharp breath. "Oh, gods, Danny, what did she do?"

Danny's eyes were swollen shut, one cheek was so bruised Cheveyo worried it might actually be broken. Blood lined Danny's mouth, difficult to tell if it was from the cuts on his lips or from something more serious indicating serious internal damage.

Cheveyo carefully pulled back the blanket, and the violence continued. Deep cuts lined Danny's arms, his familiar flannel shredded. The T-shirt underneath was torn and bloodstained. If this was Hadley's work, then she used more than simple fists and knives to create such damage.

For a moment, Cheveyo froze, afraid to touch Danny for fear of adding to his pain. There didn't seem to be a spot left untouched. Uttering a sharp curse, he twisted around, searching the hogan for anything that he could use.

Seeing the pot on the fire stove, he rose and confirmed it was water. Probably to pour over the smooth rounded river rocks piled at the stove's base for a makeshift sauna. Using the edge of his T-shirt, he brought the pot over and set it beside Danny.

A bit of frantic searching turned up a ceremonial knife. He put it to use cutting an extra blanket into makeshift cloths.

When the wet cloth touched Danny's face, he groaned and one of his arms rose weakly to bat at Cheveyo's hands. Realizing the swelling was so severe that Danny couldn't open his eyes to see who was at his side, Cheveyo spoke up. "It's just me, Danny." He caught Danny's hand in a gentle grip. "I've got you."

Danny's mouth worked but nothing came out.

The hair on the back of Cheveyo's neck quivered and the urge to call out to Tala rose in a suffocating wave, but he fought it down. Just because he couldn't see any threats, didn't mean they weren't out there. He couldn't risk them both.

First things first, he needed Danny aware so he could figure out what happened.

Using another strip of blanket, Cheveyo soaked it in the water and then waited for it to cool before dribbling the moisture into Danny's mouth, all the while keeping up a running monolog of comfort.

Eventually, Danny managed to hold Cheveyo's wrist in a weak grip and get out a rough rasp. "Cheveyo?"

"Yeah, Danny, it's me."

As if his confirmation was all Danny was waiting for, the older man began struggling to sit up.

Cheveyo scrambled to keep him in place. "Stop, Danny. You need to relax, man. You're in no shape to be moving about."

"Got to leave—" Danny gasped, his struggles fading fast. "Can't stay here. Not safe."

Danny's fear was palatable and left Cheveyo's jaw clenched as his anger clawed at his control. He laid a wet strip of cloth over Danny's eyes.

"What happened?" He blocked Danny's hands as they rose to touch the cloth covering his eyes. "Leave it, it might help the swelling."

Danny's hands fluttered uselessly before he turned his head blindly toward Cheveyo's voice. "Hadley called."

Seeing how difficult it was for Danny to talk, Cheveyo tried to fill in the blanks. "She asked you to come here to help her?"

"No, sent her here to meet me," Danny corrected before

a harsh cough left him groaning. Cheveyo propped up his shoulders until it passed. When he laid Danny back down, the older man continued, "Said she was attacked by a wo—wolf."

Right, because Danny would drop everything to help Hadley, especially since he had no idea about the geas laid on Teagan or the mirror spell directed at Tala. It wouldn't be a much of a stretch for Danny to believe a wolf attacked Hadley, especially considering how pissed the wolves were at losing their previous alpha. "And when you got here, was Hadley hurt?"

Despite all the swelling and bruising, Cheveyo still caught Danny's frown. "Wasn't Hadley waiting for me."

The unexpected answer stilled Cheveyo's hands for a moment before he continued his ministrations. "Do you remember who was?"

"Doesn't make sense," Danny muttered.

"Right now, not much does." Cheveyo lifted the damp cloth from Danny's eyes, relieved to find some of the swelling gone. Then he replaced it with another one. "If it wasn't Hadley, who was it?"

"Andrew." Confused anger mixed with disbelief.

That wasn't the answer Cheveyo expected. His hands stilled as he tried to keep his shock from his voice, "Andrew? Tomás's Second did this to you?"

Before Danny could answer, a whisper of warning blew across his spirit, and a noise from the hogan's entrance brought him to his feet as he spun around. The quick move left the world wavering for a second before it settled.

Tala stood in the doorway, backlit by the fading evening light. "Cheveyo?"

"Why are you here?" he growled, furious she wasn't

heeding their agreement to stay back until they could lure Hadley into the open.

She came farther inside, her eyes widening as she caught sight of Danny behind him. Instead of answering him, she rushed in and dropped to her knees next to Danny. She tilted her head back. "What happened?"

Cheveyo sank back down by Danny's side. "He was attacked."

An unusual reluctance filled him to say anything more, and the strange whispering in his head continued. Danny's story just didn't make sense. Not to mention Cheveyo's skin was threatening to crawl off his bones. Something wasn't right but damned if he could figure out what was wrong.

Before he could reach out to Raine to see if she could pick up on anything, Tala huddled over Danny. "Who did this, Danny?"

"Tala," Cheveyo voice was a low whip of command. "Why are you here?"

"Why wouldn't I be?" she snapped back, glaring at him. "Danny is mine, Cheveyo."

"We had an agreement."

Her eyes narrowed as she straightened and leaned in close. So close the image of her face wavered then steadied. "This is not the time or place for an argument. Either help me heal Danny or get the hell out of my way."

The niggling warning grew in strength, pressing against the inside of his skull, like a beetle trying to bore its way free. The sense of wrongness grew, but he couldn't figure out why. Cautiously, he nodded his head.

Some of the tension left Tala, and she went to place her hands on Danny's chest.

Cheveyo moved until he was sitting at Danny's head, his attention centered on Tala. He waited for her to draw on her magic, but when no familiar brush of wind swept juniper and desert emerged, he frowned.

Dark, chocolate eyes turned to his. A sickening sense of foreboding hit him, and following an instinctive warning, he struggled to keep his reaction hidden. The smile she gave him carried a cold edge, one he wasn't familiar with. She held out her hand. "Ready?"

He nodded just as a sharp, cutting pain swiped across his skull, but he hid his wince.

When he went to lay his hand in hers, Raine's voice screamed across his nerve endings. *"Don't touch her!"*

His hand hovered in midair, unable to close the distance.

Tala frowned, her gaze sharp. "What's wrong?"

He fisted his hand and dropped it back into his lap. Her question circled in his head, gaining strength until the voice was no longer hers, but his. *"What's wrong?"* It echoed, and he followed the echoes until he found the hidden link between him and Raine.

He stood before the shimmering air where nothing seemed to be. He touched it. *"What's wrong, Raine?"*

"Illusion." The one word rippled between them until the edges of it tore at the magic woven around him.

He blinked back to the hogan to find it wasn't Tala staring at him over Danny's battered body, but Hadley. A dark anticipation curled in her gaze, one she wasn't very good at hiding now that the illusion's cover was shattered.

It hit him that she didn't know he'd broken her spell. He forced his lips to curve. "I think it's best you start the healing, I want to make sure we're not ambushed."

Hadley, still in her role of Tala, frowned, but anger lit deep in her eyes, making her words a lie. "Fine, but I'm going to need your help." She shook her head, barely giving Danny a glance. "They did a number on him."

"They?" he asked, determined to keep her occupied.

She shrugged. "Whoever did this." She stared at him. "Do you know who it was?"

He didn't bother hiding anything and gave her a cold, empty look. "Yes."

And then he lunged.

CHAPTER 33

The first time Tala ever channeled the phenomenal powers of the Ancestors, she blacked out for half a day. Now, after years of practice, she was able to remain in the driver's seat. For the most part.

The problem with being the conduit for a collection of mystical entities who considered themselves protectors of their people—namely those decedents whose bloodlines were a mix of the Nation's people and Kyn—was trying to convince them to let you stick around and participate. Getting them to heed a lowly mortal's advice was similar to asking a snail to win the Indy 500.

So, Tala developed a few tricks of her own when calling on them for help. One of which involved appealing to their protective nature for those they considered their children. Of course, their idea of protection made mama tigers look like fluffy unicorns. When Cheveyo disappeared inside the hogan and too many damn minutes passed, she made the decision to bring the Ancestors into the loop.

She sent out an SOS, surprised at the quick reaction.

"Why have you called?"

The multi-tonal voice echoed inside her skull, resonating beyond the bone. She hated holding the conversation in her head because it teetered too close to the line between sane and not so much. Not wanting to risk being overheard, she kept her response silent. *"Danny's been taken by one who's intent on harm."*

She braced as the Ancestor's affront temporarily whited out her vision, their voices and presence rising to an eye-searing, ear-bleeding brilliance. *"Ancestors, please."*

It was all she could get out for a plea of mercy. It was enough. The Ancestors dialed it way the hell down, thankfully. *"Thank you."*

"Where is our healer?"

"In the holy house with Stalking Wolf." It was always unnerving when the Ancestors took over her body. Even more so when Tala was able to pay attention. The scenery around her passed by in a barely discernible blur, and then she stood on the edge of the protection wards with the hogan to her left.

Power moved through her, and not wanting to get swept away, Tala kept her spirit still, letting the psychic wake pull her along. It was a trick she learned once she could hold her own against the Ancestors, similar to surfing along the crest of their magical waves. There was the whisper of winds through leaves, rising and falling as if a storm gathered close by.

The Ancestors were talking among themselves.

Tala waited.

"Daughter," they called.

"Yes."

"Look."

Following the command, Tala turned to the hogan and couldn't stifle her sharp gasp. The hogan's walls undulated in a vaguely nauseating manor. Tendrils of red-stained yellow, carrying a heart of deepest black, twisted through the structure. Shock wiped away all but her need for answers, "What the hell is that?"

"Something that should not be." The answer was full of sibilant echoes. *"Magic, old and sick, mixed with young and corrupt."* As alien as the Ancestors' emotions could be, their disgust came through loud and clear. Even more worrisome, was the ripples of trepidation curling underneath.

Tala's mind raced, trying to put the clues together. *"Leo and Hadley?"*

A soft hum of approval, then a change in the Ancestors, as if catching the scent of prey. *"The Weaver. She is here?"*

For a moment, Tala scrambled to place who they meant. *"Raine? Yes, well, she's here, but not."*

"Good. You and Stalking Wolf need a weapon."

Before Tala could decide what they meant, the Ancestors took control.

Between one blink and the next, she found herself across the wards and at the doorway of the hogan. Knowledge that wasn't hers swirled around her, but the sound of a scream being choked off had her reaching to tear back the blanket before she could process the move.

The scene hit her like a series of photos.

Cheveyo had a dark haired woman who looked eerily familiar pinned against the wall. His face contorted into a snarl, while death crouched on his shoulder. A battered body lay motionless at his feet. A flash of metal in the woman's fist hit Tala's eyes, and her heart stopped. "Cheveyo!"

Her warning was too late. Whether it was her sudden appearance or her cry, Cheveyo's attention fractured, giving the woman he pinned a chance to slam the blade deep into his side.

His pained bellow roared through the enclosed space.

Tala didn't even stop to think, simply gathered the power singing through her veins and whipped it around the woman still dangling from Cheveyo's hand. Her magic coiled like an electrical serpent, sinking its fangs deep into the woman. The woman's pained cry echoed Cheveyo's. When his hands fell away, and he stumbled back a step, the woman hung on the wall, suspended by the fury of Tala's magic.

The Ancestors were strangely quiet, or maybe it was simply that Tala's panic and fear drowned them out. She rushed to Cheveyo, catching him as he dropped to his knees, a grimace twisting his face.

A noise from the woman on the wall drew Tala's attention. She turned her head, fury coloring her vision red. She tightened her hold until the woman began choking.

"Daughter." The Ancestors' voice bled through her haze of violence. *"Look."*

She turned back to Cheveyo, her hands covering his as they gripped the hilt still embedded in his side. Blood stained the edges, darkening his shirt. Fear tightened its choking hands on her neck. If they pulled the blade free, chances were good he'd bleed out.

When she felt his fingers flex under hers, she tightened her grip, stilling them. "Don't move, Cheveyo."

His normally copper-colored skin was pallid, and a fine line of sweat beaded his brow. "I can't leave it in."

She shook her head, ignoring the tearing pain in her chest. "We can't pull it out."

"Look, daughter." Insubstantial fingers closed on her chin drawing her attention down to the knife. *"Look."*

Unable to ignore the Ancestors, she blinked away the hot press of tears and focused. What she saw made her stomach drop. "No."

Her denial came out choked, but Cheveyo caught it. "What is it?"

An unrecognizable spell knotted around the knife's hilts and etched into the blade disappearing into Cheveyo's skin. The tendrils went from the blade to the woman still pinned to the wall. The same woman who was glaring at her with malevolent glee through a mask that mimicked Tala's features. Recognizing the illusion spell, Tala shredded it with one word, "*Exsero*."

Hadley's mouth twisted into a sneer. "You're too late, Tala."

Refusing to allow Hadley's hateful delight to add fuel to her fear as Cheveyo held grimly on, Tala buried it under a towering wave of wrath. Everything inside her froze under the onslaught, until all that was left was an insatiable need for vengeance. "What did you do?"

Muscles along Hadley's neck stretched as she fought against the power holding her in place. She managed to push her head forward. Her fingers curled into useless fists. "Destroyed you." Then her sneer turned sharp. "Again. Maybe this time you'll go down for good."

Tala didn't dare leave Cheveyo's side, but it didn't stop her from using the depth of power at her disposal.

Hadley's face paled, probably because if the Ancestors were bolstering her power, Tala's eyes would glow.

Inside her head, the Ancestors muttered among themselves, but Tala was more concerned with the man lying in front of her and the witch on the wall to worry about the ones haunting her head.

Even as she split her power, trying to hold on to

Cheveyo and keep Hadley in place, she still caught the whisper of an old spell. Without pausing to think, she cast it.

Hadley's body arched against the wall. Blood began to trickle from her ears, nose, mouth, and eyes.

Tala kept the pressure up until Hadley's screams broke the hum of magic. Another flex of power and Hadley's head was jerked up by an invisible hand, her skull hitting the wall with an audible thunk.

"What did you do?" An echo of the Ancestors' dismay deepened Tala voice.

"Go ahead and kill me," Hadley taunted, a chilling eagerness twisting her familiar features into something monstrous. "Please, I beg you."

It wasn't begging Tala heard, but an anticipatory eagerness. It made her heart seize. "Not until you tell me what you've done."

Hadley's crazed laugh ripped through Tala's bitter loathing, giving her pause. "Oh come on, Tala. Do I really need to give you another reason? Because I can if you really want me to."

Tala sank her magic into Hadley again, until her screams were harsh, choked gasps. "Talk, Hadley."

At first, Tala thought Hadley was crying, but when she lifted her head, Tala was disturbed to see she was laughing. "What are you waiting for, oh great Magi?" Hadley mocked. Her lips curled, revealing bloodstained teeth. "An apology? Where should I begin? With Tomás?" Her gaze slid to the unmoving bundle on the floor. "With Danny?" Then her attention dropped to Cheveyo, who stared at her, jaw locked. "With him?" She looked back to Tala with an unnatural slyness. "Or should I start with Aponi?"

The verbal strike arrowed home with lethal accuracy.

Tala's heart began to bleed with an awful truth. Before she could find her voice, Hadley's head snapped back against the wall, but this time it wasn't Tala doing it.

She looked down at Cheveyo to find him, pale and sweating, but his eyes, focused on Hadley, raged with a frightening mix of power and fury. "What did you do to our daughter?"

"What do you think?" she choked out.

Tala's world shattered on a silent scream of heartbroken wrath. It was echoed by a violent blast of power that whipped past her and tore through Hadley.

"Daughter, stop him or lose him."

The Ancestors' warning pierced her grief and had her moving despite her crippling grief. She couldn't lose everything. Her soul wouldn't survive it. She released the hilt and cupped Cheveyo's face, forcing his gaze to hers. The storm of pain, grief, and anger hit her like a physical blow, but the Ancestors' anxiety held it at bay. "*Bił hinishnáanii,* stop, please. Cheveyo." His name came out on a soft sob.

He blinked, and the rigid line of his jaw flexed against her hands.

"Stop."

His power pulled back, leaving him slumped against her. She held him close.

Behind them a frustrated scream broke from Hadley. "No, dammit, kill me, you bitch."

Instead, as power rolled through her, she cut off Hadley's venomous diatribe with a thought. Still holding Cheveyo, she examined the spell and asked the Ancestors, "What is it?"

"A life for a life, laced with a subtle but sure death."

Another hit, this time barely felt. Haley designed the spell to drag Cheveyo into death with her. Unfortunately, whoever was pulling her strings decided to ensure her death in a lethal double-cross. Keeping the bitch alive would be the only way to keep Cheveyo breathing. Tala gathered the fractured pieces of her heart and soul. Aponi was gone, never to be saved, but Cheveyo was here, in her arms, and she wouldn't lose him to another's madness. "Can you destroy it?"

"Not us. Ask the Weaver."

How the hell could she ask Raine when the woman wasn't here, and Cheveyo was barely hanging on thanks to the spell and the number he did on Hadley? The answer came on a memory. She managed to connect with Raine once before when they worked to save Cheveyo from the Soul Stealer. "Cheveyo, I need your help."

"With?" His voice slurred.

She needed to hurry before he succumbed to the spell. Carefully laying him out on the floor, she brushed her fingers along his face. He closed his eyes and turned into her touch. "Bring me into your world. I need to walk your dreams."

"Dangerous." Even standing at death's knees, he could be so stubborn.

Choking back her impatience, Tala leaned in and whispered next to his ear. "Dream with me, beloved, or we'll both walk the bridge to the next world."

His hand rose and curled over her neck, holding her against him, his psychic walls sliding aside, letting her in. She closed her eyes and fell into his dream.

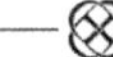

When Tala opened her eyes, a sharp stab of disappointment hit. It took a moment to realize the familiar surroundings weren't so familiar. It was her front porch, but her front yard was filled with the wild beauty of the beach stretching below Cheveyo's home. Not that she'd ever been there, but this—the contained power of waves lapping at a shore where stone, wood and the elements held dominance—was the heart she held more precious than her own.

A storm crawled along the horizon. Angry clouds twisting over the endless ocean, while salt-encrusted wind picked up the approaching fury, and added a sting to their cold touch. Lightning danced among the raging skies and the press of encroaching danger lapped against her mind.

She wrenched her gaze away from the danger, her attention centered on a couple coming up the beach, their shadows trailing behind them like specters of death. Tala rose from the wooden rocker.

"Peace, *awéé*," Cheveyo's voice turned her head. Sitting in the other rocker, his face was pale but determined, his hands gripping the armrests. "They aren't here to harm. You needed to talk to Raine."

She turned back to the railing, and now the couple was closer. Close enough to recognize the dark hair, now streaked with silver, that matched the unearthly gray eyes that belonged to one woman, Raine McCord.

The formidable woman walked beside an equally indomitable male. Hair the color of good whiskey framed the stark features of Gavin Durand, his green eyes sharp as cut glass. They came to a stop at the foot of the stairs.

Raine spoke first. "Tala."

"Raine." Her voice was stiff. Too many betrayals made her wary.

Instead of being offended, Raine smiled, but it was predatory. "I see His Nuisance managed to get himself into another bind."

Folding her arms across her stomach, Tala managed to shrug her shoulders. "He's seems attracted to them in a very unhealthy kind of way."

Gavin curled an arm around Raine's waist. "Not to rush things, but considering Cheveyo looks a bit worse for wear and the mother of all storms is bearing down, I'm assuming there's a time limit to this meeting. Shall we get to the point?"

"I need your help." Ignoring Raine's shock, Tala stepped back and waved them up the stairs.

The two deadly warriors came up and leaned back against the railing as Tala retook her seat. She laced her fingers with Cheveyo's, not as a claim but for comfort. Here in this dreamscape, she couldn't escape the whispering of the Ancestors or Hadley's threat perched menacingly at the edges, while the other spell circled with deadly intent, a reminder of time running out. It wasn't easy working on so many levels, but she managed.

"Hadley tied Cheveyo to her through a mess of spells. Some I can recognize, others I can't. Neither can the Ancestors. All we know for sure is if Hadley dies, so does Cheveyo. Problem is, someone wants Hadley dead, too."

A vicious curse slipped from Raine, and her gaze landed on Cheveyo, full of too many things. Not unexpected, considering the bond she shared with him. This layered spell meant her life might also be threatened. And if Cheveyo was right, Gavin's in turn.

Gavin's face hardened as he turned to Cheveyo. "Did you forget what Raine said?" There was a bite to his question.

Despite his condition, Cheveyo managed to glare back. "Don't worry, I'm not planning on taking Raine, or you, with me."

"I'm not planning on anyone going anywhere," Tala interrupted. She looked at Raine. "Cheveyo told me what you two did to save him from the Soul Stealer. All of it." She held up her hand when Raine went to speak. "I don't care. Your secret is safe. Right now all that matters is can you use your ability to change Hadley's magic?"

Raine shared a long look with Gavin. Tala got the sense they were talking. When Raine turned back, she said, "In what way?"

The Ancestors' whispers fell silent, waiting. Taking a deep breath, Tala dove in, "I want you to reweave the magic. Untie Cheveyo to Hadley."

An inscrutable mask dropped over Raine's face. "This spell has more layers than a Russian nesting doll. I can reweave it, but I can't undo this mess, there's not enough time." As if to emphasize her point, a deafening crack of thunder rolled over the frothing waves. "The primary spell links two lives together, that part can't be undone. We remove Hadley, who do I tie his to?"

Tala didn't hesitate. "Me."

"Tala."

She left her chair and knelt in front of Cheveyo, impending loss making her uncaring of what the position revealed to the couple watching. "I can't lose you, *bił hin-ishnáanii.*" Her hand tightened on his, until she was afraid she'd break his fingers, but she couldn't stop. "You promised we would see things through together. I won't let that twisted bitch shatter what's left of my soul. She's taken too much already." She dropped her forehead to their clasped hands. "Please don't ask me to, Cheveyo." It was as close to begging as she could get.

He tugged his hand free as she kept her face hidden,

feeling the burn of a tear slip down her cheek. Then his hands were cupping her face, lifting it to his.

He leaned in until their foreheads touched, his gaze searching hers, his voice a low thread of sound between them. "Are you sure, Tala?"

She tilted her head up and lifted her hands to caress his jaw, dropping every guard she possessed. If it could save him, she would tie them together tighter than any weave ever created. "I love you, Cheveyo. Stay with me."

Then she caught his lips with hers, pouring everything into her kiss.

CHAPTER 34

Tala's kiss poured into his broken soul, even as grief and rage heaved against his precarious control. His promise to her battled against his need for vengeance. His darker needs crawled with delight in the fissures between.

Then, in a shimmering wave of heat, her love curled into the cracks, holding the ragged edges together and drowning out the whispers of how he could make Hadley hurt and hurt. Tala's gift became a delicate, unbreakable chain woven with an unconditional acceptance and tempered with a practical ruthlessness. He hid nothing from her, letting the links sink deep and take anchor. Her kiss changed with his surrender, becoming less of an offering of solace and more a vow.

"Hate to break up this Hallmark moment, but we need to get a move on, folks," Raine's voice cut in.

Cheveyo slowly lifted his head, his gaze holding Tala's for a moment longer. He drew in a shuddering breath and shifted his attention to their surroundings. Behind Raine and Gavin, the approaching storm drew closer, its fury slowly dominating the surrounding scenery. "What's next?" he asked, directing his question to Raine.

She studied him, her thoughts so well hidden even with the bond they shared, he couldn't pick up a thing. Coming to some internal decision, she said, "This won't be fun."

And that fast the scene shifted.

The storm closed in, capturing them in its raging heart. He could feel the press of magic against his protective shells, trying to burrow in. Each attempt a cruel rake of agony. Lightning struck nearby, leaving strange aftermath images in its wake. Snapshots of Tala, Aponi, and even Raine. Despite Raine's warning, the first tug against his soul left ice curling through his veins. Pure instinct drove him to strike out.

A hiss sounded nearby and he swung in its direction. Another burst of light illuminated Raine's face, twisted with pain. The deafening roll of thunder almost, but not quite, drowned out her shouted words. "Don't fight me, Cheveyo!"

Gritting his teeth, he didn't fight the next tug, or the next. They bled together into a relentless tide of inescapable pain. Pieces of him were changing, reforming, and it was happening so fast he couldn't keep up.

"*Bił hinishnáanii*, breathe." Tala's familiar whisper seeped under the pain. "I'm here."

"*Awéé*." It was the only word he could get out from behind clenched teeth, but it was enough.

Her familiar presence crept in, giving him an anchor. Bit by bit, she appeared out of the raging storm until she was pressed against him, her arms around his waist, her head against his heart.

He buried his face in her hair and held on, while Raine continued her torturous changes.

The storm continued to rage, the winds shrieking in protest, lightning and thunder adding their bellows of denial as Raine became an unstoppable force of nature in this strange world.

He sank into Tala and felt her do the same, shared memories and emotions laying their hearts bare until it was hard to tell where he stopped and she began.

"Brace yourselves." Raine's warning was a fleeting whisper, then the world went white.

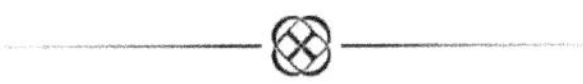

"Nooooo!" The maddened scream brought Cheveyo back, and he managed to peel his eyes open. His body felt heavy and uncoordinated, but he was back in the hogan. Fire burned along his side, but not the agonizing level it once held.

"Enough." Sharp and cutting, Tala's command directed at Hadley had him lumbering to his feet.

He stepped up behind her as she faced Hadley writhing against the hogan's wall, his chest sore but strangely full. There was an incandescent hum of power singing in his bones.

On some level, he recognized it didn't belong to him, but it was so strong it bled over. Heeding some unknown instinct, he moved in until Tala was pressed against his front, his arm curling around her waist. In his other hand there was the weight of a blade. A glance down confirmed it was the same one Hadley had buried in his side. Distantly he realized Raine managed to heal the wound to some extent.

Tala's hand covered his at her stomach and the hum of power hit a resonating level. She turned her head, and, when he met her opaque gaze, he realized the power he felt belonged to the Ancestors. "Stalking Wolf."

"Ancestors." His voice was rough.

Tala's blind gaze moved over him, peering beyond skin and bone. There was a pause, then an illuminating smile broke over her face. "Ahhh, the Weaver's creation is remarkably stunning but strong. Good."

That the Ancestors approved of Raine's reweaving of the spell eased his worry. Granted, he could feel the bond tying him to Tala, but the spell required payment. A life for a life. So whose life was now tethered to Hadley's?

A whisper of a name brushed across his mind. He opened his mouth to ask, but some instinct warned him to stay silent. For once, he heeded it. Some things were best left unspoken.

A strangled sound drew the Ancestors' attention back to Hadley. "The blade's magic was not yours. Who gave it to you?"

Understanding bred fierce satisfaction. Looked like he woke up in time for Hadley's interrogation. Hadley's eyes were wild as she struggled against the invisible bonds. Her mouth worked, though nothing came out but strangling gasps, as if fingers were tightening on her throat.

A niggling memory rose, and before he could say anything, Tala's hand on his flexed and the Ancestors' changed tactic. "Calm, child."

Hadley's jerky movements stilled and her gaze filled with fear.

"You're right, Stalking Wolf, the name of the one she schemes with is buried deep. It will kill her before we can unearth it."

Frustration rose, but he set it aside for logic. They

needed the name of her partner. Something they wouldn't get if the same safeguard being used matched the spell that killed Mulcahy and almost killed Natasha. Tala's hand tightened on his, and he realized that, while not ideal, it wouldn't just be his and Tala's word to the Council, but the Ancestors. A witness the Council would have a difficult time denying.

He stepped away from the Ancestors. "Ancestors, I request a witness."

"We witness." Their affirmation reverberated through the hogan.

He moved to stand in front Hadley. When her attention came to him, he held her gaze, letting her see his resolve. "There's no escaping this time, Hadley." This close, he didn't miss the panic seeping around the edges of her fear. "Leo lied to you."

A flicker of acknowledgment was enough to add weight to his suspicions, and he continued, "Even had you succeeded and sat in Tala's place, you wouldn't have lasted long. Your jealousy makes you blind, makes you weak." He leaned in until he could whisper in her ear. "Leo never meant for you to survive, you were only a tool."

He pulled back enough to see her face, to watch hope bleed away and acceptance of what was coming drain the last of her resistance.

Her lips twisted into something bitter. "Leo will burn the world before he lets you have it."

Hearing the name, he buried his dark joy. "I know." He didn't look away as he sank the blade deep into her chest.

"Nooo!" Her hands covered his on the blade's hilt as shock replaced her perverted triumph. "You can't."

But he could, because Raine had somehow managed to

find a loophole for the spell, finding the one thing he and Tala had always shared. With a twist of wrist, he sliced through her heart. "You called a life for a life?" The light slowly dimmed as he murmured, "We'll take yours for Aponi's."

"So mote it be," the Ancestors' multi-tonal voice echoed softly.

Hadley's lifeless body slid to the floor.

The last flicker of flames sputtered and died. Cheveyo and Tala watched from the edges of a warding circle. Ashes from the hogan's remains danced along the wind and drifted away. Behind them, the horses' chuffs broke the soft chorus of night sounds. Cheveyo laid a calming hand on the paint's neck, trying not to look at the bundle draped over its back.

After Hadley's death, Cheveyo had turned to tend to Danny, only to realize Danny had not survived Hadley's brutal treatment. Guilt at not moving faster or doing more threatened to throw Cheveyo back into the turbulent storm, until the Ancestors shared that Danny was gone before Cheveyo ever stepped into the hogan.

"I spoke with him." It wasn't wise to argue with the Ancestors, but he knew what he saw, and Danny had been alive.

The feminine hand on his shoulder burned. "An illusion, Stalking Wolf, one meant to entrap." True grief softened the Ancestors' voice, something he'd never heard before. "His spirit is safe among the stars."

Cheveyo bowed his head and let the loss of an old friend wash over him. The Ancestors left, and Tala sank down next to him. She leaned against him as they knelt by Danny, her face awash in tears. Together they wrapped Danny's body to return home. His death and Hadley's twisted magic left the hogan desecrated, and so they used the fire to purify the remains. To ensure the flames wouldn't spread, they circled the clearing with a containment ward.

Laying the warding magic was a revelation. Their power was so interwoven, they couldn't separate the two. It was a profoundly intimate connection, but neither one complained. Instead, it felt natural and right.

After ensuring no embers remained, he waited while Tala sent another breeze through the clearing, taking the scent of burning wood away. Without a word, he helped her mount then sat behind her, the paint's reins tethered to them as they headed back down the canyon. Going down the trail at night might not be the smartest move, but neither one wanted to stay. The first hour passed in quiet, each lost in their own thoughts.

When his cell vibrated from his back pocket, he startled, and Tala turned to look at him. He managed to get it out and answer it. "Hello?"

"Cheveyo, where are you?" Raine's voice came through the line.

He held Tala's gaze, confused. "On the way back down the canyon."

Raine's sigh of relief echoed through the line. "Oh, thank gods."

"Why are you calling me?"

"In case you didn't notice, our personal calling plan's been revoked."

Shock rocketed through him, and when he reached out to Raine on the psychic plane, he found only Tala. "What happened?"

"Well..." A strange hesitation entered Raine's voice.

"Reweaving the magic had an unexpected side effect. When the last thread was set into place, something changed. It severed the connection between us. Almost has if you had to make a choice."

Her answer sent a disconcerting sorrow through him, but it was quickly replaced by relief because he knew what choice he made. He held Tala's questioning gaze with his. "A choice?"

"Um, yeah," Raine sounded as if she wasn't sure if he was going to be thrilled or pissed. "I think you and Tala are bonded now. Should I apologize?"

Bonded. It made sense.

Tied at the soul level, a level deeper than the mated bond of Shifters. It was a rare connection in the Kyn world, but one he wouldn't question because the woman in front him was necessary to him at every level. The connection he forged with Raine couldn't be divided between two anchors, something he should have realized when Tala suggested tying their lives together.

Tala, intertwined with him as she was, picked up what was happening through their connection. When she bit her lip, he realized she knew it was a possibility and had chosen to tie herself to him regardless.

Her eyes widened, and apprehension darkened her gaze. "Cheveyo?"

He smiled, easing Tala's worries. "No, Raine. No apologies needed."

"Okay, good." Raine's voice went back to normal. "Then keep an eye out for Chay, he's heading your way." With that, she hung up.

His smile grew as he pocketed his cell, never taking his gaze from Tala's. As soon as his hands were free, he cupped the back of her head and took her lips, kissing her with all the love and need surging through his soul. When he finally let her up for air, her cheeks were flushed, her eyes bright.

"I love you, Tala Whiteriver, and I am honored to travel beside you through this life and the next."

CHAPTER 35
TWO DAYS LATER

Cheveyo and Tala sat in a condo in Flagstaff with Rio Castle, the Southwest Amanusa leader, sprawled in a well-worn recliner, while Toby paced behind a couch.

On a laptop screen on the coffee table the blonde, icy beauty of Natasha Bertoi, the head of the Northwest Kyn, stared back. "We can't afford to confront Leo without more support on the Council and an alliance in place with the rest of the American Kyn."

"Which I'm sure you're working on," Rio drawled as he cleaned his glasses on his shirt. "You planning on making your point at the next Council meeting, Natasha?"

Her smile was more a bearing of teeth, revealing the beast that rested under her pretty skin. "In more ways than one, Rio, yes. However—" her attention shifted to Cheveyo and Tala. "I can't be the one visiting the other American houses, or Leo will know exactly what we're up to. I'm not giving that bastard a chance to slither out of our reach again."

Tala sat on the couch, her legs curled under her, while Cheveyo perched on the sofa's arm. He sighed. "No, it won't be you, Natasha. I'm sending Chay back to Oregon, between him and Cassandra, my house should be stable. If not, sic Raine and Gavin on them."

Natasha's blood red nails drummed against her desk. "Those two have a few other things I need them working on."

He didn't bother asking, she'd share when she was ready.

Natasha's attention went to the pacing alpha. "Toby, are you certain the mess with the land deal is now put to bed?"

Toby stilled, his hands curling against the couch's back. "Yes, we found the paperwork Hadley had in her office. Leticia is already working with our lawyers to negate the contract based upon false representation. The humans' bid for Kyn land is legally done. I'll be meeting with the rest of the alphas in the next two weeks."

Natasha nodded. "Warrick asked me to offer his help, should you need it."

Toby's lips curled. "Thank you, but I'll be fine. However, I will be sure to touch base with him soon."

"As for the Magi," Tala cut in. "Cheveyo and I have meetings of our own to attend to. We need to see how far Leo's reach extends into the U.S., and it's best we do so on our own. If you have need of the Southwest Magi, please let Wyatt or Teagan know. They'll get word to me."

Natasha's unusual lilac eyes narrowed, her lips thinning with dismay. "I'm not certain I'm comfortable sending you both out."

"Not your choice, Natasha," Cheveyo countered. "The Magi don't trust you. As it is, our presence together will raise enough eyebrows. However, if we want to unite the

American Kyn, we have no choice but to lessen the secrets among our people. Otherwise, Leo wins by default."

"It's not just Leo we have to worry about. The humans are getting suspicious. We can't afford to have our attention split between two fronts." Natasha's words weren't just for him and Tala, but for Rio and Toby as well—a warning of what they were ultimately facing by agreeing to this unusual alliance.

"Don't be greedy, girl," Rio advised, his eyes bright behind his glasses. "Remember, one threat at a time, Natasha."

She glared at him but dipped her head. "Agreed."

Taking in the somber faces, Cheveyo looked at Tala. She held his gaze with hers, her determination mirroring his. Their lives and their people were worth the fight.

"Then let the games begin."

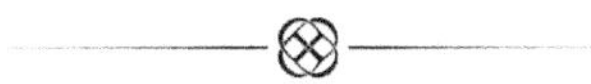

Rejoin Raine and Gavin as they face one final threat before the Kyn step out of the shadows in SHADOW'S FALL.
Now available at your favorite bookseller!

KYN APPENDIX

GLOSSARY

Amanusas:
One of four Kyn races, delight in chaos, half-demon and half-human or Kyn. Six bloodlines—War, Earth, Secrets, Enticement, Death and Inequity—referred to as 'Blood of'. For example: Natasha is Blood of Secrets.

Amá:
Navajo for "mother".

Ape':
Shoshonee for "father".

awéé':
Navajo for "baby".

ayóo-aniínishní:
Navajo for "I love you".

Baide':
Shoshonee for "daughter".

Between:

The second realm between the mortal and magical worlds, accessible by the Kyn.

Bitten:

Humans transformed to shifters through vicious attack. Magic needs human to be on brink of death to complete conversion. They are lower in the pack's structure as the control of wolf is tenuous at best. Tend not to live long.

Biovita:

A biotech lab in Hillsboro, OR where Brant Sutler, a human geneticist worked creating drug to turn Kyn wolves feral.

Blood ward:

A magical construct based on a castor's blood to defend or protect a place or person.

Bonded:

Rare metaphysical tie between Kyn, generally shifters, that connects two individuals at soul level. A step above mated. Partners generally don't survive the passing of the other.

Born:

Kyn Shifters who are born, some are Pure Bloods—rare few bloodlines.

Bound:

An Amanusa, caught in a casted circle by a summoner who uses all their names, to enslave—body and soul—to do the summoner's bidding. If a name is missed, they become half-Bound.

Chindis:

Vengeful spirits of the dead, raised by witches, however can be done by anyone with the ability, controlled by their summoner. Torment victims and rip them apart psychically. Generally are spirits of those who died violently or before their time. Once vengeance is taken, they'll rest.

Cinar International:

European based corporation.

The Council:

The ruling eleven members of the Kyn, chosen from around the world and headquartered in Turkey.

Division:

Preternatural Crimes Division, a group of talented and/or psychic humans who work for US Government and assist the Kyn on supernatural crimes.

Feral:

Wolves whose animal nature has taken control. Tend to attack humans and those closest to them. Nothing of the thinking man is left behind.

Fey:

One of four Kyn races, Sidhe descendants.

Kyn:

The entire preternatural community, composed of all four houses: Fey, Lycos, Amanusa, and Magi.

Lycos/Shifters:

One of four Kyn races, shape shifters, generally predator animals.

Magi:
One of four Kyn races, made of witches and wizards.

Mated:
Emotional bond created when two shifters commit.

Mavericks:
Lone wolves who have chosen to leave packs and roam on own. Can be Born or Bitten.

Mirroring:
Ability to send part of yourself into another by merging two magics, can add strength, but only as passenger. Empathic magic, deep level merger gives access to individual's mind/heart. Witches can mirror.

Pinnanku tease em puinnuhi:
Shoshonee for "See you again next time."

Sarielian Order:
The ultimate group of Wraiths, made of nine of the most dangerous Kyn of the world.

Shadowed Paths:
The walkways in Between, used when Shadow Walking.

Shadow Walking:
Ability to travel in the realm that exists between the waking world and the magical one.

Side:
A realm accessible to the Amanusa, not easily borne by other Kyn, completely unbearable by humans. A third plane of existence.

Sisna:
Sanskrit demon slur, lewd version of tailed demon or phallus-worshipper.

sitsi':
Navajo term for daughter.

Soul Stealer:
Nomâhtsé' héõo' Adanta - Eater of Souls, a psychic being created by black magic from the remains of a soul, tied to summoner. Gains strength eating the souls of others.

Taliesin Security:
The public security company housing the Northwest Kyn.

Tachair:
Gaelic word for "light", Raine uses it for light spell.

Three-fold Law:
Witches follow concept: What you do, will come back to you three-fold.

Tracker:
Shifters who are outside Pack hierarchy, their duty is to hunt/execute rogue shifters and threats (internal/external) to Pack.

Witches:

Practitioners of natural magic/white magic who follow the
Three Fold law.

Wizards:
Practitioners of spells, potions, tend toward dark magic, use
science and rituals.

Wraiths:
Twelve member highly skilled collection of North American
Kyn who serve as the ultimate police for the Kyn and
human monsters. They are not publicly acknowledged,
basis of Boogieman stories for Kyn, even human not sure if
they exist.

Yázhí:
Navajo equivalent of "little one".

88 Ivories:
Music/dance club in downtown Portland

CAST OF KYN

NORTHWEST KYN

Ryan Mulcahy (d.)
Former Head of Fey House,
Captain of the Wraiths,
Chief Executive Officer (CEO) of Taliesin

Natasha Bertoi
Head of Amanusa House,
Current Chief Executive Officer (CEO) of Taliesin

Warrick Vidis
Head of Lycos House,
Chief Financial Officer (CFO) of Taliesin

Cheveyo
Head of Magi House,
Chief Information Officer (CIO) of Taliesin

Carys Iver
Current Head of Fey House, Chief Legal Council for Taliesin

NORTHWEST WRAITHS

Raine McCord
Gavin Durand
Xander Cade
Jamie Ryder
Axel Kayser
Niall
Gideon
Dorian
Chayton
Fahd
Kevin Sullivan
Killian

SOUTHWEST KYN

Rio Castle
Head of Amanusa House

Tala Whiteriver
Head of Magi House

Tomás Chavez
Head of Lycos House

KYN COUNCIL SO FAR...

Leopold DiMarcco
Zayn Aimeric
Corwin Westbrooke
Malachi
Antonia

SARIELIAN ORDER SO FAR...

Darius Abazi

KYN KRONICLES

Welcome to a world where the supernatural walks alongside humans, their existence kept secret behind the thinnest of veils. Now modern man's scientific curiosity is determined to rip that curtain aside, revealing the nightmares in the shadows.

SHADOW'S EDGE

Raine's spent a lifetime hunting monsters, but can she stop her prey from exposing the supernatural community one bloody corpse at a time?

SHADOW'S SOUL

When a simple assignment turns into a nightmare, can Raine and Gavin unravel old vendettas before they both pay the ultimate price?

SHADOW'S MOON

Compromise isn't in Warrick's vocabulary and Xander won't abandon the hunt. As the line between instinct and intellect blurs, will they survive the fallout?

SHADOW'S CURSE

When the queen of chaos locks horns with death's justice, Natasha and Darius set a dangerous game in motion, leading two predators into a lethal dance of secrets.

SHADOW'S DREAM

Tala can't forget the past. Cheveyo can't change it. As the dreams they shared linger, can they escape the encroaching nightmare before it's too late?

SHADOW'S FALL

A trail of missing Kyn leads a powerful new threat into Raine's backyard. Will she and Gavin be able to hold their own or fall under the weight of secrets haunting the shadows?

About the Author

Jami Gray is the coffee addicted, music junkie, Queen Nerd of her personal Geek Squad, Alpha Mom of the Fur Minxes, who writes to soothe the voices crammed in her head. Her series combine high-stakes urban fantasy and edgy paranormal romantic suspense into books you don't want to put down. Buckle up and get ready for a wild ride through the fascinating worlds of the Arcane, the Kyn, the PSY-IV Teams, and the Collapse.

Come visit Jami's website at **https://www.jamigray.com** and stay up to date on what kind of trouble she's getting into and when you can expect to join in.

amazon.com/author/jamigray

instagram.com/jamigrayauthor

facebook.com/JamiGrayWriter

threads.com/@jamigrayauthor

goodreads.com/JamiGray

bookbub.com/authors/jami-gray

www.ingramcontent.com/pod-product-compliance
Lightning Source LLC
Chambersburg PA
CBHW051003180726
48291CB00006B/1952